THE UNEXPECTED LIST

*The Difference Between Being Calm and Being Chaotic
Is Clarity*

BY CHRISSY ANDERSON

ISBN: 978-1-4912-3884-4 (sc)
Spellbound Books, LLC rev. date: 10/17/2013

THE LIST TRILOGY

The Life List

The Unexpected List

The Hope List

For Eva...My fearless and tireless touchstone.

TABLE OF CONTENTS

Tousled
Uncharitable Heart
What the Heck?
Burnt
Pummeled
HELP!
End of an Era
Lube and Tune
Onward and Upward
Almost
Stupid, Stupid Girl
Reminiscing
Oh, NO You Didn't!
Numb
Wait, What?

FOLLOWING
Big Gaping Hole
Done
Tough Love
Five Minutes
Tainted Love
Vomit
SAY WHAT?
Hush Little Baby
It's Time
Interrogation
Unraveling
Exposed
Stubborn
Heart of Hearts
Disoriented
Great Aunties
Welcome To My World
Ready?
Answers
Mommy
Far, Far Away
April Showers
Knights in Shining Armor

In (adverb) \in\:

In or into some place, position, state, or relation.

Listen

September 11, 2002

"What are you gonna get?"

"Thinking we share the usual — buffalo wings and some nachos. Sound good?"

"Duh! But this time make sure you tell them we want ranch dressing with the wings, none of that blue cheese crap!"

Some things never change. Kelly and I have been sharing the same two things at Chili's for like a hundred years. I always give her a lot of shit for dragging me here, but I have to admit, there's something really comforting about our usual table, the bottomless beverages and the never-ending trash talking about our former high school classmates/current servers.

"Look! Look! Look, Kel! Isn't that the guy you went to homecoming with when we were sophomores?"

"Oy vey…would you look at him?" Shaking her head at the now thirty-two year old man-boy. "…After all this time, still a waiter. Jesus, to think I let that guy touch my boobs in the back of his mom's Toyota Celica."

This is the way it's always been with us. The greasy food, the ruthless revolting chitchat that makes Courtney and Nicole roll their eyes, it's my very favorite part of the week. I'm secretly glad those two had to work late tonight so we can say

1

whatever we want to without their smug looks and smarty-pants doctor jargon.

"Oh my gosh, Kel, I almost forgot to tell you! I had this horrible dream about you the other night. You had cancer. It was that one that sounds like a pancake or something."

"It's called a pancreas, you moron! It's a good thing Court and Nic aren't here; they would've made fun of you until you ran away in tears."

"Yes, that's it! You had pancreatic cancer! Man, it was brutal Kel. You got all skinny…and mean too! I wanted to help you and stuff, but you completely shut me out."

"Sounds like something I'd do."

"Didn't work though, I sat on your front porch and wrote you a bunch of mushy letters telling you how much I loved you. You totally hated it."

"No doubt. So did I die?"

I tilt my head and say, "Odd, I can't remember now."

Bored of my boring dream, Kelly looks at me over the rim of her Diet Coke and asks, "So, tell me what's been going on with you? I mean, besides the obvious."

I roll my hands down to my belly and give my bump a little rub.

"Is that husband of yours in town or are you alone again this weekend?"

"Alone again. He's working his ass off to get that new division off the ground."

It's sorta the truth. He's in Nevada taking a crash course to get his pilot's license for I have absolutely no idea why. Seriously, where the hell does he plan on flying off to when this thing pops out?

"Let us know when you guys have a free weekend. Craig wants the gang to go camping one last time before the fall."

Lovely. I hated camping enough when I didn't have an extra twenty-five pounds to drag around. But never one to ruin everyone's fun, I enthusiastically nod my head like sleeping on rocks and peeing in the woods is the most super fantastic thing I can possibly think of doing at this stage of my life.

The food arrives, and after yelling at the idiot for bringing us blue cheese dressing, I proceed to tell Kelly the most hilarious story.

"So get this...I'm at a bar a couple of weeks ago—"

"*A bar?* But look at you! And you can't even drink!"

"I know, right? It was for my co-worker. She was having some sort of mini-meltdown and she begged me to sit with her while she drank her troubles away. I don't know why, but I went."

"And....so?"

"So she bailed on me the second we got there! Yep, ditched me for some little Korean guy. Oh man, he had the funniest name. *What was it again?* Ho-gab...Ho-dog...Ho-Bag! That's it, Ho-Bag! Anyway, when they took off, I started talking to the Korean guy's friend, and you're never gonna believe this...HE HIT ON ME!"

"Was the dude blind?"

"Nah, the countertop on the bar was totally huge." Rubbing my belly again, "This thing was comfortably tucked underneath. Anyway, we actually had a nice conversation. Don't laugh...it was about ghosts."

"Oh, brother, you and your ghost stories."

"Actually he was the one who brought them up."

"Whatever. So what happened with...*what was the dude's name?*"

"Leo."

Saying his name out loud sends chills up the back of my neck and rousing thoughts of that evening begin to flash through my mind. It causes me to pause long enough for Kelly to bug her eyes out at me to continue.

"Oh! We talked until my bladder was about to burst, that's what happened..." My voice trails off as I add, "...Something about him was...I dunno...special."

3

"*Hoooold on!* Back the story up, you bar hopping Barbie! Sounds like you're leaving something out."

I'm leaving a lot out. He was mysterious and sexy and totally into me. Our conversation was packed full of things we had in common and the way my heart pounded whenever he looked at me...

"Okay, okay...I left out the fact that he was only twenty-two!"

"Holy Hannah! You could almost go to jail for that!"

"Calm down! All we did was talk!" Looking from side to side and lowering my voice to a whisper, "Can I tell you a secret though?"

"I don't even repeat the things you want me to repeat, so what do you think?"

"I kinda can't stop thinking about him, Kel. He had these hypnotic eyes..."

"Wow, this isn't like you. It's freakin' me out."

"Freakin' me out too." And then my voice trails off. "I had so much in common with him. Almost more than anyone I've ever met."

"*Hellooooooo?* What about your husband?"

Snapping back to reality, "Except for him, obviously!"

Wiping sauce from her lower lip, Kelly points to my stomach and says, "So when did he notice that thing?"

"When the bar was about to close I—"

"*You stayed until closing time?*"

"I'm telling you, his eyes were crazy beautiful! Anyway, he suggested we talk outside for a while. I was like, HELLS NO! But I still didn't have the guts to stand up and show him that he wasted his entire evening on me. This bar was crawling with chicks! And trust me; this guy could've had his pick of the lot."

"You chick-jacked him!"

I'm looking at Kelly like she's an idiot.

"What? You get to say stuff like that and it's cute. But when I do, it's lame?"

4

"Well…kinda."

"Oh, whatever! So, what the heck happened?"

"I peed my pants."

"You're kidding me, right?"

"Nope, peed all over the fucking floor. You know how it is when you're this far along."

"Oh my God! Did he notice?"

"No. I pretended to spill my water and asked him to hurry and find some towels. When he was gone I made a run for it."

After a laugh so intense that no sound emits from either of our bodies, I catch my breath and say, "I feel bad though."

"About?"

"Bailing on him."

She's looking at me like I've lost my mind.

"I know, I know…I'm married and…" pointing at my gut, "I have this. But still, it seemed like he was relieved to meet me. Like I made him feel something he never felt before. Like I saved him. I dunno…I wish…"

"You wish what, Chrissy?"

Catching myself before I say something Kelly can't even comprehend, I backpedal with, "I wish that damn waiter would bring the bill. I gotta get home and catch up on my sleep while Kurt's gone. It's like the only time I can get a solid ten hours."

Standing up to flag down the waiter, my pregnant belly bashes into the table, spilling our drinks everywhere.

The commotion jolts me out of my sleep and straight up in bed. My head darts all around to try and figure out what the hell is going on. My hands clutch my stomach and relief washes over me. Flat as a board.

"Thank you, Lord Jesus, who I'm still kinda struggling to believe in."

I'm thankful only until I remember that my best friend Kelly is dead and Leo, the man who stole my heart, is long gone.

Wounded

September 11, 2002

I have dreams like that all of the time, and everything about them is so real. *Kelly's so real.* Her frank assessment of whatever Chrissygan...Oh wait, must pause to explain what a Chrissygan is.

Over the past three years, my name and the word shenanigan have become so synonymous that my friends have made a word out of it, Chrissygan. Anyway, whatever Chrissygan I'm talking to Kelly about in my dreams, she gives me her tell-it-like-it-is take on the matter. It's very comforting. But with Kelly's comfort comes a lot of weird stuff, like being pregnant, and it makes me crazy.

While I'm in the shower trying to make sense out of my latest dream, I do my usual morning drill: pick up the shampoo that Leo left behind, squirt one teeny tiny dot of it into the middle of my shampoo, mix them together, rub until my scalp hurts, and numbly stare at the drain as it sucks down the suds.

His razor is still here, but it's so dull it cuts me whenever I use it. For a moment, it made me consider being an actual cutter. Gross, right? Well, hear me out. I read somewhere (probably in one of those useless self-help books that I picked up back in 1998) that cutting helps freaks relieve the intense emotional pain they're feeling internally. Yep, cutters feel so dead inside that seeing their own blood actually helps them to feel alive. And well...after Leo was gone, feeling alive was something I really struggled with. I was willing to try anything. One day, I picked up the damn razor and thought, *"What if?"* Who was I kidding though? I'm way too vain to scar up my body. Besides, the last time I felt dead inside, yoga (sprinkled with precisely the right amount of alcohol) worked just fine as my emotional pain crutch. Plus, there's no place in my life for masochistic thoughts like cutting. And the plastic bin of colorful toys suctioned to the side of my bathtub is one more reminder of why that is.

As I exit the shower, I knock over the garbage can next to the toilet and stare for an eternity at the waste that's now scattered all over the floor. My mind flashes back to the day I picked Leo's phone number out of my garbage can. Even though it was only four years ago, it seems like a lifetime away. I woke up that January morning stunned that I had spent so much time talking to him at Buckley's, bewildered that we continued our conversation in my car after the bar closed, and mortified that I had broken my vows as a wife and kissed him like I had never even kissed my own husband. He gave me his phone number and made me promise to call him. It seemed unbelievable...*I was six years older than him.* God, I was so scared to make that call, but what my heart needed at the time crushed all trepidation, and so I picked his phone number out of the trash and dialed. Who knew that phone call would change the course of my life and lead to so many firsts...and so many lies.

Snapping out of my funk, I scoop up the garbage and tediously wash my hands. Almost everything I do these days is tedious. I gently push Leo's towel over on the bar, careful not to disturb it. It's still hanging in the same spot and still hardened from the water he quickly dried off of his body the last time he used it. I shiver at the memory of watching him do it, wishing I had savored the moment...but knowing it would've been inappropriate given all that was going on at the time.

I prepare to leave my cozy cottage with the same feelings I've had for way too many days in a row now; glad I have somewhere to go, but pissed that I can't just stay locked in my bathroom with what's left of Leo's belongings.

Oh crap, eight-fifteen, already! I better get moving. So much to do today.

8

I toss my super special crochet yoga bag and the rest of my crap into the empty leopard print toddler seat that's tethered to the backseat, throw the car in reverse and head out.

I'm tuned into KKSF, which is jazz I barely like. It's all I allow myself to listen to anymore though, no words to drag my mind into the past. Although…today of all days, it's impossible not to think about the past. Reminders are tied in yellow bows on every overpass on my drive down Highway 680.

It's a typically beautiful late summer morning in Lafayette, California. The sky is robin's egg blue and sprinkled with clouds so perfect they look manmade. The store owners are out watering their hanging flower baskets and sweeping their store fronts. Starbucks is bustling with over-anxious patrons, and the smell of over-priced coffee is oozing out of the front door and into my car. I almost want to stop to grab a cup, but can't. *Too much to do…too much to do.*

Entering the on-ramp to the freeway, I pass hundreds of American flag-waving patriots dedicated to honoring our country and the victims of 9/11. I want to stop my car and hug every woman and man I see in camouflage and thank them for the sacrifice they'll most likely be called to make on my behalf. But I don't, because I'll just cry. Nearly every car, including my own, is proudly displaying some red, white and blue. One minute it fills me with an overwhelming sense of pride, the next it makes me mad as all hell that it took the deaths of nearly three thousand of us to make it happen. I turn the shitty jazz music a little louder to drown out my thoughts of that horrific day, and the consequences of it that changed the course of my life just as much as that day in January, 1998, when I picked Leo's phone number out of my garbage can.

I finally arrive at one of my yoga studios where my rag tag team of yoga bitches is waiting for me to start our weekly meeting. They were absolute lifesavers after the confusion of 9/11 when I disappeared for a while. When I finally came back, I returned to two very packed studios, both with waiting lists and lines out the door. Sure enough, in a gross twist of fate, the tragedy of 9/11 made people crave the peaceful healing powers of yoga and meditation, and it prompted the need to open a third Forever Young Yoga Studio. Just as my girls have done every single day since the bottom fell out of my world, they spring into comforting action as I enter the room.

"Hey Doll! I'm *loving* how that tie-dye tunic exposes your matching tankini! And turn around so I can get a look at your ass in those cute little reverse-seam leggings!"

Oh, how I love my Slutty Co-worker. Sure, she's still a big fat whore and I have a hard time wrapping my head around the amount of men she dates/fucks/accepts expensive gifts from, but the woman supports the hell out of me, so I continue to ignore the parts of her sex life that I find disturbing. Why do I love her so much, you ask? Well, for starters, she didn't bat an eye when I asked to use her apartment to rendezvous with Leo; she knew I needed time to sort out my feelings for him. And she was the one with the great idea to track him down at the Red Devil Lounge so that I could win him back; she knew it was a mistake to break up with him. She even dragged me to his hang out, P.J. Clark's, in New York after he moved there to show me all I was missing out on. And then she gave me her shoulder to cry on when I saw it all with my own eyes. Slutty Co-worker has always been there for me and not just personally, but professionally. I never could've made Forever Young, Inc., the success it is had it not been for her passion, dedication, and willingness to expose more of her ass than necessary to attract a larger than normal male crowd.

Trying to put on a brave face, I smile over at my little worker bee, Megan.

"Well, I have you to thank for my outfit. There's nothing you can't make look good, girl."

I can't believe I used to hate the girl I'm staring at right now. To quote myself, I wanted to "stab her in her childlike eyes." Looking back, I don't think I hated Megan so much because she was in love with Leo. I think I hated her because she reminds me of me, and we all know what a pain in the ass I am. Yep, Megan's a mini-Chrissy. She's stubborn, determined, and definitely a lot stronger and smarter than she looks. She's also incredibly energetic. Which is a good thing because when it comes to her job as designer of Forever Young yoga wear, she has to handle solo trips to New York to sell the collection, which she does—a lot. Even after 9/11, she boarded flights without a moment of hesitation or an ounce of fear. Nothing was going to stop her from following her dream of becoming a respected clothing designer, not even a pack of angry Islamic extremists. And because of her commitment, she's definitely becoming known within the industry. Her one-of-a-kind designs set our yoga collection apart from anything else on the market. Not many twenty-five year olds can handle the kind of pressure Megan does. Yep, when I look at her, it's like looking in a mirror!

My gaze now shifts to the beautiful woman across the table who speaks to me.

"Wow, and who knew that crocheted bag I made for you last week would coordinate so well with that outfit, too!"

Never in a million years would I have thought that the woman sitting across from me is the same woman who used to sit next to me in the lobby of my therapist's office. Thank God there aren't any more rope-like strands of grey in her hair. That stuff was nasty. Nope, she's all brunette now and proud of it, too! Her old denim capri pants are now denim cargo shorts, to show off her super toned yoga legs, and her smile is oftentimes the first thing I see in the morning and the last thing I see at night. Sad Frumpy Lady is no more and Barbara Cooper has become a very important person in my life.

Barbara came on board at Forever Young, Inc. shortly after she delivered the first batch of crocheted yoga bags I asked her to make on the evening of my last therapy appointment with my beloved Dr. Maria. Jesus, she looked so scared when I asked her

11

to make them, and I had to hold her hand through the entire process, but it was worth it…for the both of us. Barbara prefers her self-made title of 'yoga trinket maker' and backs it up by managing the production of hundreds of crocheted yoga bags, hair ties, and other hand-made accessories to sell in our studios. And being the granola-eating Berkeley freak that she is, she's also working on some new kind of biodegradable, PVC-free yoga mat. I don't even know what the hell any of that means, but our clients are super excited about it, so that makes me super excited about it, too. If you ask me Barbara's title though, I'd tell you she's really the Chief Financial Officer of Forever Young, Inc. She literally keeps track of every cent that comes and goes from our business. I've ceased asking her if she wants to go back to her Professor of Finance days at UC Berkeley, because every time I do she laughs at me. And I'm glad, because I adore her and trust her with my life. Actually, I trust all three of these women with my life. On days like today, it feels like I have to. Sensing I'm having a rough morning, Barbara walks over and settles in next to me.

"Hanging in there, Hunny?"

"Hanging *and* kicking myself in the ass at the same time."

Slutty Co-worker interjects with, "I guess you can thank yoga for the ability to do both of those things at once huh, Doll?"

I give Slutty Co-worker a fake smile and then suggest we get on with the meeting. But Barbara knows I need a little more love.

"What happened wasn't entirely your fault, Chrissy."

All three of these women know how much Leo loved me. Barbara never got to witness it quite like the other two did, but she definitely heard about it after she came on board. Oh, the fun we had crammed in my cottage after Leo moved in! The girls and I would strategize over expanding our current business while he barbequed for us and opened bottle after bottle of wine. The love he had for me was in plain sight, visible to everyone when he did things like gently rub my back as I studied our second year projections and when he kissed me every time he re-filled my wine glass (which was a lot). Leo always had to leave for work at four o'clock in the morning so he'd be there by the time the morning bell rang on the Stock Exchange. So by the time I woke up, I'd find my leftover barbeque lunch in a bag on the kitchen counter with a sweet little note attached to it. He'd regularly show up to the studio with flowers or meet up with us after work for cocktails. No matter where we were or what we were doing, Leo always made sure I was happy and taken care of, and my co-workers always reminded me that I had better fucking appreciate it.

I'm grateful for Barbara's encouraging words, but that's all they are…words. What happened was absolutely, one-hundred percent, my fault, and that's why I'm kicking myself in the ass. Despite how much these three women care about me, I can't help but think they might want to give me a little kick too for what I did.

Despite my broken heart and the melancholy 9/11 undertone of our meeting, it's productive as usual. We never talk about problems with our company, only challenges that one of us is always up to tackling. No one ever say's "It's not my job" and there's never a "HELLS NO!" Well…maybe when we're poking fun at the past. After the meeting, I do my best to make the best of the remainder of the morning by attending one of Slutty Co-worker's hot yoga classes. Then, after a quick shower, I hit the road. *Lots to do…Lots to do.*

Ritual

September 11, 2002

W hen Kelly died, my remaining best friends, Courtney, Nicole, and I made a pact that we wouldn't cry in her presence, which meant at her funeral and at her grave, which is where I'm headed right now. It was really hard to honor the pact at the funeral. I remember almost losing it during the eulogy when I started thinking about not having her to share all of the useless bits of information and gossip that fill my head every day. Then, like an idiot, I turned to look at her casket. I still thank God, *and Kelly*, for littering the funeral home with faces from my past to take my mind off what was really happening. I'm not sure I would've made it through the eulogy if I didn't have all of those people as a distraction. Kelly absolutely hated tears, and since her death, I've done a remarkable job of hiding them from her. Every month when I visit her grave, I keep them in my back pocket, only releasing them when I get in my car and drive away.

Like always, I arrive earlier than Courtney and Nicole. The actual monthly anniversary of Kelly's death was two days ago, but Nicole got stuck in the ER trying to save a freak, who in some sick sort of bondage maneuver, spread peanut butter all over his genitals for his black lab to lick off while his wife watched. Their good/masochistic time came to a screeching halt when the lab confused the dude's dick with his Kong toy (that the idiots typically filled with peanut butter for long lasting play time) and bit half of his fucking schlong off. So we had to postpone until today, which now I'm kind of glad about. I can talk to Kelly about the dream I woke up to this morning.

I lay a blanket on top of her, open up the picnic basket, dish out our spicy chicken wings and nachos, and crack open a couple of beers. I place her beer on her tombstone, and so as to not make anyone feel left out, I place the other beer on top of the tombstone next to Kelly's. (We always did like a good party.) Normally, I'd open a third beer, which would get quickly deposited down my throat, but there hasn't been any drinking for me for some time now...Well, except for my recent God-awful slip up, which caused my whole world to turn upside down and which I'll do *anything* to forget about.

Shaking off thoughts of the night I fell off the wagon, I crack open a bottle of water for myself and then lay in on my old friend.

"So Kel, are you ever gonna reveal the meaning behind these dreams?"

Silence.

"That's what I thought."

Sometimes she answers me though. No, I'm not delusional. I'm fully aware she's not actually talking to me, but I know her so well that it's not hard to speak for her. I always know what Kelly's thinking...*Except when it comes to how she would interpret these damn dreams.*

"Work's going good. We have three studios now. That one in Alamo finally opened last month."

"Took long enough don't you think?"

Ahhhh, there you are.

"Yep, way longer than I wanted, but things kind of came to a screeching halt after 9/11. I don't have to explain that to you though...you're up there...you saw the commotion."

"Speaking of screeching halt...seriously, Chrissy? *Again?*"

"It's not what it looks like."

"Dude! I'm up here! You don't think I know what happened to him?"

Shit, that's right. Lying to Kelly, (even if it's only in my mind) has to be one of the more pointless things I've tried to do.

16

I can hear her giggle as she says, "Nahhh, there've been way more pointless things."

After a long pause, I look up at the sky, exhale and say, "Oh, Kel, what have I done?"

"Looks like you lost him for good is what you did."

"I know it's crazy, but sometimes I think he might come back."

Kelly's quiet for a minute before she starts back at me.

"Hmmm. How do I put this? Getting him back would probably be just as difficult as getting me back."

With that declaration, I close my eyes and hang my shaking head low.

"Sorry, Chrissy. It's probably about time to start looking for the silver lining of his departure."

"We're calling it a departure now? Wow, you make everything sound so formal up there, Kel."

"I'm serious Chrissy. What happened to your silver linings? You found plenty after I died."

"Ran out I guess."

"Bull! What about what happened nine months ago? You've been silver lining the crap out of that, so don't give me the 'I ran out' line."

That's the closest she's ever come to acknowledging the unexpected gift bestowed upon me nine months ago and for a minute I consider talking openly about it, but then I glance at the beer bottles sitting atop the tombstones and resist the temptation. I'll cry and I made a promise that I would never cry here.

"C'mon, Kel! Tell me, do you honestly think any good can come out of what happened to Leo?"

"I'll answer your question with a question. Do you think any good came out of what happened to me?"

"That's not fair and you know it."

"Sure it is. Answer it."

"I won't."

"Okay then, I will. In the process of trying to take your mind off of my illness, you fell in love with yoga, and that led to the three yoga studios you have now!"

"C'mon, Kel, I—"

"Not done! You wouldn't have had the money to open the first studio if you didn't finally get off your butt, file for divorce, and sell your house. Another thing you probably wouldn't have done if I hadn't gotten sick. And by the way, I'm still waiting for my thanks for getting sick when the real estate market was on steroids!"

"Stop!"

"Nope, I got more! The only reason you went to New York to find Leo and tell him you still loved him was because I was near death and told you to. And yes, that little trip didn't end up like we wanted it to, but lucky for you, I died and that stubborn man opened his heart and mind to second chances and forgave you. See all of the lovely silver linings I'm talking about here?"

"Whoa! Did you just say I was *lucky* you died?"

"Yep. I have a much better sense of humor up here than I did down there, one of the perks of a stress-free existence." Along with the giggle I miss so much she says, "C'mon though, Chrissy, you get my point, right? You dug deep and created some good stuff out of what happened to me. You can do the same with Leo…If you just try."

"Can we change the subject?"

"Hey, it's your imagination. Do what you want."

I want to continue the conversation, but I hear Courtney and Nicole approaching. Actually, I hear Courtney chastising Nicole for spilling her mocha in the car. I swear, I still don't get how that klutz is a doctor.

"Hey Mamas! Over here! I got started without you again."

I hug Courtney first, mostly because she's clean. Then I lay in on her as she's tackling the picnic basket.

"Are you ever gonna wear make-up again?"

18

Opening a beer as if relief is washing over her like a waterfall, she drinks and answers at the same time, "Are you *ever* gonna stop asking me that?"

Courtney looks as stressed as usual. She left her position as Assistant Professor of saving the world (or whatever it was called), at University of California San Francisco School of Medicine and took on the gigantic job of Chief of Medicine at the local community hospital. She's the youngest person to EVER fill the job. Nobody ever sees her anymore, not even her family. If, for whatever reason, I can't make it to these gravesite visits, I can forget about seeing her for a month. If you want into Court's life, you have to be penciled in *waaaaay* in advance. I'd worry about her if she wasn't so damn happy.

"I'd hug you too, Nicole, but I don't feel like getting chocolate all over me."

Nicole, on the other hand isn't so damn happy. Like me, she went through a little bit of a metamorphosis when Kelly got sick. She realized that being a doctor isn't something she completely loves being every day. She felt like she had a different calling, and after much soul searching, revealed it was to be a junior high science teacher. While she'd be an amazing role model to a bunch of seventh grade freaks, she's completely saddled with student loans and stuck in the ER until she wins the lottery. Looking at her chocolate-stained shirt, I don't know who I feel sorrier for her, or her patients.

I reach over and pluck what looks like a muffin crumb out of her hair.

"Jesus, girl, are you ever gonna pick that fro out?"

"I don't have a fro, you dumbass. And you better watch it...you're not looking so hot yourself these days."

She's right. To say I've let myself go is an understatement. After plopping down on the picnic blanket and sharing a moment of silence, mostly because we're all exhausted, we begin our usual chit-chat.

"We saw you when we walked up. Talking to her again?"

19

"Of course, Court. I don't know why you two think it's so weird. She can hear us, you know."

Drinking the rest of her beer in one gulp, burping and then reaching for another one, Courtney says, "What's she sayin' today?"

"Buncha crap about Leo, silver linings…same ol', same ol'."

Rolling her eyes, Nicole chimes in with, "Tell me this, John Edwards, does she ever ask about you-know-who?"

"Nope, and I'll never bring her up, doesn't seem fair."

Looking up at the beer bottles perched atop the tombstones next to us, Courtney whispers, "Nothing about what happened is fair."

With her admission, we silently toast our surroundings by clinking our own bottles together. And then it gets quiet again. For the ten months after Kelly died, we laughed a lot at her gravesite. We knew that's what she wanted us to do and because of the memories we shared, it wasn't that hard, really. But then, for the second time in our short lives, death reared its ugly head and the laughter came to a screeching halt. Now, no matter what Chrissygan or flashback to our carefree days we chat about at her grave, the laughter is missing. Outside of the giggles that take place in my cottage, I'm beginning to wonder if the laughter will ever return.

Must stay focused right now though. *Lots more to do today. Lots more.*

Muddled

September 11, 2002

The sun is setting on the way to my last pit stop of the day. The sky is burnt orange, and the air is thick with the smell of a thousand backyard barbeques. As I enter the neighborhood in Walnut Creek that my ex-husband, Kurt, now calls home, I scan the faces of all of the seemingly happy suburban families enjoying the last days of summer. I see proud fathers washing their cars and squirting their children as they ride by on their bikes. The kids who aren't on bikes are tending to their lemonade stands and hopscotch games. It's total suburban utopia. The scene makes me forget about graveyards and Muslim terrorists, and for a split-second I almost forget about what happened just two weeks ago and why I'm so mad about being here.

Rounding the corner to the house, I see the mothers. They've come to recognize my black Land Rover, and when they see me pull into the neighborhood, they cling a little tighter to their small children and give me a sympathetic courtesy nod. As much as I always wanted to be a pretty suburban soccer mom, complete with all the suburban bells and whistles, these women make me think otherwise. They're always out here, *doing absolutely nothing* except drinking Starbucks coffee and what looks like gossiping about each other. Truthfully, I'd love to punch one of them in the face. At least tending to their wounds would give 'em something to do for a few hours.

This kind of neighborhood is *sooooooo* not where Kurt wanted to be, but he made the move for her. I pull into the driveway, put the car in park, exhale, and then let out an exhausted sigh. The last time I was here, so much bad happened. Yep…my latest Chrissygan was a doozy, and it spawned a question that I pray to all that's Holy remains unanswered for the rest of my life. I can't know the truth. It'd fill the big gaping hole in my heart that Leo left with a big shame-filled mass and I might never recover.

When I open my car door, it hits the white picket fence that surrounds the front yard, and I let out a defeated laugh wondering if he put it up to hurt me. I was the one who always wanted one of those things, and he knows it. It makes me think of that damn Porsche and I laugh again. But you know what? Regardless of his intentions for the fence, I'm glad it's here. It makes it safer when she plays outside.

Most of her favorite things are already on the porch – the new Barbie suitcase, The Dora the Explorer backpack and her Berenstain Bears fishing pole – and I'm wondering what the hell he expects me to do with the pole. Like, does he really think I'm going to go down to the fishing hole to drop a line in? Even after all of this time, does he *still* not know me? Shaking off the irritation of the pole, I get started loading everything into my trunk. It's better to do it before I ring the bell. Since this all started, it's been an awkward transition, and now, thanks to my latest Chrissygan, it's a million times more awkward. Just when I slam the trunk of my car shut, the front door opens.

He's holding her hand, and although I hate to admit it, it's just about the sweetest vision imaginable. From the moment he got the word, he's wanted to protect her. Would've made my life a lot easier if that wasn't the case, but he has every right to the grip he has on her, and I'd never do anything to yank it away…not even after what happened just a few weeks ago. Doing my best to hide the big gaping hole in my heart from her and the contempt I have toward Kurt for contributing to its existence, I plant a huge smile on my face.

"Hi Sweetie! Did you have fun at Marine World yesterday?"

"Soopa doopa fun!"

In classic carefree Kurt style, he chimes in with, "We sure did. Would've been more fun if you were there!"

Looking at him like he has a lot of nerve for saying that since he knows perfectly well I'd rather electrocute myself than go to Marine World, I hiss "Right, cuz I like that place so much."

They're the first words I've spoken to him since that morning, two weeks ago.

He gives me a look that says, *C'mon, not in front of the kid.* I just shrug my shoulders and say, "It's okay, Kurt, we have our own fun time!" Then, poking her in the belly, "Like, at the mall when we're shoe shopping…when we're at the movies…when we're at the studio doing big girl yoga!"

She lets out a giggle and I'm comforted knowing I'll have that sound around me for the next five days, until the next exchange happens. After I have her buckled safely into the leopard print car seat that Kurt mocked me for spending over two hundred dollars on, I turn to grab the last of her stuff, doing my best to ignore his presence.

"Is this how it's gonna be from now on, Chrissy?"

"I already told you, I don't have anything to say to you, unless it concerns her."

"Would it have been this way if you didn't get caught?"

In the harshest whisper I can get away with so as to not alarm the little one, I hiss, "I guess we'll never know the answer to that, will we?"

As I grab the car door handle to get in and get away, he touches my hand and says what I already know to be true.

"What happened wasn't my fault, you know."

Ignoring his attempt to get me to open up, I keep the conversation focused on her.

"Just tell me how it went the last two nights."

"Great."

I look at him like, *really?* He realized the goof the second he made it.

"Oops! Sorry, I forgot everything can't be "great" all the time. Honestly though, everything went fine. She slept through the night, no nightmares or scary thoughts. Her appetite was ferocious, and it was fun...I promise, we had a fun time, Chrissy. I think we're turning a corner."

I reach out to grab a stuffed animal from him. Instead of handing it over, he hangs onto it as he asks, "So how'd it go for you the last two nights?"

"I think you know exactly how it went."

When I grab for the stuffed animal, he gently takes hold of my finger and says, "Why don't you just stay for dinner. C'mon, I feel bad about what happened. I'll even set out a nice big bowl of chips and salsa, and I won't care if you devour the whole thing and ruin your appetite. I promise, Chrissy, I really don't care what you eat now."

How did this happen? Four years after I had an affair, three years after I moved into my cottage, two years after we're officially divorced...we're parents.

I yank my finger away in frustration at that thought and at his invitation.

Smiling from ear to ear, he jabs, "So, what? No chips and salsa then?"

"No. None now and none later. None, ever. And besides the obvious reason why that's the case, I need to get her home. I like to keep her on a schedule. You know that."

"Just so you know...I'm glad you forced me to set up a schedule for her over here. I think it helps with the transitions."

"Right." Chucking a little, "Like you really think that."

Looking deep into my eyes like he never did during all of the years we were together, he says, "You were right about that and so many other things."

When we were together, I would've craved a compliment like that from him, but experiencing it so long after I thought the dust had settled between us just makes me feel…stagnant.

After I buckle myself in, I address him one last time through my open window.

"Honestly Kurt, I don't even understand how you could ask me to stay for dinner. Didn't you listen to anything I told you the other day when I stormed out of here?"

"C'mon, Chrissy! You know me, I try not to listen to most of what you have to say!"

And there it is, his amazingly perfect smile. I think one of the soccer moms with nothing better to do than stand around on the street and watch our exchange just fainted.

Spying

September 11, 2002

Just like that, my car goes from a place that's usually so quiet it makes my head hurt to a giggle factory filled with Elmo songs, farm animal noises, and my favorite of all car games, I spy with my little eye. Things I used to make fun of my friends for are now the things I look forward to the most. Children are magical that way. Everything around you can be falling apart, but one smile...one cheery song, one tight grip of their tiny hand on yours, makes you stronger than you thought possible and reminds you of what's really important. At the top of the important list – make sure my kid doesn't fuck up her relationships like I have! And speaking of fucked-up relationships...

"So what did you guys eat for dinner last night, Sweetie?"

"Mmmmmmmm....chicken....tatoes....cookies!"

Not wanting her to perceive a problem, I think long and hard before I ask the question.

"Yummy, cookies! Tell me...how many bites of chicken did you have to eat before you got the cookies?"

Staring at her in the rear view mirror, I watch her struggle with the question before I rephrase it.

"Did you guys count your bites out loud or did you just eat until your tummy was full?"

"Tummy full."

Relief sets in. Nevertheless, it's too early to give Kurt the benefit of the doubt when it comes to his parenting skills. After all, it was the very fear of them sucking so bad that played a role in our demise. But I have to admit, the long discussions we had about how to handle this little girl and to NOT be a food Nazi with her, went far and deep with Kurt, and he's been nothing but a caring and sensitive parent to her. So far, so good. Unlike how he pestered me all those years; he hasn't made her clean her plate yet.

We arrive at the cottage. The same cottage I moved into after I left Kurt and the same cottage Leo moved into after Kelly died. I've been here since November, 1998, and I'm beginning to wonder if I'll ever leave, which is a peculiar prospect considering just a month ago I bought my dream home in Lafayette. Now that everything has happened, I have no idea what to do with the house, and it seems that I'm all alone to figure it out. I drop the load of kid crap I'm carrying onto the floor of my tiny living room, instantly overwhelmed with all of the decisions I'm now forced to make.

After unpacking her little suitcase and shoving the stupid fishing pole under the bed, I make her a delicious frozen corn dog dinner and then clean it off of her face and hands in a luxurious bubble bath. After she dives into the plastic bin of toys suctioned to the side of the tub and plays until the water is lukewarm, I tuck my precious gift into bed.

"Hold on Sweetie, I'll be right back."

This is when I always lose it. When I'm tucking her in and she looks all cute and cozy...my self-deprecation snowballs. I have to excuse myself and run to the bathroom so she can't see me. I always look in the mirror and ask myself if the little girl that I'm trying so hard not to screw up will be worse off for knowing me? Will she be just another undeserving casualty of my fuckedupness? Staring at myself in the mirror, I think of Francesca, from *The Bridges of Madison County*. I thought I had long since said good-bye to her, but she magically reappeared in my life when the little girl in the other room did the same. Like Francesca, I have a child now. And like her, my choices are made with my child's best interest in mind. Unlike Francesca though, it seemed that I could do that *and* live a fabulous life at the same time. Everything had finally fallen into place for me regardless of having a child; miraculously, none of my personal happiness had to be sacrificed in order to give her everything she deserved. In fact, there were days when I would walk around the Lafayette Reservoir (that I've come to know and love so well) and stare into the faces of all of the modern day Francescas and feel empowered by the risks I took to be different from them. Up until a few weeks ago, I honestly believed I could have my cake and eat it, too. But then, I pulled a Chrissygan and totally fucked myself. And now it seems that all I can do is wait for a *Bridges of Madison County, part II* to tell me what to do next, because I'm all out of ideas. With that thought, I wipe the last tear off of my face and set off to my little angel's room to try not to screw her up.

Lowering her lights and tucking her in tight around every inch of her body just like she likes it, I kiss her on the forehead and tell her I love her very much and that I'll always be here for her. I reassure her that I'm not going anywhere. Like every normal little girl, she moves right past my heartfelt words.

"One more game! *Pleeeeeeeeezzzze!*"

"Okay, just one more then it's time for night-night."

"I pie wit my widdle eye...somediiiiiiiiiin' happy!"

"A bird!"

"Noooooooooo."

"You!"

"Noooooooo."

"I need another hint!"

"Ummmm, it's somedin' super dooper pwetty!"

"Are you sure it's not you?"

Giggling, "It can't be!"

"Why's that?"

"Cuz I'm spyin' somedin' dat's dead.

Already (adverb) al*read*y:

Indicating that something has happened before now, happened in the past before a particular time, or will have happened by or before a particular time in the future.

I'll never forget, I'll never regret you and me…
For one moment
("For One Moment," *MaryAnne Marino*)

Recapitulating

April, 2001

"For the third time, lady, you can't park here! Keep it movin' or I'm gonna ticket your ass!"

Punching the gas, I think, *Jesus, when did this place turn into New York?*

No biggie though. Driving in these circles gives me time to think about everything that's happened since Kelly died in February. Honestly, I still can't believe I made it through the last two months without her. If it wasn't for the three years of physical and mental torture-conditioning that I put myself through with my Leo affair and my Kurt divorce, I doubt I would've been prepared to handle the demands of her funeral and the shit show that followed it.

Courtney and Nicole were a mess at the funeral. I warned them months in advance that they better start shedding some tears, but *nooooooooo*, they had to act all tough and doctor-like during her cancer. Well, while they went along with Kelly's wishes and stayed as far away from her as possible during the last months of her life, in classic Chrissy style, I barged in for some closure, told her I loved her (more times than she cared to hear) and said my good-byes. Even though her death ripped my heart out, I was way more prepared to handle the pain of it than my two shell-shocked doctor friends.

Immediately after the funeral, I dragged my brokenhearted friends to Mexico so they could get out privately what they should've been trying to get out the minute Kelly was diagnosed. Boy, did their floodgates open on that trip! And as the self-proclaimed emotional core of the group, I led the surge of tears. I'm actually surprised the Mexican authorities didn't slap a Section 5150 on us and declare us a danger to the hotel property, others, and ourselves and then hold us against our will for psychiatric evaluation. That's how big of a mess the three of us – the remaining member of the A-BOB's – were.

Kelly's death wasn't the only thing I mourned on that trip to Mexico. One night when Courtney and Nicole were drinking themselves to sleep, I ventured down to the beach and paid a little respect to my girl, Francesca. That woman has haunted me for the last three years, and it was time for me to say good-bye to her, too. But before I made my way down to the beach, my friends and I had a little Life List burning ceremony. Chugging from the same bottle of wine and sharing a cigarette, I grandly stood up on the bed in my undies and rattled off my seven point Life List for the last time while Courtney and Nicole jokingly booed and hissed. Once our bottle was empty and I was done with my dramatic diatribe, I shoved the old tattered up piece of paper that I'd carried around with me since I was sixteen years old into the wine bottle, dropped the lit cigarette on top of it and watched intensely as it went up in smoke. Then, at the beach, I kissed the bottle, whispered "good-bye, Francesca," and chucked it as far into the ocean as I could.

The day I returned home from Mexico, I drove straight to Kelly's house to check on her husband Craig and their child, my three year old Goddaughter, Kendall.

Craig actually moved Kendall out of the house and in with his parents two months before Kelly died. Even though his folks are super old and almost incapable of caring for a toddler, Kelly's condition became so fragile and scary looking that he thought it was for the best. By doing that, Kendall has in some of ways, gotten used to the loss we're all just being introduced to now. She's gotten used to Mommy not giving her a bath, Mommy not cooking dinner for her, Mommy not reading her a bedtime story…Mommy not kissing her goodnight. And being so young, Kendall's tears and confusion are already almost gone. Sometimes though, when she wanders around the house and notices the pictures of her mother that are still scattered about, you can see the commotion going on in her little head. Her inquisitive eyes dart from one photo to another, but her vocabulary isn't mature enough to express her thoughts. No one knows if it's best to talk her through the ordeal or yank the pictures away. Both seem so terribly wrong. For now, simply popping in a video about a stupid purple slow-speaking idiot dinosaur seems to put a quick end to the heartbreaking moment.

A car honks from behind and shakes me away from my sad thoughts of the funeral and of Kendall. I begin to obstinately stare into the huge glass window to try to make sense out of the crowds of people on the other side, but almost immediately, the mean fat guy yells at me again to "KEEP IT MOVIN'!" so I hit the gas and round the bend one more time. Right away, thoughts of the days immediately following Kelly's death fire away in my head again.

Kurt, who also happens to be Kendall's Godfather, called me just hours after Kelly died to see if I was okay and to ask if I wanted some photos of our old camping days. For some stupid Kurt-type reason he thought camping pictures would cheer me up. Anyway, it was a nice gesture and I agreed to meet up with him at a coffee shop for the photo exchange, which I did a few days after I got back from Mexico. Since he didn't say a word to me at the funeral or at the memorial service afterward, it surprised me when he wrapped his arms around me and whispered, "I've been so worried about you." Why on earth that man would give two shits about me after what I did to him is beyond me. And to my surprise, his two shits turned into three shits as we sipped our lattes. He commended my effort to boost

Courtney and Nicole's sprits in Mexico, he congratulated the success of my yoga studios, and he even complimented my Dolce and Gabana sling-backs. I didn't ask why. I just graciously accepted all of the attention I had been seeking since our first dance at his high school graduation party back in 1986. As I drove away from the coffee shop that day, I marveled at how much Kurt had grown in such a short period of time.

After that day, Kurt and I exchanged a few concerned emails about Craig and Kendall, and for a minute it seemed that maybe we could be friends despite everything that happened. But all of Kurt's good nature went out the window when he found out that Leo showed up on my doorstep and was moving back from New York and into my cottage. I abruptly stopped hearing from him, and I guess it's a good thing. With Leo back in my life, Kurt can't be, and so I'm relieved he made things easy for me by cutting off contact. It's nice not to be the bad guy for once. Even nicer not to have to come up with a lie to avoid being the bad guy! And speaking of lies…telling them is something I vowed I'd never do again. We all know keeping vows hasn't exactly been my strong point. But I have to give it everything I've got. My recently resuscitated relationship with Leo depends on it.

My effort to blend in with the other cars that are loading and unloading fails once again and the mean fat guy furiously taps his flashlight on my window to tell me to leave. Pulling back into the fray, I once again get lost in my thoughts of Kelly.

Shortly after she died, I was helping Craig pack up a few of her personal belongings. Don't EVEN get me started on how heart-wrenching it is to decide which one of your dead best friends belongings get packed up to decay in the attic, get to remain in plain sight, or get donated to Goodwill. There are no words. Anyway, it was during this task that Craig broke down and told me the demands of his job required him to increase Kendall's hours in daycare. I had to figure something out! There was NO WAY in hell Kelly would've had her daughter in daycare all day when she was alive, so there was NO WAY in hell I was going to allow her to be in it all day now that she was dead! So, I worked out an arrangement with Craig where two days a week he'd pick up Kendall at two-fifteen and three days a week I'd pick her up at two-fifteen and keep her until Craig was done with work. I admit, with the workload at the yoga studios, some days it's a challenge and most days I'm exhausted. But I wouldn't give up my time with Kendall for anything in the world, and I can't think of a single person who would ask me to.

It's only been a few weeks since I said good-bye to my therapist, Dr. Maria, but I already miss her so much. What a weird way to end our time together, with an audio tape of the frantic message I left her after having phone sex with Leo. The thought sends shivers up my spine, and I shake off the mortification of the whole thing by turning the radio louder. I don't have one second to be sad, embarrassed, or beat myself up, because right now I'm circling the arrival terminal at Oakland International airport looking for Leo and I want to look and feel my very best. He's been going back and forth from New York since we got back together to tie up some loose ends at work and pack up the apartment that he used to share with his best friend, Taddeo. When Leo told him he was moving in with me, I think the words Leo told me he muttered were "fucking idiot." I'm sure it was worse than that, but since I don't have the ability to hack into any of his communication devices anymore, I'll have to take his word for it.

In anticipation of the rush of my Leo drug, I twist the pewter Banana Republic ring that he bought for me in Mill Valley – which I gave back to him in Monterey – which he gave back to me in front of my cottage last month. He told me I can only take it off when he buys me the "real deal." Not believing I'll ever need more than I have with him right now, I can't help but wonder…*what does that mean exactly?* It's definitely a thought "old Chrissy" would obsess over. But "new Chrissy" is too satisfied, too busy, too focused on the here-and-now to be consumed with things she can't control. Besides, when I was trying to control my life, it always got in my way of really living it. From all that I learned from Dr. Maria, Kelly, and my own experiences, I plan on living the shit out of my life, and I plan on doing it with the man who just grabbed his luggage off of the conveyer belt and is walking toward my car. With every step, I feel my Leo drug slowly seep in and melt my heart.

Finally

"**B**aby, over here!"
    Forgetting for a minute that I'm in Oakland and there are about twenty people in a five foot radius that would have zero problem jacking my car, motor still running, I jump out of it and attack Leo's face.

"I missed you so much!"

"Not as much as I've missed you, Chrissy."

Then, pointing to the rolling cart behind him, he adds, "Is that cottage of yours prepared to handle this last load?"

Clinging to him tightly, I whisper, "You mean…that cottage of ours."

After getting my final earful from the fat ass wanna-be police officer traffic guy for taking too long to load the car up, we set off for what I hope is a never-ending sex filled night. You see, Leo and I haven't "been together" since we got back together last month. Crazy as it sounds for two people who used to maul each other, but it's the truth.

Last month when he showed up on my doorstep and asked me if I was finally ready to be afraid with him, we spent the entire evening talking about, *and being sorry for* (that would be me) everything that went wrong between us. I'm not sure if it was exhaustion from anticipating his arrival or exhaustion from the last three years of my life that caught up to me, but I fell asleep in his arms on the couch and didn't even wake up when he left for his early flight back to New York the next day. We never even made it to the bedroom. I woke in the morning to a bunch of wild flowers he picked from the creek below my cottage and a sweet note on the coffee table that said…

"Have to wrap things up in NY. Until I get back home, dream about me."

Truthfully, if it weren't for the note, I would've thought everything about that night was a dream. Leo was back in my life and I could hardly believe it! Like a modern day Snow White, I cheerfully spent the next few weeks preparing the cottage for his impending move-in day. I cleared everything out of my medicine cabinet that contained the words: wrinkle, itch, zit, rash, and flare-up. I disposed of all of my big ol' period panties, hid my super absorbent tampons and heavy flow maxi pads, and promptly started receiving Depo-Provera injections. Now that sex is on the horizon, I've got to protect myself and Lord knows I drink way too much alcohol to be trusted to take a pill every day. No babies, not yet, no thank you. It's time for me to have some long overdue fun, not change diapers!

Seven days ago when Leo returned from New York with his first load of items to move into the cottage, you can bet your sweet ass I had huge plans for him to see my sweet ass. I was NOT going to fall asleep this time! And I didn't, and not because I was having constant sex, it was because I had Kendall's sweet little ass with me. It wasn't the plan, but Craig had a last minute business trip and his folks weren't able to help him out. That meant Chrissy, or as Kendall calls me, Ki-Ki, to the rescue. Kendall would be with me for Leo's entire two-day visit before he had to go back to New York one final time. Suffice it to say, my big plans to handcuff Leo to the bed and do things to him he had better hope to all that's Holy no woman ever did to him in New York, were squashed.

Kendall was apprehensive about Leo at first. And being a man of few words, he didn't do much to convince her not to be. The ride from the airport back to my cottage that day was about as odd as odd could be. Just me...driving along in silence with my dead friend's three year old daughter and the twenty-five year old guy I'd barely seen in the last year and eight months and just reunited with. AWKWARD! Leo wasn't trying to be rude on that drive home. In fact, I think it was just as weird for him to be around Kendall as it was for Kendall to be around a big strange guy. You see, this was the first time Leo ever met anyone associated with my old Freakmont days. Not that he doubted it for a minute, but Kendall was the proof that I *did* have a best friend who died, that my best friend *does* have a husband who is still horribly grieving, and that her husband has a best friend who *happens* to be my ex-husband. No shit it was a quiet drive.

And the quiet continued once we got to the cottage. Just as I was about to suggest to Leo it might be best for him to stay at a hotel, he tenderly opened up his carry-on bag and started playing with a bunch of shitty airport gift shop toys. Kid gold! Kendall's eyes lit up at the mountain of florescent plastic crap that Leo so obviously bought when he got my call about her being with me just minutes before boarding his plane. I watched from the kitchen as Kendall slowly walked over to the pile. When she got there, Leo said, "My favorite color is blue, what's yours?" Within an hour, the two of them were on the back deck overlooking the roaring creek with flashlights in hand hunting for snipes. By the time I tucked Kendall into bed, she made me promise that "Weo" would hunt for the imaginary creatures again with her tomorrow.

That weekend, Leo and I agreed it would be in poor taste to sleep together with Kendall under the same roof, and it was torture watching him play with her, knowing the entire time he wouldn't be able to play with me. While he slept on my super pretty, but annoyingly uncomfortable wicker couch, I curled up next to Kendall in my bed and forced myself to forget about the man on the other side of the wall. But you know what? Despite being celibate for more days than I care to count, the three of us had a fantastic time that weekend. We went boating at the Lafayette reservoir, we ate dinner at one of those cook-at-your-table Japanese restaurants that ALL kids love, and of course, we hunted for snipes. There's nothing that could've made those forty-eight hours any better. Well, maybe one thing, and with Kendall sleeping at her own house tonight, I'm ready to collect.

Knowing tonight was finally going to be the end of my celibacy tour, I wanted everything to be perfect. I waxed nearly every square inch of my body and spent a hundred and seventy-five bucks on lingerie that barely weighs an ounce. Seriously, there's no point to it other than "Hey look at me, going to all these extremes to turn you on." I scrubbed every inch of my cottage and my body, set up candles anywhere there was space, and prepared a dinner for us that hopefully wouldn't come back to haunt me later while trying to bust a compromising move in bed (like in the form of a Chinese-firecracker-type fart). Before I left for the airport to pick up Leo, I put on my lingerie, my cutest jeans, my sexiest shoes, sprayed on the same Carolina Herrera perfume I had on the night we met at Buckley's, and then I eagerly hit the road. And now, here we are!

Pretending to listen to Leo talk about the new job he's about to take at Robertson Stephens in San Francisco while he drives my luggage-packed car back to the cottage, I can only hear my own thoughts and they're saying the same thing over and over again…*One year and eight months after the love of my life slammed the door on my face, I'm finally gonna get laid!*

("Beautiful," *Me'Shell Ndegeocello*)

Glowing

April, 2001

"Wait outside until I call you in."

His face is screaming, *Dear God, please don't tell me you have a husband to hide*, but he'd never say it out loud. He'll do anything to forget about the fact that I used to have one of those things.

After a kiss that reassures me I'm about to get pounced on, I scurry inside the cottage to light the three thousand candles I set up a few hours ago. Then, hurriedly picking my thong out of my butt while simultaneously applying lip gloss, I give the place one final look-over.

Once I'm satisfied that everything's exactly how I envisioned it would be, I yell, "OKAY, LEO! YOU CAN COME IN NOW!"

Not knowing what to expect, he cautiously peeks his head inside. As his whole body enters the shimmering retreat I spent hours constructing, I can visibly see the strain of the last three years of his life (courtesy of me) melt away from his body.

"Wow, Chrissy. This is…incredible."

And then out of nowhere, nerves hit me. He hasn't seen my naked body in almost two years! Granted, it's undergone extensive yoga remodeling, but still…what if it's not as great as he remembers it to be? Maybe I should've consulted with Slutty Co-worker about my plans for tonight. You know…gotten some sex advice, some new moves…something. *Hmmmmm*, I vaguely remember her talking about sucking on a couple of Altoids while giving a guy a blow job, and she said he really liked it…or were they Tic-Tacs? *I wonder if it matters!* Jesus, should Leo wear a condom? I mean, I'm not worried about getting pregnant because I got that Depo-Provera shot the minute we got back together, but do we need to have some kind of "talk" about the sexual relationships we might have had between ours and now? Obviously, I've had none, so he's definitely not going to catch anything from me. *But what if he has?* Aw, who am I kidding? My nerves aren't about getting gonorrhea, Leo always plays it safe. I'm anxious that maybe he screwed around when I didn't! Dammit, I knew I should've forced myself to sleep with that tatted-up defense attorney, Mark Wisely, or that Cal Berkeley Quarterback (whose name I totally can't remember) so I'd have something in my back pocket. I mean, if Leo's been with other women, I'm going to have to lie about being with other guys! Welp, so much for my vow to be totally and completely honest. But I have no choice! He can't have the sex leg-up on me, can he? *Would I be okay with that?* HELLS NO! Son of a bitch, I don't think I can be with Leo if he's been with someone else. It's not in my DNA!

"Baby, you okay?"

But I really, really, really need to have sex, and I need to have it with him. Aside from death and yoga, it's all I've thought about for almost two years. The last time we were together was in this very cottage, and it was as sensual as the first time we were together at his rundown apartment in Moraga. Every time I had sex with Leo it was sensual. But it won't be sensual with him anymore if I know he's been with another woman. That mental block will get in the way of any pleasure I'll ever be able to feel with him. Yep, it's official. We're through.

"Chrissy, talk to me. What's going on in your head?"

"Wine! Want some? I feel like I need a glass."

Actually more like *four* glasses.

Reaching into the drawer that houses the bottle opener, visions of the night I brought Leo home from The Round Up flash through my mind. Well, the good ones before Kurt started pounding on the door, anyway. I want to feel like I did that night again. But it'll never happen if I know he's face-planted another girl against her kitchen wall and seduced the shit out of her. I NEED WINE, NOW!

"Chrissy, please come back over here. This is the first time we've been alone in a long time. I just wanna sit with you for a minute and enjoy that this is really happening."

Carrying our glasses to the couch and sucking mine entirely down on the way, I settle in next to Leo's better-than-I-remember body. He was always in great shape, but the embraces we've shared since we got back together tell me there was a helluva lot of working out going on while he lived in New York. His neck is thicker, his forearms are wider and...*what the hell is going on under that shirt?* Seven little buttons on that thing are all that's separating me from total paradise. Will I be able to get a peek before my thoughts of him ram-charging another woman from behind get the best of me? Doubtful. Oh, Jesus! I need a distraction!

"Guess what? Kendall called me today and told me she can't wait to play that snipe hunting thing with you again. You made quite an impression on that little girl."

He moves even closer to me, and the smell of him is like ten thousand needle pricks of heroin hitting my body at once.

"I'm glad. I can't wait to see her again too, but I don't wanna talk about her right now. I wanna talk about you. No, scratch that. I don't wanna talk at all."

The lips. They're strong and hungry and they're on me. They're exactly where I'd want them to be if I wasn't stewing about them being on someone else.

"Leo, I'm sorry! I can't!"

He pulls away with his hands in the air like he's afraid he hurt me.

"Whoa, what's going on, Chrissy?"

"Don't you wanna know if I've been with anyone else while we were apart?"

"Okay, one…you should know the thought of that makes me psychotic, so I'm not sure why you'd bring it up. And two…I know you haven't."

There's that un-cocky confidence that hypnotized me the night we met.

"How do you know that?"

"How could you be with someone else?"

"What do you…but how could…hold on, can you explain so I can stop having my own psychotic thoughts?"

"Chrissy, you being with another guy makes about as much sense as me being with another girl. It makes no sense. I'm sure you tried, just like I did, to date and put yourself out there, but it's not how you and I operate to sleep with someone we're not in love with."

"But you told me in New York we were done! You made me believe I had to move on! Jesus, Leo, you made me believe you already had! You might as well have said, 'Go have sex with other guys, Chrissy, because you'll never have it with me ever again!'"

"Yeah, and in my mind we were done, but in my heart, it just wasn't happening."

I'm looking at him like I ain't buying what he's selling.

"Baby, for the last year and a half you've been stuck in the middle of my heart, leaving no room for anyone else. And you should know I can't have sex with a woman when my heart isn't in it. Haven't I proven that to you?"

I think back to April, 1998, when he rejected my pleas to come to his apartment. He thought I was engaged at the time and knowing he could never have my whole heart if I was, he couldn't give me his. So, he rejected me...and my sex.

"Sex with some girl would've only tainted what we had together. I've never been ready to do that. So, no Chrissy, I don't think there's any way you'd be sitting here with me right now if you slept with someone else. I don't think there's any way you would've tainted what we had."

"Everything you're saying makes sense, but you're a guy, Leo! Isn't it impossible to, you know...go that long?"

Just asking that question makes me chug my re-filled wine glass in one gulp.

"Damn near! Especially with thoughts of you and what we did together running through my mind. Made me quite the master of my domain, if you know what I mean."

Who knew being told your ex-boyfriend jerked off to thoughts of you for over a year and a half could be so romantic! And you know what? I guess that's why the motor on my vibrator fried out...TWICE!

After a sharing a gentle laugh at what he just said, he takes my hand and places it over his heart like he's done so many tender times before.

"Feel that? That was made for you. Sometimes I think God watched you on earth for the first six years of your life and was like, *Crap, there's still no one who's perfect for her*, so He made me."

"Sure would've made my life a lot easier if you were born in Freakmont six years earlier and went to my same high school."

"Probably would've made my life easier too. But so what if the hand you were dealt required you to trade in a couple of old cards for new ones. All that matters is that you had the courage to do it."

"So you're not mad at me for *anything* that happened?"

"I'm mad that some things had to happen the way they did. But no, I'm not mad at you. If I was, I wouldn't be here right now."

47

With my hand still glued to his heart, he says "It's wild, but sometimes it feels like I loved you long before I even met you."

Nodding my head in agreement, I confess, "No one I know could possibly understand us."

"Does that make us crazy?"

"I think it makes us lucky."

After a gentle kiss that reassures me he's not mad at all, Leo takes my hand and leads me to the bedroom and without a word he undresses me. The only light is coming from the electric moon outside and the only sound is that of the roaring creek below the open window. That is until he explores my naked body with his eyes, takes a deep breath in and says, "My God, you are so beautiful."

Reaching out for him, I speak modestly when I whisper, "I bet everything you look at through those green eyes is beautiful."

"That's absolutely not the case..." Taking my hands, "...I see very few beautiful things. That's what makes you so special to me, Chrissy."

After tranquilly assisting with the removal of his clothes, we kiss and settle onto the bed in one intertwined motion, with him softly landing on top. My fingers trace up and down the length of his back, his hands cradle my neck. Our kisses are sometimes halted by long gazes at each other, acknowledging this almost didn't happen.

If forced to make the choice, I would gladly take the long gazes into Leo's eyes over sex with him. They're what tell me he loves me so much. But...thank GOD I don't have to make the choice! It's been one year, eight months and glancing at the clock as he kisses my neck, three hours since the last time I've been with him. Not usually one to bypass the thrill of foreplay, with every ticking second, I get more and more restless.

"Leo, please. I miss you so much. I don't think I can..."

And he can't either because there it is. Holy mother of mercy! I NEVER should've deprived myself of this feeling for this long. I should've fought harder to be with him sooner! I should've done whatever it took to have...this. I don't care what type of woman you are (minus lesbos), the feeling of a muscular man laying on top of you who is able to enter your body without his hands ever leaving your side and his eyes never leaving your gaze, is the single most electrifying sensation EVER. Momentarily lost in the pleasure, I close my eyes and roll my head back. Not ready to lose the control he has over me, he gently bites my lower lip and kisses it back to where he wants it as he says, "Look at me, Baby." I do, but I can't see him. I can't see anything. I'm completely blinded by what he's doing to me and my love for him.

Shitshow

May, 2001

I'm not a great pooper. I don't bring a magazine in with me to relax. I don't keep the door open so I can watch my shows while I'm going. In fact, I'll even put off doing the deuce until it absolutely positively can't stay inside of my body for one minute longer. Then when I finally do go, I force it out as fast as I can. I've got more important shit to do!

On top of never finding the time to poop, I hate talking about it with people or acknowledging that it even happens. Unlike Slutty Co-worker! That woman will literally excuse herself from the middle of a yoga session by announcing to the class, "Be right back, gotta take a crap." And when teaching certain positions, she'll shout out, "If you're not farting, you're not doing it right!" At first I was mortified, but apparently our clients find all of her potty-talk charming because she's booked solid every single week. But me, if I have to go at work, I'll sneak off when I know everyone else is out to lunch and that's ONLY when it's an absolute poop emergency! I'll never drop a bomb at a party, a friend's house, or a restaurant. I'd rather die than shit in public! Which is why 99.9% of my pooping occurs when I'm alone in my cottage. Which is why, now that Leo has moved in, I'm up shit creek. And it's with his suggestion that we grab some Mexican food for dinner that I nervously wonder...*will I ever poop again*?

Yeah, yeah...I know it's natural to poop and everyone does it. It's the very fact that everyone DOES poop that's gotten me through a lot of personal challenges in my life. No matter who I'm in a business deal with or what beautiful movie star I'm

51

admiring on TV, I can never get too intimidated or awe struck because in the back of my mind I'm thinking...that person sat on the shitter this morning and wiped his ass. Jennifer Aniston does it, the President of the United States does it, every single human being does it! That being the case, NOBODY can ever be better than me. I'm serious! Look around the room right now and zero in on the most attractive person you can find. Now, imagine them squeezing one out. *See?* They aren't so great now, are they? Well, for a long time I relished in the thought that Leo didn't think anyone could be better than me. But now that I'm sitting at Senior Colorado's and staring down at my burrito especial, I bet that won't be the case once I turn into his Mexican food-shitting girlfriend. Shit.

"What's wrong Baby, not hungry?"

I'm super hungry, starved actually. But my hope is that two bites of this stuff won't piss off my colon and I can hold it together until he leaves for work in the morning.

Then I look at his plate of food, beans and all, and realize, holy shit, Leo poops, too. I mean, I don't mind. He's a man and men shit. But the bathroom in the cottage is right next to the bedroom! WILL I HEAR IT? When will he do it? Tonight? Tomorrow before work? Jesus, what a nightmare! *Shhhhhhh,* calm down, Chrissy! Remember what Dr. Maria said...When you go from one relationship to another you just trade in one set of problems for another. Okay, I realize pooping isn't technically classified as a problem, but it sure is the beginning of this relationship turning into something ho-hum. I've been watching the clock and counting down the days until Leo officially moved in, but now that it has happened, I sure wish I had eaten more burritos and shit a whole lot more while I was waiting for it.

Returning to the cottage after dinner, I pretended to need something from the grocery store, and I slipped out to give Leo time to settle in privately. No need to propel this living arrangement into something that feels like we've been together for twenty years quite yet.

An hour later, I sink in next to him in bed where he's freshly showered, smelling heavenly, and drifting off to sleep. As I'm lying on his chest listening to him breathe, I'm so grateful for the second (or I guess, in my case, fifth) chance to be with him. I start thinking about the first nervous night I walked into his apartment. As he gently placed his hand on the small of my back to guide me in, I nervously wondered what would happen next. Once inside, my eyes darted around in every direction looking for clues about him. Everything about that night was exciting, and I envied single people everywhere for being able to have that anxious rush all of the time. I vaguely remember experiencing the same rush when Kurt and I were first together. It died off pretty quickly though…right about the time he took me four wheeling and rifle shooting a few months after we met. I never want the rush to go away with Leo, and I wonder for a second if I stupidly fast-tracked the whole moving-in-together thing. I mean, now that we're cohabitating, I'll never be able to experience the rush of him picking me up for a date. You know that exciting moment when you open the door after having spent hours showering, drinking wine, listening to loud music and picking out the most perfect outfit and you imagine him doing the same (well…in a fraction of the time and with beer). Those moments are already gone for us because we'll be getting ready together. And there's no mystery about whose bed we'll be waking up in. I've already ripped myself off of that thrill by narrowing the choice down to one. I bet it won't be long before Leo realizes I actually do poop, that I have incredibly unforgiving periods, that I prefer to sleep in baggy sweats over lingerie, and that I'm secretly obsessed with reruns of *The Golden Girls*. And what about his weird stuff? What if he farts in his sleep? What if I catch him picking his nose…scratching his balls…hawking a loogie when brushing his teeth? Before I fall into my own deep sleep, I wonder...*Did I rush into this living arrangement?*

"I miss you!"

"You just saw me three months ago. You can't miss me that much."

"We usually do this every month, though. Why did we get off schedule?"

Kelly's always been a pale girl, but not right now. Her eyes are bright and her cheeks are rosy. She looks more alive than ever.

"There really is no schedule here. They say it takes time to adjust to that."

Shoving garlic cheese fries into my mouth, I wonder, "Who's they?"

"You'll find out one day."

"Dude, what's going on with you? It's like you're talking in circles or something."

Playfully throwing pieces of bread at me she says, "What's going on with me? More like, what's going on with you?"

"What the heck did I do?"

"You stayed with Kurt."

I abruptly stop dodging the bread and stare at her, confused. "No, I didn't. *Did I?*"

"Didn't look like you were going to, but you did."

Shaking my head in frustration because I can't seem to remember shit from crap to set her straight, I press her for information.

"Kel, how come I don't know what my life is like?"

She stands as she says, "I don't think you have it figured out yet."

"Wait, why are you leaving?"

"I'm still busy settling in, and I don't have a lot of time."

"Settling in where?"

54

"Sorry, Chrissy, but I don't know if I can be here next month either. Things are constantly changing."

"What are you talking about? Nothing's changing! This is what we do! We eat the same crappy food and drink the same stupid drinks. It's a tradition!"

Totally confused, I stand up and watch her walk away. But then she turns, runs back to me giggling and whispers in my ear, "Guess what? You're about to be a mommy." And then she disappears into the mad rush of happy hour at Chili's.

With the sheets drenched in sweat, I bolt straight up in bed and scream at the top of my lungs,
"KELLYYYYYYYYYYYYYYYYYYY!"

"Baby, Baby, Baby, it's me! You're having a bad dream!"

Leo grabs me tightly to try and stop the trembling.

My eyes dart around the room looking for her, before I exclaim, "Kelly was here!"

"She's not, Chrissy. You were having a dream."

"No, it wasn't a dream! Her voice was crystal clear!"

"Baby, I just came back from getting a glass of water, you were sound asleep."

"NO, LEO! SHE TALKED TO ME!"

"Okay, okay, okay, I believe you. What'd she say?"

Clutching my stomach, "She said...she said..."

"It's okay, you can tell me."

Yeah right, tell you I'm about to me a mommy? I don't think so!

"She said...she loves me."

What? It's not a lie. It's an omission. Completely different.

With Leo gently rubbing my back as I try to fall back asleep, I think, wow...dodging poop and talking to dead people. Yep, probably rushed things a little.

Shit...*heads*

May, 2001

"*Okayyyyyyy* and what are you gonna do the first time you get the stomach flu?"

I remain silent.

"You're gonna shit your pants is what you're gonna do!"

Sitting on the picnic blanket on top of Kelly's grave for the third-month anniversary of her death, I continue to endure a verbal beating from Nicole and Courtney.

"Everyone poops Chrissy! Do I have to let you borrow the book on the subject that I bought for my two year old son?"

With beer nearly snorting out of her nose, Nicole chimes in with, "So...like does Leo think he landed the only non-pooping human being on earth?"

Going in for a gulp of my beer, I murmur, "Are you guys done yet?"

"No! It sounds like you're up to the same old shit, no pun intended...that you were up to with Kurt!"

"What's that supposed to mean?"

"You're pretending to be something you're not."

"Yeah, Chrissy. Seems like you're trying to be all perfect."

"Hey, guys! It's not like I'm taking up ice hockey or scuba diving for the guy! Is it so wrong that I wanna keep the passion alive in this relationship for as long as possible?"

"Whoa, thought you weren't afraid of the passion disappearing with this guy!"

"I'm not, Nicole! Jesus, if it makes you guys feel any better, Kurt didn't think I went number two either."

"Girl, you need to be studied."

And then Courtney, "No, more like committed!"

I gulp down the rest of my beer as I trace the outline of Kelly's name on her tombstone while the two of them try to compose themselves. When they can finally breathe again, I ask the question I've would've thought the two of them would've asked me by now.

"So do you guys wanna meet Leo or what?"

Their quick glances at each other before pointing their heads down to their bottles offers me no assurance that they're in a hurry.

"What's the problem?"

"Oh, it's not us. Trust me, we're dying to meet the guy who stole you away from Kurt."

"Let me clarify this for the millionth time, Court! Leo didn't steal me away from Kurt. I just happened to meet him at the exact moment I realized Kurt was totally wrong for me. Now it's your turn to clarify…if you want to meet Leo so badly, what's stopping you?"

I sit in irritated silence as I listen to the two of them stumble through their answer.

Court's first with, "Well, you know how far back we all go…"

Nicole then stutters, "…Yeah, and it's hard for our husbands to…."

And then Court butts back in with, "…You get it right? They just don't want to lie to Kurt about…you know…"

Now it's my turn to laugh at my friends.

"So let me get this straight. Your husbands *forbid* you from meeting my boyfriend?"

"No way! Kyle doesn't forbid me from doing anything!"

"Yeah and neither does Guss!"

Sure looks like I hit a couple of doctor nerves. Never one to back down to their over-achieving asses…

"Great. So then you guys have no problem meeting me and Leo for drinks on Friday night, then?"

Their nervous glances scream, HUGE PROBLEM!

"Wow, thanks so much for your support."

"It's not like that, Chrissy. You know we support you!"

"Yeah, you just have to try and see things from Kyle and Guss's perspective. They still want to protect Kurt."

"He's a grown man! He doesn't need their protection. Shit….Kurt barely cared when I left him, why should they?"

"I don't know, maybe it's because they're husbands."

Hopeful she'll lend some mature perspective to Nicole's stupidity, I ask Courtney, "What's that supposed to mean?"

"They sort of think Leo should've walked away the minute he found out you were married, like he broke some kind of guy code or something."

Now I'm the one with beer snorting out of my nose!

"Do they actually think Leo walking away would've made a difference in the end result? You know what? Why don't you refresh their memories and remind them that Leo did walk away, and he stayed away for over a year and half…until Kelly convinced me to beg him to come back!"

Their disgraced faces tell me they already tried this route and it didn't work.

"So that's it, then? Kyle and Guss are choosing sides?"

It's almost comical until a nauseating thought occurs to me and my jaw literally drops to the dirt that's covering Kelly.

"OH MY GOD! But you know who didn't leave for a year and a half?"

If shame had a face it would look exactly like the two of theirs.

"Did they meet *her?*"

Courtney, the tougher of the two, speaks up in their defense.

"Guss and Kyle are two of Kurt's best friends. Of course they met Kayla."

Searching for some kind of common sense, my heads snaps in the direction of every tombstone within sight. I scramble to my feet and yell like I've never yelled before!

"AND YOU TWO ARE SUPPOSED TO SHOW ME YOU'RE MY BEST FRIENDS BY BEING EXCITED ABOUT MEETING THE GUY WHO STOLE MY GOD DAMN MARRIED HEART!"

But their married hearts tell me their hands are tied. I quickly shove my shit in the picnic basket and mumble, "Your husbands can go fuck themselves," and then I turn and make my way to my car. But another nauseating thought sucker punches me on the way there, and I instantly run back to confront my fraidy-cat friends one more time.

"The two of you have never lied to me before so don't start now..." They can see it coming, and they hang their heads low when I scornfully ask, "...Did you meet her, too?"

Their non-response tells me everything I need to know. This time I DON'T mumble when I sneer, "On second thought, you can ALL go fuck yourselves!"

Puffalumpa

May, 2001

"Why do you care?"

"What do you mean, *why do I care*? They're my best friends!"

"Is it that you feel like they lied to you or is it that you consider it a betrayal that they hung out with the other woman?"

"Kayla isn't *the other woman*! It's not like he left me for her or anything!"

"Exactly, so then why do you care?"

I'm staring at Slutty Co-worker like she's lost her ever-lovin' mind.

"Did they get to you? Seriously, this isn't like you to be *alllllll* let go and let God-ish."

Wrapping her arms around me she lovingly says, "I'm just screwing with you, Hunny. I'd be pissed too. Maybe you should just give it some time to work itself out though. Men are big fucking babies, and sometimes it's just easier for the women they're with to let their poo-poo baby shit go away on its own rather than do something about it. Sure as hell explains why I've never wanted to be in a relationship. Committed men are way too much work if you ask me."

I wonder if that means it's only a matter of time before Leo's too much work for me. Dammit, why are thoughts like this suddenly haunting me? *What am I so afraid of?*

"So, how come I've never met these best friends of yours?"

"Are you kidding? I'm doing you a favor. They'd hog tie you, blindfold you and take you to some secret science lab in the desert to test you for a new strain of venereal disease! Trust me, I'm doing you a favor."

Or, more like I'm doing myself a favor by keeping my two worlds separate, but she doesn't need to know that.

Focusing back on work, Slutty Co-worker points to a box in the corner that Barbara Cooper dropped off before any of us arrived to work this morning.

"Are Megan and I ever gonna get to meet that woman?"

"Let's just give her a little more time to adjust to the production deadlines before I scare her with a face to face introduction. Lord knows, meeting you could set her back years in therapy!"

With that, I head out to Kendall's daycare. It's my day to pick her up at two-fifteen. On the way, I leave Barbara a message thanking her for the delivery and that I'd like her opinion on other handmade crap we could offer in the studios. She calls me back within minutes of the message, giving me her ideas and sounding as nervous as the first time I talked to her in Dr. Maria's parking lot two months ago.

"...Oh, and Barbara, I have one more thing to tell you."

"What's that?"

"My partners really want to meet you. They're impressed with the work you've done so far and like me, want to talk to you about being more involved with the business."

"Will you be there when I meet them?"

"Of course! And I promise...you'll love them."

Pulling into Kendall's daycare I'm reminded of something she needs to know.

"Actually, there is one more thing I should tell you."

Sensitive to Barbara's tragic loss, I feel it's necessary to reveal...

"I have a three year old Goddaughter. In fact, she's my best friend's daughter...the friend of mine who died."

She's silent.

"I think you need to know that Kendall...that's her name...is with me a lot. I hope this won't be hard for you if you decide to work with us."

After a long pause, Barbara slowly speaks. "It'll be very hard for me."

Thinking that's that and I'll never see Barbara ever again, she continues, "But maybe not any harder than crocheting again. I guess we'll have to wait and see, won't we?"

"I'm so glad you're willing to give this a shot! I'll call you next week to arrange a meeting!"

And then I hang up in just enough time to grab the call coming in from Leo on the other line.

Sexy as ever, he says, "Hey, Baby! Put on some of those cute shoes of yours and meet me in the city for drinks!"

Staring at the entrance of The Happy Hearts daycare center, my all at once unhappy heart sinks.

"It's my day with Kendall."

"Oh, damn, that's right. A bunch of people are meeting after work, and I wanted to show you off. Next time, I guess. Tell Kendall that I got us some night vision goggles so we can get all Rambo-like next time we're snipe hunting."

Not that thirty-one is old or anything, but the sounds of the children streaming out of The Happy Hearts daycare center and the fact that one of them is preventing me from getting my drink on tonight makes me feel...thirty-one. If it was my own child causing the road block to my fun, I'd get a babysitter, but...*I am Kendall's babysitter*. With a long sigh, I tell Leo to have a good time without me...even though I don't mean it.

I feel sorry for myself for ten minutes, exactly how long it takes to sign Kendall out of Happy Hearts and strap her into the car seat that I still can't figure out how the hell to use properly. Seriously, the child only has one head and yet there are four straps and three buckles to work with. It makes me wonder what strange/horrific accident must've happened once upon a time to have necessitated all of this equipment. After Kendall talks me through the process for the millionth time and I'm able to give my little mini-Kelly a kiss, all misery over missing out on happy hour with my super sexy investment banker boyfriend at some totally hot bar in San Francisco flies out of the sunroof. Looking at Kendall in the rear view mirror, I let the good times roll.

"What's the plan, Stan? Do you wanna go back to the yoga studio, go to the park…get some fro-yo? You name it!"

"Puffalumpa!"

"Puffa…what?"

Waiving a piece of paper at me, she demands me to, "Get my Puffalumpa, Ki-Ki!"

I open the note and sink down into my seat as I read it.

Don't hate me, but can you drive to Kurt's house and get Kendall's stuffed animal? She left it there yesterday and she can't sleep without it. She was up all night! Thanks a million! Craig

Oh, you've got to be kidding me!

Mustering up all of the fake happiness I can, I sing, "Sure, Sweetie! Let's go rescue your Puffalumper."

"No, Ki-Ki! It's *Lumpa!*"

No. It's more like, Puffa-I'm-gonna-fucking-kill-Craig-Lumpa! I never knew where Kurt moved after we sold our house in Danville, and I didn't want to know. I'm the type of person who functions better when I can't visualize the realities of people I could potentially be jealous of. Don't get me wrong, I don't want to be married to Kurt anymore. But just knowing he bought that Porsche after we split up and that Kayla's driving around in it in all of her 34-D cup glory was enough to make me lose sleep. I'll shit my pants if anything else in Kurt's life is better than it was when he was with me. And given the fact that Leo doesn't think I shit, going to Kurt's new home poses even more of a nuisance than my jealousies.

Rounding the corner to the address that Craig supplied, I pull over in confusion.

"Oh, you've GOT to be bleeping kidding me!"

Must keep the language clean; kid in the car.

"What, Ki-Ki?"

"A flipping gate?"

"Can I pwess da buttons?"

"Is this *really* Kurt's house, Kendall?"

"Yep! Ku-Ku's house is soopa fun!"

For some retarded reason, Kelly thought it would be cute if Kendall had special names for Kurt and me as her Godparents. Hence the Ki-Ki and Ku-Ku bullshit.

I'm in freaking Orinda! How the hell can Kurt afford a house with a gate in this city? Doctors and lawyers can barely do it! How can a moderately focused, overgrown child with a job that never paid as much money as mine, afford all of this? Beyond irritated, I hit the button on the gate expecting to hear his gloating voice. Instead, I get the luxury of hearing someone else's stupid one. *Jesus, shouldn't she be the one in daycare right now?*

"Oh, hey Kayla, it's Chrissy. I'm here to pick up Kendall's Puffa...thingy."

Kayla's silent for a long time before the line eventually drops and the gate slowly opens. Apparently Kurt communicates with this chick as much as he communicated with me. It's obvious by the look of pure shock and terror on her face that she's completely surprised I'm here. The poor child is still scared to death from the one and only time I ever encountered her, when she was riding bikes with my ex-husband and my dog at my then-home in Danville. I remember nearly fainting when I saw her bra dangling off of the edge of my wedding picture. I guess since she can hang her bra wherever she wants in this house, I'll take it easy on her...this time. After I slowly roll into the driveway, the big boobied dummy cautiously walks up to my car window.

65

"Kurt didn't tell me you were coming."

I'm immediately reminded of how stupid this girl is by her outfit. Pink sweat pants with some lame word printed across her ass, a white tank top with glitter splattered all over it, and of course, a big freaking bra that's visible from every direction.

"You're surprised about that?"

"Yeah, since he tells me everything."

I'm sure he tells her everything she can comprehend, which probably isn't much. Seriously, I wonder how this girl got into Stanford. Must come from money. *Ahhhhh*, maybe that explains this house.

"If you'll just give me the stuffed animal, I'll let you get back to..." I want to say Sesame Street, but figure I'll be the bigger person for a change. "...Whatever you were doing."

"I was making dinner."

"I don't really care, Kayla. I just need the Puffaloompy."

"Ki-Ki! I told you, it's my Puffa-*lumpa*!"

Given the fact that five minutes ago I thought I'd die if anything in Kurt's life was better than it was when he was with me, I'm actually surprised I don't feel an ounce of jealousy about this place now that I'm staring at it. I mean, I can see the sparkling pool beyond the wrought-iron fence, the private tennis court to the right of the four-car garage, and clearly the residence is a good four thousand square feet. I'm even a little surprised that I'm not jealous of the fact that Kayla is evidently some kind of stay-at-home-something or other – a gig that Kurt was never supportive of me landing. But what's *not* surprising is the overwhelming amount of rage that exploded inside of me when Kayla handed Kendall her stuffed animal. She extended her head inside of the car and said, "I miss you *sooooooo* much, and I can't wait for our next pizza party!" And then she planted a HUGE kiss on her forehead.

OH NO YOU DIDN'T, BITCH! It's one thing to be living the life I'd been planning for myself since I was sixteen, but you DON'T get to smooch on my dead best friend's daughter!

Taking control of the situation the only way I know how, I start to shut the window on her head. Sadly for me, she manages to wiggle out just as it's about to close in around her neck. So much for taking it easy on her.

Doing all I can to control my smile, I begin to gush, "Oh my goodness! I'm soooooo sorry Kayla, I hit the wrong button!"

"NAH-UH! You did that on purpose! I'm telling Kurt!"

Part of me wants to call her a tattle tale, but that would reduce the conversation to the second grade level she's clearly accustomed to. Although…I wonder what level a window closer person is? Probably a higher level. It involves mechanics and critical thinking and stuff.

Knowing full well she'll do anything she can to prevent me from speaking to Kurt ever again, I apathetically reply, "Alrighty, I'll be home later tonight if he needs to talk to me about it."

As I drive away, Kayla picks up a basketball and with boobs bouncing everywhere, she starts shooting basket after basket after basket, never missing a shot. I think she's trying to show me how much Kurt must love her awesomeness, but it only makes me happy for him...and wanting a boob job. The whole scene has me cracking up in my car, but I stop the second the gate opens to let me out. Suddenly everything's not so funny anymore.

Different

May, 2001

As the gate to the property inches open, I see Kurt sitting in his Porsche on the other side. Our eyes lock and my smile withers away. At once, all of the blasé feelings I had about being here vanish and my past emerges.

The gate causes dust to kick up into the air, and it takes me back to Kurt's motorcycle accident in December, 1999, and how his body was covered in it. He thought the accident would reunite us, but when I brought him home from the hospital I asked him to let me go. I begged him to believe in the peace, sanity, relief, and safety that wraps around you like a cocoon when you're with the right person. It took some convincing, but eventually he told me he believed in the kind of love I was talking about and agreed to a divorce so that he could be free to find it. Now, looking at Kayla in my rearview mirror, I don't see how he's found all of those things I was talking about. Something's seriously wrong with this picture.

It's been almost three months since I saw Kurt at that coffee shop for the camping photo exchange. Like always, his hair is cut super short so as not to interfere with his recreational activities. His arms, it seems no matter what time of the year, are golden brown. His smile is as carefree and bright as it was when I met him fifteen years ago. But his ordinarily lively eyes…just turned noticeably weary. I can tell he *just* realized that he forgot Craig told him I'd be dropping by to pick up Kendall's Puffalumpa. The absentmindedness would've made me mad

69

when I was married to him, now it just makes me chuckle. Just like I thought the overly casual outfit he wore to Kelly's funeral was a little endearing, I sort of think the absentmindedness is, too…now that I'm not responsible for it anymore. Slowly pulling up to each other's car, I roll down my window.

"Nice digs, man. Who knew you were such a heavy roller these days."

"I wish I could take credit for all of it, but it belongs to her parents."

Aha! I knew it!

Peering into the back of my car he sweetly asks, "Hey there, Kendall! Got your guy back?"

"Puffalumpa's a *guuuuurl*, Ku-Ku!"

"Oh, that's right! How could I have forgotten that?" Nervously looking back at me, he asks, "So, how'd it go in there?"

"I almost decapitated her, but she made it through alright."

"Yeah, Ku-Ku! Ki-Ki squeezed Kayla's head! It was funny!"

I wish I had a camera to capture the look on his face.

"Dude! We're kidding…sorta. Don't worry, it went fine. She was obviously caught off guard, but she triumphed in the end by walking into the house all by herself without falling out of her shoes, grabbing the *correct* stuffed animal…which by the way must've been difficult because I bet she has a lot to choose from on her bed, and then she walked the *whooooooole* distance to my car without losing her way the entire time! You should be proud, really."

"Having fun?"

"Kind of. But c'mon! It's too easy."

"She's actually pretty smart, Chrissy."

"Smart enough to get into Stanford on her very own?"

Now laughing a little himself, he confesses, "Not that smart. Both of her parents went there."

His honesty was *always* something I appreciated.

Looking back toward the house, I marvel, "So, what's up with this place, Kurt? Seems kinda fancy for you."

"Kayla's folks are gone six months of the year. It was too hard to pass up the accommodations while I figured out my next steps."

I don't really want to know, but thanks to Craig, I'm now forced to visualize Kurt's reality. I'd rather just hear it straight from him that it's FAN-FUCKING-TASTIC than torture myself with manufactured thoughts. I don't know why, but I feel an intense need to hear it straight from him that Kayla represents the peace, sanity, relief, and safety that we set each other free to find.

"So, like…is she in your next steps?"

"Would it bother you if she was?"

"Not at all. I was just curious. I mean, it seems serious. You've got her buddying up with my best friends and all."

"Does that bother you?"

"You knew it would. Remember? I'm a truly, madly, deeply kinda gal."

"About that…Are you ever gonna explain to me what that means exactly?"

I get the sense he's trying to be charming, but I can tell he really doesn't know what it means to be a truly, madly, deeply kind of person. But I'm no dummy. All energy to continue to explain it to him would be wasted. That was a lesson I needed to learn…let's see…forty-seven times!

"Been there. Done that. Failed miserably, Kurt. Don't worry, though. I'll manage the expectations of my friendships with Courtney and Nicole directly with them. Go ahead and invite them to *allllll* the backyard barbecues you want. I can just divorce them too if they don't see things my way."

I was trying to be funny but it looks like I hit a nerve because his smile is gone.

"You expect too much from people, Chrissy."

Mine is gone too now. Glaring directly into his eyes, I profess, "Obviously not enough."

Then I turn to Kendall who's in hog heaven with her rescued Puffalumpa, and tell her, "Say bye-bye to Ku-Ku, he has to go babysit now."

Then looking back at Kayla through my rearview mirror, I continue to press Kurt's buttons and tease with, "Looks like we're both on duty today, huh?"

"You're something else, you know that?"

"Like I said, it's too easy."

Before my window makes its way to the top, Kurt yells out, "What are your next steps?"

Not wanting to have this conversation in front of Kendall, I put the car in park and tell her I'll be back in a minute. Then I make my way over to Kurt's passenger side window, tap on it and wait impatiently while it rolls down.

"Are you wondering about my career or my love life?"

"I already know about your career."

"And you also know Leo lives with me. There! Looks like you're all caught up on my next steps."

"Don't you think you're rushing things a little with that guy?"

Laughing like I hadn't laughed in a very long time, I roar, "Wow, Kurt, your hypocrisy has no limits. What do you call your living arrangement here with Boobs? And let's not forget about your trip to Mexico with her after you made me feel like an irresponsible slut for wanting to go to Mexico with Leo? And here's a good one, how about sleeping with her in *our* house? I've known Leo a lot longer than you've known that girl, so don't even get me started on the who's rushing things with who bullshit. You'll lose the argument and you know it."

Struggling to say what's on his mind, he stares at me for a lot longer than I'm comfortable with.

"Jesus, Kurt, if you have something to say, just say it! For once, just speak from your fucking heart!"

72

And then, in an insightful tone that I don't think I've ever heard, he says, "I call all of those things convenient distractions from the pain of losing the love of my life and watching her move on with who she thinks is the love of her life."

Okay, I was completely NOT expecting that. The old Chrissy would get a little mushy about what Kurt just said. She'd question the choices she made over the last three years and doubt most of them. She'd worry that maybe she threw away over a decade of her life because she got impatient...or that her expectations were too high. She'd hurt for Kurt...she'd desperately want to help him. But I've learned too much about myself...I've become too happy with where I am in my life to let a few seemingly sincere words from Kurt pull me back to a place that wasn't good for me. Besides all of that crap, I'm in deep, deep, deep love with Leo. Even so, I'm taken aback by this raw side of Kurt that I've never seen before.

Clearing my throat, I ask, "Did you ever think that maybe you're where you're at today because you always have convenient distractions in your life?"

"Look, Chrissy, I'm not trying to start an argument here. I'm just saying it seems really fast for you to be seriously living with a guy."

"His name is Leo and yes, it's fast, but it's real...." Looking back toward the mansion, which all of a sudden does have me a little jealous, I scoff, "...Nothing like the convenient distraction you have going on here."

"Fuck. Maybe you're right."

Whooda huh?

Running his fingers through his hair, he exhales, "I really do have to figure my shit out. Kayla's parents are coming back in a month, and I'm not really sure what she expects."

Surprise, surprise.

"I don't think I'm ready to seriously settle down with someone, and she's gonna be pretty pissed about that. She thinks we should be doing what you're doing."

My frustration is now replaced by curiosity.

"I don't get you, though, Kurt. When our divorce was final, you told me you were falling in love with her. You made me think she was the one who could give you all of that peace, sanity, relief, and safety we talked about."

"I said a lot of things when our divorce was final."

Not wanting to go down this beat up, chaotic, emotionally charged road with him again, I don't pursue an explanation to that comment.

"Just be honest with her, Kurt. If she's not the one, let her go. You both deserve to be happy."

Signifying the end of the conversation, he revs his engine. As I back away, he says, "You look different, Chrissy…in a good way," and then he drives off in the car of my dreams toward the girl with the rack of my dreams.

As I make my way out of the Orinda compound, I think, Kurt sure looks the same, but something about him, too, is very different.

Bwamp-Chicka-Bwamp-Bwamp

June, 2001

L ast month, when I arrived back at the cottage after rescuing Kendall's Puffa-thingy, I was going to tell Leo the truth about how I spent the afternoon. I mean, things are different now, I'm officially divorced and we live together. There's no reason why I should have to hide the fact that I did something that made Kendall happy, even if it meant coming face to face with my ex-husband, right? Right. But when I walked through the door that afternoon to find a very agitated Leo holding the shoebox that I was 99.9% sure I hid so well so he'd never find, I changed my mind.

"Okay...don't be mad."

No response. Only the sound of the heavy shoebox going THUMP on the kitchen counter where he threw it.

"Baby, c'mon...you didn't expect me to throw everything away from that part of my life, did you?"

"Yep."

"Leo, that's ridiculous! Those are just pictures of all the places I've traveled...Europe, Japan, Hawaii...They're my memories! You don't expect me to forget I ever had them, do you?"

"He's in those fucking pictures."

I want to be sympathetic because if the tables were turned, I'd be pretty upset too if I stumbled upon pictures of Leo kissing a girl in a bikini. But I can't help but be sarcastic.

"Ummmmm, yeah! I didn't go alone!"

"Damn it, Chrissy, I thought we were on the same page about this kind of stuff."

"We are. But it doesn't change the fact that we've been with other people and that we might've shared a few good memories with them. Leo, as pissed as it makes us, *you* have to accept that I was married, and *I* have to accept that you…dated a couple of girls."

I *soooo* hoped he'd consider that even-steven, but nope.

"Right. You were married. You even dated that guy for what, like almost a decade before you got married! Which I don't get AT ALL! But Chrissy, I only dated three girls before I met you, and I think the longest I could stand any of them was three weeks. Shit, you don't even know if I slept with any of them."

WHOA! Is he insinuating *I'm his first?* Shit, if I am, the dude must've watched a lot of porn because he's sure got some innate mad skills in the love-making department.

"And I don't wanna know if you slept with any of them! The idea that you might've even bought an ice cream cone for one of those girls makes me crazy. That's what makes us so perfect for each other – we're completely insane. But Leo, I'm thirty-one years old. You have to start appreciating the fact that I have only been with one person…" Then calmly placing my arms around his neck, "…And I was committed to that one person until I met you."

Kissing his neck, I softly remind him of his old saying, "And if you take care of business…you'll never go out of business."

He gently, but convincingly, grasped my wrists and in a tone that did more to turn me on than shock me said, "The same rule applies to you."

Leo's words that night were the truly, madly, deeply kind I've always craved to hear from a man and two minutes after I started kissing his neck we were in bed. The love spell we cast over each other that night worked and all of my contemplation about telling Leo where I had spent the afternoon and all of his anger over the old photos of me and Kurt went out the window when we started to make love. The only thought racing through my mind as he rhythmically worked his magic on me was...*There's no fucking way I'm this guy's first!*

What? It's not like I lied about my whereabouts that day! It's simply another omission. I'm still good with that honesty vow I made. Rest assured, if Leo *specifically* asks if I drove to Orinda and rescued a stuffed animal from Kurt's girlfriend's parents' house last month, I'll tell him yes. But I'm glad that hasn't happened, and probably never will, because there's no doubt my honest answer would've prevented the last few amazing weeks from happening. Actually, amazing is an understatement.

Even though Leo's been beyond busy at work since he landed at Robertson Stevens, our weekends have been nothing short of remarkable. Over the last few weeks we made some trips down memory lane with a visit to Mill Valley. And of course, we rocked out to live music at The Sweetwater Saloon when we were there. We drove down to San Louis Obispo and did all of the things we did at Shell Beach in April, 1998, which included skinny dipping and a brand new wine club purchase, compliments of him this time now that he's earning a pretty nice paycheck. Then, as if life couldn't get any more exhilarating, I finally got to meet his co-workers. He's part of a confident, successful, ass-kicking investment team, and the entire night was something out of a Hollywood movie. Fancy bars, over-priced-artsy-fartsy looking food, hard liquor, dirty jokes, and dirty dancing. And the fast-paced, action-filled night ended with fast-paced, action-filled romance in the back of a limo. After we dropped the last drunken person from his office off on the curb outside his house, Leo opened a bottle of champagne, that we drank while staring at the city lights from Coit Tower. Then, once back in the limo, he poured himself another glass which he took a small sip of and then ever so smoothly deposited into my mouth when he kissed me. It was an unexpected move that once again made me think there's no way Leo hasn't been classically trained by a woman twice my age! (Right then and there I made

a mental note to learn a few new moves from Slutty Co-worker.)
When some of the champagne dripped out of the corner of my
mouth and down the center of my chest, Leo didn't hesitate to
clean up the mess by removing the shoulder straps of my dress
and tracing the direction of the trickle with his tongue. The
driver must have sensed that our make-out session was about to
turn into something a little more bwamp-chicka-bwamp-bwamp
so he gradually raised the volume of the music and rolled up the
privacy window. Frankly, I wouldn't have cared if he watched.
When I'm with Leo, it's like he and I are the only people in the
world. Everything about my time with him, starting from the
moment we met, makes me feel seventeen again.

Besties

June, 2001

"I'm telling you, Kel, it was super weird. It was like the first time he laid his feelings on the line, and to be honest, it didn't seem that hard for him. Maybe he did learn a lot from the divorce, or...and it pains me to say this, maybe Kayla is good for him."

Courtney and Nicole couldn't come to the cemetery today, which is fine with me because I'm still pissed at them. Besides that, it gives me a chance to talk out loud to Kelly about all that stuff that happened at Kurt's house last month. Even so, it's super creepy being here alone.

Placing a beer on Kelly's tombstone like always, I gripe, "I wouldn't be alone if you didn't have to leave."

The sound of a lawnmower humming in the distance brings the creepy factor down a notch and makes me feel slightly better. Still, I sigh.

I really wish I had Kelly to talk to about Kurt's weirdness at his "house" last month. She'd have something sensible to say that would put everything into perspective. I also wish she was around for me to bitch about Court and Nic. She'd totally be in my camp and NEVER hang out with Kayla. She was very team oriented that way. But mostly I wish Kelly were here so I could tell her in person how good things are going with Leo. Instead, I have to settle for telling her bones which are buried six feet below me.

"So Kel, he keeps bringing up house hunting, and I saw on his calendar that Taddeo's coming for a visit in August. The two aren't exactly correlated, but combined with the fact that he's been more pensive than usual makes me think something's up."

I had my first pretend conversation with Kelly last month when my doctor friends were late. I was rattling off a bunch of questions, and it felt so unproductive not to get any answers, so I just started answering them as if I were her. Peculiarly, I heard the answers in Kelly's voice—*like she was right there with me.* It was the voice of reason that's been missing from my life since the day she died. Lord knows there's no reason coming out of Courtney and Nicole! Since their husbands turned into little bitches, the two of them SUCK at talking about Leo. For example, if I just said all of that stuff to Miss Problem Solver Courtney, she'd deduce that Leo simply wanted a more comfortable living situation, that he misses his best friend, and that work is probably stressful, hence the being pensive nonsense. Miss Sarcastic Nicole would simply say Leo's probably contemplating breaking up with his cougar girlfriend. Then, because I'm Miss Emotional Chrissy, I'd show her the cougar I am by ripping her frizzy-ass hair out.

I'm sorry, but the whole calling an older woman who dates a younger man a cougar is nauseating to me. Think about it. A cougar is a big, wild cat animal that hunts, prowls, and kills its prey. *That's what I'm being compared with?* How come older men who date younger women get a nice sweet name, like sugar daddy? All I'm saying is, it's not right!

"He's probably gonna ask you to marry him."

Yay! There's my girl!

Looking down at my pewter Banana Republic ring, I exhale, "I've been thinking the same thing too, Kel."

"Doesn't it make you happy?"

"It makes me worried."

"That isn't what I expected you to say."

It wasn't what I expected to feel, but that's the great thing about having these "conversations" with Kelly. I say the first thing that comes to my mind and it's usually pretty authentic. Dr. Maria would be so proud.

"What are you worried about?"

"Failing…again."

"Like, that you'll cheat on him?"

"No way, that would NEVER happen. He's it for me."

"Then, what?"

"When Leo showed up on my porch in March right after you died, we agreed to let the vulnerability that existed when we first met drive the relationship. We agreed to be afraid together, and I thought that would be enough to…"

"*To what?*"

"Make me forget that he's six years behind me."

"Oh, for the love of Pete!"

"No, listen! What if I'm not what he wants when he's my age? What if he has as much growing to do in his life that I had to do in mine? I don't know, seems like I'm forced to be the more vulnerable one in the relationship, and it scares me, Kel."

"Jesus H. Christ! *Are you really doing this?*"

"I'm really doing this."

"Anyone can grow and change at any time, Dummy! You don't have to be six years younger than someone to screw up a relationship. You're living proof of that! Chrissy, if you're a match, you're a match. Age has nothing to do with it."

I should know all of this. But still, I'm scared he's going to leave me and then I'll be divorced…AGAIN! I don't think I can handle that kind of failure twice in my lifetime.

"Let's just drop it. If it happens, it happens, and of course I'll say yes. But for now, I just wanna keep enjoying what we have…a monogamous relationship without all of the paperwork and public humiliation if it doesn't work out!"

I go on to tell Kelly about the last few amazing weeks with Leo. I recap the trip to Mill Valley, the dreamy weekend at Shell

Beach…The Sweetwater Saloon. And even though she's not here with me, when I tell her about the sex in the limo, I blush. When I'm done getting her all caught up, I ask her the question that's been on my mind since last month.

"So, Kel, what's up with that dream I had the night Leo and I went out for Mexican food? Does it mean anything?"

"Do you want it to mean something?"

"Not if it means I still have feelings for Kurt or if there's a baby in my near future. There isn't…right?"

"How the hell do I know what's in your future?"

God, I miss her. After a loud laugh that makes the lawnmower dude give me a creepy look, I whisper, "But seriously, Kel…the dream felt so real." After thinking for a minute, I curiously ask my dead friend, "What do you think dreams really are anyway?"

"Hmmmm, good question. Maybe they're the release of our deepest secret desires, or maybe they're the place we go to solve the problems we couldn't solve when we were awake. Or, I dunno, maybe they're just a montage of bits and pieces of our day mixed in with the crap we watch on TV. Why? What do you think they are?"

"I have no clue, but I have a weird feeling you're gonna teach me."

Packing up the picnic basket, I hear Kelly's voice say, "Call your best friends. Yes…when it comes to matters of the heart, they're dumb as stumps, but they love you like a sister and they're worried about you."

"Sorry old friend, I'm not backing down on this one." A few feet down the path, I turn and yell, "They can call me!" And then, "Don't forget to tell my Grandpa I love him and I hope he's enjoying this nice long vacation from me!" After getting another weird look from the lawnmower guy, I hop in my car to pick up Kendall – someone I still can't bring myself to talk about with Kelly. And I never will, unless she brings her up.

Like most of my afternoons with Kendall, we end up at the mall. After Craig helps me unload the shopping bags, he puts on a cartoon for his daughter and pops open a couple of beers. Like usual, we hunker down on the front porch. The minute Kelly got sick, it became our special spot.

"You know…that closet of Kendall's is starting to look like a Stride Rite store. You might wanna ease up on the shoe shopping."

"Hey, you better watch your mouth ol' pal! It should look like a Nordstrom! Besides that, a girl can NEVER have too many pairs of shoes!"

Our laughing then escalates when I recap my encounter with Kayla.

"Oh my God, Chrissy, you're gonna give that chick a heart attack!"

"Like I told Kurt, it's just too easy!" After a big swig of beer, I add, "Fun too. But unless you send me there again to retrieve Kendall's Puffa-thingy, I can't think of a reason why I'd ever see her again."

Knowing me better than I thought, he's quick to say, "*Are you kidding?* I can't deny you that kind of entertainment! I'm definitely leaving it there the next time those two make dinner for me and Kendall!"

The sick feeling in my stomach catches me by surprise.

Before I finish saying, "Will Nicole, Courtney and their douche bag husbands be there too?" He's nodding his head.

"Seriously, Craig…*what's up with that?*"

"Okay, okay, Kitty…Keep your claws in. Everyone just needs a little more time to adjust to the break up."

"But why is everyone welcoming her with open arms?"

"Baby steps, Chrissy."

"More like bullshit steps if you ask me."

"C'mon, we've been one big group since like, high school! I doubt if Guss and Kyle have even changed their underwear five times in that length of time and you want them to all of a sudden meet your lover?"

"*My lover?* Jesus, what am I, a character in a romance novel?"

"Shit, I don't know what you call that guy!" Thinking really hard and scratching his head, he quips, "I got nothin' else to add to the lover stuff, but…I'd like to meet him though."

Nearly spitting my beer out, I ask in astonishment, "*Are you serious?"*

"Absolutely. I mean, even though I trust you with Kendall's life, I'd be a shitty dad if I didn't get to know the guy who's spending so much time with my daughter."

"That's understandable."

"That's not all."

And then he gets a little somber.

"It was my wife's persistence that brought you and that guy…"

Trying to make him cheery again, I interject with, "You mean…*my lover!"*

But he stays serious.

"Right. It was Kelly that got you and Leo back together. I wanna see what all of the fuss is about. How about a barbeque over here next week?"

"You know what? That sounds like exactly what we need to unite everyone."

After high-fiving on the plan, I grab Craig's wrist watch to make sure I'm not running too late. When I look at it, I'm taken back in time.

"Oh my gosh, Craig. That's the watch Kurt and I gave you for your wedding. I had no idea you still wore it."

Kurt and I bought Craig and Kelly his and hers matching watches which we had inscribed with, "*To our best friends…it's about time,*" on the back. In return, they bought us matching robes for our wedding a year later. They had the word "ball" inscribed on the back of Kurt's and "chain" on the back of mine.

Kurt and I always did buy better gifts for people. Correction. *I* always bought better gifts for people.

"I never take it off. You know how Kelly was…she liked it when we wore matching gear."

It suddenly occurs to me that Kelly must've been buried with her watch on. Well, I'll be darned. She did take a piece of me with her.

After leaving a somber Craig alone with his thoughts on the front porch that evening, I made my way home to my love, feeling pangs of guilt the entire drive that mine was alive and I'd be able to wrap my arms around him. The only thought that lifted my spirits was that my old friend genuinely wanted to meet Leo. If Leo can make a good impression with Craig, maybe he can talk those other idiots into accepting him. I know Leo could give a shit if they like him or not, but I'm not ready to let my past die along with Kelly and my marriage. Those meatheads and their dumbass doctor wives are my family. I may act all tough in front of them when it comes to defending my relationship with Leo, but when it comes right down to it, I love them and I need them.

Exposure

Still not a poop out of me since Leo moved in (well, at least not in the cottage anyway) and still not a peep out of Kurt since I ran into him. And that's just fine and dandy with me. I can't be exposed to Kurt. Bad, bad things happen when there's exposure. If Craig leaves the Puffa-thingy at Kurt's girlfriend's parents' house, he's on his own. I was almost scared the subject would come up in front of Leo when we had dinner with Craig last week because I forgot to tell Craig that Leo has a little bit of an issue with the fact that there is a Kurt. Luckily, Kendall hijacked Leo the second we got there to show him her swing-set in the backyard, and I was able to tell Craig to zip it. The night ended up being better than I could've imagined, but it definitely got off to a rocky start in the car on the way there.

The last time I saw Leo that nervous was also the first time. It was when I went to his apartment in February 1998, when I knelt down in front of him and nudged myself between his legs. His entire body trembled when I started to kiss him. Though he didn't tremble when we pulled into Craig's driveway, he definitely appeared anxious.

"Baby, relax. It's Kelly's husband, *Kendall's father*…not Attila the Hun."

"Yeah and he's also Numb Nuts' best friend."

Ahhh, Numb Nuts. Been a while since he busted that one out.

"I can't help but think this is some kind of set up."

Almost cracking up, I tease, "Just how much Miami Vice *did* you watch when you were a kid?"

Doing the quick math in my head, I calculate that I was sixteen when that show was on and Leo was...oh shit. Leo was ten. PURGE THE THOUGHT CHRISSY! PURGE IT! You're not screwing a ten year old. You're screwing a twenty-six year old. Perfectly legal.

"There's no set up, Leo. Craig genuinely wants to meet my boyfriend and the guy who his daughter has so much fun hunting snipes with. That's it. Please have an open mind and show him the man I fell in love with."

And that he did. After a two second territorial eye stare and some butt sniffing, the two men quickly determined they were compatible and there was no dog fight. Other than the one eyebrow raise and neck twitch when Leo walked past a framed picture of Craig, Kyle, Guss, and Kurt on a fishing trip, the evening went off without a hitch. We talked about our jobs, football, the sluggish economy, and the main reason I got on the red eye to find Leo in New York last December. It was the first time Leo heard about just how much time I spent on Craig's porch when Kelly was sick. I had told Leo about the letters I wrote to Kelly, but he had no idea of just how many there were. Craig talked about the flowers I planted in her garden, the grocery shopping, the babysitting, and the long talks he and I had over beers after Kelly fell asleep. Leo had no idea how much Craig really knew about him and no idea that had it not been for Kelly's one and only letter back to me in which she wrote, *"Go find him Chrissy. I know he's waiting for you...get moving on those second chances,"* I wouldn't have.

After an amazing dinner that Kelly would've been very proud of her husband for preparing on his own, Craig and I watched from the kitchen window as Leo and Kendall were getting in their last snipe hunt of the evening.

"I can see why you like that guy so much, he adores you."

"Correction. I love him."

"You should. He's the real deal. Good with kids too. Look at them out there."

Craig and I smile at the silliness we're witnessing in the backyard.

"So, the big thirty-two next week, huh?"

"Yep. Life's flying by."

"Flies by faster with kids in the picture. Still want any?"

"Totally. But I don't plan that stuff out anymore. Bogs me down."

"You might wanna jump on it. You're not getting any younger."

Punching my old friend in the arm, I warn him, "Hey, watch it, buddy!"

"C'mon, I'm serious. He might be young, but he seems ready. Fuckin' in love with you, that's for sure!" And then he tries to put my worries at ease with, "Don't worry about Kyle and Guss, they'll come around."

"You know...I'm really torn about that."

"Why's that?"

"I don't think Leo wants them to come around. I think he wants all of the reminders of Kurt to go away."

"And you?"

"I wish my past didn't hurt him so much, but without it, I wouldn't be who I am, and I certainly wouldn't have been at Buckley's that night. All of my experiences, mostly the ones with Kurt, put me there..." Thoughtfully inhaling as I watch Leo outside, I admit, "...I can't resent them the way he does."

Laughing like I hadn't heard in a long time from him, he roars, "Sure bet Kurt wishes you stayed home that night!"

"Doubtful! He's got Boobs and a big free mansion. That guy's not wishing anything different."

"If you say so."

"What are you talking about?"

"Forget it. I don't wanna stir anything up. I like that guy out there and I can see why you do too."

"But?"

"But Kurt knows what he did wrong. He's learned a lot about himself since the snipe hunter came around."

Annoyed, I grab a stack of dishes to wash.

"I'm not really sure what you're driving at Craig, but it's too late. If Kurt didn't want me to end up looking for love at some dive bar, he should've paid more attention to me on the phone that night…and for that matter, for the twelve years before it…" Scrubbing a dish like it's nobody's business, I gripe, "…If he didn't wanna go out of business, he should've taken care of business."

"Wow, that's a good one. You just think of that?"

Breaking from the dirty dish, I glance back out at Leo and whisper, "Can't take credit." Then, mauling the dirty dish again, I sneer, "But why don't you reiterate it to that old friend of yours so he doesn't make the same mistake twice."

"Don't have to. He already knows…" Looking back outside at Leo and Kendall, he adds, "…Kurt did a lot wrong, but he's a good guy."

Annoyed, I slam down the dish and snap, "C'mon Craig! Why are you doing this?"

"Let me finish. I was *gonna say*, and it seems like Leo's a good guy, too. You're a pretty lucky woman to have found him. Me…I can't imagine I'll ever go down that road again."

Jesus, I'm such a self-important bitch. Here I am, talking about myself AGAIN! I did it with him when Kelly was sick, and I'm doing it again now that she's gone. What the hell is the matter with me? With soapy hands, I walk up behind him and place one of them on his shoulder.

"You just made me realize how similar I am to those jerk offs, Guss and Kyle."

"How's that?"

"I don't want you to go down that road with anyone new."

Turning to me with tears in his eyes, he confesses, "I don't think anyone has to worry about that, Chrissy. She was my life. No one could ever come close to what she did for me."

Now, with my own tears, I tell my old friend, "I just want you to be happy again, Craig. Please tell me what I can do."

"There's nothing." And then he loses it when he says, "Dammit...this is so much worse than I ever imagined. I'm completely lost without her."

Just then Leo walks in with Kendall and sees me embracing a grieving Craig. Quickly realizing we need another minute, he claims to have seen another snipe and hurriedly escorts her back outside.

Aside from the emotional moment I shared with Craig at the end of the night, our evening was a pleasant success. Craig thought Leo was cool and Leo said, "As much as I don't wanna like the guy, it's hard not to." We left with plans to do it again soon. The drive back to the cottage that night was quiet. The only question Leo had was, "Why didn't you tell me you spent that much time on Kelly's porch and about all of those letters?" My honest answer was, "I might seem okay, but it's still too hard to talk about." After that we were both silent, deep into our own thoughts.

Whadididoo?

August, 2001

By most accounts, it's been a relatively uneventful year. Let's see… In January, Apple announced something called iTunes. They actually think people are going to buy some little contraption called an iPod and give up Tower Records in order to purchase music on their computers. Like , idon'thinkso! Last time I checked, this was Earth! Hmmm, what else has happened this year? Oh, in April, the Netherlands became the first country to allow same sex marriages. To be honest, I'm surprised I didn't notice a decline in the population of San Fransissyco…the way those people bitch about equal rights for gays-n-shit. I'm serious, there's like a parade or a nude march every other day. I thought the year was about to take a turn for the interesting last month when Craig invited me and Leo to his house to hang out with the gang, but according to the message Nicole left me obviously lying about having the flu, the evening was canceled. I didn't call her back, and I visited Kelly's grave a day earlier than the July anniversary day to avoid my best friends, and I did the same this month. I can't see Nicole or Courtney until I can make sense out of what's going on. I'm the one in the friendship who's supposed to be the liar! I'm the one who's supposed to be the wimp! I'm the one who's supposed to be emotionally challenged! It's like they're me all of a sudden, and it's throwing all of the planets out of whack. Craig tried his best to mediate between the two parties, but as of last week, he quit. Said he had too much of his own shit to deal with and for me to let him know when I have my head out of my ass. I assume he told all of them the same thing.

Let's see, what else is going on…Oh yeah! Last month, Leo told me the London Stock Exchange went public. Whoopdidoo. Let's see if I can shake things up a bit tonight at my thirty-second birthday party.

I'm in my bedroom getting ready for tonight's birthday festivities while Leo's at the airport picking up Taddeo. Why that Italian pain in my ass had to fly in today is a mystery to me. But not wanting to be "that girl" who gets in between her man and his best friend, I grudgingly changed my birthday plans to include the guy. Leo and I were going to have a romantic dinner at the brand spanking new Ritz Carlton in Half Moon Bay, but Taddeo messed all of that up when he switched his flight. And since he can only be in town for one night, he wants to take a trip down memory lane and hit up, drum roll please….The Round Up. It's the place the guys always go when he comes to town and God forbid Taddeo change his ways. So tonight Leo, Taddeo, The Ho-Bag, Slutty Co-worker, Megan and I are going to that dilapidated piece of shit wanna-be saloon bar. The girls came to the cottage early to pre-funk and calm me down.

"This was the dress I was gonna wear to Half Moon Bay."

As the two of them *oooh* and *ahhh* over the black strapless beauty I just pulled out of my closet, I bend down and grab my old cowboy boots and toss them on the floor.

"But lucky me, I get to put these shit kickers on instead."

"You kill me, Hunny. If you don't wanna do this on your birthday, then why are you?"

"Yeah, sounds like something you would've done when you were dating Kurt, and we don't have to remind you how that turned out."

After slamming my fourth lemon drop and burping, I tell them, "Guys, there's a big difference here! I'm not pretending to be happy about this. Leo knows exactly how I feel. This is a situation where I'm simply doing something *for* him because I love him, not because I *want* him to love me."

"But are you gonna be able to keep your annoyance under wraps long enough to survive the evening?"

Slamming shot number five, I brag, "Totally."

Boyyyyyyyyy, was I off on that assertion! I'm not sure if it was because I underestimated my hatred of The Round-Up, the displeasure of giving up my birthday for a guy who clearly still detests me, or the outcome of the three additional shots of random alcohol I consumed once we got to the shit hole, but my annoyance toward Taddeo was as unmistakable as a fart in church. When Leo went to grab more drinks, I pounced on the fucker.

"So Taddeo, manage to screw up any other birthdays this year or just mine?"

As if they're back-up singers, Slutty Co-worker and Megan let out a simultaneous, *"Ooooooh, shiiiiiiiit."*

Not backing down as usual, Taddeo mutters, "Nope, just yours."

The back-up singers shake their heads and let out an exasperated and synchronized, *"Here we go…."*

"When are you gonna give me a break, Taddeo?"

"When I'm done waiting for the other shoe to drop."

"What's that supposed to mean?"

"You'll screw this up…again."

"Nope! Pretty sure I've got everything under control now. I mean, Leo does live with me after all!"

"Chrissy, you have more baggage than a 747. Something from your past will eventually cause a disturbance."

Oh that's it! This asshole has GOT to go! I knock over a glass as I reach across the table to try and grab Taddeo's arm, but all of a sudden it looks like he has seven of them.

Being the older and allegedly much wiser one in the group, Slutty Co-worker quickly stands and interjects the only way she knows how.

"Taddeo, why don't you and I go for a walk?"

Knowing exactly what the hell that'll entail, The Ho-Bag pulls the cigarette from behind his ear, throws it on the table and says, *"What the fuck?* I wouldn't have come if I thought you weren't gonna go home with me!"

Slurring my words, I point at Taddeo and let the blame rip.

"Now see what you did? Nobody wants you here. Why don't you just go back to New York where you can blend in with all of the other mean people!"

"Because I don't want him to."

The back-up singers are at it again with, *"Uh-oooooooh"* as we all turn to see Leo fiercely glaring down at us.

"Chrissy, what's going on?"

Pointing at Taddeo...or somewhere in his direction, I continue to slur, "It's his fault! Make him go away, Baby."

Looking at Taddeo, Leo sternly asks, "Dude, is there a problem?"

"No problem, man. Just defending myself."

Standing up to show off my slender figure, I sway from side to side as I try to say, "Oh...what Taddeo? Am I so scary?" But it sounds more like, *"Oh..whaddeo? Mysooo scaaaaaaaaary."* And then I plop back down in my chair.

After he says "Actually, yeah," the Ho-Bag, Slutty and Megan literally freeze when Leo bends over, rests his hands on the table in front of Taddeo and says, "What the fuck is your problem, man?"

"She's the problem. How come you can't see it?"

Dramatically rolling my eyes and causing myself to get so super dizzy, I nearly fall out of my chair, I cry out, *"Whadididoo?"*

Knowing he's not gonna be able to get to the bottom of things with my drunk ass in the picture, Leo tells Slutty Co-worker and Megan to take me home and put me to bed. On the way to the door Slutty yells to The Ho-Bag, "I'll be back to get you in thirty minutes!"

Damage Control

August, 2001

The argument that ensued the day after my birthday wasn't nearly as bad as the one that took place on Leo's graduation night, but it was up there. When I woke up, Leo was sleeping on the wicker couch in the same clothes he had on the night before. I tip-toed to the fridge to get something to hydrate with/pour over my head, and that's when he woke up.

As he rubs his eyes he sleepily asks, "Why did you have to do that?"

"I'm sorry, what?"

"You knew he still needed time to get to know you. Why'd you have to push his buttons?"

"Leo, first, he's had plenty of time to get to know me. And second…what about my buttons?"

Ouch. My head hurts.

"Chrissy, have you forgotten about all of the times you screwed me over and who was there for me *every single time?* If a girl did that to him, she'd never have a chance to get on my good side. At least he's giving you that."

"I'd rather he not give me the chance than taunt me with future failure! Because that's what he did, you know! He said I'm gonna screw this up…AGAIN!"

And then a crazy thought occurs to me. Maybe I'm not angry about what Taddeo thinks. Maybe I'm scared that he might be right. Maybe that's what triggered my ridiculous reaction, which is what I'm assuming I had since Leo's so angry with me that it made him sleep on the couch. Actually, come to think of it, I don't remember much about last night, not even how I got home. Last thing I remember is Taddeo telling me I was about to go on an airplane...or was it that I needed to buy new luggage?

"Baby, you're not gonna screw this up. Look...I don't want to fight about this. There was enough of that last night."

"What are you talking about?"

When he sits up, I see his black and blue face.

"OMIGOD! What happened?"

Exhaling like he's super disturbed, "Defending your honor, I guess."

Oh shit, he got in a fight with the only other person in the world he loves! What the hell did I do last night to have made that happen? Think, think, think...

Rushing over to him to get a better look, I'm horrified at what I see.

"Are you hurt?"

I hate fights! I hate them so much, my body actually feels the blows of the punches when I see them happening on TV. They're savage and primeval and they have no place in my life.

"Not as much as he is."

"Why Leo? He didn't do anything that bad!"

Did he?

"It never should've come to that!"

Should it have? God dammit, why don't I remember anything?

"I'm not gonna let anyone, Taddeo included, disrespect you to my face. After you left, I told him to take it easy...warned him to back off."

"But he didn't?"

"Does it look like it?"

When Leo clasps his hands behind his neck it causes his biceps to flex and it stirs something inside of me. I walk over to him in anticipation of trying to make him forget about last night, but before I get there he leans back on the couch, closes his eyes and shakes his head. My sweet, loving, noble knight in shining armor is hurting and it doesn't look like it's from the black eye.

"Leo, please tell me what can I do to fix this? I know! Gimme his number, I'll call him and apologize. I'll tell him he's right about…whatever it was he was accusing me of being. I'll do whatever it takes to make things good again with you two."

Snapping his head up, he barks, "No, Chrissy, he wasn't right! I never would've beaten the shit out of him if he was…" Standing and pacing the small living room, he runs his fingers through his black hair and grumbles, "…Fuck. This is a mess."

That should be my middle name, Chrissy Mess Anderson. I thought I would've shed it, along with Gibbons, when I got a divorce, but for some reason it's globbed onto me.

Doing the only thing I ever know to do when Leo gets super mad, I wrap my arms around his neck and kiss him.

"I guess there's one good thing that came out of last night."

"Oh yeah, what's that?"

"You found out I'm a really bad drunk."

I knew things were bad when Leo barely cracked a smile at my joke, broodingly took the Gatorade bottle for a swig, and then silently walked down the hall for a shower. It's been almost a month since that morning and the same amount of time since he's spoken to his best friend. However, the same cannot be said about me and my best friends. Courtney and Nicole caught onto the fact that I'd been going to Kelly's grave a day earlier than anniversary day, courtesy of the creepy lawnmower dude, and to my surprise they were there waiting for me yesterday. The minute I saw them, it hit me how much I've missed them. There were massive amounts of apologies on both sides and a speedy invitation to get the gang, *plus Leo*, together. They hated the fact that Craig had met him before them and said they talked some much needed sense into their unnecessarily loyal and idiotic husbands, hence the pool party Leo and I are invited to attend tomorrow night at Nicole's house.

Even though it's totally the wrong time to spring this on Leo because he's crazy busy at work *and* still stewing from the Taddeo nightmare, I accepted the invitation anyway. I had to! I'm the one who caused the big stink to make it happen! Here's to hoping I still look good in a bikini and that it's enough to distract Leo from the probable shit show I'm about to put him through.

Do hast mich gefragt
Do hast mich gefragt und ich hab nichts gesagt
("Du Hast," *Rammstein*)

Gangness

September, 2001

"Holy crap...What's the occasion?"

Leo walked in from work at precisely the right time and apparently I did, too. A second earlier and I wouldn't have been ready. I showered, got pretty, and quickly changed into my bikini with barely enough time to refresh my lip gloss and make him a double scotch on the rocks before he walked through the cottage door.

"You look amazing in that thing. Get over here."

Grabbing my waist and already untying my bikini top, I wiggle away and hand him the drink.

"Here, I made this for you!"

After taking a sip and nearly choking to death, he puts the drink down and makes a joke about me taking the movie *Boiler Room* way too seriously because not all investment bankers chug hard liquor. Then he attempts to untie my top again.

"Hold on there, big guy. I actually have to *get* dressed."

Chasing me into the bedroom he yells out, "Unless we're about to catch a plane to Hawaii, nothing's gonna stop me from taking that thing off of you!"

As he catches me and throws me on the bed, I blurt out, "Would a car ride to Freakmont do the trick?"

The mood in the room changes faster than a cat can lick its own ass. Climbing off and standing over me, Leo's all of a sudden, all business.

"What are you talking about?"

"My friend Nicole invited us to her house for a pool party." And then, as cute as I can muster, I ask, "Doesn't that sound fun?"

"I assume it won't just be the three of us swimming…who else is involved with this?"

"Uh…All of them."

"All of who, Chrissy?"

"The gang…minus Kelly and Numb Nuts, of course."

Naturally, he didn't find that a bit funny.

"And you found out about this…when?"

"Does it matter? Your reaction would've been then same if I told you now or a week ago…" Sliding off of the bed and peppering his neck with kisses, "…See what a good girlfriend I am to have spared you the aggravation?"

"Yeah, how thoughtful."

"C'mon Leo, it won't be that bad. Please…they're my friends." Still kissing his neck, "Can't you just throw me a bone? I mean, I never complain when I have to hang out with The Ho-Bag."

"Okay, one…I was trying to throw you a bone two minutes ago and you rejected it. And two, give me a break! It's not like The Ho-Bag is best friends with one of my ex-girlfriends. But even if he were, it wouldn't matter because it's not like I ever had one for more than five minutes." Now heading back to the suddenly appealing scotch, he reminds me, "Chrissy, I told you before, I could give a shit about meeting those people."

I pull the waistband of his pants to turn him around, look him in the eyes, and tell him, "But I do. *Please?*"

I won. Twenty minutes later we're sitting in traffic on the way to Freakmont and listening to the overly annoying German heavy metal band, Rammstein. It's angry and violent and normally it would turn me on, but right now it makes me wonder what the hell Leo's preparing for in his mind. When I reach out to hold his hand that's resting on the center console, his focus doesn't budge from the road ahead.

"It'll be fun. Please try not to worry."

"*You think I'm worried?* Chrissy, my mood right now has nothing to do with being worried. I'm annoyed. I wanted to be alone with you tonight, I wanted to…" And then his voice trails off.

"You wanted to what?"

"Forget it."

"Please tell me."

"It's not important anymore. But one thing's for sure, I didn't want to have to meet…" and then he takes his hands off of the wheel and sarcastically does those mid-air quote thingies, "…'The gang' tonight." Then turning the music down, he wonders out loud, "You don't get it, do you?"

All of a sudden I feel like a fool. "No. I get it."

"*Then, why?* Why is it so important to you that I fit in with these people?"

"I don't know, Leo. I guess there are things I still need to hold on to. Not because of Kur…Sorry. Numb Nuts. It's because of Kelly."

"But you have Craig, you have Kendall. And you have your friendships with Nicole and Courtney. They'll keep her memories alive for you. Why do you need the whole package?"

Snapping my head at him, I shriek, "*What did you say?*"

"The whole package. What? Is something wrong?"

I think back to the one and only conversation I had with Kelly on her front porch when she ripped my head off for always needing her, Courtney, Nicole and Kurt as some kind of package. She chastised me for relying on them too much to feel

103

good about myself and she ridiculed my need to always mend the package when it was broken…even when none of them asked me to. But she reminded me that I didn't function like that when Leo was in my life, because he was all I needed. What was so amazing about the ass-ripping she gave me was that when I thought for sure Leo wasn't going to be in my life after he told me to take a hike in New York, I was hell bent on proving her wrong by not running back to my package to feel better. I dug deep and became my own package by way of my yoga studios. Kelly was right about everything she said that day, and she changed my life.

"Why are you suddenly so quiet, Chrissy?"

And Leo's also right. I have Craig and Kendall to keep Kelly's memory alive, and I still have my friendships with Courtney and Nicole that he thinks are fabulous. I'm all of a sudden sick to my stomach because this pool party wasn't the gang's idea, I made them do it. Here I am again, with my glue and tape, trying to fix something that nobody asked me to fix. And I think I know why. This has everything to do with feeling vulnerable with Leo. I want the gang to like him, and I want him to like the gang so he's tied to more than just me. He might think twice about leaving me one day…if it's more than just me he'd be leaving.

But Leo's actions and words are so over the top convincing that I'm it for him. The way he makes me feel is proof that I don't need outside influences to keep us together. So why the hell do I need the gang as some kind of safety net to keep him around? If anything, he should be the more vulnerable one in this relationship! I'm the one with the track record of leaving marriages! God, I'm such an idiot! I need to channel Kelly's words of wisdom and fuck the gang! In fact, the gang is probably the only reason Leo might want to dump me!

"Turn the car around."

"What?"

"I don't wanna go, Leo. This was a stupid idea, and I'm sorry I brought you this far. Let's just go home."

Turning the music loud again, he roars, "Nooooooo way, Baby. You told them we're going, so we're going. I'm not about to make them think I'm intimidated by their..." And here he goes with the quote thingies again, "'gangness.'"

Nice going, you vulnerable jackass. Leo's acting like he's about to encounter the Mexican Mafia and your friends are only having this pool party to appease your needy ass. For some insecure lame reason, you thought the gathering was going to make your relationship with your boyfriend more *solid?* If anything, it's bound to do the opposite. Those morons waiting for us at Nicole's house are...a bunch of morons! Jesus, Leo's not going to stay with me for fear of losing "the gang." If anything, he's going to associate me with their idiocy and bolt faster. Nervously staring out of the car window at the dilapidated spray-painted trains along Oakland's thunderdome-esque stretch of Highway 880, I think...It's so pretty compared to the utter mess I'm about to step foot into.

Group Love

September, 2001

"What's it called again?"

"The Hitachi Wonderwand. It's also a body massager. I love all of that dual purpose stuff! You really get your money's worth!"

"Where do I buy one?"

"No worries, Hunny! I have a few lying around."

"Gross! I'm not gonna use one of your second-hand vibrators!"

"No, no, no Sweetie! I always have a few on hand for last minute hostess gifts!"

After shaking off the shock of *that* information, I wave at Slutty Co-worker to continue, and whine, "Just tell me how I'm supposed to use the damn thing on him."

Two things raced through my mind when Leo and I left Nicole's house last night. One, although individual members of the gang mean a lot to me, the need to hang onto the group in its entirety is no longer important. And two...I need to learn some new sex moves to make Leo forgive the fact that I tried to make him a member.

Thank goodness Craig was already at Nicole's house when we got there. He handled the introduction of Leo to Guss and Kyle and was the one to promptly smack Guss in the back of the head after he asked Leo if he could get him a free checking account. Nevertheless, the smack *and* Craig's explanation of the difference between being a bank teller and an investment banker for one of the most prominent boutique investment firms in the world did nothing to curb Guss and Kyle's stupid questions. It wasn't until Nicole and Courtney made the two of them go away to start the barbeque that I was able to exhale. Like the good friends they are, they handed us ginormous vodka martinis and in unison, told Leo how happy they were to finally meet him. I was surprised to see Courtney wearing make-up and Nicole without a stain on her clothes. It showed me their effort, and I appreciated it. Leo ended up spending most of his time with Craig and a case of beer at a picnic table. Guss and Kyle kept to themselves watching ESPN on the outdoor TV, turning around every so often to size up Leo. And I spent my time running between those two groups and my girlfriends who, after finally getting a look at my boyfriend, were very interested in my sex life. Eventually, after caving into Nicole's curiosity about whether or not Leo and I have used whip cream on each other, it was time to call it a night. Their husbands grunted something from their lawn chairs as we waved good-bye and my friends kissed us at the door, with Nicole's kiss to Leo lasting a little longer than necessary. Craig walked us to our car and being the stand up guy he is, apologized for his friend's idiocy. Leo, being the sharp guy he is, reminded him that he used to work in a rock yard so he's used to it. The two guys shook hands and off we went. Seeing as though Leo didn't blow up the house, the evening went off without a hitch. But I don't have the desire to ever do it again and neither does he. When he turned to me in the car and said, "Satisfied?" I looked at him and said, "Yes, and now I'll do whatever I can to satisfy you to make you forget I ever dragged you into this." Hence the sex lesson from Slutty Co-worker that I'm having in my office right now.

"Okay, so tell him to lie down on his stomach. Naked of course! Then, start using the wand on his back and shoulders, working your way down to between his legs. Don't worry, he'll naturally spread them apart when you apply pressure to his inner thighs."

"Easy so far. What's next?"

"Well, you just put the wand right up there and start to wiggle it around!"

"Are you fucking crazy? You want me to stick that entire thing up my boyfriend's butt?"

Slowly and methodically placing her non-fat latte on the table, my dear old friend tediously looks at me and says, "Yeah, Hunny…I want you to shove a vibrator up Leo's ass. OF COURSE NOT! You edge it up to the area between his balls and his asshole!"

Now it's my turn to methodically put my latte down.

"Hold on…There's an entire *area* right there?"

"You're kidding, right? How do you not know this?"

Not wanting to rehash all of the reasons why my sex life was so boring for most of my life, I anxiously wave my hands at her to continue.

"Alrighty, I see that we're gonna have to have a little anatomy and physiology refresher course here."

Then sketching out what looks like a disfigured penis/rectal area, Slutty Co-worker uses her pencil as a pointer and taps at the area in question.

She gets all teacher-like as she explains, "Some people refer to that space as taint, although it's more of an abyss to me. You can really get lost in there! Sooooo much fun to be had!"

Just realizing I've been massively short-changing Leo in the lovemaking department, I anxiously wave her on again. My curiosity causes her to excitedly sit up and clap her hands while she continues to coach me through sexually violating Leo.

"Okay…no matter how badly he wants to turn over and fuck the shit out of you, don't let him! If you want this to be about him, then make it about him and keep on gently wiggling that thing around. Don't start getting all selfish."

"I won't! And then what?"

"Only after he begs, *and I mean*…BEGS, let him turn over, but then quickly straddle his upper thighs so he can't move.

Then grab his dick…" She leans toward me and whispers, "…Tell me though, Hunny, what does it look like?"

I whisper back, "What does what look like?"

"His dick."

Not whispering anymore, I bark, "NO WAY!"

"Come on! I bet it's big!"

"You get nothing, just keep coaching, Lady."

Dejected she slumps back in her chair.

"Fine. I'll tell you this much…it's in direct proportion to the rest of his body. Satisfied?"

Clapping her hands some more she smiles and admits, "I am…and I bet you are too, Hunny!"

"Can we please continue now?"

Sitting back up to the edge of her seat, she resumes her lesson.

"So you gently grab his dick and run the wand, on low speed of course because we don't wanna make the damn thing fall off, run it up and down his shaft…"

Spitting my latte all over the desk, I almost choke when I ask, "I'm sorry, did you just say *shaft*?"

Megan walks by my office door laughing, "Yep, she said shaft alright."

"Oh my God, I don't think I've heard that word since sixth grade health class!"

"Well, Jesus Hunny, with all of these elementary questions I thought that's what this was!"

After composing ourselves, class resumed with everything I ever needed to know about blow jobs (yes, it was Altoids I was supposed to use), balls in the mouth (who knew you could fit both of them) and…gulp…anal sex. I told my dear friend that I'd gladly oblige on everything but the anal. Tain't no fucking way! Just as she was telling me I'd be making a huge mistake because that's probably the thing he wants more than anything in the world, Megan peeks her head back in again.

"Hate to break things up just as they're about to get interesting, but Chrissy, you have a visitor. Singing the words as she walks away, *"And you're not gonna liiiiiiiike it..."*

Slutty Co-worker and I round the corner to the front lobby at the same time, and we're both shocked to see Kurt standing there. She whispers, "What, no flowers this time?" before I shove her away.

"Kurt, what are you doing here?"

"I need to talk to you. Can we go in your office?"

Once there, his eyes zoom right in on the picture of me and Leo cuddling in a booth at The Sweetwater Saloon. Part of me wants to slam it down on my desk to hide it. The other part of me feels like that would be such a betrayal to Leo. As uncomfortable as the moment is, I leave it upright.

"Sweetwater, huh?"

"Yeah."

"So, does he think you went there for the first time with him?"

"Kurt, please don't. It's too uncomfortable. Can we just talk about why you're here?"

After staring at Leo's face in the picture for a lot longer than necessary, he turns to me and confides, "It's Craig. I'm worried about him."

"I saw him a few days ago, he looked fine."

"He's not. He's been missing meetings at work, calling in sick all of the time. I need to get him out of town, maybe take him camping. Can you take Kendall for about a week? His parents can't handle her that long."

"Worse than that, they're so damn old they could die in a week!"

"*Really?* Do you always have to be so crass?"

Smiling at his displeasure, I inform him, "Told you that you wouldn't like authentic Chrissy."

Ignoring my comment, he continues, "Well, can you?"

111

"Of course. I'll do anything to help Craig out. But like I said, he seemed in okay spirits the last few times I saw him. He even made dinner for…"

Oh crap.

"Chrissy, relax. Craig can break bread with whoever he wants to and I'll still be his best friend."

"So you don't care at all that Leo hung out with Craig and Kendall? Not one single thing about that bothers you?"

"Why would it?"

Why does that make me so angry? Why do I even want him to care? God dammit, why am I making this conversation all about me?

"You know what? You're right. Why would it? You have Kayla and I have Leo and we should all be able to be friends with whomever we want, especially Craig and Kendall because they need all of the support they can get right now. In fact, to show you how untruly, unmadly, undeeply I can be about this, I'll even invite Kayla to go to lunch with me and Kendall when I'm watching her."

Of course that's a total lie. But hey….my no lie vow only applies to Leo!

Cracking a brilliant half-smile, he chuckles and says, "Sounds great. Just don't kill her."

"Kurt! I've watched Kendall for long periods of time before and she came out just fine!"

"I'm not talking about Kendall."

And with that, he taps the photo of Leo and me just hard enough so it knocks over and he walks out of my office.

You are mine, I am yours
Let's not fuck around...
("Draw Your Swords," *Angus & Julia Stone*)

Bravado

September, 2001

The magical Wonderwand and all of the necessary training that went with it could NOT have come soon enough. I thought I needed it to make Leo forget that I dragged him to that pool party and to cushion the blow of the fight he got into with Taddeo, but I really needed it to turn his mood around when I told him we'd be watching Kendall for a week because Kurt wanted to take Craig camping. No! It wasn't the fact that we'd be taking care of Kendall that appalled him, he adores that little girl. What set him off was hearing me say Kurt's name out loud. It still bothers him to the point that he wants to punch a hole through a wall. While he went to the gym to work out his frustrations, I took two shots of something brown from the liquor cabinet to get my nerve on and then I changed into my outfit.

There have been several times over the course of the last three years when I tried to make Leo's jaw drop to the ground, but when he walked through the door two minutes ago, I succeeded in making it drop the farthest and the fastest. Playing homage to his Catholic school education, I was suddenly dressed as the girl I never thought I'd be, but secretly thrilled to become. Judging by the expression on Leo's face, I nailed the part and should send Slutty Co-worker flowers for giving me the idea.

113

Quickly slamming the door behind him so that no one from the street can get a peek at me, a totally focused Leo walks toward me.

"The last time I walked in and you were wearing something sexy like this, I had to go to Freakmont. Just so you're clear: we're not going anywhere tonight."

Standing there, feeling more vulnerable than I ever have in my life, I dig deep into my sexual bravado and tell Leo to go and take a shower. And then I walk my sexy Catholic school girl wearing slutty-slutty-bang-bang outfit self into the bedroom to gear up for the evening's festivities.

Everything's ready to go. My fishnet stockings are securely attached with a garter belt just below my teeny tiny plaid skirt, my black satin bra is peeking out of my crisp white blouse that's tied at my belly, my black stiletto heels make me feel in charge, and the Hitachi Wonderwand is ready to go on the nightstand. Time for me to go and find that abyss. By the end of the night I want this man begging me to never leave.

Fortunately, for my sexual sanity, I didn't have to wait until the end of the night. Within fifteen minutes of firing up the wand, I had Leo nearly threatening me with my life if I didn't let him take control. Still, I followed Slutty Co-workers advice and made it all about him. I found the special spot that I'd ignored on him for so long and used all of my strength to keep him in position while I drove him crazy. But my strength was nothing compared to his, and I didn't stand a chance when he flipped over and straddled me. Not the plan, but I had made him beg long enough to take the lead, and because of the work I just performed, I was now more than satisfied I would be a part of his life for *at least* as long as he had a sex drive.

With one hand, he firmly held both of my wrists above my head and with the other he recklessly ripped every piece of fabric off of my body and then forcefully entered me. We've had a lot of sex together, but nothing and I mean NOTHING, compared to what we were doing to each other. Looking down at me while nearly crushing my pelvis with the thrust of his, he keeps saying, "Is this what you wanted?" over and over again. Despite my cries of "Yes, yes, yes," without warning, he pulls out of me, flips me over and reaches for the wand. I never thought about the thrill of being dominated before, but after this, I have a feeling it's all I'll ever think about.

After delivering right back to me everything I had given to him, he throws the wand against the wall, pulls me up to my knees and enters me from behind. Reaching my arms behind my head to grab his neck for stability, he begins to kiss mine as my weary head falls to the side. In an instant, the triple X-rated porn we had been acting out in our cottage bedroom transforms into something meaningful and slow. With each thrust, Leo whispers "I'm never letting you go." My repeated response is, "I won't let you." Finally reaching the end of our journey, we fall softly to the bed with his arms wrapped tightly around me. Before he drifts off to sleep he whispers one more time, "I'm never letting you go, Chrissy." For the first time since we got back together, I'm assured that our six year age difference will never interfere with our love. I'm no more vulnerable in this relationship than he is, and it's that very vulnerability that will keep us together, forever.

Speechless

September 11, 2001

"Kelly!" Banging my glass on the table, "Why so sad?"
"I don't know, they won't tell me."

"For cripes sake, enough with the "they" business and just tell me why you're sad."

She's been gnawing on the same fry for over a minute, and she keeps looking over her shoulder at the door like she's expecting someone.

"C'mon, woman, stay focused! I have a lot of stuff to tell you about last night."

"I'm sorry, it's just that I thought they were expecting a lot of people today."

"It's Chili's, Kelly! Not the Nordstrom's half yearly shoe sale!"

And then I see the tears in her eyes. I've only seen them once before, and it's a weird sight.

"Sorry, Kel, it was just a little joke…" Reaching my hands across the table to hold hers, "…Please tell me what's going on."

She looks intently at the salt shaker for a few seconds before she pops her head back up. Now she's smiling.

"They're starting to come! I have to go and you should to."

"But we're not done with the awesome blossom yet!"
Yelling at her as she runs out the door, "I STILL HAVE TO TELL YOU ABOUT THE WONDERWAND!"

The phone ringing yanks me out of my deep fried onion dream and I mumble, "I've got to get to the bottom of these damn things. They're really starting to freak me out."

Blindly reaching for the phone, I find the note instead. Ignoring the annoying sound, I sit up to focus on Leo's words.

If I could whisper in your ear right now I'd say the same thing as last night. I'm never letting you go. I love you. Leo

Happy that the ringing stopped, I clutch the note to my heart and fall back into bed. My happiness only lasts for two seconds, when the phone starts to ring again.

I grab at the phone and yell into it, "This better be important!"

"WHERE'S LEO?"

I laugh and fall back on my pillow.

"Megan, please don't tell me you still have a crush on him."

"Have you turned on the TV yet?"

"No, why?"

"You need to turn it on."

"But I haven't had my coffee yet and…"

"TURN ON THE GOD DAMN TV, CHRISSY!"

Reaching for the remote I mumble, "Our yoga collection better be on *Good Morning America* or I'm gonna kick your ass."

Confused by the special effects I'm watching, I switch to channel 4, then to channel 7 and then back to channel 4 before I slowly say, "Megan…*what's going on?*"

"We're being attacked! Have you heard from Leo?"

For a second I think it's all a big joke. Nobody can attack us. We have eyes and ears everywhere, and we have missiles and bombs that can easily destroy whatever those eyes and ears see and hear. Still confused, I flip through the channels again and make out that the plane I'm watching slam into the World Trade Center, over and over again, is one of ours. Piecing together everything I'm looking at, Megan's question now jolts me to my feet. Leo works on the top floor of the Bank of America building, the tallest building in San Francisco!

"OH MY GOD, HE'S IN HIS OFFICE! I have to go Megan! I have to find him."

Frantically pushing the end call button so that I can enter Leo's office number, the line just rings and rings and rings. No answer. After my tenth attempt, I call Megan back.

"He's not picking up in his office!"

"Did you try his cell?"

"It's Leo, remember? He doesn't have a fucking cell!"

"Oh shit…that's right."

"Megan, I can't turn on the TV and look. Did he get hit? Please tell me we're okay here. Please tell me this is only happening in New York! Oh my God, he's not answering his office phone! He got hit, didn't he? Oh my God, Oh my God, Oh my God."

"Chrissy, take a deep breath. I'm pretty sure he's okay. So far it's just New York…Oh, and the Pentagon."

"Holy shit…*the Pentagon?*"

"Yeah. Chrissy, I'm scared. Can I come over?"

"Of course. I'll call Barbara to make sure she's okay. You call everyone else from the studios and tell them not to come in today."

"Okay. But Chrissy…"

"Yeah?"

"Doesn't Taddeo work in the World Trade Center?"

Instantly my knees give out from under me and I crumble to the floor. It's a reaction that I've only experienced two other times in my life, at the baby killing clinic when I was seventeen and the night of Leo's college graduation when I thought I had lost him forever. Please, Jesus, who I'm still struggling to believe in, please don't let Leo lose his best friend. I'll never forgive myself.

Scramble

September, 2001

I don't think the morning of September eleventh was any different for me than it was for anyone else. From the moment I realized what was happening, everything began moving in slow motion. Awaiting Megan's arrival, I called my family and my best friends to make sure they were alright. And of course, I continued to call Leo's office line. After twenty unsuccessful attempts to reach him, I finally left a message.

"Leo! I know where your head is right now, and I need to make sure you're okay. I love you so much. Please hurry and get home to me."

I knew Leo's head was with Taddeo's...in the rubble at the bottom of The World Trade Center. Of course, I couldn't substantiate Taddeo's *exact* whereabouts, but deep down I knew where he was. And when Leo came barreling through the cottage door two hours later, that's where he told me he was going.

"Now? But there aren't any flights, and no one knows when there will be!"

Rushing past me to pack a bag he mumbles, "Then I'll be the first one in line when they start selling tickets."

Borderline begging, I grab his arm.

"Leo, please! What if it's not safe?"

Then scrambling to say whatever's necessary to delay his effort to leave, I yell out, "Wait! Have you tried his cell phone?"

Startling me and Megan, he slams his fist into the wall and screams, "Damn it, Chrissy! There is no fucking cell reception where Taddeo is! Don't you get it? He was on the top of that building! He's dead!"

I'm torn between being scared for his potential loss and the one I might have to endure if he boards a plane.

"You don't know that, Leo! Please, just call his parents, they might know something!"

Now hanging his head low and speaking in barely a whisper, he tells me, "I already did. I borrowed someone's cell phone when we evacuated our building."

"What'd they say?"

Looking up at me, scared and brokenhearted, he continues to whisper, "They told me to please go and find their son. Which is exactly what I'm gonna do. I have to find their son...my best friend...who..." His words were muffled, but I knew exactly what he said because I was thinking the same thing, "...who I beat the shit out of last month."

Grabbing his shoulders to try and talk some sense into him, I beg, "Please, just wait a few days."

But he says nothing. I turn his face to look at mine so he can see how serious I am when I admit, "Leo...I'm scared. I don't want you to go there right now. What if...what if it happens again?"

"Chrissy, do you realize I was working at the top of those same buildings just a few months ago?"

I do. And the thought of him jumping out of a window, blowing up or burning alive has entered my mind about a hundred times this morning. The second the images hit my head, I boot them out and then silently thank my angels in heaven for getting him out of harm's way. My head *cannot* go there. I'll fall apart if it does.

"Chrissy..." Tilting my chin up with his finger, "Now it's your turn to look at me."

I don't want to because I'll be forced to give him my blessing. I can't say no to him. Ever since the moment I met him, I've not been able to. The nanosecond my eyes confront his, I know I've lost this battle.

"If the tables were turned, he'd be looking for me."

"I know."

"I have to go."

"I know."

And then he walked to the bedroom to pack his bag. The bedroom that just fifteen hours ago belonged to the happiest place on earth.

Thirty minutes later, after a long hug and kiss, a very overwhelmed Leo told me he loved me and then abruptly left for the airport.

Megan and I called Slutty Co-worker to make sure she was okay, but surprisingly The Ho-Bag beat us to it. She was with him at a bar watching the news with all of the other single people who didn't want to be alone and had nowhere else to go. But unlike all of the single people surrounding them, they held hands and squeezed them tightly together whenever the reporter mentioned potential fatalities. When I finally got through to Barbara it was evident she was very afraid. I told her I'd come and get her, but she said she'd rather hide in her home in Berkeley and pretend nothing bad happened.

Megan stayed at the cottage with me for four days. I was too scared to be alone. I was scared for Leo who had been sleeping on the floor at Oakland Airport waiting to catch a flight to New York. I was scared for Taddeo, who still had not been heard from. And I was scared because thanks to a few Muslim extremists, life as I knew it would never be the same again.

After saying good-bye to Megan this morning, I closed the cottage door and thought how crazy it was that just four nights ago I finally found the kind of contentment with Leo that I was sure nothing could disturb. Lying in his arms, I imagined the children we would have. I thought of all things perfect on my old Life List and started crafting a new one in my mind, knowing this time around I'd achieve every single line item. But when I turned on the TV the next morning, I was reminded of how quickly the good things in life can vanish. (Actually, I'm surprised and saddened I needed that reminder given the fact that Kelly died just seven months ago.) The morning of September eleventh reminded me of how little I'm actually able to control. I was reminded that the only thing I have control over is my happiness, and as I watched the horrible images of the airplanes crashing into the twin towers over and over again on TV that day, and for the next three, I sure as hell couldn't find any. And even though Leo called me five minutes ago from a cell phone he purchased inside of JFK to tell me he landed safely, I'm still struggling to find any happiness. Everything is completely upside down, and I have a sick feeling it's going to stay that way for a very long time.

Fifteen minutes after telling Leo I loved him and begging him to be safe, my phone rang again. Thinking it was him and scared that another plane was falling from the sky, I lunged at it.

"Baby, are you okay?"

"Sorry to disappoint, but it's not Baby."

I already knew Kurt was okay following the 9/11 attacks. When I called Courtney the day it all happened, she told me he was on the way to her house to pick up Guss who was going camping with him and Craig. September eleventh was the day I was *supposed* to start watching Kendall. Obviously, that never happened.

"I don't have a lot of time right now, Kurt."

Despite having a semi-decent conversation with him at his "house" in May and at my yoga studio the other day, I kept both of them from Leo and that didn't feel decent at all. I decided the other night during my triple X performance with Leo that, barring anything to do with Craig or Kendall, I would not have contact with Kurt anymore. That decision starts now.

"Just wanted to make sure you were okay, Chrissy, that's all."

"You don't have to do that anymore."

It's not like he ever did, but that shit ship has long since sailed, and I'm not about to bring it back to the harbor and remind him.

"Chrissy, I know you're alone, and I know why and unless you've changed more than I thought, you're probably a little emotional."

Before I can ask how he knows I'm alone, he interjects with "Don't worry. I'm not frantically trying to figure out your personal life. Courtney told me "Baby" has a friend in the towers and he went to go find him. It's pretty intense stuff and I just wanted to make sure you were all right. Is that a problem?"

"His name is Leo and why wouldn't I be all right? I'm...not...the one...buried at the bottom of those buildings!"

And then I lose it like the Chrissy he's known his entire adult life.

"I'll be there in twenty minutes."

And then the line went dead.

I'm forgetting the way you moved
The way I felt
I'm forgetting the time we spent…
Cause it's too late to try to change your mind
And there's nothing else I can do
I'm forgetting you
("Forgetting You," *Nathan Angelo*)

Destructive Distraction

September, 2001

My cottage is a place that's completely separate from the life I shared with Kurt. In it, there's no trace of the stupid appeasing girl I used to be and there's no room for her return. I am who I was always meant to be, a successful-business-woman-slutty-Catholic-school-girl-costume-wearing-overly-adored-porn-princess, and that's why I'm happiest when I'm in it.

Kurt's only showed up to my cottage twice in the past, and those two times felt like I was being pulled back to something that didn't feel right. In spite of how much I used to love him, each time he came here and said, "Pack your bags, you're coming home," it felt like a death sentence. Even though he has no legitimate reason to say that to me anymore, I don't like him in this space, and I knew that's exactly where he was when I heard the knock on the door. This cottage belongs to Leo, too now, and the knock felt like a betrayal the minute I heard it. Opening the door I pledge to myself to honor the decision I made the other night to keep my ex-husband out of my life.

"Kurt, you can't be here."

But dammit, despite the pledge, it still hurts to hurt him.

"I'm just checking on you, Chrissy. That's all."

"Thanks for the concern, but I'm fine…really."

"Let me come in for a minute."

"*No way.* I don't think I have to tell you how mad that would make Leo."

"Let me get this straight. He can sleep with my wife, but I can't drop by to see if she's doing okay after he left her to go to New York?"

Whoa! That's the first time he's ever verbally acknowledged my affair. I want a plane to hit *me* right now.

"Okay, first…he didn't *leave* me to go to New York. He went to find his best friend. HUGE DIFFERENCE! And second, I'm not your wife anymore, Kurt. It's not your job to check on me. You really need to go."

When I try to close the door, he puts his foot in the way to stop it.

"Look, I didn't come here to upset you. I'm sorry."

He's sorry? Didn't he listen to his own words? I slept with someone else when we were married! Good Lord, *I* don't even know how he can even be standing here right now!

"Kurt, you can't be here. It's just not a good idea."

"Fine. Then let's go get some coffee."

Is he freaking kidding me with this?

"C'mon, Chrissy, you look like shit. You need to get out of here for a few hours."

"Of course I can use a break, but not with you! Kurt, we're not friends! We decided we couldn't be when we got a divorce, remember?"

"Jesus, I'm not here to get in the way of what you've got going on. I just wanted to see if you were okay. Has anyone else tried to do that?"

Come to think of it, no. My friends suck.

"Thanks a lot, Kurt. First you tell me I look like shit and then you remind me I have no friends. Good job cheering me up."

128

Laughing a little, he puts his foot in the door when I try to close it again.

"Actually...first I reminded you that you cheated on me."

In addition to Kurt's honesty, I always appreciated his sense of humor.

After releasing a small smile that I tried really hard to contain, I tell him again, "Kurt, you really do need to go. This doesn't feel right."

"I'm not taking no for an answer. C'mon, one of your biggest complaints about me was that I never fought hard enough for you. I'm tired of proving you right."

"The fight's over, remember?"

"That one is, but not this one. C'mon let's just grab some coffee, get you outta here for a few hours."

I have been in the cottage for four days straight...A coffee break might not hurt.

"C'mon...I can tell you want to."

"Okay, but just ONE cup."

Three cups later, Kurt was up to speed on what I *think* happened to Taddeo in New York and what *really* happened between Leo and Taddeo at my birthday party in August, and I was up to speed on his surprising break up with Kayla. Apparently, not long after her parents came back, she was expecting an engagement ring and a house like the one Kurt and I used to own in Danville. When he tried to gently set her straight, she freaked out and broke up with him.

"She wanted what you and I had, but I told her I already had it once and blew it. Why would I go down that road again?"

"*Are you crazy?* You go down that road to find what was missing between the two of us. Maybe you didn't find it with Kayla, but you will with someone else. I guess the good news is, until you find her, you still have the Porsche, right?"

I'm trying to lighten up the conversation, but he's not having it, and what he says in response shocks me.

"Nothing was missing between the two of us. I just blew it."

129

Okay, now I'm really freaking out. This is not the guy I knew in high school and certainly not the guy I married. It would be a massive understatement to say something's different about him.

"Kurt, I'm just so confused. When we split up, it really seemed like you were falling for her. And then, at your "house" in Orinda you talked about her being some kind of convenient distraction. What's going on with you?"

He abruptly places his coffee cup down on the table.

"*What was I supposed to say, Chrissy?* I already told you a million times before the divorce was final that I thought you were making a terrible mistake. I already asked you for another chance…told you I can give you everything that guy can and more. Once the divorce was final, it felt better to just tell you I had moved on."

Following suit with my coffee cup, I bark back, "Again…I'm confused! Why would you have even wanted another chance? Look what I did to you!"

Staring intently at me, he says the unexpected.

"Chrissy, look what I did to *you*."

Shaking my head in shame, I mutter, "Believe me, it didn't warrant my behavior."

"It must've or you never would've done it."

In an attempt to set him straight, I unload things that I thought for sure I'd keep a secret my entire life.

"Kurt, I snuck out of our house to meet with Leo in the middle of the night."

"I know."

"I left that surprise party you threw for me to go and find him."

"I know."

"Dammit! I fell in love with him!"

"And at one time you fell in love with me, and that just doesn't go away."

"You know what? Maybe you're right. Maybe I'll always love you, Kurt. Maybe I'll always be concerned for your happiness. Maybe I'll always be disgusted with myself for all of the lies and betrayal. Is that what you wanna hear? Will that make you happy?"

"Actually...it—"

"Well don't let it. Because just because I love you, it doesn't mean you're right for me."

"Is that you or Dr. Maria talking?"

"Sorry to disappoint you, but no one put the thoughts in my head and no one put the words in my mouth."

"Tell me this then, how can you divorce someone that you might always love?"

This conversation has gone *wayyyyyyyy* over his untruly, unmadly, undeeply head and it's beginning to break my truly, madly, deeply heart.

"Funny, because that's the very thing I had to come to terms with in order to finally leave you."

"What do you mean?"

"You wanna know what happens to unrequited love, Kurt? Well, just like Dr. Maria tried to explain to you the one and only time you went to see her, it turns into resentment and once that happens, the relationship is over. No matter who's in love with whom or how much. In my heart, I knew I'd always crave more than you could give to me, and it just seemed like a love life not worth living. That's how I could divorce someone I might always love."

"But you never even tried to explain it to me like that. It's like you never even gave me a chance to fix the damage."

"By the time I realized what was wrong with us, it was too late. I already met Leo, and it was like all of these missing pieces in my life magically appeared right along with him. Our marriage didn't stand a chance."

"Ouch."

131

"I'm not trying to be mean. I'm just trying to give you the truth you deserve. I wish you knew how hard it was for me to do that."

All of a sudden it feels like a heavy weight has been lifted off of my shoulders. But I feel like I deserve some truths, too...I wonder if hearing them will add the weight right back.

"As long as we're being honest with each other, maybe you can fill in some blanks for me."

"Like what?"

"How come you let me move out of our house so easily? No wait, how come you *helped* me move out of our house? And you never called after I moved out...never even went to one single therapy session alone like I asked you to. Seems to me like there were a few opportunities to try and fix some of the damage."

Cracking a tiny half smile, he admits, "I feel so stupid. But I honestly thought I was giving you your space. I thought I was giving you what you wanted and it would make you happy and then you'd come home."

I offer him no hint of enjoyment when I respond to what he just said.

"I couldn't risk losing another twelve years of my life by thinking your intentions were anything other than simply not caring. I had already given enough of myself to you. Even if Leo and I didn't work out, I knew I'd be happier alone."

Looking down at my watch, I'm reminded that I'm not alone and that Leo and I did work out and that I really have to get back to the cottage to see if he called. I abruptly scoot my chair out from under me.

"Thanks for the coffee, but I really have to get going."

Now standing himself, "Wait...There's something else I need to talk to you about. Stuff that I thought I was gonna have the opportunity to make up to you, but everything just fell apart."

"What are you talking about?"

"This is hard for me, Chrissy. Remember, I'm the guy who thought letting you move out was a good idea."

"Talking isn't supposed to be torture, Kurt."

"I'm learning that. Look…that thing that happened in high school…I have to make it right."

Why? Why? Whyyyyyyy did he have to go there and *WHY NOW?*

"MAKE IT RIGHT?"

Realizing that people are now staring, I lower my voice back down.

"How the hell are you gonna make it right, Kurt? I had an… an…"

It's still so hard to say that vile word.

"I can't tell you how sorry I am that I acted that way. I was young and stupid. I didn't handle it the way I should've."

"Stop! I'm not doing this with you! You had your chance to make that situation and so many others right. In fact, you had over a decade of chance! You ran out of time, Kurt. When are you gonna realize that?"

"I realize it already, I just thought that—"

"You realize NOTHING! Three years ago I took you to Dr. Maria so that you could figure yourself out and get shit like this out of your system. But you chose not to say one helpful thing or share one compassionate thought and because of that I got on with my life."

Reaching for the receipt on the table I scribble Dr. Maria's phone number.

"Here! Try again! Believe me…she's the only one who wants to listen to what you have to say."

Having coffee with Kurt has been a distraction from the shitty things happening in New York, but it's been a destructive distraction. Bad, bad things happen when there's exposure to him, and this is the absolute last time I plan on playing with fire. He says nothing as I grab my things and storm out of the coffee shop with more weight on my shoulders than I had when I walked into it.

There weren't any messages when I got back to the cottage, but there were five missed calls. Leo picks up on the first ring of my first attempt to reach him.

"Where were you? I called like a hundred times!"

"Ran out to grab some coffee."

Technically…just another omission.

"Is everything okay? I didn't expect to hear from you so fast."

After a longer than comfortable pause, Leo's voice cracks as he says, "I didn't expect to find him so fast."

And then he breaks down.

Frantic

October, 2001

After failing to get anywhere near Ground Zero, Leo frantically started asking where the nearest hospital was. He was told that most of the 9/11 survivors were taken to The New York City Downtown Hospital. Before he rushed there, he pinned up a picture of his best friend, along with his new cell phone number, at the make-shift lost victims gathering place. Sadly, there wasn't one single lost victim there hoping to find a family member or a friend, there were only the people looking for them.

The hospital was crowded and chaotic, two things Leo hates the very most. He tried to be patient and wait his turn in line at the reception desk, but that only lasted five minutes. He offered a hundred dollars to a nurse to take him to the rooms of every male victim of 9/11. After the ninth room, the nurse had to leave him for an emergency, but for another hundred, he let Leo search on his own. It was during my phone call with Leo, when he interrupted his recount of searching for his friend by reminding me of how shady the people are in New York, that's when I knew, Taddeo was alive. That phone call was twenty-five days ago.

I flew in yesterday. It had been almost a month since I saw Leo, and I couldn't take being apart from him any longer. I could also tell by the sound of his voice that, as each day went on, he'd grown increasingly more depressed about Taddeo's condition. His best friend had been laying in a coma for nearly a month with no signs of waking anytime soon.

Leo arrived to my room shortly after I checked in last night. His face unshaven, his clothes coffee stained and wrinkled, and his eyes sunken in. He looked ten years older than the last time I saw him. We embraced for a long time and then proceeded to a light dinner where he tried to prepare me for what I was going to see the following day. After dinner, he excused himself to go and pray at the small church he found down the street from the hotel. He said, "It's the only thing I can think of that will help him." I declined his invitation to go because, well…after all of the sins I've committed, I'm afraid I'll light on fire if I step foot inside of one of those things. I decided to contribute to Taddeo's recovery by doing what I do best; I raided the hotel mini-bar, shook myself a martini, and begged Kelly to pull some strings. Clearly our prayers worked last night because two hours ago Leo called me at the hotel with the remarkable news that Taddeo woke up.

Apparently, a few minutes before the first plane hit the towers on 9/11, Taddeo, who recently left Goldman Sachs to start his own hedge fund, went to the lower level of The North Tower. He was called down to meet a very lost furniture delivery guy. Once he was down there, tragedy struck. Everyone, including Taddeo, very slowly started leaving the building and no one really panicked until they got outside and realized what had happened. Even so, it seemed like such a small hole in comparison to the size of the building and he even contemplated going back to his office to grab his laptop. When he turned to ask a police officer if he could re-enter the building, that's when The South Tower was hit. He stayed nearby to witness the catastrophe…too close actually. When The South Tower fell, it crumbled to the ground as quickly as a Jenga game gone bad. He ran as fast as he could to avoid the debris, but knew his efforts were hopeless when it started steamrolling around him. He dove under a car and held on for dear life. Apparently, Taddeo held on good enough because finally, after

136

nearly a month of drifting in and out of consciousness, he woke up this morning to his grateful best friend sitting beside him.

After a few minutes of gathering his surroundings and several more of doctors poking and prodding him, a very confused Taddeo finally turns to Leo and asks, "Dude, what the hell?"

"Terrorists, Man. It was really bad. The Towers are gone."

"Holy… A lot dead?"

"Almost everyone."

After absorbing the enormity of what he survived and telling Leo the story of how he did, he asks, "When did you get here?"

"Bout' a month ago. Took the first flight out."

"Jesus Christ…I've been out that long, huh? How do I look?"

"Like you got the shit kicked out of you."

"So I guess I look just like I did before that building landed on me, huh?"

"Damn it, Taddeo, I'm so sorry that happened. We never should've fought."

"It's all in the past. Forget about it."

Realizing he came as close as he did to losing one of the most important people in his life, after doing one of the most foolish things in his life, Leo conceals the sorrow in his eyes with his fingertips and hangs his head low.

In barely a whisper he tells his best friend, "I don't know what came over me, and I don't know if I can ever forgive myself."

And like all good best friends, Taddeo lets him off the hook.

"Love, Man. Does crazy shit to people."

Leo's job at Robertson Stephens, although sympathetic at first because everyone there seemed to have known someone that died on 9/11, had become tired of waiting for him to come back and gave him an ultimatum – be at work on Monday or we have to let you go. That was two weeks ago. It would've been a devastating blow to most guys who had worked their entire adult life toward becoming an investment banker at one of the most prominent firms in the country, but he barely felt an ounce of pain from the loss. It paled in comparison to the potential one he sat next to at the hospital every day for the last month.

By the time I arrived to the hospital this afternoon the two old friends were already joking about the fight they got into back in August. Feeling awkward about the position I put the two of them in, I excused myself almost as quickly as I got there. But before I left the room, I put my hand on Taddeo's and said, "I don't ever want to interfere with your friendship with Leo. You mean too much to him and he means too much to me. When you get back on your feet, we're going to have to work something out." And then I kissed him on the forehead. When I reached the door he said, "I think we just did."

After I left the hospital, Leo stayed to talk to the doctors who informed him that Taddeo appeared to be out of the woods and if everything stayed the course, he could possibly resume his life within a couple of weeks and go back to work. Now, preparing for his first restful night of sleep in nearly a month, Leo's changing into a clean white t-shirt as I talk to him from the hotel bed.

"*Resume what work*? His new business is blown to smithereens."

"Yeah and so is my career at Robbie."

Sensing he's hinting at something, I slowly put my wine glass down on the room service tray, pull my hotel robe tighter and wait for it.

"After you left today, Taddeo talked to me about joining his hedge fund group. Well, *technically* I'd be the group because the rest of the group is dead." After shaking off the insanity of the situation, he continues. "He's still got an incredibly viable business, it just needs to be rebuilt and he can't do it alone."

Trying not to sound nervous, I admit, "Wow, sounds like quite an opportunity."

As he walks over to rummage through his suitcase he continues to talk about the potential in what Taddeo was just starting to get off the ground, about the likelihood of making far more money than he ever could've made at Robbie and about his commitment to helping his best friend that he feels like he so horribly mistreated outside of The Round Up on my birthday.

"There's just one problem, Chrissy."

Oh, crap. Here it is.

"What's that?"

"I have to be where the big clients are...in New York."

Fifteen years ago, I fell in love with Kurt. It was also when I fell out of love with myself by agreeing to do, say and be everything that man wanted just so he'd love me back. Four years ago, I realized how wrong it was to be that way when I sat next to Leo at Buckley's. And almost a year ago, I fully realized the damning effects of not being true to myself by finalizing a very painful divorce. I'm not really sure how Leo expects me to react to what he just said, but I will not be true to myself if I say I'm okay with him living in New York. We fought too hard to finally be together again and he had to make huge career moves to work in the Bay Area. Besides all of that, New York is a God awful, mean, terrorist-laden location! I feel like I need to remind him of all of that stuff. *But what would that make me if I did?* What does it say about me to be the only one in this relationship to question those things...to be the only one afraid of losing everything we worked so hard to get back? *Does it make me true to myself or truly desperate?* On top of these concerns is the promise I made to Taddeo just yesterday, where I said I wouldn't get in the way of their friendship. All of a sudden a familiar feeling hits my stomach. I'm losing Leo...again.

"I don't really know what to say."

Leo turns from his suitcase, walks toward me and gently gets down on one knee. And then he hands me a beautiful black velvet box.

"Say you'll marry me."

Relief

November, 2001

I guess the good news about being alone in my cottage is that I can peacefully poop in it again. Aside from that, there's not a whole heck of a lot of good about it. I'm lonely and I miss Leo like crazy. He hadn't lived in the cottage long enough to unpack most of his belongings and aside from his business suits, he shoved what he did unpack into a bag when he quickly left for New York in September. Then, when he decided to stay in New York to work with Taddeo, I shipped off his suits so he'd be prepared for all of that business rebuilding, and I put his boxes in his mother's garage where I wouldn't have to trip over them every day. Aside from a few toiletries in the bathroom, it's like he never even moved in.

There is plenty of good news outside of my cottage though. We're opening our third Forever Young Yoga Studio in Alamo. Yep, the land of the rich! We're going to hit those suckers with some relaxation and we're going to hit em' hard…after we make them commit to a contract and take their money up front of course!

Things became so weird after 9/11. Eating in with family and friends became more important than hitting up the newest and hippest restaurants and hopping on a plane for an exotic vacation was all of a sudden as enjoyable as getting your wisdom teeth extracted. People are craving family, stability, and peace. People want stuff like yoga and meditation to calm their nerves and almost overnight both of our studios became too crowded to

141

handle. The minute I got back from New York we got to work securing our newest location. I was super happy about the distraction because I sort of didn't want to think about the weirdest of all things that occurred after 9/11...my engagement.

Everything became blurry when Leo got down on his knee. I kept saying the words over and over again in my mind...*No, not yet! No, not yet!* I don't know why I thought that, because ever since I laid eyes on Leo, I wanted him to be my husband. But I guess the immediate idea of becoming a wife again scared the crap out of me. There's a lot of responsibility with that role, a lot of things that can potentially go downhill...the possibility that more failure could creep back into my life. But when I opened the black velvet box and saw the ring, a vintage 2.5 carat square cut diamond engagement ring with enough tiny sapphires surrounding it to probably make an entirely separate 1 carat ring, *No, not yet* turned into *Give it to me! Give it to me!* and all of my fears went out the window. Without ever having a serious conversation about rings, Leo bought me exactly what I would've picked out on my own. He nailed it. And then I let him nail me. I suppose you could say it was my "Yes, I'll marry you!"

The remainder of my time in New York was filled with a bunch of Hedgehog, or whatever it's called, talk. There was no talk of a wedding and that was just fine with me. *What would we have discussed?* I have a thriving business on the west coast, and he has a bunch of hedge-thingies he's trying to get in order on the east coast. I have a Goddaughter that I'm responsible for three days a week, and he has a friendship he's trying to repair. I hate New York, and he wants to live in it. See? Everything's blurry and grey. And I know from experience, you can't have a productive conversation about anything, let alone a wedding, when things are blurry and grey. So, two days after the proposal, I caught a flight home without having once talked about our future.

I remember for a time near the end of my marriage to Kurt, I compared us to two dots, one black one and one white one, because that's how different we were and as time went on, our dots kept moving farther and farther away from each other. So far that by the time we had officially separated, our dots were almost undetectable.

But from the moment I met Leo, we were the same bright color dot. Even when were thousands of miles apart and not talking it seemed like our dots were moving in the same direction – toward each other. That's how connected we were since the very beginning. That's how in sync our dreams and goals were. But all of a sudden our bright and shiny dot has turned grey and grey has NEVER looked good on me! All of a sudden it feels like we're moving in opposite directions. I don't function well when there are two different color dots in a relationship. I know better than anyone that's what a grey dot eventually turns into.

I tried to hide my fear of grey from Leo when I was in New York because he's got so much on his plate right now, but he saw right through it when he walked me down to catch a cab to the airport.

"It's gonna be okay, Baby. Maybe it'll be like this for four…five months tops. But after that it'll be like how it was before 9/11."

"Sure…if you're still alive."

He's just as scared as I am about the whole terrorist thing. Shit, everyone is. (That's why I flew that day with my pointiest boots on. One swift kick to the groin and that extremist would rue the day he ever tried to take my plane down.) Still, Leo did his best to calm my nerves when he said, "I don't wanna be in New York any more than you do. It's just the right thing to do right now. I'll get this business set up as quickly as I can and then I'll get home to you. I promise."

His *Braveheart/The Last of the Mohicans*-like demeanor pulled me into engagement dreamland, and for a few minutes I

143

forgot about all of that grey area stuff. Our kiss at the taxi stand that day was epic and so was my flight out. As my plane ascended into the air, I thought about the last time I had departed from JFK. It was last December, right after Leo told me to take a hike outside of P.J. Clark's. As I sat on the airplane a few days ago, I nervously twisted my new engagement ring as I stared down at the massive gaping hole in the ground where the towers used to stand. Given my tumultuous history with Leo, I thought to myself, "Who would've thought *that* would be the thing I'd never see again?" Life is so crazy sometimes that it scares the shit out of me.

And speaking of having the shit scared out of you…While I was busy getting engaged in New York, Slutty Co-worker was busy with a few things of her own. While I was gone, the studios were shorthanded so my dear old trampy friend was forced to call people she didn't even know to help her out and on that list was Barbara. I'd been trying to get Barbara to make an appearance in the studios since last May, but it seems like ever since I told her about Kendall, she's come up with every excuse in the book to postpone a visit. She's continued to drop off her handmade gadgets at the back door before anyone arrives or I've gone to her home in Berkeley to pick them up. It was evident that the idea of being around Kendall was too much for Barbara, so I never pushed it. Apparently, a little pushing was all that was needed though, because Slutty Co-worker succeeded in doing something I've failed at for six months!

"Who the hell is that?"

Standing outside of the glass window that separates the yoga studio from the reception area, I'm pointing at a woman who's getting a private lesson from our most experienced and attractive yoga master dude.

Smiling from ear to ear, Slutty Co-worker boasts, "That's your home girl, Barbara!"

"Uhhhh, no it's not. Barbara has more grey hair than…whoever has the most grey hair! And besides that, she's scared to death to step foot in this place, let alone take a private class from that guy! Hold on, is that even yoga? *Is he supposed to touch her like that?*"

"Why do you think his classes are always so full, Hunny?"

"Nope, no way that's Bar—"

With welcomed assistance from the yoga master, the woman whom I so appropriately used to call Sad Frumpy Lady transitions into Warrior One, then sees me and starts wildly waving.

"Oh…my…God, what did you do to her?"

"Told her she looked like shit."

"And?"

"And I also told her no man would ever fuck her if she looked like shit. Then I took her to my stylist and out for a chardonnay. Now, here we are!"

"Holy crap, you must've scared her to death."

"Totally…but her fear disappeared pretty darn fast when she looked in a mirror. I said to her, 'Now there's a face I'd wanna fuck!' You know what she said?"

"Oh God…what?"

"She said, 'You're right. I really do need to get laid.' And then I think she laughed for the first time in her life."

Megan then joins us at the window to stare at Barbara in total disbelief. It's a nice, quiet moment until Megan grabs my left hand and shoves it in my face."

"WHAT THE HELL IS THAT?"

"HOLY SHIT, HUNNY, IS THAT WHAT WE THINK IT IS?"

The commotion causes Barbara to fly out of the studio to see what's going on, but I postpone the inevitable by complimenting the unbelievable.

"I like your hair Barbara. You look…Jesus, you look fantastic!"

Twirling around in a happy circle, she laughs like I've never heard her laugh before.

"I know, unrecognizable, huh?"

Wrapping her arms around Slutty Co-worker, she gushes, "Who needs therapy when you have friends like this?" Then, noticing the other two women marveling at my ring, she changes the subject to me with, "Oh my goodness, Chrissy, is that an engagement ring?"

I proceed to tell my rag-tag team that Leo asked me to marry him three days ago, but he's staying in New York to rebuild a business and restore a friendship...or vice-versa or whatever.

"Hold on! This happened three days ago? But you called us every day to give us an update on Taddeo and bark orders at us! How come you never mentioned it?"

"Because...I'm scared, Megan."

"Scared of what? Seriously, look at the size of that sucker!"

"I'm scared he's never coming back."

("Here I Go Again," *Whitesnake*)

Simplicity

November, 2001

Singing at the top of my lungs to my 80's music, *"Here I go again...blah, blah, blah...going down the only road I've ever known,"* actually puts me in a good mood for a few minutes. It ends when the guy at the gate motions his finger across his neck to turn it off. The jerk doesn't have a clue how much Kelly would like to hear what I'm playing, and I flash him a look that tells him how irritated I am. I make my way to my usual parking spot and settle in next to Courtney's and Nicole's cars. We're gathering today to recognize the nine month anniversary of life without our voice of reason, and I've packed plenty of nachos and beer for the occasion. I sure hope Nicole didn't forget the cigarettes. It's still so much fun when the three of us smoke together. It takes me back to when we were young, to when lighting up a cigarette was the most forbidden thing I could possibly do. It takes me back to when things were simple.

I left New York three weeks ago, and I've barely spoken to Leo since. He's been working twenty-four hours a day on the hedge thing-a-ma-jig with Taddeo, but progress has been super slow. Everything is still such a mess in New York, and he's worried that it's going to take longer than expected to get things going at a pace where he's comfortable moving back to California. But staying true to my promise to Taddeo to not get in the way of their friendship, I haven't said a word about how much our new set up scares me and about my fear of him never coming back.

Another thing moving along at a slug's pace is our wedding. In fact, there's still been no mention of it. With all of the 9/11 business and Leo's hectic schedule, it just doesn't seem right to bring it up...it doesn't feel right to be happy. Besides, what am I going to bring up? Our parents haven't met, my friends have never met any of his friends...Shit, half of my friends haven't even met the other half of my friends! And what the hell am I going to wear? I can't wear white again. Been there, done that, and I'll just have to remind Leo of that little tidbit if I bring up dresses, so it's best not to. There's no reason to register for gifts. It'd be pretty tacky of me to do that twice in a lifetime. Sigh...Something tells me Barbie doesn't get two dream weddings in her lifetime. Nope, all of the tasteful divorced Barbies quietly elope.

The closest Leo and I have come to the subject of our wedding is when we talk about the engagement ring. He's asked me a few times over the phone if I love it and of course, the answer is yes. It's spectacular! Whenever I wear it, I even get stopped by strangers who ask to take a peek at it. Yes, you read that correctly...*whenever I wear it.*

Leo bought the ring back in June, right about the time I mentioned my suspicions to Kelly that he might ask me to marry him soon. Apparently, right after we went on our trip down memory lane to Mill Valley and San Louis Obispo, he ran out and bought it. Last month when he got down on his knee and proposed, he adoringly said, "The next time I go back to those places I want to bring my wife" and then he slipped off the pewter Banana Republic ring I'd been wearing since we got back together in March and slipped on the diamond sparkler. His original plan was to ask me to marry him at the Ritz Carlton on my birthday, but it was scrapped when Taddeo came to town. Then, the fight happened, and he wanted to wait until his black eye went away before he made another attempt. That next attempt was set for the night I sprang Freakmont on him, which explains why he was as mad as he was about it. By the time he simmered down from that night it was already September. He made reservations back at the Ritz Carlton for the weekend of September fourteenth, but we all know what got in the way of that. Knowing it would probably be weeks until he saw me in person again because of his new business partnership with Taddeo, he decided to do it when I visited New York last month. I'm glad he did, because it'll give us an endearing story to tell our kids one day. But and I'll only admit this here, even though I'm scared about him being stuck in New York for more than five months, I'm a little relieved that he'll be there for at least the next few. It gives me time to drop the M-bomb on my best friends...who I know will be quick to drop the M-bomb on Kurt.

I've been trying to figure out why I want to keep my engagement from Kurt. For the past few weeks I've been sitting in my cottage listening to every love song ever written, drinking wine and trying to make sense out of feelings that should've been left on Dr. Maria's couch. One drunken minute I think I'm hiding my engagement because of guilt. Marrying the guy I had an affair with makes me feel bad. Sure, marrying Leo makes me look like less of a whore, and it's proof that I really did fall in love with the person I chose to break my marital vows with. But it seems like one more undeserved slap in Kurt's face. I struggle with defending my union with Leo without feeling the shame that encases it. But then the next drunken minute I think I'm hiding my engagement from Kurt because I have a feeling, given his recent come to Jesus moment at the coffee shop about being an emotional lame ass for the last fifteen years, that he'll knock my cottage door down to tell me I'm making a huge mistake. Of course I'd stand up for my choice, but it's just one more emotionally-charged encounter with him I don't want to have. Bad, bad things happen when I'm around Kurt. Buried feelings surface, and he makes me think about stuff I don't want to think about anymore. But when I turn off my persuasive love songs

149

and sober up and really reflect on why I'm hiding my engagement from Kurt, I know the answer. And boy, I'm sure as hell glad I don't sit on Dr. Maria's couch anymore because she'd kill me if I revealed it to her. I don't want Kurt to find out I'm engaged because...I don't want to hurt him. Even after all of this time, I'm still trying to protect the feelings of a man who never asked me to. What's scary is that in the process of doing that, I continue to assault the feelings of the man I love and the man who has vulnerably asked me time and again not to break his heart.

Right now I only wear my engagement ring at the yoga studios. When I'm around my rag-tag team, I get to celebrate my excitement about becoming Leo's wife. I get to talk about how far we've come and about how far we plan on going. I get to start over. But outside of the studios, when I'm around Craig and Kendall or Courtney and Nicole, I hide my fresh start.

Cracking open my beer and reaching for the cigarette Nicole's handing to me, I whisper to Kelly, "For now, it's just our little secret." And then I allow myself to enjoy the simplicity of the moment while we all light up.

Fur Reals?

November, 2001

It's beginning to look like things in Chrissy-land are getting back to normal (which, by the way probably isn't saying much because that's only half of what's normal in Normal-land).

It's been almost two months since I ran out of that coffee shop and away from Kurt, and the guilt or fear or whatever it was that I had about him finding out about my engagement has since subsided. In fact, the longer I've been able to sit and think about it, how dare he try to make up for the past like that...and in a coffee shop! I loved Kurt more than anything in my life, for most of my life, but not anymore. And if my new marriage stands a chance in hell, I had better start acting like that. And I have. I never bring the subject of Kurt up around my friends and whenever they do, I leave the room. So far, Craig seems to be the only one who's noticed my valiant effort, and he even complimented me on it at the last get together with the gang. He continues to support my relationship with Leo, and I've actually decided that he'll be the first gang member I'll tell of my engagement...when it's the right time. Baby steps...

My friendships with Courtney and Nicole are completely back to normal now that we all agree that Leo will never be a gang member *and* I now know the full reason why they met Kayla. If I hadn't had a full blown Chrissy meltdown at the cemetery that day and driven off so quickly, they would've been able to tell me that Kurt brought her, unannounced, to a barbeque at Courtney's house. They hated every second of her and told Kurt to keep her infantile sorority-ass as far away from them as possible. (Their husbands, however, totally enjoyed her and her boobs.) I have no doubt that my best friends will jump

151

up and down and clap at the news of my engagement…when they hear of it. Baby steps…

My special time with Kendall has come to mean so much more to me than I ever thought possible. Since I've started picking her up three days a week, she's adopted so many of my characteristics and Craig has even forgiven me for most of them! Shoes are her number one favorite accessory, she never leaves home without her Mac lip gloss and pathetically, "HELLS NO" has escaped from her mouth on a few occasions. The staff at The Happy Hearts daycare center greets me by first name and sends me invitations to all of her special events and you can bet I'm at each and every one. I'm even mistaken as her mother by new staff and when it happens, Kendall and I just look at each other and giggle. Even though I hide it from Kendall, being called her mother is like a straight shot to my heart. But for some reason she really enjoys it, so I follow her lead every time and laugh away. Kendall misses "Weo" and the snipe hunting marathons they used to get into, and she's at the top of the list of people who will be overjoyed to know that he's soon to become my husband…when the news hits the stands. Baby steps…

And speaking of my future husband…his dot is becoming less grey now as talk of the wedding has commenced. As we were wrapping up our phone conversation tonight with twenty-six "I love yous" and forty-seven "No, you hang-up firsts," Leo blurted out with, "Oh, wait…I almost forgot! Tell me some place you've never been before."

"Why?"

"Just tell me."

I've traveled to so many places with Kurt and with my old job, it takes me a few minutes to hone in on an answer. Before I'm about to say, Russia, Leo interjects with, "Make it somewhere tropical."

Looking down at the plastic water bottle I'm drinking out of, I think, *hmmmm*, that looks like a nice place.

"Fiji."

"That's crazy because that's *exactly* what I was gonna suggest!"

"For what?"

"The place we get married. Just you and me…"

"…All alone on a beach. Oh, Leo, it sounds perfect. "

And it does. No wedding dress, no wedding cake, no gift registry, and no thank you cards. But mostly…no guests and no laughing at me for the second walk around the block. Oh, c'mon, we all place bets on every second marriage we're invited to! We all scoff at the big whoop-di-doo the second chance bride makes of her big second wedding day! We all kick our date under the pew as the second chance bride takes that second walk down the aisle in her big fat white second chance dress. We all say the same thing, "Honey, you shoulda got married on some remote beach like all of the other self-respecting second chance brides!" Which, is where I'll be thanks to my overly private fiancé who hates large crowds and chaos.

I hang up the phone with Leo happier than I've been in a very long time. After taking a long energized sip of my wine, I reach for the remote. But the second I click on the TV, I click it off, fearing I'll catch some of the 9/11 footage that continues to run twenty-four-seven. Wanting to hang onto my happiness for as long as I can, I reach for a piece of paper and get to work.

1) Marry Leo on the beach in Fiji.
2) Find our dream house together.
3) Have a baby.
4) Get a dog.

Yes…things in Chrissy-land are totally back to normal.

Acceptance

December, 2001

According to all of the books I *tried* to read when Kelly was diagnosed with terminal cancer, there are five stages of grief. First you've got your denial. I imagine this is what I experienced when I turned my office at the clothing company into a medical research lab and tried to find the cure for pancreatic cancer. For a girl who never got better than a C- in science and was told by her high school counselor that she wasn't even qualified to chew gum, I'd say I was in serious denial. A few days into my research, I remembered how scientifically challenged I was and realized my efforts to cure Kelly were useless. All hopelessness was reinforced when Internet search after Internet search yielded the same results, "SHE'S GONNA DIE!" As you can imagine, this made me mad...really, really mad. I was kicked in the ass to the next stage, anger. For as angry and negative of a person as I am, one would think I'd still be sitting in this stage. Surprisingly it was a short one for me. I figured since, at that point in my life, I had so many demons and lies at my disposal due to my underground relationship with Leo, it would be a better use of my time *and* Kelly's time to skip anger and get right to the bargaining stage. And that I did. "Please, God, I promise to start believing in you if you'll just let Kelly live." And "Please, God, if you make the cancer go away, I won't have another drink as long as I live." And "Please, God, just take me. I'm the lying cheating childless person who deserves to die, not Kelly." God didn't listen to me. Shocker. When Craig stopped returning my calls a few weeks before Kelly died, I knew I was out of bargaining chips, and I became pretty depressed – stage four. I was depressed, but it was weird though, because at this point the depression wasn't about losing Kelly. One of the perks (yes, I just called it a perk) of pancreatic cancer is you get used to dealing with loss pretty quickly. It's one of the deadliest cancers and since I already learned that way back in the denial stage, I multi-tasked and took care of my depression about losing Kelly then. The reason for the depression I was experiencing at stage four was from feeling powerless. But I kind of got lucky again with this stage. You see, because I had so much therapy with Dr. Maria about feeling powerless with Kurt for all of those years, I kind of knew how to handle it. And thousands of dollars of therapy taught me to handle it by…simply refusing to feel it. And that I did by jumping into the fifth stage, acceptance. Acceptance was peaceful, and I was glad to have quickly arrived. My journey through the five stages of grief was very strange- *Mostly because I was already at the end of the stages when everyone else was just beginning.* I guess it explains why I could deliver Kelly's eulogy without freaking out. I guess it's why I could take care of Nicole and Courtney in Mexico. I guess it explains why Kelly's death immediately made me want to take risks…live life…find love.

That old saying, what doesn't kill you makes you stronger, is super true. And since I know this so well from personal experience, I know I'll eventually get to the acceptance stage of what Kurt just unexpectedly showed up to my cottage to tell me. The difference this time though is I'll probably arrive at acceptance at the same time as everyone else.

I was on the phone with Leo. He and Taddeo had been hard at work rebuilding the hedge fund business, and the work officially started when they renamed it T.L. Capital. Hearing that Leo's initial was now in the title made me think his stint in New York was going to be longer than the four or five months he promised. But when I nervously asked if I should change his mailing address, he said "Baby, like I said, I'm coming home." He was still on target to open up a west coast division of the

156

business in March. I was relieved to know that my drugs would be back at my disposal in three months. It was during my explanation of comparing being with him to injecting heroin that the walls started vibrating.

"I'm serious Leo! Heroin is like taking the best orgasm you've ever had and multiplying it by like…a billion, and you're still nowhere near how good it makes you feel! Yep, you're like my heroin! I tried you once and now I'm addicted for life!"

His deep and sexy laugh makes me want to crawl into the phone and end up in his mouth!

"But Chrissy, have you ever *tried* heroin?"

"Well no, but—"

The pounding startled me so much that I let out a little scream.

"What's wrong?"

"Someone's at the door."

"What the hell? It's ten at night!"

I thought the same thing and it scared me. There are only two reasons for a ten-at-night door pounding; a booty call or a scare-the-wits-out-of-you emergency. Seeing as though my booty call is currently an airplane ride away, I knew the night was about to take a turn for the worse.

"CHRISSY, OPEN THE DOOR! PLEASE, I NEED YOU!"

That's Kurt's voice. Oh shit, he found out about the engagement! *But how?*

"Talk to me. What's going on over there, Baby?"

Remember Chrissy, you made a vow…no more lies.

"I don't know, Leo. I think it's…I think it's Kurt."

"Open the door and put him on the phone."

"Seriously? There's no way I'm…"

"OPEN THE GODDAMN DOOR AND PUT HIM ON THE PHONE!"

You know what? Leo has every right to be mad, and I think this time I need to let him handle his anger directly with Kurt. I wonder though…would I be thinking so rationally if the ass-kicking had the potential to be anything more than a verbal one? Uhhhhh, that would be a BIG no! Honest to God, I fear the day these guys have a face-to-face encounter. I don't think either of them could hold back the urge to punch, and the thought of them hurting each other is too much to bear. Reaching for the door handle, I think…*until then, let the verbal war begin.*

Nothing could've prepared me for what I saw when I opened the door. There was Kurt, trembling, with tears streaming down his face and large pools of dried blood covering his sweat-drenched shirt. I dropped the phone at the same time Kurt dropped to the ground. Yes, I knew the night was about to take a turn for the worse when I heard the pounding, but there was absolutely nothing that could've prepared me for how bad a turn the night – no, scratch that. There was absolutely nothing that could've prepared me for how big of a turn my life was about to take when Kurt opened his mouth and starting screaming.

Again

December, 2001

My eyes crack open to the sun piercing through my sheer curtains and my mind goes right to the dream I just woke from.

There I was at Chili's with my big platter of fried appetizers and my bottomless fountain drink. As usual, disgustingly fat patrons with their obnoxiously loud children were strewn about the joint. As usual, the losers from my old high school days in Freakmont delivered food to me, and as usual I was supposed to meet Kelly. Only this time, she didn't show up.

I hear the coffee pot signal it's ready and for a second I wonder why it went off so early. But then I suddenly remember and my heart sinks. I thought I had already gone through hell and back with the Kelly stuff, the affair, the lies, the divorce, the....oh, you get my point. But here I am, back in hell. This time though, I'm scared I'm not going to make it back. This is literally going to be the longest and most painful day of my life.

After a laborious brush of the teeth and a long, drawn-out sigh at my worn-out reflection in the mirror from having stayed up most of the night, I grab my old lime green French terry robe and set out to try and get everything straight. My coffee cup, already poured and prepared just the way I like it, is waiting for me on the kitchen counter. After a short search, because my cottage is only six hundred square feet, I find Kurt on the deck. He's shirtless and staring at the partially frozen creek below.

"Kurt...you're freezing. Why don't you just put it on?"

Last night, after calming him down enough to tell me what had happened and then him calming me down enough to absorb the news, I helped him out of his shirt. It was only serving as a horrible reminder of what he just went through. I offered him one of Leo's old shirts that I sleep in almost every night of the week, but he was quick to say, "No fucking way. Get it out of my face." I suppose I would've had the same reaction if he offered me one of Kayla's bras. Even though he didn't snap at me for making the offer again right now, the look on his face is saying the same thing he said last night.

"Then here...take my robe."

"Chrissy, I don't need the robe. I can't feel anything."

I remember that same numb feeling when Courtney and Nicole broke the news to me about Kelly. You think it's going to last forever, but it passes...as you pass through the stages of grief.

Gently taking hold of his arm, I nudge him to walk with me.

"Come on, Kurt, let's go inside. We have a lot to talk about and it's too cold to do it out here."

Leo was remarkably calm last night. It took about fifteen minutes for me to pick up the receiver that I dropped to the ground when I saw Kurt. But when I did, he was still on the other end of it. He told me he heard every word that Kurt spoke and while he was obviously frustrated about my ex-husband standing shirtless in front of me, he didn't feel like it was the right time to be angry about it. He asked if I wanted him to come home and help me, but I told him to stay put until I knew what I needed help with. This is exactly what Kurt and I have to figure out this morning. After two pots of coffee and two hours of back and forth phone calls between Craig's parents, Kelly's mom, Courtney and Nicole and their husbands, I think we have a tentative plan.

"...So, I'll go and pick her up tonight. That'll give you and everyone else time to make the arrangements."

"What are you gonna tell her?"

My own courage catches me by surprise.

"The truth."

"Jesus, how is she gonna be able to handle that?"

"She won't. That's why, first thing tomorrow, I'll call Dr. Maria."

"She's a marriage counselor. What the hell is she gonna be able to do?"

"Please don't snap at me! I'm just as confused and upset as you are right now!"

"I'm sorry... I don't know what I'm..."

And then his tears let loose again. It's a sight that's so foreign to me that I still don't exactly know how to act when it happens. I gently put my hand on his bare shoulder to soothe him.

"I'm sorry too. Look, I'm not sure if Dr. Maria's qualified to handle this kind of situation, but she'll know someone who can. That's a good start, right?"

Vigorously rubbing his face with his hands, he asks, "And then what?"

"I guess we have to talk to a lawyer and the sooner the better. We have to initiate some kind of stability...we have to give everyone some answers."

"So...we're leading the charge on this?"

Even though I'm scared to death, I can tell he's more scared. So scared...that I think *I'm the one actually leading the charge on this.*

"It's the responsibility we signed up for."

Realizing that I'm losing him to the first stage of grief-denial, I put my hand back on his shoulder to bring him back to the hand we were dealt.

"Kurt, look at me...I'm pretty sure everyone's relying on us to figure this out."

Staring at each other like two people who just got stranded on a deserted island with no possibility of a rescue, I hesitantly continue.

"I *think* we have first right of refusal on this, or maybe we don't have any choice at all in what happens. As far as I know, their Will stayed the same, but I don't really know what that means. Do you?"

"No."

Now it's his hand that touches my knee when he asks, "But what do you want to happen?"

I answer without hesitation.

"I want her."

Still stunned and still shirtless, Kurt left my cottage at two in the afternoon with plans to meet me and the rest of the gang at Craig's house later that afternoon. I'm supposed to bring Kendall back to my cottage and everyone else will stay to make the funeral arrangements. Now I know why Kelly didn't show up in my dream last night. She was busy welcoming her husband, Craig, to the place she's called home for the last ten months.

Crash

December, 2001

According to everything Kurt told me, they were supposed to have a good time yesterday – just two lonely guys out on the town. Kurt wanted to give Craig something fun to do to take his mind off of Kelly for a few hours. He also wanted to meet some chicks and attempt to jump back into the dating scene again. On top of his wanting to shed the sound of my voice telling him he sucked as a husband, Kayla told him to never call her ever again unless he had a house and diamond for her. Now even though I've made my fair share of relationship mistakes (like, for example, pretending to enjoy mountain climbing in scary animal infested forests just so Kurt would fall madly in love with me), *even I know* Kayla's a friggin' idiot to make demands like that! Seriously, it's like the girl's boobs sucked the common sense right out of her brain. No dude worth marrying is going to give in to an ultimatum like that. Ever.

First, Kurt and Craig hit up a sushi restaurant in Palo Alto and had a great time doing sake bombs on table tops with the pretty Stanford girls. Initially, it took some convincing to get Craig to join in on the fun, but one co-ed in particular had a way with words and it gave him one of his first genuine smiles since his wife died. After that they continued their ego boosting/mind distracting tour at a nearby pool hall where seemingly pretty white trash girls hit on the two of them. I say *seemingly* pretty because had the boys managed to keep their alcohol consumption to shall we say…less than what an entire stadium full of football fans would drink, they would've realized the pool hall girls were total floozies.

163

The two guys drove separately to Palo Alto. Kurt had a meeting with his biking club, (please…don't even get me started) in nearby Menlo Park earlier that afternoon, so Craig made the drive over the Dumbarton Bridge to meet him. By late afternoon it seemed like the ego boosting/mind distracting mission had been accomplished because the boys were cracking jokes and laughing like it was 1987 all over again. It was just what the two of them needed.

Now, I've enjoyed my fair share of beer with Craig in the old days and on Kelly's porch, but he was never one to push the limits. Especially since Kelly died, because he was the only one left to keep a close eye on Kendall. But yesterday Kendall wasn't with him. She was at his parent's house. A place Craig didn't relish leaving her unless it was super important because they weren't as sharp as they used to be – they were freaking old! In fact, Kelly used to jokingly call them his "prehistoric parents." But Kurt deemed yesterday's festivities necessary and convinced Craig to go against his better judgment and party the day away in Palo Alto – so he left her there. Then, Craig went against his better judgment again when he got behind the wheel of his car and drove back home to Freakmont when the party was over.

Craig knew better than to drive drunk. In fact, it was always him who policed us in the old days. He'd be the first one to stop drinking to make sure everyone who was drinking either stayed the night at his house or was okay enough to drive by the time they left. But at around seven o'clock, the drunkenness that for a brief time made him forget about his heartache faded into a somewhat coherent buzz. Kurt told me he started missing Kelly again, and he started to get anxious about getting back to his parents' house before they dozed off – something that usually happened around eight o'clock. He promised Kurt once he got there he'd tuck Kendall into his old bed and sleep on the couch. He thought the foolish deal he made with himself to just make it to his parent's house was practical and he gave himself the green light to drive. Kurt stayed behind at a coffee shop to sober up and as far as he can remember, Craig appeared in control when he said good-bye. How would he have really known though? He was way too hammered to be the judge of anything. The two guys gave each other a good-bye bro hug at the coffee shop and made plans for a round of golf on Sunday. That was the last time Kurt ever saw Craig alive.

After four cups of coffee and a nice little cat-nap on a park bench, Kurt was sober enough to return to his brother's house in Freakmont where he'd been shacking up since his break up with Kayla. Personally, I'd rather call that park bench my home than live with anyone in his family, but we've already covered my revulsion of the Gibbons clan, no need to digress.

Traffic was super backed up on the bridge, and what would normally be a thirty minute drive to Freakmont, was more like two hours. Finally, when he got to the other side of the bridge, just a few feet west of the toll plaza, a tired and frustrated Kurt saw what all the fuss was about. There appeared to be a two car collision and by the looks of the stretcher with a haphazardly covered body on it, it was a fatal one. Driving by at a mere two miles per hour, Kurt who was totally sober by now, but a little nervous about the smell of his breath, hunkered down low in his seat as he slowly passed the cops who were milling around the crash site. He got so low that his eyes were directly in line with a hand sticking out from underneath the sheet – a hand wearing the watch he bought for Craig as a wedding gift. Despite seeing what he knew was Craig's lifeless body, he acted just as I did when I was told Kelly had pancreatic cancer, he tried to save him. He jumped out of his car, ran to the stretcher and immediately started performing CPR on the mangled and bloody body. Paramedics ran to pry the crazed stranger away, but Kurt fought them off so he could continue his hopeless effort. He was finally subdued by the police, and after calming down and explaining who he was, he was told what happened to his best friend. It appeared that Craig plowed into an abandoned car stranded in the right lane of the two-lane stretch of the bridge. Witnesses to the accident were shocked that Craig didn't notice the bright hazard lights of the broken down car, and they said it appeared he was driving about eighty miles per hour, twenty-five miles per hour over the limit. Despite his seatbelt and air bag, he was dead on impact.

Head swirling with the news, Kurt was finally allowed to return to Craig's stretcher where he cradled his best friend in his arms and repeated over and over again, "I love you, man. Please come back. Please come back. Please don't leave Kendall..."

At last, the paramedics painfully told Kurt they had to take Craig away and peeled him off his body. Without thought, he got into his car and drove straight to me.

Happening

December, 2001

"Chrissy, I have to come home. You can't possibly handle all of this on your own."

Even though I'm on my way to Craig's house to retrieve Kendall and tell her the horrible news about her daddy, I'm not so messed up to have forgotten how stupid it would be to have Leo anywhere near this scene. "The gang" is going to be very entwined in the next few weeks and we all know Kurt's a member.

"I would love that, Leo, but I have to focus on Kendall. I'm taking her back to my cottage tonight, and it's best if I'm alone with her."

Although crushed, my beautiful, heartfelt Leo agrees to go along with whatever I think is best. Hoping to continue to ride his wave of warmth, I spontaneously decide there's not going to be a better time to tell him the news, so I pull my car over to the side of the road.

"Leo, I never told you this, but Craig's parents are very old."

"I remember he mentioned something about that when we had dinner at his house."

"And…Kelly's mom has never been the same after she died."

"I'm sure this is gonna be incredibly difficult for all of them. Honestly, I can't even imagine the grief."

"That's not why I'm telling you this. Leo…you know how I'm Kendall's Godmother?"

"Yeah."

"Well…Kurt's her Godfather."

167

"I never wanted to ask, but I suspected as much. Why are you bringing this—*Oh my God, are you two the legal guardians of Kendall?*"

"As far as I know, yes."

The tone in his voice takes a subtle shift from warm to worried.

"When will you know for sure?"

"First thing tomorrow morning, I'll call the attorney listed on my last version of their Will. But Leo, you have to know something."

He doesn't need to wait for me to tell him, he already knows.

"You want her, don't you?"

"Try not to spit your coffee out, but I'm the only shot that child has at living a life that's remotely close to what her parents would've wanted for her."

"You don't think Nicole or Courtney can do it?"

All of a sudden a maternal instinct to protect kicks in that even I didn't know I possessed.

"Are you insinuating I should even *suggest* it to them?"

"I don't know…they're married, they already have kids."

"Yeah, kids they barely have enough time for because of their jobs! Kelly would roll over in her grave if Kendall was in daycare for even half the amount of time their kids are!"

"Baby, Baby, Baby! I'm not trying to upset you. I support whatever you decide. I care for Kendall too, and I'll do whatever I can to honor her parents and be the best…I guess the best father-figure I can be. I mean, that's what we're talking about, right?"

Hearing him say that makes me wonder for the millionth time in nearly four years, what the hell have I gotten this guy into? Seriously, if Taddeo thought I had baggage because I was a divorced chick, he's going to have a field day about this. Worry about it later, Chrissy! There's still more to tell him.

"I don't think it's gonna be as easy as that."

"I don't think there's gonna be anything easy about this, especially for her. But I want you both to be happy, and I'll do whatever I can to make that happen because I love you."

"I love you too, Leo, but that's not why I said this isn't gonna be easy." Here we go…"I'm pretty sure, once he's had time to deal with everything that's happened, that Kurt's gonna want her, too."

It's quiet for a long time as the two of us process the millions of what-ifs shooting through our heads. He's first to break the silence, and he does it like he's a man on a mission.

"I'll fly home tonight, and we'll get married tomorrow. We'll prove we can offer her the most stability, and if we have to, we'll fight him for custody."

How did I know a fight would be involved?

"Leo, if their Will stayed the same, it won't be that easy."

"So, what are you saying?"

"I'm saying we're gonna have to stay calm and strong for Kendall, no matter what the outcome. I won't allow one more minute of chaos into that child's life."

"I understand, but are we talking about split custody here? Chrissy, are you saying he might have to be a part of our lives…*forever?*"

"I don't know what I'm saying. Right now, I don't know anything."

I take that back. I know the familiar sick feeling brewing in my stomach. It's telling me I'm losing Leo all over again.

After a frazzled good-bye, I set my phone down and resume my drive to Craig's house. On the way, I play sick head games with myself like, if someone told me we could have Craig and Kelly back if I remarried Kurt, would I? And to make this news to Kendall easier, would I break up with Leo right now? And on and on and on.

I'm the last person to arrive at the house. Kurt, Guss, and Kyle are standing in the middle of the garage talking, and Courtney and Nicole are sitting on the front porch. With both hands extended out in front of her, Nicole motions for me to go to them first. Kurt's eyes stay worriedly focused on every step I take toward my best friends.

Focusing on Courtney, I see a sight hardly ever seen before. I bend down to comfort my problem-solving pal.

"Court, talk to me. Where's my touchstone? C'mon, girl, I need you to guide me through this. Just like you did with Kelly. Can you do that for me?"

My typically sensible and tireless friend lifts her head up and hopelessly shakes her head.

"Court, it's gonna be okay."

Nicole wraps her arms around Courtney, looks up at me and says, "Kendall has no parents, how can you say that? Actually, hold on….*how is it that you're the one saying that?*"

I can hardly believe it myself. How is it that, I, the emotional core of the group, am the only one not crying right now? And then I see the answer peering at me through the curtains. The same curtains her mother peered through and gave me a shaky thumbs up just a year ago.

As I motion to Kendall with my finger that I'll be inside in a minute, I whisper to my friends, "She needs me to be strong."

I've lost my shit over a missing tube of mascara before. I've called in sick to work because I had a zit. I literally lost twenty pounds in two months from being such an emotional wreck when I met Leo. I've bawled my brains out over stuff that in the grand scheme of things didn't matter. I could melt down because deep inside, I knew life wasn't going to end over stupid shit. But life will end—well, the chance at the happy one Kendall deserves anyway—if I lose my shit right now. I feel Kelly's strength weighing heavy on my heart, *and my tear ducts*, and I feel the force of her thumbs-up. She's giving me what I need to take control of this situation and do what's best for her daughter. I just know it.

Stepping away from my best friends I walk to the garage. I give Guss and Kyle quiet hugs and then speak directly to Kurt who still hasn't taken his eyes off me.

"Do her grandparents know I'm gonna tell her?"

"Yeah. Kelly's mom is at the funeral home and Craig's parents are at their own house. They're a mess and don't want to scare her."

"Does she have any idea what's going on?"

"I don't think so. I brought a bunch of toys over, hoping to keep her preoccupied until you got here. She's been so busy with them she hasn't even noticed Craig's not here."

Courtney and Nicole slowly walk up and are now in the garage with the rest of the gang, and all eyes are on me. This is really happening. I'm really about to tell a four year old little girl, who lost her mother to cancer just ten months ago, that her father is dead.

Please Don't Make Me Do This

December, 2001

U p until the minute Kelly got too sick and tired to tend to her daughter, she'd always been a hands-on mom. Of course Kendall was in daycare until two-fifteen because Kelly worked, but after that, every day of Kendall's life was filled with a craft, or a trip to the park or story time on her mommy's lap. The weekends were filled with trips to the zoo, Mommy and Me gymnastics classes and good old-fashioned family time in the evening with Craig. But Kelly's energy ran out in the last two months of her life and the fun came to a screeching halt…she also became pretty scary to look at. After Kelly shaved her head due to hair loss from chemo, she did her best to keep her wig on to hide the look from Kendall, but slipped up on one occasion. And that occasion freaked Kendall out – big time. One night, after a bad dream, Kendall tippy-toed into her parents room for some comfort, but got the opposite when her startled mother sat up in bed and revealed her bald head. Despite Kelly's effort to calm her, Kendall cried, "Make it go back, Mommy! Make it go back!" According to Craig, that's when Kelly started wanting to die. She was frightening her child who, up until that time, she'd done everything in the world to protect from terrifying things. That's when she decided to move Kendall out of the house and in with her grandparents. The only night Kendall came home in those last two months of her Mommy's life was a few days before Kelly went into the hospital where she died and that's only because the grandparents got the flu and couldn't look after her. She came home the night Kelly begged Craig to take a bath with her, but he didn't. He was too busy doing everything he could to keep Kendall away from Kelly. It wasn't what he wanted, but it's what Kelly made him promise he would do.

After Kelly died, I asked Craig why he didn't ask for my help instead of relying on his ancient parents. He said, "Kelly didn't want our problems to become yours. She thought you had enough on your plate." It always bothered me that Kelly thought I had so much going on in my stupid love life that she didn't ask for my help when she needed it the most. It's why I jumped at the chance to help Craig care for Kendall by picking her up at daycare three days a week. It's why I'll fight anyone, legal or otherwise, who gets in my way of raising Kendall now that her father is dead, too.

Tippy-toeing into the house, I find Kendall playing with one of the new dolls Kurt brought over to keep her occupied while the gang figured out their next moves.

"Ki-Ki!"

"Hi sweetheart! Come over here and give me a big kiss. Remember...just like the fancy ladies do it!"

Kendall scrambles to her feet, runs over, and plants a wet one on my right cheek, then my left, and for our own personal touch, a big one right on the kisser.

"That's the way I like it! Whatcha' doing over there?"

"Ku-Ku bought me dis fun stuff. Can you pway wit me?"

"I have a better idea! How about we pack it all up in a suitcase with your favorite pajamas and we have a sleepover at the cottage!"

Jumping up and down, she can barely contain herself.

"Yay, yay, yay! Can Weo come too so we can hunt for snipes?"

"Well poop, he's still in New York. But we can call him! How's that sound?"

Definitely not as happy as she was two seconds ago, Kendall says "Alllllright," grabs her bright pink Barbie suitcase and starts packing.

The gang is gone by the time I get Kendall outside. I made them promise to leave because if I saw them it would only make what I have to do that much more difficult. I need to be focused, not have their concerned faces staring at me as I load up my Goddaughter.

"Wait, Ki-Ki! I forgot to tell my Daddy about the sleepover!"

"You know what, sweetheart? Daddy knows."

"*He does?* Can I say bye-bye?"

I can't do this. I can't do this. I can't do this. STOP IT, CHRISSY! You don't have the option to back out. Look at her. Who else is going to tell her the news? Her crypt-keeper grandparents? Kelly's mom who's probably seven pills deep on Prozac and on the verge of a mental breakdown? The gang? A stranger? No! You're the only one she'll feel comfortable clinging to. Looking back toward the curtains in the living room, I can visualize Kelly giving me a shaky thumbs up, and I can hear her saying, "It has to be you, so get your shit together!"

"Da…" Clearing my throat, "Daddy told me to tell you bye-bye. He had to go see someone."

"Who?"

"Ohhhhh, someone *very* special."

"Who?"

"How about if I tell you over hamburgers and French fries at the cottage? We can snuggle up in warm blankets and have a picnic on the deck and throw rocks into the creek."

"And hunt for snipes?"

"Yes, Sweetie, and hunt for snipes."

175

I didn't think I wanted you
But I want you now…
You will always be mine
("Ballerina," *Leona Naess*)

I'm Doing This

December, 2001

"You sure do love your French fries, don't you?"
Kendall is covered in ketchup. While I'm wiping her
face, I turn away to wipe my own. The tears just keep building
up and I can't stop them. I close my eyes and say my usual
prayer. Dear Lord Jesus, who I should probably start believing
in, please make this as painless as possible for this little girl. She
doesn't deserve to hear what I'm about to tell her. Deep inhale.
Eyes now open. It's time. Grasping my Goddaughter's ketchup
stained fingers, I stare lovingly into her big blue eyes.

"Kendall, remember when I told you Daddy went to visit
someone super special?"

"Was it Barney?"

"No, not Barney."

Chrissy…you have to do this. Go.

"Daddy went to visit…your Mommy."

Her eyes move slowly from the basket of fries to my eyes.

"Can I do that?"

"No sweetheart, you have to be invited."

"By who?"

It's okay, Chrissy. You can say it. It might help her.
Whatever it takes…

"God."

177

"Daddy talked to God?"

"I...think so."

"What did God say?"

"No one will ever know for sure."

"We can ask Daddy when he gets back!"

Excited at the prospect of asking her Daddy what God said to him, she jumps up and down in front of me.

Scooping her up in my arms, I place her on my lap facing outward toward the creek so I don't have to look at her anymore. I can't. Then whispering in her ear I begin to do the unthinkable.

"The thing is Kendall, once God invites someone to Heaven, they have to stay."

Physically feeling the excitement secrete out of her body, she timidly asks, "My Daddy...isn't coming back?"

I squeeze her tighter and choke back my tears.

"No, sweetheart. Kinda like Mommy, Daddy can't come back. I know it makes it *really* hard for the people on Earth because we miss them so, so much, but one day we'll get our invitations..." Well, probably not me. "...And everything will make sense."

Turning to face me, she pleads, "But my Daddy didn't say bye-bye."

God dammit. Looking up at the star-dusted sky, I plead for Kelly's help as Kendall begins to cry, "I want my Daddy! I want my Daddy!"

Pulling her into my chest and holding her as tight as I can, I cry as well when I tell her, "I want him for you Kendall, and I'd do anything in the world to bring him back, but God has a super important job for Daddy..." Now holding her even tighter, "...And he has to stay there. I'm so sorry, sweetheart."

Wiggling out of my grasp, she looks up at me with her quivering lips.

"That job is more impotant din being wit me?"

Son of a bitch.

"No, no, no, Kendall! There's nothing more important than that!"

Now inconsolable, she demands, "Then why did God inbite him to his house?"

Pulling her back into me so I don't have to look at her, I answer like God's got another thing coming when He/She/It meets me.

"I promise you, Kendall, that's the very first question I'm gonna ask when I get there."

Kendall was barely three when her Mom died, and while Craig said it was awful for the first month after she passed away, Kendall seemed to get used to life without her pretty quickly. At first she'd sort of wander around the house looking for Mommy. When Craig tenderly reminded her that she was in Heaven, she'd throw a temper tantrum. But Craig did an amazing job of showering Kendall with love and maintaining a secure environment for her and, as much as it pains me to admit, life went on. But Kendall is a year older now. She turns four in two weeks. And she's a very emotionally in-tune child when it comes to the finality of death. When I told her that her Daddy died, she knew within seconds he was never coming back.

Getting Kendall to bed was excruciating. The poor child literally cried herself to sleep as I gently sang "Hush, Little Baby" over and over again. Of course I made up every single line because I don't know where the fucking diamond ring goes or when the God damn Billy goat gets bought (clearly I have a lot to learn in a very short time), and obviously I removed any reference to "Daddy" as being the one buying any of that crap. I stuck Ki-Ki in as a replacement. The only thing that persuaded me to slink away from Kendall's worn-out sleeping body was the non-stop faint knock on my door. Peeking through my kitchen window, I'm relieved at the sight I've dreaded seeing here a few times in the past.

It takes me less than three seconds to break down at Kurt's concerned face and not much more than that for him to comfort me. I'd do anything for his arms to be Leo's, but since I can't have those, I'll take any that give a crap about me right now. After settling me onto the couch, he disappears to the kitchen, returning a few minutes later with a cup of tea.

"I hate tea, Kurt. Remember?"

"Look, I'm not trying to shove eggs down your throat. Just drink it, it'll relax you."

Taking a sip, I think…Damn, that is good. I'm not going to tell him, though.

"I bought a box of that stuff when I was in Nepal last month. Good, right?"

"Nepal?"

Aged, worn out, and eyes swollen with pain, he answers…seemingly thankful for the short reprieve from talk of death.

"Yeah, I went there for some charity first-aid thing right after Kayla gave me the boot. Camped all over the country and helped people who have little or no access to medicine. Thought it would be nice to get away and at the same time, help people. Mount Everest was beautiful. Blew me away."

Charities…mountains…camping. As if over a decade of my life came flooding back to irritate me, I exhale, "God, Kurt, you have such a weird life."

"If that's not the pot calling the kettle black."

"Yeah, I guess I don't wanna go down that road, do I?"

The small talk was a nice distraction, but our tired and soft laughter causes Kendall to stir. After checking on her to make sure she's okay, I return to the couch and to a fresh cup of tea. Staring into each other's embattled eyes, we know what we really have to discuss.

"I almost don't wanna know, but how did it go?"

"I can't talk about it. Kurt…I'm so scared. How do I make this better for her?"

"I don't think you can. It's just gonna take time. Did Dr. Maria give you the name of a good children's counselor?"

Bursting into tears again, I sob, "I forgot to call. Oh my God, I've only had her for five hours and I already suck at this."

"Stop it, Chrissy. You don't suck at this. You're just in shock. We all are."

Hugging me until I get control of my emotions, he takes another detour from what we should really be discussing.

"I need to apologize to you for that little display at the coffee shop. Maybe I was looking for some kind of closure. I don't really know."

Wiping my nose on his shirt, I mumble, "Isn't that what the divorce was supposed to give you?"

"When did you get so funny?"

"Weird how my humor seems to show up at the most inappropriate time, huh?"

Ignoring me, he continues with his original thought.

"I just thought you deserved to hear how sorry I was about…you know…what happened."

Pulling away from him, my first instinct is to tell him to leave. I can't go back to the horrible memory it took the greater part of my adult life to put behind me. But at this very moment, he's all I have and I'm too scared to be alone with my huge Kendall thoughts.

"You don't have to be sorry about anything. I put myself in the irresponsible position to get pregnant and I'm the one who made the choice to make it go away."

"But I shouldn't have ignored it after it went away. I should've been there for you, and I guess I'm trying to—"

"I appreciate what you're trying to do, Kurt, I really do. But and I mean this in the most sincere way…if I still wanted something from you, I'd still be married to you. For me, divorce was the end of my expectations."

Slowly nodding his head, he wonders out loud, "When did you get so smart?"

"I've always been smart, I just needed to grow up."

Looking around the quiet cottage he asks the awkward question I just knew was coming.

"So when's he coming back?"

"All right, down boy. He'll be here when I need him."

"You do know that I have every right to be pissed off about what happened."

"Yeah, I do, and I think I reminded you of that at the coffee shop. But be pissed at me. Leave him out of it."

"That's a little easier said than done."

Pointing to the bedroom, I make it clear, "This isn't the right time to be talking about this stuff."

Would telling him right now that I'm engaged be a bad idea? Maybe he just needs to hear it. Maybe that'll put an end to these uncomfortable conversations that seem to pop up whenever we're around each other.

"I didn't come here to upset you, Chrissy." Somberly rubbing his worn out face, "I'm just a mess right now. He was my fucking best friend, you know..."

Yep, it'd be a bad idea.

Putting my hand on his knee, "I know *exactly* what you feel like right now."

"Jesus, that's right. Looks like we have more in common now than we ever did when we were married, huh?"

It's morbid...but it's kinda true.

"Are you gonna be okay tonight, Kurt?"

Without looking at me, he says, matter of factly, "No." Then he gathers up his leather jacket, tosses the box of tea to me, and warns, "Take it easy on that stuff. It'll put you to sleep for a week if you're not careful."

Then right before he walks out the door, he turns and says, "I wanna help Kendall through this, too. Call me first thing after you talk to Dr. Maria. I promise, you're not alone this time."

And then he ever so gently shut the door behind him so as to not wake her.

Bawling Brawling

January, 2002

Turns out Craig had been taking Xanax to manage the anxiety and depression that developed when Kelly got sick. And it turns out, when Kelly died, he started popping those things like I used to pop St. John's Wort...like Tic-Tacs. Surprisingly, his blood alcohol level wasn't nearly as high as Kurt assumed it was when he left Palo Alto that day and it most likely wasn't the sole cause of him ramming that other car from behind. What probably did him in was the lethal combination of alcohol *and* Xanax. The coroner's judgment was that Craig unexpectedly fell asleep from the concoction. This was the information Courtney was giving to me as the handful of guests started to arrive for Craig's memorial.

Craig was very clear after Kelly died that when he kicked the bucket he didn't want a big funeral like she had. Sitting in the pew and staring at her coffin made him physically sick, and he said he could never put anyone, especially Kendall, through something like that. He wanted to be promptly buried next to Kelly, no big shoveling ceremony, no eulogy, and no hanging around the casket and crying. When they were sitting around drinking beers one night, he told Kurt, "When I go, I want a good old fashioned barbeque at my house and if anyone starts bawling, kick em' out." No one would've ever thought it would come so soon.

After hugging Craig's decrepit mother, I glance over at his picture. It's been one week since he died. The morning after I told Kendall the news, I woke up very early to call Dr. Maria. For the first time ever, I used the special number she gave to me

183

years ago in case of an absolute emergency. While I certainly felt like I went through a lot of code reds during my years with her, I could never justify calling the number with any of my problems. I always felt like the line should be kept open for the Sad Frumpy Ladies of the world. Staring at my haggard and make-up-less face in the mirror as the line rang that morning, I thought…there's one. Her voicemail picked up and in as loud of a whisper I could muster up so as not to wake Kendall, I got right to the point.

"It's me, Chrissy Anderson. Kelly's husband has died, and I have their daughter in my possession. I told her about her daddy yesterday, and it didn't go so well. I need to see a children's counselor right away. I don't know what the hell I'm doing and I need to know fast."

Within five minutes of hanging up the phone, it rang again and it was a child psychologist. Dr. Maria heard my message, contacted the best one she knew and told her to call me immediately. Our conversation was brief. She identified herself as Dr. Vikki Ester and told me to bring Kendall to her that afternoon and to not let her out of my sight.

Kendall was quiet as we got ready to go to Dr. Ester's office. I could tell she was wondering, "What happens to me now," but she doesn't have the vocabulary to express those kinds of big thoughts. I wanted to put her mind at ease and promise her that I'll take care of her for the rest of her life, but without knowing the exact details of Craig and Kelly's will, I knew I couldn't make that promise. I just kept hugging her and told her I loved her.

I called Kurt on the way to the psychologist's office, and as promised, he joined us. Dr. Ester directed Kendall to a toy room that magically made her happy and she directed the "grown-ups" to a different room to talk. When the psychologist referred to me as a grown-up, I literally froze. Wasn't I the one who just four years ago met a twenty-two year old guy at a bar and tried to take his pants off in my car? Wasn't I the one who used to hack into that guy's voicemail account and sabotage his plans to hook up with other girls? Wasn't I the one who, up until I was thirty years old, pretended my name was Prudence, Maude, Guadalupe, and Nell? Wasn't I the one who verbally assaulted Kurt and Boobs outside of my old house in Danville while my neighbors watched? *How can someone as psychotically challenged as me be called a grown-up?* Furthermore, *can someone as psychotically challenged as me be a good mother to Kendall?*

"Chrissy, you coming?"

Kurt motioned for me to sit down next to him so the "grown-ups" could get started. After instructing us to call her Dr. Vikki because it's more casual for the children, she went on to tell us how she thinks Kendall will react over the next month or so, and then she gave us an action plan to deal with it. The bottom line is we have to provide her with a stable routine, keep things calm and shower her with love. She recommended I bring as many of Kendall's belongings to my cottage as I could and keep the illusion of a really long sleepover going for as long as possible. Illusions are definitely something I have experience with creating, so no problem there. Everyone's hope is that we can determine guardianship as soon as possible to provide Kendall with long-term stability as quickly as possible. But when Kurt's cell phone rang during the meeting with Dr. Vikki and it was the attorney, "as soon as possible" went out the window.

"Well, what did he say?"

Dr. Vikki and I were on the edge of our seats.

"Well, we're still her legal guardians."

"Did you tell him we're divorced?"

"Yep. He said he thinks he remembers an update to the will that tackles that subject."

"He thinks?"

185

"He's knee deep in another case and can't pull the file until the first week of February."

"Are you kidding?"

"Nope. Apparently the asshole is too busy until then to solidify the future of a four year old little girl. He told us to do the best we can with her care until he can see us to work out the logistics."

Nicole breaks a plate in the kitchen and it snaps my mind away from Dr. Vikki's office and back to the memorial. Staring at Kurt, who's helping her clean up the mess, I feel relief that the asshole attorney can't see us until February. I still haven't told him, let alone any of the other people in this room, I'm engaged to Leo *and* that we want sole custody of Kendall. I mean, it would be the most stable, calm and loving set up for her, but the challenge is going to be convincing Kurt of that. He already lost one girl to Leo, I'm not so sure he's going to give another one up to him so easily this time. Oy vey, I definitely have a few logistics of my own to figure out before February.

"What are you thinking about?"

It was Kurt. He stopped on the way to the garbage can to throw the broken glass away and saw me staring pensively down at my drink.

"Kendall."

"Are you sure it was such a good idea to leave her there today?"

Dr. Vikki thought it would be too difficult for Kendall to be around the gang because she'd expect to see her father, so Kurt and I agreed she should be somewhere else for the barbeque/memorial. I dropped Kendall off with Slutty Co-worker and Megan at one of the studios this morning. They're the only people she knows outside of the ones with me here.

"Of course. Kendall loves it there and they love her."

What I wasn't counting on this morning though was Barbara being there. To this day, she has a very hard time being around little girls. Despite all of her years of intense therapy, the pain of losing her three year old daughter has been something she could never deal with. The only thing that's made coping somewhat tolerable was staying as far away from little girls as possible. But Barbara's years of dodging them came to an abrupt halt this morning when Kendall opened the front door of the studio and it hit her in the nose. I thought the head on collision was going to be disastrous. But in actuality it seemed to be therapeutic. A visibly traumatized Kendall clung to my leg and Barbara just stood motionless, staring at her for what seemed like forever. Finally I interjected with, "Maybe this isn't such a good idea" and started to usher Kendall out of the studio. But Barbara softly touched my hand and said, "I'm okay, Chrissy," and then looking down at Kendall, "This can't be about me." In coming face-to-face with the little girl who lost both of her parents, all of a sudden Barbara set aside anguish she'd been carrying around for nearly two decades. She lovingly took Kendall's hand and asked her if she'd like to learn how to crochet. Before I set off for the memorial, I gave Kendall a big kiss and told them all to start planning her birthday party celebration. Between the crocheting, party planning and Slutty Co-workers silly antics, I left there knowing Kendall was in very good hands.

"Can I get you another drink?"

"Kurt, I'm fine, really. Please don't worry about me. Here…." taking his glass, "…let me get you one."

The truth is, I haven't put a drop of alcohol in my body since the night before Craig died, and with Kendall in my life, I can't imagine another drop will go in it. I can't take any chances that something bad will happen. As I'm pouring Kurt a glass of wine and refilling my club soda, I listen to the whispers of questions being thrown around like…

"What do you think will happen to the house?"

"Who's paying the bills?"

"Should Kendall ever come back here?"

"Should Kendall live here?"

I snap the whisperer of that question a firm look that says HELLS NO, I'M NOT LIVING IN FREAKMONT! But then I turn to Kurt who's giving me a look of, it might not be such a bad idea if she continues to live in her own house. I sigh and think, yep...gonna be *lots and lots* of logistics to work out.

All of a sudden, the whispers come to a screeching halt. Well, except for Nicole's when she murmurs over to Courtney, "Instead of no *bawling* at this thing, Craig should've said, no *brawling*." Wondering what she's talking about, I turn to find Leo standing in the door-way.

It's been almost two months since I've seen him, but instead of running and jumping into his arms, my gaze shifts to Kurt whose eyes are planted on the man who took his wife away.

My Worst Nightmare

January, 2002

The room is silent, but I can almost hear the clicking of twenty shocked eyeballs shifting between the two men as Kurt and Leo come face-to-face.

Since Leo has already met Guss and Kyle, his eyes impulsively zoom in on Kurt, the husband he's heard so much about, but never seen in person. When their eyes lock, Kurt's stance becomes noticeably rigid. Out of the corner of my eye, I see Guss shift slightly toward Kurt and give Kyle an eye roll to do the same. Their ridiculousness triggers my own eye roll.

"Hey, girls…why don't the two of you go over there and tell the Cobra Kai's to stand down. We're all grown-ups here, maybe we should start acting like ones."

Dr. Maria, and I guess now, Dr. Vikki, would be so proud.

As if it's my twenty-ninth surprise birthday party all over again, my best friends, sans Kelly this time of course, make a beeline for Kurt to try and engage him in meaningless conversation so I can have an important one with Leo.

I thought I knew how much I missed him. But seeing him in the flesh stirs something inside of me. The same something that stirred the first time I laid eyes on him and every other time since. Forgetting for a moment that Kurt's eyes are probably glued to the back of my head, impulsively, I walk toward my drug.

Things have been so confusing since Leo and I got back together last March. I had a bout of insecurity about our age difference and a stint of fear of exposing just how normal and boring I can actually be on a regular basis. There was his uncomfortable first encounter with Kendall, the fight between

189

Taddeo and me at my birthday party fiasco, *and then* the one between him and Taddeo right after my birthday party fiasco. There was the uneasy introduction of him to my best friends and their husbands. Then, after that, there was the shock and chaos of 9/11, Leo's spontaneous career move that kept him in New York and, of course, the marriage proposal that I feared was a bit sudden.

It isn't until I'm a few steps away from him that his eyes finally shift from Kurt's to my own and it worries me. But hearing his poised voice whisper, "Hi, Baby" calms my rattled nerves. And magically, when he wraps his arms around me, all of the confusion of the last nine months disappears.

"Why didn't you tell me you were coming?"

"Why didn't you ask me to?"

Duh, obviously I didn't want my old life and my new life to collide.

"I'm sorry. Everything just happened so fast."

As he glances back at Kurt, rather agitated, he asks, "Are you sure that's it?"

I pull away and try to play it cool.

"What do you mean?"

He doesn't have to say a word. His eyes have this mystical ability to speak for him.

"Leo, this has nothing to do with Kurt. This is a memorial service for my friend, and if the two of you can't put aside whatever it is you have to put aside to make this day be about what it's supposed to be about, then you're *both* a couple of numb nuts."

"I can do that…for you." And then he pulls me back into his chest and whispers, "Is it inappropriate to tell you how beautiful you look and that I can't wait to be alone with you?"

Smiling from ear to ear, I profess, "A little bit."

The time alone with him is way overdue, but I need to remind him of something more important and I pull away from his chest to do just that.

"I have to pick up Kendall on the way home. I'm sorry, but I don't think there's much alone time in our future."

"All that matters is that I'm with you guys. I've missed you so much."

And with his eyes squarely concentrated on Kurt's, he kisses me on the forehead before he pulls me back into his chest.

I ask Leo how he even knew the memorial was today. We haven't talked for days...long before it was even organized.

"Yesterday, when I couldn't get in touch with you again, I had enough with the not knowing what's going on. I called the studio and Megan told me about it. So, I flew in."

"But I just saw her two hours ago, why didn't she tell me she talked to you?"

"I told her I wanted to surprise you and asked her to keep it a secret."

Trying to be cute and coy, I tell him, "I'm not so sure I like you having secrets with Megan. She used to have a huge crush on you, you know."

"Yeah well, I don't like you being in the same room with your ex-husband. Looks like both of us have to put aside our annoyances for the day."

Cute and coy sure backfired. I tenderly hold up his hands to about mid-chest height, kiss them and tell him how sorry I am for his annoyance and that I'll do whatever I can to make it up to him. His head tilts down to kiss my hand in return and that's when all hell breaks loose.

"Chrissy, where's your ring?"

Holy...shitballs. Leo's staring at my ring finger and instead of looking at the whopping diamond ring he spent more money on than he has in his bank account, he's looking at the fifty-five dollar Banana Republic ring he bought for me three and a half years ago. I am soooooo screwed. Either I lie and break the honesty vow that so far I've done an impressive job of keeping or I tell the truth and get murdered. Both options put this relationship in jeopardy.

191

A little louder now, he asks again, "Chrissy, where's the ring?"

Leave it to Nicole to start a fire, *"What ring?"*

I look up and see the entire gang, including Kurt, staring at me. Sensing I'm struggling with an answer, Leo, who now grasps the fact that I'm hiding the wedding from my friends, looks right at Kurt and answers for me.

"Her engagement ring."

Oh shiiiiiiiiiiiiiiiiiiit.

Speaking gravely slow, Kurt looks at me and asks, "You're getting married?"

Then, Nicole and Courtney say in unison, *"ALREADY?"*

I swear. It's like I have back-up singers wherever I go.

Leo directs my attention back to his face and warns, "I swear to God, if you answer him before you answer me, it's over."

I'm in total shock! Leo's seriously threatening me with a break up if I so much as address Kurt's question! And I guess thank God for the shock, because I don't even know how to answer either one of their questions!

Kurt puts down his drink and very cynically says, "Answer me first then, Chrissy."

Closing my eyes, I think, *Oh, Kurt. Why? Why did you have to say that?*

Letting go of my hands, Leo takes a step toward Kurt and lets it rip.

"What the hell did you just say?"

Kurt, Guss *and* Kyle all take a step toward Leo, and my heart literally jumps out of my chest. This has been my worst nightmare since the morning after I met Leo at Buckley's. The love triangle I created and the jealousies I stirred up would only result in one thing if Kurt and Leo ever came face-to-face: a fight.

I had outlined a list of possible outcomes for myself the moment I knew I was in love with Leo, and because I feared what would happen if my husband and him ever met, number three on that list was the only sensible option: Divorce Kurt and break up with Leo. Back then I knew I had to end it with both of them in order to avoid a moment like this and right now I wish so badly I had had the courage to do that. I cannot bear to see either one of them get hurt. And dammit…looking at their size and their anger and knowing their pride…someone is about to get very, very hurt.

"STOP! Leo come back! We'll leave and talk about this at home!"

So calm it has me more worried than I was two seconds ago, he says, "No. If he has something to say, he should say it."

And then all of the men take another step toward each other.

"Courtney, Nicole! Make them stop!"

My friends scramble to their husbands and urge both of them to let Kurt and Leo handle this on their own. If it wasn't for Kurt telling Kyle and Guss to listen to their wives, I know they wouldn't have.

Now just a few feet away from each other, Leo asks Kurt a different, although just as provoking question, "Do you have a problem?"

"Hey man, no problem here. I mean, I'm not the one who sleeps with married women."

"Can't help it if I'm the one married women want to sleep with."

If the floor were made of sand, I'd bury my head in it.

"Are you fucking kidding me with this? *You hear that Chrissy?* Sounds like maybe you're not the only one." And then taking another step towards Leo, he sneers, "Why don't you tell us, Romeo, how many others are there?"

Cool as a cucumber, Leo doesn't back down.

"None. She's it for me." And now he takes one step closer to Kurt and jabs back, "And I think you need to start accepting the fact that I'm it for her."

Oh my God, I can't take this anymore.

"LEO! STOP THIS! We've all been through enough over the last four years. This isn't making things better!"

Eyes blazing with rage, Leo turns to address me.

"Remember Chrissy, I didn't start this. You did by not telling me you were married, and now it looks like he doesn't want to end it."

Then, without warning, Kurt taps Leo on the shoulder, says "You're right, I don't," and then sucker punches him on the chin.

There's nothing my hundred-and-ten-pound-body can do to stop the almost four hundred pounds of force aimed at each other. My screams for them to stop the insanity go unnoticed and with each punch my heart is electrocuted. I close my eyes so I don't have to look, but I'm tortured by the sound. My hands press firmly over my eyes as I scream uncontrollably for them to stop. Desperate, I run outside to Guss and Kyle and beg them to do something.

"We will, Chrissy, but Kurt said he wanted five minutes."

Staring widely at them, I scream, "LEO COULD KILL HIM IN FIVE MINUTES!"

Alone, I run back inside and find Leo straddling Kurt, but I turn away as fast as possible so I don't have to see what's happening. I scramble to the beverage table and one-by-one start throwing bottles of wine on the wall behind them, screaming at the top of my lungs, "YOU'RE KILLING ME!" over and over again. The shards of glass hit both of them and within seconds they scramble to get out of the way. Just then Guss and Kyle run back into the room and help Kurt to his feet. His cheek and chin are already showing signs of black and blue, his left eye has a deep cut, and is already swollen. His shirt is ripped, his hands are bloody, and he's clearly still full of rage. Guss and Kyle tell him to calm the fuck down and take him outside.

Leo doesn't appear any different from Kurt and from the looks of things, I'd say the fight was a draw. Unable to move from my bottle throwing spot, I crouch down into a ball and do my best to find a happy place in my mind. Courtney and Nicole rush over to console me, but Leo's quick to peacefully say, "I'll take care of her."

He takes his blazer off, and as he wraps it around my shoulders he says, "Come on, Baby. It's over."

As he's helping me to my feet, I mumble things like, "Why?" and "Please don't hurt anyone" and "Make it stop."

As if enough unfortunate things haven't already happened in Craig and Kelly's house, I numbly stare at the broken wine-stained family pictures on the wall.

Quivering, I turn to Leo and weep uncontrollably as I say, "Look at what you made me do."

Sensing I'm on the precipice of completely crumbling, he picks me up and carries me to the car.

Tousled

January, 2002

The drive back to the cottage was quiet, the only sound coming from Leo's hand on the fabric of my pants as he rubbed my leg to comfort me. It didn't help. My nerves only started to calm once I was on my couch and sucking down a cup of the magic tea Kurt brought back from Nepal.

"Chrissy, please talk to me."

I love him so much, and I hate that he got hurt, too, but I'm so upset I can barely look at him.

"I have to go get Kendall."

"I called Megan and told them they should take her out to dinner. I said you were upset about the memorial...we have some time to talk."

Dazed, I look at him over the rim of my cup.

"Upset?"

Dropping to his knees, he takes the cup and places it on the table. Then, with his bruised hand, he shifts my face to look at him.

"Chrissy, you can't be mad at me for defending myself."

My eyes well up as fragments of the nightmare that just came to life before me flicker through my mind.

"You could've just walked away...let him be the bad guy."

"That's not how it works, Baby. Guys aren't wired that way. If someone hits, you have to hit back."

"Leo, you guys didn't hit, *you destroyed*...and for what? Kurt and I are divorced. You and I are getting married. What the hell is there to fight about? The dust was supposed to have been settled."

Suddenly remembering that he has every right to be mad at me, too, he takes his hand away from my chin.

"Oh yeah, Chrissy? If the dust was so settled, why'd you hide your ring from all of them?"

"I guess the engagement just happened so fast for me. I mean, don't get me wrong, I want to marry you, Leo. It's all I've wanted since the moment I met you. But I felt like it was just one more thing I'd have to explain...defend almost. I've been explaining and defending myself to those people for four years. I just wanted more time in a peaceful place. They just met you for God's sake and I knew this would be hard for them."

"Be honest, Chrissy. This wasn't about them, it was about Kurt. You were putting his feelings ahead of mine, again."

Be honest, be honest, be honest. Why the F does *everything* require so much damn honesty?

"Okay, fine. I didn't want to hurt him."

Pissed, he tries to stand and walk away but I grab his leg to stop him.

"Leo! You have to understand! He just lost Craig...he's worried about Kendall! It's a lot for someone to have to deal with. I didn't want one more thing for him to..."

Oh, crap. I went too far.

"To what? *To have to worry about?* If all of that dust is supposed to have settled, tell me this Chrissy...why would he have to worry about you getting married?"

Walking to the bathroom to shower the blood off of his body, Leo furiously divulges what I didn't want to admit to myself.

"The dust isn't settled and you know it."

And then the door slams shut.

I thought I had let Kurt go. After his motorcycle accident, when I begged him to move on...to try and find the love that I had found, I truly thought I left my concern for his happiness behind. I ended my therapy with Dr. Maria with the awareness that my life was starting over. *What went wrong?* I'm not in love with Kurt anymore, so why do I always find myself back in this space of caring about him? Reaching for my newest addiction, the Nepalese tea, I suck it down and think…maybe I need to pay my old therapist a visit.

Leo exits the bathroom with a towel wrapped around his waist. Despite the major bruising up and down the left side of his rib cage, the red and swollen knuckles and the large cut on his chin, he's a beautiful man…inside and out. He has never been anything but honest and loyal and loving to me. Will I ever allow myself to be happy with him? Is it even possible for us to be at peace now that all of this guardianship crap exists? If the dust hasn't settled between Kurt and me, how will it ever even have a chance to with our joint responsibility of Kendall? Yep, I definitely think this psychotically challenged woman has to put aside her pride and call her old friend, Dr. Maria.

"Tell me what you're thinking, Chrissy."

"I'm scared."

"Of what? You know I'll never let anything happen to you."

"I'm scared I'm gonna lose you."

With my admission, he softens up a little and wraps his arms around me.

"Baby, I might be pissed off right now, but I'm not an idiot. We didn't come this far to let that happen."

Then lifting my chin up with his hand so that our eyes meet, he reiterates the same genuine words he said to me when I "accidentally" into him at The Red Devil Lounge.

"Remember…I'll always be where I know you are."

"Even if that means I'm at Kurt's house every few days doing a transfer of Kendall?"

The look on his face screams, *you should probably be scared of losing me if that happens.*

"Leo, I'm gonna be honest with you…" And why not? If everyone's throwing punches today, I may as well join in. "…He wants her just as much as I do and probably more now after tonight's boxing match. I'm sorry, but it looks like as long as

Kendall's in my life, Kurt will be, too..." In barely a whisper, I tell him, "...If you want the ring back, I understand."

"Are you kidding me? If I could solder that metal to your finger I would! Chrissy, we'll figure this out and if it makes you feel better, I won't hit back if he takes any more swings at me. I'll just use them to my advantage in court when I try to get us sole custody of Kendall."

Although he's trying to lighten the mood, I know he means it. I have to be serious and let him know where I stand on this. Nothing is about me anymore and what I might stand to lose, everything is about Kendall and all that she has to gain.

"Leo, you have to understand something. Kurt was her Dad's best friend, and he's just as close to her as I am. He's also one of the few ties to her parents that exists. I have the stories of her mother to tell her, but he's the one with the stories she'll need to hear about her father. I know it's not what you wanna hear, but I want Kendall to be around Kurt as much as she wants to be."

"Let me get this straight. After how loyal I've shown you I am and even though I'm willing to marry you tomorrow and be the best father in the world to her, you're not even gonna try to get sole custody?"

All I can do is shake my head.

"Then I guess there's a lot more dust than I bargained for."

I'm so scared I feel like I can hear my tea cup trembling.

"What are you saying, Leo?"

"I'm gonna take the red-eye back to New York tonight. Kendall will be here in an hour and I don't want her to see me like this."

"But, what do you mean...more than you bargained for?"

"Dammit, Chrissy, it's so opposite of who I am to have some kind of working relationship with a guy you used to love. If we're being honest here...Then, yeah a part of me wants to walk away from this."

Oh my God. He's slipping away.

"I under—"

"Let me finish. But I know I can't because you're like my drug, too. I have to dig deep and find a way to deal with this."

For the first time ever, Leo's vulnerability does little to calm my nerves. I fear that our relationship is once again on life support.

And with that, he walks into the bathroom to get rid of his towel and then walks naked into the bedroom to get dressed.

I stagger into the bathroom for some tissue. Wanting nothing to change until he returns home again, I gently push Leo's disheveled towel aside on the bar, careful not to disturb its wet and tousled state.

Uncharitable Heart

January, 2002

I hadn't seen Kurt since the memorial. Needing to know the answer to the question I asked myself when he provoked Leo, I walk up behind him and ask, "Why did you do that, Kurt?"

Turning to look at me, I see that he's still pretty banged up from the fight…we all are.

"It's called pride. I'm sure what's-his-name had the same answer."

Sigh…What's-his-name had the *exact* same answer. Men are impossible.

"Are you okay?"

"Am I okay with what?"

The thing is, I'm not exactly sure. Do I want to know if he's okay from the fight or okay with the engagement…*or both?*

"I don't know. I just haven't talked to you since everything happened, and I was…I guess I was worried about you."

Letting out a slight mocking laugh, "You're gonna start worrying about me now? Look, Chrissy, just so you're clear, I got whatever it was out of my system. I could give a shit about your engagement. I only care about Kendall." Turning away and looking at her through the window, he informs me, "Our relationship is only about her. Period. From here on out we start operating like real divorced people. Got it?"

The only thing I'm clear about it is that he's clearly NOT okay. The dude is pissed and I guess he has every right to be. His high school sweetheart-turned wife, cheated on him and divorced him. His rebound girlfriend dumped him when he wouldn't marry her, and then his best friend died. He found out his ex-wife is going to marry the guy she cheated on him with and to add salt to the wound, he found it out from the guy himself at his best friend's memorial. He lost his marbles at the news, destroyed the memorial *and* his face and now he has to put aside his rage at all of the above because he might be awarded some kind of custody of his dead best friend's child that he'll now have to share with his ex-wife and the new husband. Jesus, all of it makes me feel completely awful and wanting to punch something myself.

"Kurt, I'm so sorry for—"

"Good Lord, Chrissy, just stop already."

Not wanting this get-together with the gang to turn into another WWF event, I recoil from the heated exchange.

"Okay, okay, you've been heard. I guess I should get in there to see if Kendall's having fun."

Feeling more than a little dejected, I walk away to check on Kendall, but not before I turn and say, "For what it's worth, I'm glad you're healing nicely."

"And I'm glad to see you got creative with the birthday party theme."

This is how Kurt is. He'll push me to limits with his abrasive honesty and then rescue me from tears with a tiny dose of cynical humor. He never could stay mad at me for long.

Looking into the meditation room, I marvel at my own lack of creativity.

"Yeah, hopefully I'll have more experience with the mother thing before her fifth birthday."

"I'll give it to you though…not many kids can say they've had a yoga-themed birthday party."

We're looking at Kendall's fourth birthday party though the glass window that separates the meditation room from the lobby. Due to the unfortunate events at the memorial, I decided it would be best to have the party a few weeks late to give everyone a chance to cool off. Joining us for the festivities are the gang and their kids, Craig's ancient parents, and Kelly's now WAY overly-medicated mother.

"I guess our first order of business is to get to know all of the kids at the Happy Hearts day care center to avoid a lame party like this from happening again..." Then a thought occurs to me. "...But wait...Geez, I guess she won't be going there anymore. I guess I should look for a pre-school around here, right?"

"Guess we'll have to see what the attorney says."

"What do you mean?"

"I dunno...Maybe we should look for a pre-school around my house."

The new mama bear in me is now unleashed.

"Hold on, first of all we both know Kendall should live with me, and second of all, you don't even have a house!"

"I'll have a house in a month, and I'm not so sure it's best for Kendall to live with you anymore."

"Kurt...you don't have to act like this. I didn't do anything wrong by getting engaged!"

"Chrissy, I don't have time to list all of the things you've done wrong. Excuse me, looks like they need help bringing in the yoga mat cake."

"Let him go, Hunny."

I turn to see Slutty Co-worker and Megan in the office. They were so sweet to come in today to help me set up. Now that the whole gang knows I'm now engaged, there's no need to keep my worlds separated anymore. There aren't any more secrets...right now.

"What's his problem? It's not like I'm the one who punched him."

"Aren't you though?"

Looking at Megan like she's got a lot of nerve for saying that, she's quick to defend her words.

"Chrissy, it's like the guy can't catch a break. C'mon, you said it yourself a thousand times, he didn't deserve what you did to him. Crap, you've been begging him to feel something for like fifteen years, let him feel this anger."

"You know what, you're right."

Taking a sip of her drink, Megan changes the subject with, "And you know what YOU'RE right about? This tea you brought in...It's the bomb! Where the heck did you get it?"

"Kurt bought it in Nepal when he was there for some charity, camping, mountain climbing, first-aid bullshit thing."

Noticeably more impressed with the charity thing than she is with the tea, Megan sits upright in her chair.

"Wow, Nepal. I've always wanted to go to a third-world country and do something like that."

I look at Slutty Co-worker, who's wrapping her lips around a limp balloon like she's going down on a man, and ask, "What about you?"

She pulls away from her project and inquires, "What about me?"

"Would you go to Nepal for charity?"

"What do the men in Nepal look like exactly?"

Frustrated with our uncharitable hearts, Megan chimes in with, "I'm serious you guys. We should do that!"

In unison, Slutty Co-worker and I say, *"Do what?"*

"We have so much extra fabric in the back room, we could make clothes and send them to poor people! I know Barbara would totally be up for it."

Before she dives back into her balloon, Slutty says, "No shit, she'd be up for it! She's one of those Berkeley-giver-people!"

Megan appeals to me to take her seriously. But I annoy her even more when I curiously ask, *"Can we make money doing that?"*

At my preposterously selfish question, the balloon releases from Slutty's mouth, flies over our heads and deflates. Laughing her ass off, she mocks, "No Leona Helmsly! That's why they call it charity!"

But there's not a trace of a smile on Megan's over-achieving, Catholic college alumni, fashion designer face.

"I'm serious, Chrissy! Would you mind if I talked to Kurt about which charity organization he used for his trip? So many of them can be scams."

Thinking of how weird that would be, I shake my head, and defiantly say, "No way!"

"C'mon, it might cheer him up."

Staring at him while he swings Kendall around in a circle, my heartstrings get pulled in a million directions.

"I dunno, Megan. It could get weird."

"Oh, c'mon! Think about the tax write-off you'll get!"

I knew there had to be a perk. As I walk out of the office to re-join the party, I yell out, "His number's in my rolodex!"

How will we laugh just like before
When there's water rising up to our door
And we may never see each other again
My dear old friend
("My Dear Old Friend," *Patty Griffin*)

What the Heck?

January, 2002

K endall's birthday party ended on a somber note. After she
made her birthday wish and blew out the candles, her eyes
slowly scanned the room. We all knew she was looking for
Craig. If it wasn't for Barbara's awkward timing of popping in
to surprise Kendall with her very own big girl crochet starter kit,
everyone would've burst into tears. While loading Kendall's
presents into my car, my work friends and my best friends, who
were *more* than excited about finally meeting, talked about a
girls's night out to get to know each other better. The idea of it
gave me the heeby-jeebies, and I said I'd get back to them with a
convenient date…which will be NEVER! Work has always
been, and always will be, my refuge from all of the shit I stir up
outside of it, and I feel an intense need to keep it that way.

After the birthday party, I needed to go to Kendall's house to
pick up more of her stuff so I asked Kurt to take her back to my
cottage to play with her and all of her new toys. It was our first
joint effort task in caring for her and despite his animosity
toward me, there was none detected from him in Kendall's
presence.

I barely packed anything in Kendall's Barbie suitcase that first day I brought her to the cottage. I was completely oblivious to anything other than the news I had to tell her. But now that the news has been delivered and life is trying to resume, more clothes, toys, and Barney videos are required to make life manageable. Quite frankly, I'm totally blown away with how much stuff it takes to get a kid through the day. In fact, I've only had Kendall with me for twenty-two days and already I've ceased saying, "must be nice to be you" whenever I see a mother pushing a stroller. I now realize there's a helluva lot more going on in that woman's day than rolling that thing along. I'm definitely starting to think there's *a lot* of takesies-backsies in my future with regards to this motherhood business.

Kendall's definitely been struggling since she lost her daddy. She has some good days, but most are bad. There's a lot of crying and long periods of time where she just sits and stares out of the window at the creek. My solution is to sit and cry with her. Heck, Lord knows I'm a pro at that, right? When we're done crying, we talk…mostly about what Heaven is like. My visions of turquoise unicorns, angels with cotton candy wings, and rivers flowing with chocolate milk soothe her aching heart. And I have to admit, they soothe mine, too. When we're done talking we write Craig letters and draw him pictures that we hang all over the cottage. We bake him cookies (the kind that come in a container that you just pop open, of course) and then eat them all up because I tell her that's what he'd want us to do. Tending to Kendall leaves very little time for all of the things I used to do, like go for a run, get my nails done, wax unwanted hair off of my body, read my own books or bust out my Wonderwand. And what's weird is that I don't mind at all. However, what I do mind is all of that the mommy stuff makes me more tired than I've ever been in my life. Usually, just after Kendall falls asleep, I doze off myself. Oftentimes without making a goodnight call to Leo.

Kurt's been diligent about keeping his commitment to attend the sessions with the child psychologist. He has asked meaningful questions and requested guidance on so many of the choices we'll have to make on Kendall's behalf. I've been more than impressed with his thoughtfulness, and I was proud of him when he bowed out of the last two sessions for fear of scaring Kendall with the cuts and bruises he got from the fight. We've actually had a very amicable relationship in dealing with her, but after his threatening words today at the birthday party about wanting more custody than me, I'm on edge. I just hope I can keep my composure in check until we meet with the attorney next month.

My car is unusually quiet. No Kendall and no radio, just my thoughts. This will be the first time I've been back to the house in Freakmont since the memorial and I'm uneasy about going inside. The house was eerie enough for the short time I was there for Craig's disastrous memorial; I get shivers thinking about what it's going to feel like now. I pick up my cell phone to call Leo. He has a way of making me feel safe…like everything in my life is going to work out perfectly. But before I even finish dialing, I hang up. I just remembered he made me feel those things *before* all of this custody business. Now he'll probably just ask where Kendall is and then I'll be forced to say Kurt's name out loud. He's still trying to "dig deep" and be okay with this set-up, and saying Kurt's name definitely won't help with the digging. Under normal circumstances, like picking up Kendall's Puffalumpa at Kurt's house or going for a cup of coffee with him while Leo was in New York after 9/11, I'd know how to deal with this. I'd simply omit a few key pieces of information, like Kurt's name, and quickly move past the subject. But these aren't normal circumstances. A little girl's happiness is at stake and her happiness is dependent on one hundred percent sincerity between me, him, *and* Kurt. There cannot be an ounce of resentment between any of us or she'll suffer, which is ironic, because sparing a child from resentment was another reason why I divorced Kurt. Yet, here we are. Right now, since I assume Kurt is one of her legal guardians, I have to focus on easing the resentment he feels about my engagement. I never thought I'd say this, but I can't deal with making this sticky situation better for Leo. I'm struggling with trying to deal with the stickiness of it myself.

I park my car in the driveway and warily make my way to the front door. I feel guilty, apologetic actually, for being here. It's so, so wrong that Craig and Kelly don't get to raise their little girl. I put my key in the door, close my eyes and push it open. It's cold and dark, and all I can hear is the soft hum of the refrigerator. Turning the lights on, the first thing I notice is the pictures on the wall...the ones that broke during Kurt and Leo's fight. They're all re-framed, clean, and hanging just where they're supposed to be. Had to have been Kurt.

On my way to grab Kendall's gear, I pass Kelly and Craig's room. I've already been through Kelly's stuff, once at her own memorial and again when I helped Craig pack up her belongings after she died. But I've never been through Craig's stuff. *Why would I have?* But maybe I should poke through now. Maybe there's something of value that I should put in the safety deposit box with Kelly's jewelry. One by one, I open the dresser drawers. Just the usual...socks, underwear, t-shirts, nothing out of the ordinary. Thank God, because how weird would that be if I found a big stack of condoms or a bunch of porn?

I make my way over to the nightstand and notice Craig's wedding ring. I carefully pick it up and read the inscription on the inside: *My first. My only.* And I'm reminded of just how young Craig and Kelly were when they met. I gently place the ring in my pocket for safe keeping and then open the top drawer...Just some reading material, ear plugs, Chapstick, and loose change. I swipe my hand along the back of the drawer to scoot the materials toward the front, and that's when I get a paper cut. I reach back in and carefully remove an envelope. Once I get it out, I'm surprised to see my name on it.

"What the heck?"

I pull the papers from inside and immediately sit myself on the bed when I see the handwriting.

Chrissy,

If you have this letter in your hand it means one of two things. Either Craig is dead or he lost his friggin' marbles and is no longer capable of taking care of Kendall. I know the man misses me, but I bet my entire estate he was able to keep his shit together and take care of our baby girl. So, if you're reading this, I'm pretty sure he's gone. It's hard for me to imagine how or why Craig would be dead, but it's even harder for me to imagine a life for Kendall without either one of us, and I pray to God you never have to read this letter. But if you are...be prepared because your life is about to get really chaotic.

I flip the envelope over and see Craig's handwritten words, FOR ATTORNEY. He must've forgotten to give this letter to him. Or...he was damn sure nothing would ever happen to him and shoved it in this drawer. After a deep breath, I read on.

As you recall, when Craig and I asked you and Kurt to be Kendall's Godparents, we also made you guys her legal guardians, and guardians of our estate should something ever happen to us. But since you and Kurt are heading toward divorce, (and it doesn't look like you're going to reconcile) it leaves me and Craig with a lot of decisions to make in a very short period of time. According to the doctors, I only have a few months to live and since Craig is a wreck right now, he left the decision up to me what to do with Kendall if something should happen to him. So, here it is: You will be named the sole legal guardian of Kendall.

"Oh...my...God."

213

*But and this is VERY important, Kurt will be granted
visitation. Kendall has to have a father figure in her life. Trust
me, I've watched enough Dateline and 20/20 to know that girls
who don't have a positive male role model in their life end up
dead in ditches and other messed up stuff like that. Yes, it would
make your life easier if I didn't set things up this way, but for
once, this isn't about you. You're just going to have to deal with
it and work out the dynamics of this relationship. My only
requirements are as follows:*

*1) Until Kendall turns eighteen, she has to stay with you
from at least Sunday night until Friday morning. Consistency is
important.*
*2) I don't want Kendall to be left alone with any man unless
you are 100% sure you're going to marry him. Same rule
applies to Kurt. (Between you and me, I sure as hell hope he
doesn't end up with that Kayla chick. Craig has NOT said great
things.)*

*Believe it or not, that's it. It would be silly of me to think I
could control your lives beyond those two requests. As far as our
estate goes, the will has also been changed to make you the sole
executor of that as well.*

This information has me on my feet and pacing the room.

*Since Kendall will be with you a majority of the time, it
makes sense that you manage the finances. Sell the house and
the cars and keep everything else in a storage facility. When
Kendall's old enough, she can decide what to do with
everything. By the way, you wouldn't know it because Craig and
I chose to remain in Fremont and live a very frugal lifestyle, but
when my Dad died, he left me two million dollars.*

"Ho-ly crap."

Our lawyer will give you all of the details. But Chrissy, if one dollar of that money is spent on highlights for your hair, you'd better believe you're going straight to hell. However, since I love you and want nothing more than for you and Kendall to be as close as I could've been with her, the estate will pay for one pedicure a month for the both of you and one seven-day vacation a year. Girl bonding time is important. My best friends taught me that.

"You taught me that too, my friend."

Okay…I guess since you're reading this letter, it's time you finally knew why I never had time to join you on my front porch. Put the letter down and open my closet.

I place the letter on the bed, walk to the closet, and cautiously open it like she's in there waiting for me. Of course she's not. But what's there is almost as shocking. Not taking my eyes off of what I'm looking at, I walk backward to the letter.

Each video represents a year of Kendall's life that I'll be missing. As of today, I'm at her sixteenth year. Yep, when I get done with this letter I'm heading out to my car to videotape myself in the driver's seat. I'll die all over again if I know my child is operating a vehicle the same way we did when we were teenagers. My head spins with worry just thinking about not being there to keep an eye on every move she makes. I know I won't be, but with these videos I can show her how much I wanted to be and how good of a mother I would've been. I made these videos for Craig, but since you're reading this letter, they're yours now. I need you to promise that you'll watch each and every one and implement my lessons, my ideals…my love. Kendall can start viewing them when you think she's old enough

215

to handle it. I know this is an unexpected list with staggering expectations, but say you'll promise, right now.

Looking back up at the videos I let out a nervous, "I promise."

Good girl. Now...Since I know you better than you know yourself, your mind is screaming, "WHY ME?" Okay, one...get over yourself! Sometimes shit just happens. Look at what's going on with me. And two...through the confusing events of the last few years of your life, you showed me that the difference between doing something and doing nothing is everything. I wanted to give up the minute those doctors told me I was going to die. But I mustered up the courage to make these videos for Kendall. By putting my anger and helplessness aside, I hope that doing something will, in the end, mean everything to my daughter. Make good choices for her. I trust you. K.

Slowly I rise and walk toward the closet, pondering everything I just read. Not once since Craig died have I asked myself, *"Why me?"* In fact, the only thought going through my mind has been, *"It can only be me."* From the moment Kurt dropped to his knees and told me Craig was dead, I've been prepared to take care of Kendall. But as I now glide my fingers across the videos, I worry that I will never be prepared to watch my best friend deteriorate before my very eyes.

Burnt

February, 2002

"*That's all I get?*"
    The attorney is looking at Kurt like he should be happy he only got Kendall for a couple of days a week. And I'm looking at him like he better not ask for more. This is what Kelly wants and this is what Kendall is going to get.

Clearly, he's not satisfied with the news he's just been delivered, and he sits upright in his chair when he infuriatingly addresses the attorney.

"Hold on a minute, I just need to get this straight…If Chrissy gets married, Kendall will basically live with the guy for…*five days a week?*"

Addressing him like he's a fool for not seeing the bright side of this set up, the sleazy attorney says, "Yeah…and conversely if YOU get married, you and your new wife will have the child for *two* days a week." Then addressing us both, "However, according to the Will, Kurt, you have the option to back out of visitation at any time, by simply signing this piece of paper."

Kurt takes the paper the attorney is dangling in the air and tosses it in the garbage.

"What about Chrissy, can she opt out?"

"Are you joking with that, Kurt?"

"Hey, it's a reasonable question. You're the one starting a new life…" Insistently speaking back to the attorney, "…Well, *can she?*"

"It's not that easy for her. She can contest the guardianship, but it would most likely mean Kendall would be put into foster care until the court determines new caregivers. You, or her grandparents, could fight for that role, but clearly, this is not

217

what her parents wanted to happen. They've chosen your ex-wife."

"Can Chrissy decide to give me more visitation?"

"Kurt, what are you doing?"

"What I think is best for Kendall."

"What's that supposed to mean? You don't think I'm the best for her? Do you think I'll...what was it you said years ago, 'have to bum a bagel off of someone in the school parking lot to feed her?'"

"It's not you I'm worried about."

"Jesus Christ, Kurt, he loves her, too!"

"How the hell can he love her? He just met her like five minutes ago!"

The attorney holds up his hands in the air and interrupts our spat.

"Ahhhh, so I take it there's a new Mr. Chrissy on the horizon..."

"Yeah, and what if I'm not happy about that for Kendall?"

The unsympathetic sleazebag attorney tells Kurt exactly what he didn't want to hear.

"Sorry my friend, but you're just gonna have to be unhappy like the other three million ex-husbands out there. The will of Kendall's parents wants what it wants. You have no say in this arrangement other than opting out of your visitation. But just know, once you opt out, you can't opt back in. Mr. and Mrs. Chrissy will have the child one hundred percent of the time."

"What about the appointments with the child psychologist? Can I still go to those?"

"The choice is your ex-wife's. The only thing this document gives you is the right to have Kendall with you on the weekends. However, the will doesn't specify *every single* weekend, only that the schedule needs to be consistent. The exact rotation has to be worked out between the two of you..." Looking down at the will, "...within thirty days. If you agree with this, you just need to sign here."

Kurt irritably grabs the last page of the document from the attorney and signs his name at the bottom, effectively agreeing with the terms of it.

Before he storms out, he turns to me and says, "I will never opt out of my time with Kendall. The only opting out will be from your engagement when that guy finds out I'm not going anywhere."

After Kurt slams the door shut behind him, the attorney turns to me.

"That tough guy act didn't fool me."

"Excuse me?"

"Looks like someone still wishes they could play house with you."

As I sign my part of the document, effectively making me Kendall's legal guardian, his rudeness continues.

"I guess since you're getting married though he can wish in one hand and crap in the other, huh?"

I ease his curiosity as I hand the papers back to him. I say, rather numbly, "Yep, that house burned down a long time ago."

Pummeled

February, 2002

"Holy shit, *two million dollars?"*
        It's the one year anniversary of Kelly's death and the first time Courtney, Nicole, and I have been to the cemetery since Craig died. And as we walk closer to the gravesite, we see that he's parked right next to his wife now. The three of us stare at the morbid setting for a minute before we quietly start setting up the picnic. Once we're settled in with our greasy food, Courtney's the first one to start asking questions.

"Jesus, with all of that money why the hell was she hanging on to all of those fluorescent clothes from high school?"

Always one to ask the nitty-gritty questions, Nicole dives into the cash management.

"So how does all of that loot get doled out?"

"It's in a trust. I get a fixed amount every month to pay for the necessities: school, food, entertainment stuff…and the amount increases a little every year until she turns eighteen. That's when the rest is hers to do what she wants."

"Wow, lucky kid."

Before Nicole notices the disgust on Courtney's face and mine, she's quick to reach her hand out, touch Kelly's tombstone, and recant.

"Omigod, I'm such an asshole. I didn't mean that AT ALL!"

I give her a kiss and tell her, "She knows."

"What? That I'm an asshole or I didn't mean it?"

"Both."

After a few quiet minutes of my friends processing the fact that I'm Kendall's legal guardian, I ask them if they're okay with it. It's Courtney who puts my worries at ease first.

"We kind of assumed you'd be the one to get her. I mean, she's been living with you since day one."

"Yeah, it's okay, Chrissy. You don't have to feel bad. We knew Kelly didn't want Kendall in daycare and that's where she would've ended up if either of us got custody of her. Plus, we know how much you love her. You're gonna do a great job of raising her."

"I wish I was as optimistic as you two about this. I'm scared to death I'm gonna screw her up."

Leaning in to give me a big supportive hug, they chime, "Welcome to motherhood."

After a much needed pep talk from my experienced mom-friends, I grab two beers, one for me and one for the top of Kelly's tombstone. But then I suddenly remember, due to Kendall, I don't drink anymore. I place Kelly's in its usual spot and pause for a second before I place the other one on Craig's.

"This is so sickening."

I couldn't agree more with Nicole's claim, and I could talk about how nauseating the scene is until the sun goes down. But never one to stay in a dismal emotional state for long, Courtney changes the subject to one that only proves dismal for me.

"How did Kurt take the news about Kendall?"

"Not good. Mumbled something about never giving up his visitation and fuck Leo if he thinks he's gonna raise Kendall."

"Oh shit. That's intense."

"Probably not as intense as what Leo said though, right Chrissy?"

I know Nicole is inquiring because she truly cares about me, but I don't want to tell her Leo's real reaction for fear it'll get back to Kurt and fuel his fire.

"Leo said he loves me. He'll do anything to make me and Kendall happy."

In reality, I called Leo when I left the attorney's office, and while he told me he loves me, he's one hundred percent NOT happy with the visitation arrangement. In fact, his exact words were, "I'm not sure how much deeper I can dig on this." The minute I got back to work that day, I cried my eyes out with worry as I told my yoga team the truth about Leo's frustration. And when I did that, I created a brand new reason to keep my old best friends away from my new great ones. That girls' night out thing is NEVER happening if I have any say in it.

"That's surprising."

"What do you mean?"

"I dunno, with his short fuse and the way he pummeled Kurt…You'd think the guy would freak out if he knew he'd have to engage with him during every Kendall tradeoff."

Do'h! I hate hearing the truth! I feel defensive Chrissy kicking into gear.

"First of all, Kurt started that fight so it's not really fair to call Leo the one with the short fuse, and second of all, Leo knows exactly what he's getting by marrying me and Kendall. In fact, I can't think of anyone else strong enough to handle that kind of pressure."

"Correction, with all of that visitation, he's kind of marrying you, Kendall, *and* Kurt."

Courtney, sensing by my silence that I'm plagued by what Nicole just said, switches the subject to something she thinks is more positive.

"When do you think he'll be back from New York?"

"The original plan was next month, but it's now delayed by two months…he thinks."

"What's his relationship like with Kendall?"

Aware that she struck an irritated chord with that question, she's quick to defend it.

"I mean, we know he's a great guy, adores you, and all of that. It's hard to just suddenly be a dad, though. Just wondering how he's handling it."

"He sends her gifts, calls her all of the time. All of that snipe hunting they used to do went far to win her over. Trust me, that little girl adores him."

Throwing a potato chip at me, Nicole chimes in with, "You wanna know what I'm worried about?"

"How you're gonna get that giant stain out of your pants? Seriously, Nic, what is it with you and coffee drinks?"

"Shut up! No, I'm worried about that great big sex life of yours!"

"What the heck are you talking about?"

"Dude, you live in a six hundred square foot box…with a kid!"

"Yeah girl, Nicole's right. You're gonna have to get a longer hallway between you two and Kendall. Oh, and you should probably get some locks on the doors."

I turn my head swiftly back to Nicole who's apparently got more insight to add to my sexless future.

"Well, that's only if you have the energy to have sex. The older the kids get, the later they stay up. By the time they konk out, you're too damn tired to even lay there while he pounds away at you. It's too much freakin' work after all of the work you already did that day, half of which you don't even talk about because…you're too damn tired!"

My head darts back at Courtney looking for some kind of positive spin on this subject. But there's none to be found.

She shrugs her shoulders and continues to enlighten me.

"There's always the morning though, you know, at around six when you know for sure the kid is still asleep. Of course, you look like shit and you're breath smells like ass, but you won't look at each other anyway. He'll just pull your pj's down and stick it in from behind. The good thing about that position though is you can doze off for a few more minutes."

Nicole laughs, slaps her on the shoulder, and admits, "You do that, too?"

Horrified, I stare at my friends before I say, "C'mon you guys, it's not that bad…is it?"

Reaching for another beer, sarcastic Nicole replies, "You were married before. Tell us, did the sex get better as time went on?"

"Well...no! But with Leo it's different!"

Looking at me like she ain't buying what I'm selling, Nicole keeps at it.

"There are those occasional nights though, you know...when you get hammered at a girls' night out or something. You come home all drunk and crawl into bed and have crazy sex like you used to have *before* kids."

"Yeah, but he's the only one who gets something out of it though, because you're usually too drunk to feel anything."

"Damn right about that, Court! And the other downside to those drunk nights is he just expects it like two nights later when you're completely sober and all you want to do is watch your TIVO."

It's quiet for a minute, and I'm relieved that it looks like we're going to change the subject. But they're not done.

"It's when you have a brand new baby that you can kiss that sex life good-bye."

"So true, Nic! So, what do you think? They probably have what...like a year or two of semi-good sex left?"

I heatedly throw my hands in the air to halt the sex—or should I say—NO sex talk.

"*A baby?* We just got a four year old! There won't be any babies anytime soon!"

"That's what you think! You can get pretty lazy about birth control once you're married!"

"Yeah and not to mention how forgetful you can become when you have a four year old!"

Rolling my eyes at my friend's over the top scare tactics, I tell them to shut up.

"Stop worrying about my sex life and start worrying about you own! Sounds like you need to!"

225

I thought I made it clear we were done with the subject, but Courtney dives in for a little more information.

"Speaking of sex and babies and stuff, what do you and Leo use?"

"For protection? Oh, my last Depo shot was…" Counting the months on my fingers, I'm shocked to realize how right Courtney was when she said a four year old would make me forgetful. "…Wow, it was in September. My next one was supposed to be last month, but crap, I just realized I forgot to get it. I've been so busy, I guess it just slipped my mind."

Clapping her hands, Nicole roars, "Oh girl! I see a baby in your near future!"

Help!

April, 2002

So much has happened in the last few months, and at the same time absolutely nothing has happened. Now that I'm caring for a child, my days are filled with a million seemingly insignificant tasks that make life fly by.

Before Craig died, I used to wake in the morning to a nice quiet cup of coffee, go for a relaxing run, followed by a very long hot shower. I'd take my time picking out an outfit for the day and leisurely set off to work, arriving unfrazzled and with all sorts of ideas to move the yoga business and my life forward. Sure, sometimes the evenings were challenging if I had to help Craig out by watching Kendall, but there was always an evening in the near future that I looked forward to.

Before Leo left on 9/11 we'd spend our nights cooking dinner together or overtly flirting at a restaurant. If he had to work late, I'd get a pedicure or go out for drinks with the girls from the studio. There were all kinds of options! But no matter what, the nights always ended with some sort of romance. Even after Leo left for New York, we'd find a way to be intimate on the phone. It seemed that all of my days ended with me feeling satisfied and empowered, professionally and sexually. Now I end my days feeling ineffective and scared to death that I forgot to do something important. In order to get Kendall to pre-school on time, I rush out of the cottage in the morning without coffee *or* a matching outfit, and I usually trip over toys on the way because my cottage isn't structured to deal with seven thousand of them. During my lunch break, I quickly grocery shop or chaotically browse the Internet searching for advice on how to raise a four year old and then at two o'clock I rush back out to pick up Kendall from school. I bring her back to the studio where we place a call to Leo so they can stay connected, and then the rest of the day is spent more on entertaining her than actually working. Instead of having sweaty sex with Leo, my nights now end after giving Kendall a dinner that pretty much consists of only one food group, an hour of Dora the Explorer so I can do the dishes in peace, and a long bath…for her. I tuck her in and then plop on my wicker couch, usually too tired to call Leo. He'd only want me to put my hands down my pants like the good ol' days and quite frankly I'm so tired I'd have to fake it and the thought of that makes me more sad than not talking to him at all. So I lay in the dark and let my mind wreak havoc on me. Millions of muddled mommy questions and concerns zip into my head like, did I remember to pack Kendall's school lunch? Did I RSVP to the four birthday parties she was invited to on Saturday? Did I remember to buy gifts for those four birthday parties? Did I pick the right pre-school for her to attend? Am I wiping her butt the way her parents did? How long until I can stop helping her wipe her butt? Did we remember to say a prayer about her Mommy and Daddy tonight? Nope, forgot. Damn it. I suck at this!

The life I had pre-Kendall was thrilling and productive. Now I just run around like a crazy woman and feel like I have zero to show for it. Yes, the days of my life are very different now that a child is in it and worrying about stupid stuff like pooping in my small cottage while living with Leo is a thing of the past. In fact, I'd give anything to find the time to poop now. Maybe Nicole and Courtney were right. Maybe my steamy romance with Leo can't survive all of these new challenges. Maybe I've been fighting my whole life to have it all—only to realize now, when you have children, you can't. Maybe that's what being a grown-up is all about…*realizing you can't have it all.*

I guess I'm about to find out. Leo's supposed to finally move back next month. He reassures me he's kicking ass and that he's going to give me and Kendall the life we both deserve. When he talks about our future it gives me butterflies, and when I listen in on the phone conversations he has with Kendall it makes me feel like we really are going to be a family...a fucking weird one, but a family nonetheless. He calms my nerves about struggling with the mom stuff and reassures me that things will be easier when he's around to lend a hand. *I just have to make it to next month and everything will go back to good.* It's after my conversations with him that I feel like I'll be able to prove Nicole and Courtney wrong and prove to myself that I can have it all. It's a constant ping-pong game of emotions I play with myself, but I'm determined to win.

But I'll tell you what I'm NOT winning at right now...the real estate game! Just like I was shocked when I pulled into the home Kurt shared with Kayla, I'm blown away as I park in his new driveway, located in a charming gated community in Walnut Creek. It's Kendall's first official visitation weekend with him.

After greeting Kendall with a balloon and a bunch of color swatches, Kurt tells her to go upstairs and pick out any room she wants and to pick a color to paint it.

Pryingly poking my head inside, I stare in amazement.

"Wow, Kurt, this place is incredible. Tack on another three thousand square feet, a pool, and a tennis court and it could be that house in Orinda."

"It'll work. It's close to Lafayette, and I assumed since the Forever Young headquarters are there, it would make our transfers a little easier."

"So, you moved here...*for me?*"

"No, *Ego*, I moved here for Kendall."

Clearly, he's still holding some kind of a grudge toward me.

"Right, that's what meant. I just said it wrong. I meant to say...you moved here to make this easier on us. But not us meaning me and Leo, us meaning all of the adults. Does that make sense?"

229

"No. You never make sense to me." Nudging me out as he closes the door, he assures me, "I'll drop her off on Sunday."

"Hold on!"

Irritated, he cracks the door back open a smidge.

"What?"

"I just realized, you can't drive her around in the Porsche, there's no room for the car seat!"

"*Noooooo*, really? Give me some credit, Chrissy, I sold the Porsche last month and bought a car fit for a kid. How stupid do you think I am?"

"You sold the Porsche?"

"Did I stutter?"

"Well, no, but I thought you loved that car."

"Not as much as I love Kendall."

Wow, he's taking this responsibility to levels I never thought he had in him. Chrissy's confused.

"Oh…okay."

As I'm yelling good-bye to Kendall, she comes barreling around the upstairs corner.

"I wuv my room Ki-Ki! I wuv it, I wuv it, I wuv it!"

"That's great sweetheart. I'll see you on Su…"

And then she was gone, back to her brand new big room in the brand new big house. Then Kurt said, "See ya" and slammed the door on me. It takes me back to that daunting day in November, 1998, when I moved into my cottage. After Kurt helped me pack up some of the furniture from our old house in Danville, I sat idling in the driveway, hoping he'd see how sad I was. But he just flashed his million dollar smile and went inside the house, giving me the independence I begged him so hard to have.

My cell phone snaps me away from the memory. It's the real estate agent in charge of selling Craig and Kelly's house. She tells me the buyers need to shorten the closing process, which means I have to have everything cleared out – like, right now! I hang up the phone and literally lose it in my car.

I'm in the process of selling a house that doesn't even belong to me and I'm in charge of storing away the entire contents of it for future use, and now I've just been told that I only have ten days to do it! Childless Chrissy can tackle anything in ten days! But now that I'm a mom, all I have available are the weekends when Kendall is with Kurt, and that's not enough time to get the job done, at least on my own anyway. I pick up the phone to call Leo, but then throw it back on the seat. What's the point? It's not like he can do anything all the way from New York.

"God fucking dammit! Will life EVER be normal for me?"

I begin to pound on my steering wheel and throw the biggest pooh-pooh baby temper tantrum in the world. The much needed moment is rudely interrupted by a slow soft knock on my window.

"Go away, Kurt."

"Roll down your window."

"No."

"Chrissy, roll it down and tell me what's wrong."

"No, you'll just tell me I deserve everything I have coming, flash that stupid half-smile and walk back into your stupid new house."

Trying hard not to laugh at my drama, he reassures me, "I won't do that, I promise. Tell me what's going on."

"Everything's wrong! I'm falling behind at work! I haven't done my laundry in six days! Don't *even* get me started on how stinky this tank top is! And you were right about me being a terrible cook – Kendall won't even eat the hotdogs I make! I've barely had the time to pack up Craig and Kelly's house and now….I have to do it in ten days! It's too hard, and I need help, but I'm all alone and no one fucking cares how hard all of this is. Just go away so I can figure it out."

He taps on my window again, "Roll down the damn window so I can hear you, please."

Giving in, because deep down I don't want to have to figure this out on my own, I roll down my window.

Rather calmly he asks again, "Now, tell me why you're crying."

After telling him everything I just said when the window was rolled up, he quickly comes up with a plan to clear out the house.

"Why don't you head over there now and get started. I'll pick up where you left off on Monday and work through the week and then—"

"But what about your job?"

"I'm the boss, I can make it happen."

Blowing my nose as I look at him, I curiously ask, "What do you mean, you're the boss?"

"You're looking at the new president of Quest Adventure Gear."

"*When the hell did that happen?*"

"It doesn't matter. It just happened."

"But you fart around too much for something like that to happen."

"Chrissy, I work in the outdoors industry. All anyone does is fart around. Apparently, I do it the best."

Well put me to bed and turn out the lights. Never in a million years did I think Kurt had the work ethic to propel himself to such a level. Then again, why am I surprised? He knew where he wanted to work the minute he graduated from college. He started at the bottom of that company and stuck with it all the way to the top. He never quit.

"Chrissy, did you hear what I said?"

"Uh…yeah…you'll do all the work."

"Uh…no, that's *not* what I said. You go now and do what you can. I'll continue to work through the week and we'll meet back there next weekend to finish together."

"What about Kendall? I don't think we should have her at the house with us."

"Guss and Kyle lost a football bet and they have to paint the inside of my house next weekend. They can start with Kendall's room and watch her at the same time. Seeing as though they have kids, they shouldn't screw up too bad."

"You'd do all of this for me?"

"No! Jesus, what is wrong with you? I'm doing all of this for Kendall."

And with that reality check, I set off for Freakmont to tackle the task of cleaning out Craig and Kelly's house, feeling more relieved than I had in a long time.

End of an Era

April, 2002

"It looks like that's the last of it."

"Yeah, and right on time. I told Guss and Kyle I'd be back to the house by five o'clock and..." he looks at his watch, "...look at that, an hour and a half to go."

Standing in front of Kelly and Craig's house with a garbage bag in one hand and a broom in the other, Kurt and I stare in silence at the home we shared a lot of laughter in over the years.

"Man, remember when they bought this place?"

"Yeah, we were so jealous. We still lived in our little shack in Half Moon Bay."

"Aw, c'mon...our house wasn't that bad."

"Kurt, we had a tarp on the roof ten out of twelve months of the year. Calling it a shack is giving it too much credit!"

"Seems like just yesterday, doesn't it?"

"Hard to believe it was five years ago next month."

"That's right...they moved in May, didn't they?"

"Oh, geez, remember the freak rain storm that day?" Chuckling at the memory, he recollects, "Craig and I were scrambling to get the couch from the U-Haul into the house before it got drenched, remember?"

"And you dropped it! Kelly and I were laughing our asses off. We were in the living room, unpacking boxes...watching you guys fumble around..." My voice trails off as I say, "...she was just pregnant with Kendall."

"Are you okay, Chrissy?"

"No. Are you?"

"No."

"Will we ever be?"

235

"I hope so, for Kendall's sake."

After a long pause, I turn to him and admit, "I don't know what the hell I'm doing, Kurt. It's really scary."

"Me neither, but she's only four, it's not like she's been through this before and can correct our mistakes, right?"

"How do you do that?"

"Do what?"

"Stay positive all of the time."

"Trust me, you taught me how to see the negative in all kinds of things."

"I knew you were gonna say that."

"What was that you said after you tormented Kayla at the house in Orinda? Oh yeah, it was just too easy."

And then he shows me a sliver of his infamous half-smile.

"I guess I deserved that."

I see his eyes shift down to my ring finger and his mood takes a nose dive.

"And a whole lot more if you ask me."

And now his smile's gone.

"And why do you do that?"

"Do what?"

"Flip-flop your emotions. It's like one minute you can go from being nice and cracking jokes with me to the next when you clearly hate my guts."

"Just drop it. I'll go lock up."

"C'mon, Kurt, I know I deserve all of the crap you throw at me and it would make more sense if you hated me one hundred percent of the time, but sometimes you give me these little signals that we might be able to have a working relationship and then other times you're cutting me down. I never know where your mind is."

"You wanna know where my mind is? It's with Kendall all of the time. And I can have a working relationship with you, for her. I think I've proven that to you. But when I remember What's-his-name is coming back, and he'll have a hand in raising her, it makes me sick. That's why my emotions flip-flop."

How will things ever be normal for Kendall when Kurt calls Leo, 'What's-his-name', and Leo calls Kurt, 'Numb Nuts?' This parenting set up is doomed.

"What am I supposed to do, Kurt? I mean, think about it, we're divorced. I was bound to meet someone eventually and probably get married again. You are, too. Is this how you expect me to act when you bring a woman into the picture? Am I supposed to give her an insulting nick name and act angry all of the time?"

"Yeah, if she was fucking me while we were married."

Yep, this parenting set up is definitely doomed.

"You know what? You're right. And I know you don't believe me, but I'd give anything for things to have happened differently. But if it's Kendall's happiness you're concerned with you're going to have to find a way to handle your emotions, and What's-his-name will have to, too. Because, I swear to God, I won't let anything stand in the way of that girl's happiness. I mean it, Kurt. I'll rip that visitation away from you faster than you can say Yosemite National Forest, and I'll break off my engagement with Leo faster than he can say capital divided if you two can't get your shit together! Got it?"

Instead of threatening me right back, Kurt doubles over and starts laughing like crazy.

"What are you laughing at? I'm serious!"

"It's Yosemite National *Park* and capital *dividend*!"

I'm only able to hold back my own laughter for two seconds and then it takes us way more than that to compose ourselves.

"Oh, man…why am I so damn stupid?"

"Oh stop, you're not stupid."

And now more seriously, I confess, "I'm gonna screw that little girl up, I just know it."

"Not a chance. All it takes is love, and she tells me all of the loving things you do for her. I hear about the places you take her, the songs you sing her...the food you *try* to cook her. You're doing a good job, so don't beat yourself up and certainly don't call yourself stupid. You're far from it."

"So, I'm not as bad of a mom as you always thought I'd be, huh?"

Clearly disgusted with himself, he confesses, "I might've said some stupid stuff to you over the years, but I hope you believe me when I tell you I never meant for any of it to make you feel inadequate."

"But can you see now how it would've?"

"Obviously. We're standing here divorced and you have that thing on your finger..." After a long pause he looks back toward the house and murmurs, "...I think we're done here. You ready to lock it up?"

Feeling overwhelming sadness at the finality of it all, I exhale, "I don't think I can."

"I'll take care of it. Why don't you head to my house to pick up Kendall."

"Are you sure?"

"Positive. My time ends with her at five o'clock sharp. I'd hate to lose my visitation because I didn't have her ready for you in time."

"Hey, I'm not that mean!"

Pausing before I open my car door, I turn back to him.

"Kurt?"

"Yep?"

"Thank you...for everything. I never could've done this without you."

"No problem."

Just when I'm about to close my door he yells back, "Hey Chrissy..."

"Yeah?"

"How come What's-his-name didn't offer to help?"

"I never asked him to."

"Why's that?"

Looking back up at the house, I sigh, "I guess I needed to mourn it without explaining exactly what it was I was mourning."

"That makes sense. I bet he hates getting dragged back into your past. One of the downsides of starting over, huh?"

"I wish it wasn't that way, but yeah."

"I remember that with Kayla. I felt like she couldn't possibly understand the pain associated with my losses because she wasn't around to celebrate the joys once linked to them."

Even though Leo is about as compassionate as any man could possibly be, Kurt's right. He'll never truly understand how heartbreaking my divorce was or how painful the deaths of my dear friends were. It's like Kurt's the only person in the world who can identify with what I've gone through.

Gazing back at the house, I tell him, "I hate to be the dramatic one all of the time, but it kinda feels like the end of an era."

"Not dramatic at all. What lived in this house was supposed to be forever, but something came along and messed things up. I can probably relate to that sentiment more than anyone else."

And then he walked inside to lock all of the doors.

I'm knocking down buildings
Searching high and low
I'm looking for a feeling
Just one more time before I go
("Back to Her," *Five Way Friday*)

Lube and Tune

April, 2002

"**H**unny, you know what your problem is?"
"That's good news—I only have one?"
"You need to get laid."
"Well unless I can screw myself, I don't see that happening anytime soon. Leo's knee deep into this hedge thing and I can't find a two-day gap in my schedule to make the quick trip to New York. Besides, even if Kurt picked Kendall up from school on a Friday afternoon, it only gives me thirty-seven hours with Leo until I have to be back on Sunday. Hardly satisfying."

"Why don't you just ask Kurt to take her for an extra day?"
"No way! It's not what Kelly wanted."
"Well I bet she didn't want your huha to go to waste either! And would you look at yourself? You're starting to look like...a mom."

Walking over to a full length mirror in one of the studios, I too am repulsed by what I'm looking at. The roots of my blond hair are grown out to Courtney Love-like proportions, my eyebrows are now an *eyebrow* and my outfit looks like something I pulled out of the lost and found.

"Tsk-tsk...You're starting to look like Barbara before I got my hands on her."

241

"Oh my God, when did this happen?"

"December. When Leo left."

"I better make some appointments and get myself back on track. He's supposed to move back next month."

Exhaling as I look in the mirror and play with the dark strands of hair dangling in my eyes, I mutter, "I've got to do something about this. One look at me and he'll rip this ring off of my finger and catch the first flight back to New York."

"Here Doll, this should help."

Taking a small red box from the palm of my sweet Slutty Co-worker's hand, I flash her a look that says, *what have you done?* Then I open it.

"Oh my gosh, this is a two day spa retreat at The Ritz Carlton in Half Moon Bay! ARE YOU SERIOUS?"

"Yep, and you better get going. Your cut and color starts in two hours! And Hunny…do yourself a favor and wax more than those eyebrows. If the carpet matches the drapes…you're in some serious trouble!"

Jumping up and down like a four year old, my rejoicing comes to an abrupt halt when I remember I have a four year old.

"Shit. I can't go. Kendall."

"Such a good mommy. But even the best mommies need a break. It's all taken care of."

"How?"

"Megan's picking up Kendall from school and taking her to Kurt's."

Adamantly shaking my head, I insist, "I can't ask her to do that."

"You didn't, I did. Listen, it's his two days with her anyway, who cares who delivers her to him. Besides, she wants to talk to him about that Nepal charity crap…" Placing my car keys in my hand and nudging me out the door, "…All you have to do is go home to pack your bag. Oh! And Hunny, here's one more little gift. But don't open it until you're told to."

"Told to by who?"

"Me. I'll call you tonight. Now get going!"

On the way to The Ritz, in between shaking the box that Slutty Co-worker told me not to open, I try to call Leo to tell him about my surprise. But to my disappointment he never picks up. Nevertheless, I make it to my afternoon of pampered bliss and immediately forget about the letdown of not hearing his voice. I get cut, colored, massaged, waxed, mani'd and pedi'd to absolute death and then float out of the spa and into my room where I order room service. After staring at myself in the mirror and proudly proclaiming, "Now there's my girl!" I get all cozy in a big white fluffy robe and then make my way to the balcony to enjoy the ocean view. My enjoyment is immediately disrupted by the countless number of couples I see walking hand in hand along the shoreline. Just as I'm beginning to feel sad about being all alone at such a fabulous resort, a loud knock pulls me away from the melancholy moment. I pull my robe tighter as I make my way to the door and open it expecting to find my Cobb salad. But I find something even better.

"Oh my God! Leo!"

Rushing into his arms, I nearly knock him over, kissing his face, his neck, his eyes, his ears...anywhere my lips land.

"Are you really here?"

He cups my face in his hands and with that voice that will forever spellbind me, he says, "Yes, Baby, I'm really here."

It's been months since I've had his arms around me and I'll die if I have to go that long without them again. There's so much to talk about, so many details about our new life together with Kendall, and so many things I want to know about his new business, but everything can wait because there is so much about each other's body that we have to get reacquainted with.

Closing the door with his foot and throwing his bag to the ground, Leo keeps one hand on my neck while he kisses me and unties my robe with the other. Thank you, Lord Jesus, who I'm still struggling to believe in...I'm *soooo* glad I paid extra to get the super lube and tune wax job! I tear off his belt and rip the buttons off of his shirt while trying to remove it. The scent of him makes my legs go weak and each inhalation makes them weaker. Every girl part attached to my body is throbbing and I don't care about anything other than having him inside me. Mercifully, within thirty seconds of laying eyes on my love, that's exactly where he is.

Over and over again I keep saying, "I never want you to stop, I never want you to stop." Breathlessly, he whispers back, "Not until you tell me to, Baby…not until you tell me to."

My hands travel from his shoulders to his forearms and then back up, taking in all of his strength. Then they trail down the middle of his back and rest on the lower part of his hips where I can feel his muscles tighten with every thrust. I'm in absolute Heaven with his intoxicating smell, his breathless confidence and his powerful focus until…

"Oh my God! Stop! Stop! Stop!"

Slowing down but not leaving me, he smiles and says "No way, Baby."

Pushing him off of me, I yell, "I'm serious, Leo! You have to take it out!"

Now lying beside me, he breathlessly admits, "That didn't go as well as I planned."

Out of breath myself, I explain, "I'm not on any birth control. I never got that other shot. Jesus, it's like I can't keep track of anything anymore!"

Climbing back on top of me like he could care less about what I just said, I push him away again.

"Are you crazy? We just got Kendall! We can't risk another one, not right now."

"Remember the night we met?"

"Yeah…"

"Did you plan for it to happen?"

"That would be a big, NO!"

"Would you say meeting me was the best thing to ever happen to you?"

"Of course."

"Do you still plan on marrying me?"

"Leo! Yes, and why are you asking me these questions?"

"Remember that one time we were in Monterey and I pointed out that woman who was pregnant and I told you I couldn't wait until you looked like her."

"How could I ever forget?"

"I meant what I said. Chrissy, not one damn thing about our relationship has been conventional." Now laughing, "The timing of us having a baby is irrelevant to me…" Moving back on top of me, "…it's the fact that we'll be together forever that matters."

"Your wooing words are charming, but I want everything to be perfect, Leo."

"And what does perfect mean?"

"It means you'll be home with me and Kendall. That she has some time to settle into our new family. Shit…so we ALL have time to settle into our new family. Perfect means you won't miss one day of my morning sickness, my first ultrasound…my expanding waistline."

"Then I guess I'm outta here."

Standing to put his pants on, I tug at his hem and ask where he's going.

"The drug store…" Smiling down at me, "…I'm not done with you. Oh, and open that box while I'm gone. The spa was my gift to you and that's your gift to me."

"So this whole thing was your idea?"

"Yep."

And then he bent down to kiss me before saying "I'll be back in ten minutes," and then he dashed out the door.

I almost opened the door to beg him not to leave, but resisted the urge because I knew there would be no sex on the menu if he stayed. So, while Leo was gone I ordered another Cobb salad for him and opened the box. When he returned, I was wearing the lingerie he entrusted Slutty Co-worker to buy for me. It was surprisingly tasteful and fit like a glove…and it came off just as easy as one.

The remainder of our weekend was a dream. We hardly left the bed and spent countless hours talking about Kendall, our wedding and the success of T.L. Capital. Apparently, not only are they going to open up an office in California, but Texas as well. The forty-eight hours we spent at The Ritz were long overdue time together needed to plan our future, and I could've continued to do it long into the future, but Sunday rolled around and Leo had to catch his flight back to New York and I had to be home by five o'clock to meet Kendall who was being delivered by Kurt. Hearing Kurt's name come out of my mouth was obviously hard for Leo to digest, but for the first time in four years he didn't clench his fists when it happened. It looks like he dug deep and things might be okay with the visitation arrangement after all. Two days after I opened the door to him, I have to open it again to let him out.

"Do you have to go back?"

"Unfortunately, yes."

"I guess it's just for one more month." Hugging him tightly, I worry out loud, "I *think* I can make it."

"Chrissy I have something to tell you. I waited until now because I didn't want to ruin the weekend."

I pull back a little.

"You're scaring me."

"It's not scary, I promise. It's just that I have to stay in New York until July to help Taddeo with the Texas deal."

"*What? No!*"

"I only need an extra six weeks and I can get what I need done. I promise. I wouldn't do it if it wasn't important."

"But it's been so long already and Kendall probably doesn't even remember what you look like!"

"But she knows what I sound like. We talk on the phone all of the time."

"It's not the same! Damn it, Leo, I don't wanna live like this anymore."

Pulling me back into him, he admits, "It's hard for me, too. But what I'm doing is for the rest of our lives. We can make it six more weeks, can't we?"

Just like I remember doing in Dr. Maria's office so many years ago, I nod my head yes like it's no biggie, but the hole in my heart that's flashing a big neon vacancy sign says otherwise.

Onward and Upward

June, 2002

“Thank you for taking care of that.”

“What? All I did was order the food.”

“I’m talking about my clothes. Thanks for not throwing them away. I just know all of that fluorescent stuff will make a comeback one day.”

“Okay…one, you’re totally wrong about that assumption. And two…how come I never know what you’re talking about anymore, Kelly?”

Giggling, she teases, “You don’t know what *you’re* talking about!”

“Huh?”

“Who’s it gonna be, Chrissy? Just pick already!”

“Who’s *who* gonna be?”

“You’re gonna have to choose or something will happen that’ll make the choice for you.”

“Are you talking about love?”

“You got it.”

“Will I ever find it?”

“It’s all around you…even about to be inside of you.”

“I’ve always had love inside of me, Kel!”

“But you’ve never had it growing inside of you.”

I bolt straight up in bed and grab my stomach, which is stupid because unless a phone can impregnate me, I'm in the clear.

There's no need to jump out of bed because Kendall's with Kurt, so I slump back down and reflect on my latest confusing dream with Kelly. I know I'm not pregnant, and I know what man I've chosen, so what's the message? Are these dreams some kind of a reflection of my insecurities? *But what insecurities?* I know who I am now and I know what I want, so why all of the creepy man/baby talk? Maybe I'll give Dr. Maria a jingle and chat about it. I've wanted to touch base with her since she set me up with Dr. Vikki, but life has done nothing but get in the way of it. Maybe next week. Too much to do today. And first on my list of things to do is to call my gynecologist and get my Depo-Provera shot so I'm ready to go when Leo moves back home. I'll do anything to avoid another condom nightmare from happening. I swear, if all of my hair hadn't been waxed off, the friction would've started a fire and burned the damn hotel down.

I make my way to the bathroom and like usual, trip over a hundred toys on the way. And like usual I groan, "Son of a bitch, I can't live like this anymore." And it doesn't look like I'll have to for much longer! Leo and I had a long talk in Half Moon Bay, and we decided I should get started on looking for a house. It makes more sense to have a home ready and waiting for him upon his return in July, there's simply no room in the cottage for a suitcase, let alone a man. Both of our businesses are doing extremely well and we're prepared to spend a pretty penny on a piece of property in Lafayette. It's where Kendall's pre-school is and in keeping with the consistency commitment I made to Kelly, I won't switch her. Not that I would anyway. My inexperienced mom ass got super lucky and picked an amazing school. She loves it there and is totally thriving. So much so that Dr. Vikki only has us on an as needed basis. As of right now, there's no need to see her in person.

Once Kelly and Craig's house was sold and all of their things were put in storage, a huge weight got lifted off of me. And spending two amazing nights with Leo helped to alleviate a lot of stress that had been building up. Almost overnight, my head cleared and I was able to better manage my days. I started setting my alarm clock for an hour earlier to once again enjoy a quiet cup of coffee and a long shower, and I started making larger grocery trips on the weekends so I didn't have to run around like a crazy woman during the week. I even enrolled Kendall and me in cooking classes and we're learning what a well-balanced meal is *together*. I also put her in an after school gymnastics program that gives me an hour more a day in the office. All of the changes have brought a great deal of sanity back into my life and it's reflected in Kendall's smile every day. She's healthy and active and for the most part seems to be enjoying life. I'm sure there are a million other things I could be doing to make her days better and I bet Kelly spelled them all out for me in those videos, but I still can't bring myself to watch them. Brushing my hand alongside the box that holds them, I mutter, "I just need a little more time, Kel."

In the shower I wash my body and like always I imagine my hands are Leo's. I've missed the touch of a man like I never thought I would. Sure I'm "mom" tired, but something about being a mom seems to bring out the desire more than when I wasn't one. Maybe it's a fear of becoming old…of becoming undesirable. I don't know, but it's an insecurity I don't want to think about right now because I'm happy and I don't want anything to bring me down. I exit the shower and push aside Leo's still hard and tousled towel from when he last went back to New York in December after the fight with Kurt. It's one of the few reminders I have of him in the cottage and I can't bring myself to alter it.

Now staring at myself in the mirror, I study the fine lines under my eyes and wonder if I look thirty-three. I'll be turning that old in two months. It's hard to believe I was only twenty-eight when I met Leo. It's even harder for me to believe, given all of the wrenches thrown at us, that the dreams he and I shared the night we met at Buckley's are about to come true. I can't believe that I sat down next to a twenty-two year old, college attending, rock yard worker and went home destined to spend the rest of my life with him. And now, four years later he's accomplished his goal of becoming not only an investment banker, but the managing partner of T.L. Capital, his very own business. And I learned to follow my heart and it led me to my very own business, Forever Young, Inc. There have been times when I thought for sure our relationship wouldn't make it, but it was always our shared dreams that brought us back together, and I know it's our shared dreams that will keep us together. Dr. Maria so brilliantly made me realize that.

Now in my bedroom putting on my clothes, my thoughts return to my list of things to do today, which starts with the house hunt. Hopefully I'll find us the perfect one and it'll close by mid-July, because I have another big thing I have to start planning: our wedding. Leo and I finally talked about it in Half Moon Bay and decided to bail on the idea of Fiji and just have a very small wedding at our new house, like with just the two of us, Kendall and a bunch of snipes. We set the date for September fourteenth. Four months from today.

Heading to my desk to get started on a list of must-haves in the new house, my mind drifts off for a second to the two amazing days with Leo in Half Moon Bay. It makes me remember two *very* important items to put on the list—long hallways and a lock on the master bedroom door! Come to think of it, we might even want to build in some sound proofing!

Almost

July, 2002

"I'm standing in it right now! It's ours Leo! I can hardly believe it, but it's ours!"

Looking out of the kitchen window and into the backyard of my new house, I'm smiling from ear to ear as I watch Kendall run around like a crazy person who just chugged two liters of Coke (which I'd never give her) and ate four cupcakes (which I don't know how to make).

"We're officially ready for you, so please come home now!"

As of thirty-one days ago I still hadn't found the right place to call home and Leo agreed with every listing I faxed to him that none of them felt right. They either didn't have enough bedrooms, the kitchens were outdated, there wasn't a pool, or the lot was too small. House after house was disappointing and I was running out of time. After touring twenty-four homes in Lafayette, I was starting to get discouraged that I wouldn't find the right house before he moved back in July.

And thirty-one days ago I set out on what I *thought* would be another exhausting house hunt with our agent, but to my surprise I stepped foot into the most perfect home to start our new lives. And today I got the keys! Yep, right now I'm on the phone with Leo and I'm standing in our three thousand square foot totally remodeled rancher. The quintessential California home! It has three spare bedrooms that are all located as far from the master bedroom as they can possibly be! The backyard is humongous and totally loaded with every toy a grown-up (because I'm officially one of those now) could ever want. It's got a pool, an outdoor kitchen and a fireplace, and it also has the most charming garden that I can already see all of our kids digging around in. Gone are the days when I long to live in Danville again. In fact, Danville can eat me!

When I faxed Leo the listing, he called me right away and said, "That's it!" So I put in a full price offer and never looked back. Well except once, when I was packing up the cottage and called him crying.

My cottage had become like an old friend to me and the thought of saying good-bye to the kitchen counter where "Holy Fucking Shit" night took place or the front door that Leo slammed in my face on "Lo Siento" night or the cozy little living room where I found out Kelly had pancreatic cancer on "Duck, Duck, Duck, Goose" night, totally depressed me. Sure all of those nights were horrific, but I got through them because I had my tranquil cottage to seek refuge in and I was having a hard time walking away from it. But as usual, my beautiful Leo had a brilliant idea. He said, "Let's keep it!" Apparently he's going to have tons of out of town guests for work and he thinks it'll be a great place to set them up. After reassuring me that his business is doing better than I could ever imagine and we could afford it, I worked out a deal with the landlord and re-signed the lease for another three years. Leo was not kidding AT ALL when he said he'd do anything to make me happy.

"I wish so badly I could come home right now, but I can't."

"I figured you couldn't come early. I guess I've waited this long, what's three more days, right? Besides, it'll give me time to unpack. I want this place to be perfect for you when you get here." Catching a glimpse of Kendall blowing bubbles in the garden, "Oh my gosh, Leo, you should see her—"

"I can't come home in three days."

All of a sudden my head is spinning.

"I know I didn't hear what you just said."

"It's not that bad, I promise! I just have a few more things to wrap up, so I have to push the date out a little."

"How little?"

"September."

"*September?* But we're getting married in September!"

"And I'll be there for it, please don't worry."

"Leo, do you realize we've only seen each other once in…"

"Three months, three days and sixteen hours. Trust me, I know."

"*Then why?* Hold on a minute, is that Italian bastard doing this on purpose?"

His laugh is deep and sexy and hearing it makes me madder than ever!

"Leo, I'm serious! This is ridiculous! Kendall doesn't even know what a fucking snipe is anymore, and I've become re-virginized!"

"Well, one of those is a good thing."

"Stop! This isn't funny. We were supposed to do this together."

Pausing for a long time because it hurts him so much that I'm hurting, he finally says, "Believe me, I don't like this anymore than you, but it's really important that I stay these extra few days. I promise, Chrissy, I'll be there on September first and not a day later."

"Can you at least come for my birthday next month?"

"I don't think so, Baby. I'm supposed to be in Texas."

Jesus Christ, it feels like I'm Diane Lane all over again and I'm back in that Lifetime made-for-TV movie. I mean, seriously, what normal person gets custody of her dead best friend's kid and has a fiancé who's resurrecting his lucky-to-be-alive best friend's business all the way across the country?

Staring at Kendall, I let out a big sigh. "What am I supposed to tell the snipe hunter about the delay?"

"The truth. That I'm doing this for you guys. I meant what I said last December. I will honor the memory of Kelly and Craig and be the best father I can be to Kendall. You know I wouldn't stay these extra few weeks if I didn't think I was doing that, right?"

"I guess so."

"You trust me?"

"Of course. You trust me too, right?"

"Are you wearing your ring?"

"Every single day."

"Quick! How many sapphires are on it?"

Knowing I wouldn't know the answer unless I actually had it on to count them, I swiftly deliver the answer that I hope, once and for all, puts him at ease.

"Eight."

"Okay, I trust you. It took four years, but I think we've arrived."

On that note, Leo and I hung up the phone, and I took Kendall back to the cottage where we'll remain until he arrives. I want our first night in the new house to be together...as a family.

Stupid, Stupid Girl

August, 2002

Leo's birthday in July came and went without more than a thirty minute conversation. He barely had enough time to talk to me about Kendall and our new house, let alone the fact that he was turning twenty-seven. In fact, he completely forgot it was his birthday until I reminded him. By the time I finally talked to him that day it was nine o'clock in the evening and he still hadn't been back to the apartment he was sharing with Taddeo to find the cookies I'd sent that Kendall had made all by herself. Clearly he's scrambling to get everything done before his move back home, and while I appreciate his drive and intensity, I don't appreciate that he's forgetting about some pretty important stuff...like my birthday too! In fact, everyone outside of Kendall and girls at the yoga studio forgot today was my birthday.

The day started off with a promising bang that it was going to be great. Kendall woke me up by loudly singing happy birthday and telling me I'm the best Ki-Ki in the world. After that I dropped her at pre-school where she told me she was working on a craft and would surprise me with it after school. Hoping to continue the birthday fun, I checked my messages, but hung up disappointed when there weren't any. After checking my watch and assuring myself that the day was still young and I'd get calls later in the afternoon, I made my way to Starbucks to treat myself to my favorite, a non-fat vanilla latte. But by mid-first sip of my delightful caffeinated creation, it dawned on me that it already is *later* in the afternoon in New York.

I sauntered into work with an irritated look on my face that took Slutty Co-worker less than five seconds to diagnose. She immediately ushered me into a relaxation class and followed it up with a masseuse that was waiting for me in my office. Once my massage was done, I bounced off of the table and grabbed my cell phone just knowing I'd hear Leo's voice. There was nothing, and my mood took a nose dive. Luckily, the girls made a lunch reservation at my favorite restaurant where Slutty Co-worker entertained all of us with a recap of her date last night which managed to take my mind off Leo for a few hours. From the restaurant I had to rush out to get Kendall and then drive to the new house to do the final walk-through with the painters I hired to help me make everything just perfect for Leo's return. But being busy throughout the day did nothing to curb the frustration that mounted from not hearing from Leo. From the moment I got off of the massage table, to five o'clock when I dropped Kendall off at Kurt's house for the weekend, my phone never left my hand...and it also never rang.

I check my phone again when I pull into Kurt's driveway and try not to sound dejected when I sing the words, "Here we are!" to Kendall. There still aren't any messages, and not just from Leo, there aren't any from my best friends either! Walking up to the front door, I mumble, "What the friggin' hell is wrong with everyone today?" I ring the bell and as usual try to steal a look inside Kurt's new home as he ushers Kendall inside, but as usual he blocks my view and makes me stay on the porch.

As he's closing the door on my lonely birthday girl ass, he groans, "I'll have her back on Sunday. See ya."

"Oh...okay. Well, you guys have a good..."

By the time I got to the word "time" the door was locked from the inside.

Back in my car I check my phone once again and then throw it on the passenger seat.

"It's nine o'clock in New York! *Where the hell is that man?"*

Maybe something's wrong. I mean, I know he's busy, but he'd never forget me like this! I grab my phone and start dialing his number, but almost immediately snap it closed.

"No! I'm not gonna be *that* girl again! I'm not gonna ask to be remembered!"

Been there! Done that! Bought the big, uncomfortable, divorced tee-shirt!

Then I start doing what any dejected birthday girl would do…I start having a psychotic conversation with myself. My mouth is moving at a hundred miles per hour and my hands are flailing all around.

"*Seriously Leo?* On top of managing my studios and taking care of Kendall, I've been working my ass off to get the house ready for you! Is this the thanks I get for all of my hard work? Is it *soooo* hard to remember me on my birthday? *WHERE THE HELL ARE YOU?*"

My rant gets interrupted by light tapping on my window and it startles me.

"Jesus, Kurt! You scared the crap out of me!"

"Sorry for the interruption, but I have to ask. Do you plan on making it habit to throw temper tantrums in my driveway?"

"No. Sorry. I'll leave."

Starting my engine, he taps on the window again.

"You should've been gone like ten minutes ago. Problem?"

Rolling down my window, I inform him, "Nope, no problem."

"Well, it's a good thing you're still sitting here…without a problem. Kendall forgot to give this to you. She made it at school and said you had to have it today."

I gently take the clay figurine from Kurt's hands and read the inscription on the bottom. It says, Happy Birthday, Mo-Ki-Ki.

"*Mo-Ki-Ki?*"

"She said she started to write Mommy because that's what all of the other kids write on their artwork, but then remembered…"

I could cry, but I don't know if it's because she doesn't have her real mom or because she's starting to confuse me with her real mom.

I whisper, "It's the best birthday present I ever got."

"*Really?* Better than that portable water purification system I bought you for that four day camping trip to Hell Hole Reservoir back in 1993?"

Knowing it's exactly what his comment was intended to do, I crack my first smile of the day.

I tease back, "I know…it's hard to believe anything could be better than that gift, huh?"

"Well then, consider it the last thing I buy you that could save your life."

"Is that a promise?"

After thanking him for the laugh and for bringing the clay figurine out to me, I start rolling the window up.

"I wonder if this means she'll start calling me Da-Ku-Ku?"

I roll my window back down and say, "Excuse me?"

"I said, I wonder if this means she'll start calling me Da-Ku-Ku?"

"God, I hope not. She'll sound like a crazy person."

"I know, right? Can you imagine if people heard her in the grocery store shouting, 'Mo-Ki-Ki! Da-Ku-Ku,' like she's friggin' speaking Swahili or something."

Ahhhh, Kurt's humor! Definitely something I needed a huge dose of right now.

After settling down from the laugh, I place my one and only birthday present in the passenger seat next to my stupid fucking phone and buckle myself up to leave.

"Thanks again for bringing that out. I'd go in and give her a kiss, but evidently I'm not allowed inside."

"Just trying to start over, Chrissy, that's all."

"No, I get it. I was just trying to be funny, too. Guess I'm not as good at it as you. See you Sunday, Kurt."

As I slowly back up he knocks on the hood of my car.

"Big birthday plans tonight?"

"Gigantic. Gonna toss in *Bridges of Madison County* and sip on some Nepalese tea. I hope my neighbors don't call the cops."

"No attention-seeking celebration?"

"Nope."

"But that's unheard of for you."

"That's exactly what I've been thinking all day."

As I begin to back up my car, he hesitantly grabs my window to get me to stop.

"You know what, why don't you come inside for a drink. I'll give you a birthday tour."

"As much as I'd love to see casa de Kurt, I haven't had a drink since Craig died. Too scared with Kendall around."

"It's your birthday. One isn't gonna hurt you."

"I don't know."

"C'mon, you know you're just gonna go home and mope, Chrissy."

"You're totally right, but it's your time with Kendall. I should just go."

Giving me what he knows I need the most—more of his candid humor, he opens my car door and says, "Chrissy, get over your martyr self and get your Mo-Ki-Ki ass in the house."

I can go inside for a drink or I can go back to the cottage and continue ranting like a woman who's already been married for twenty years.

"Okay, okay, one drink and then I'll scram.

Reminiscing

August, 2002

"Cabernet, right?"
    "Yeah, a heavy one of you've got it. If I'm gonna fall off the wagon, I want it to be with something I love."
    He hands me the glass of wine as my eyes drift in every direction. Although void of most of the essential pieces of furniture, Kurt's house is absolutely gorgeous.
    Laughing like I can't help it, I blurt out, "Kayla would've *loooooooved* this place!"
    "Not without a ring she wouldn't have."
    Enjoying my first sip of alcohol in nearly nine months, I ponder, "What is it with girls these days? Why are they in such a rush to settle down?"
    Nearly spitting out his first sip, he jabs, "*And you weren't?*"
    "Are you talking about this time or last time?"
    "Seeing as though we dated for nine years before we got married, I'd hardly say you rushed into that marriage."
    "Didn't I though? I mean, if I never stopped to ask myself if it was right or not, I'd consider that being in a rush."
    Just then Kendall comes bouncing into the room to show us a picture she colored. After both of us excessively admire her work, she jets back off to tackle another one. It's quiet for a long time before Kurt tackles a little something himself.
    "Why question something that felt right?"
    Reflecting on my old Life List and wishing for a second I had kept it to show Kendall an example of what NOT to do

263

when you're a teenager, I regretfully whisper, "I never questioned anything on my list."

"What list?"

I settle into a big overstuffed chair and exclaim, "Holy shit, Kurt! Is this from Ethan Allen?"

Ignoring me, he asks again, "What list, Chrissy?"

"Fine. I never told you this because you would've just laughed at me, but...right after I met you...I made a silly list of all of the things I wanted in life."

Kurt knows how I am with lists. He's seen me make grocery lists, weekly to-do lists, household project lists. He knows that everything I put down on a list, gets crossed off. Always.

"It was stupid. There was some nonsense on it about college and a fashion career...some stuff about you."

"Like what?"

There was a time when Kurt never would've wanted to know. He would've agreed the list was stupid and then he'd turn his attention to something I thought was stupid like buying a bread making machine or snow shoes.

"Ridiculous stuff like that I wanted to buy a house with you, marry you, buy a bigger house with you..."

"Is that all?"

"There was some stuff about kids..."

Knowing it's an emotional subject for me, he reaches over to refill my glass. Ignoring my one drink limit, I let him.

Reflecting on my old life, I whisper, "I wanted two of them. A boy first and then a girl. Silly, I know."

"It's a good thing we got a divorce because that would've been a problem...I wanted six."

His humor is off the charts, but so is his timing and the wine literally flies out of my mouth.

"Hey, watch the chair! That thing cost more than my mortgage payment!"

"Sorry, but SIX? You never told me that! That right there should be proof to you that we had a HUGE communication problem!"

"What girl is gonna marry a guy who wants six kids? No shit I never told you!"

He hasn't let his guard down around me since he found out I was engaged, and it's nice to see him relax a little.

"Well, well, well! Looks like I'm not the only one who wasn't honest about the things she wanted in life!"

And then he's serious again.

"But I still would've spent the rest of my life with you if we only had two."

"Kurt..."

"I'm sorry, I shouldn't have said that."

Refilling his own glass now, he takes another stab at me with, "It's totally out of line to say that to someone who's rushing into their second marriage."

"Very funny. Look, I'm not rushing into anything. When it's right, it's right. Please don't make me explain this to you. It's uncomfortable."

"I'm not asking you to. Look, I know it's hard to believe, but all I want is for you to be happy, Chrissy."

My eye roll speaks volumes.

"I'm serious. You deserve all of the things on that list you didn't think you could have with me. It's who you plan on having it all with that makes me pissed."

Clearing his throat, which is his usual way of signifying the end of the conversation, he invites me to stay for dinner to soak up some of the alcohol I just consumed. Kendall, who's entering the room with another picture, hears the invitation and jumps up and down with delight and begs me to stay. After checking my messages again to see that there aren't any, I accept and for the next two hours, Kurt, Kendall, and I make homemade pasta. Flour flies everywhere and so does the laughter. Everything's relaxed and fun and it finally seems like the visitation arrangement Kelly had the foresight to set up for Kendall might work after all.

Wiping the last of the pasta off of my face, I finally admit after all of these years, "God damn, you're a good cook, Kurt."

"I waited a long time to hear you say that!"

"Tell me though, now that you live alone, who do you yell at when you burn something?"

Dinner's done. Kendall's quietly playing upstairs and music is softly humming in the background.

Refilling my fifth glass of wine, he shoots back with, "Very funny. And by the way, I never yelled at *you*. I was yelling at the food. You just always happen to be standing there when it happened."

"Oh, so that's what it was, huh?"

It's quite remarkable how something that used to break my heart is something I can now joke about.

We stare at each other for a moment before I place my hand on top of his and say, "Thanks for talking me into staying. You were right; I would've just gone home and sulked."

"No problem. I think it was good for Kendall, too."

I look down at his hand which I hadn't touched in a very long time, and when I do, the song we danced to at his graduation party in 1986 starts to play on the stereo.

"Omigod, Kurt, remember this one?"

"Of course I do. I'm the one that put it in my playlist."

He sips his wine and watches me attentively, as I sing out loud…thinking I sound a lot better than I actually do, thanks to the wine.

*"We walked…the loneliest mile…We smiled…without any style. We kissed altogether wrong…no intention. We lied…about each other's dreams…*Wow, Kurt! It's like the song was written for us. Woulda saved us a lot of heartache if we listened to the words a little closer back in 1986, don'tcha think?"

"You really think we kissed altogether wrong?"

"Not at first, but—"

"And you think I lied to you about my dreams?"

"Well you never told me you wanted six kids, that's for sure!"

Unleashing one of his infamous half smiles, he admits, "I guess you got me on that one."

I'm not sure if it's the song, my singing, or the fact that I overstayed my welcome, but all of a sudden he's on his feet, excusing himself from the table.

"I'm gonna get Kendall ready for bed and then I'll put on a pot of coffee. Sound good?"

Checking my watch, I'm shocked that it's already nine o'clock. Leo's either on an airplane to or from Texas or he's completely forgotten it's my birthday. I guess there's no need to rush home…and I kind of want to hear that song again.

"Another bottle of wine sounds better."

He contemplatively stares at me for a long time before he says, "You got it. The opener's in the drawer next to the fridge. I'll be down as soon as I can."

After I blow a goodnight kiss to Kendall who's upstairs, I clear the dishes and then actually enjoy washing them in a kitchen that's larger than the size of one inside of an RV, (like the one in my cottage.) When I'm done, I rewind the music, grab a bottle from the wine fridge and search for the opener. Rummaging around the drawer, I find a stack of papers about Nepal with a post-it on top marked *'For Megan.'*

I mumble, "Charity freaks."

I shove the papers aside, and when I do I'm taken aback by what's underneath. I slowly reach in and pick up the thing that causes a rush of emotions to hit me.

"If it wasn't for you, I would've been all alone."

I whirl around to find Kurt staring at me holding a picture of the two of us from his college graduation day. He gently takes the photo from my hand and stares at it for a long time himself before saying, "That was the moment."

"What moment?"

"The moment I blew it."

This is the point where, in the past, I'd list off all of the ways I felt like he blew it, hoping he'd agree, but usually getting in an argument instead. Not this time. For once, I'm quiet.

"I didn't know it back then, but I do now."

"What are you talking about?"

"I never expected a lot from my folks. By the time they had me, they already had five kids. They were fucking tired and the novelty of stuff like little league, boy scouts, and school conferences had totally evaporated. I guess it's why I always wanted to have six kids of my own…to prove that you can give the last one just as much time and attention as the first one."

He grabs the opener out of the drawer and continues to talk as he gets to work on the wine bottle.

"Anyway, by the time I got to high school, my parents were even more tired. Plus, by then, my dad had been hitting the bottle pretty hard and my mom was in total denial about it. Things got really weird or maybe they were weird all along and I was just finally old enough to see my family for what is was. What was it you used to call them?"

Rather apologetically, I confess, "Dysfunction junction."

"That's right. Anyhow, I had to push away any expectation or dependence I had of either of them. It was fight or flight, you know?"

I remain quiet as he refills my glass.

"So I didn't have any…until I graduated from college, anyway. I made the road to that day pretty easy for them too. I mean, I never asked them for a dime, always had a job…bought my own car. I was a pretty good kid, you know?"

I so badly want to call his parents a couple of fuckers right now for not even making the effort to go to his graduation. But I bite my lip.

"It's like, all they had to do was show up that day and say, 'good job, Kurt.' I had no idea how badly I needed to hear those words until I realized I wasn't gonna get them."

Looking down at the picture, I hurt all over again for him. "But you were there…and it scared the shit out of me." Confused, I look back up at him.

"It petrified me that one teeny tiny twenty-one year old girl could have so much control over my happiness…that I could need something so badly. It's like that fight or flight thing clicked inside of me, and I pushed away expectation and dependence all over again. There was no way I was gonna allow anyone to let me down the way my parents did. So, I acted like I didn't need you and I tried to convince you not to need me. It was the moment I blew it."

Kurt and I could've had it all…if he had been willing to risk his heart. We could've had it all…if he believed in what I was offering him the day of his college graduation. We could've had it all…if he had admitted any of this stuff to me even just two weeks before I met Leo.

"And what's weird is that even though I acted like that, you married me any way. I got everything I ever wanted without having to give up anything for it. But I was too stupid to realize that there would be others out there who would offer you the things you deserved and that you'd need those things bad enough to leave me for them. I was too stupid to notice you weren't a young girl anymore."

Putting down his wine glass, Kurt now takes a step closer to me, lifts my chin and wipes a tear from my face.

"I know exactly what truly, madly, deeply love is, Chrissy. I've been at war with it since the moment I met you."

And then his perfectly molded lips kissed me.

Oh, NO You Didn't!

August, 2002

"*Guuuurl*, you really did it this time!"

Shoving chips and salsa into my mouth, I wonder, "What did I do now?"

"I told you…if you didn't make the choice it would be made for you."

"Kelly, *what the hell are you talking about now*? I swear, you never make sense to me anymore."

"Believe me, you don't make sense to me, either!"

Our drinks finally arrive, and I'm so thirsty that I immediately guzzle mine down.

"I'd be dehydrated, too, if I were you."

"Why? Did we get hammered last night?"

"Somebody did!"

"What the heck is that annoying ringing sound?"

Clapping her hands in total excitement, Kelly chimes, "Oh boy! Here it comes!"

"*Here what comes?* And would you turn that damn thing off, it's driving me crazy!"

"It's yours, you big dummy!"

I begin searching my pockets for the sound, but I can't find it. It just keeps getting louder and louder.

"Kel, why won't it stop?"

"Oh, it's about to stop alright."

271

The annoying ringing pulls me out of my dream and my eyes slowly crack open only to quickly wince shut again. Oh man, my head…it's pounding. Smacking my tongue around my dry mouth…it's like freakin' cotton, dipped in peanut butter, wrapped in tissue paper. Jesus, that noise…is that my cell phone? Eyes still closed, I reach down to grab it out of my back pocket where I'm pretty sure I last put it. Suddenly, my eyes snap wide open.

"WHERE THE FUCK ARE MY PANTS?"

Startled by mumbling, I quickly turn over to see my ex-husband lying next to me…shirtless.

"Omigod! Dude, why are you in bed with me?"

A very groggy Kurt, tells me to turn off my phone.

"I DON'T KNOW WHERE THE HELL MY PHONE IS, KURT!"

"Oh, good…it stopped."

"NO! *NOT GOOD!* NONE OF THIS IS GOOD! WHAT THE HELL HAPPENED LAST NIGHT? "

Just then a very sweet Kendall, in her very sweet Dora the Explorer pajamas, bounces into *what I think* is Kurt's bedroom, and she's holding my cell phone.

"I find her, Weo. Yes, she's right here sweeping with Ku-Ku."

WHAT? *NOOOOOOOOOOOOOO!*

Forgetting about my head pain and thirst, I leap out of bed and grab the phone from Kendall's tiny hands. As calmly as possible, I tell her to go and pick out any cookies she wants to eat for breakfast and then I run into the bathroom.

"Leo! It's me. I'm right here. Sorry about that."

My honorable and adoring fiancé sounds a little ticked off when he says, "Did I just hear what I thought I heard?"

"Huh? What's that?"

OMIGOD, OMIGOD, OMIGOD, OMIGOD!

"Chrissy, what did Kendall just say?"

"Oh, that? I was sweeping when you called and...I guess...I guess I didn't hear my phone."

"Sweeping... at seven in the morning?"

"Yeah, tons to do with the move and all. Just getting an early start."

"It's Saturday. Kendall's not supposed to be with you."

"Right, uhhh, there was a last minute schedule change."

"Were you sweeping with a cuckoo clock in your hands?"

"*What?* That's funny, why the heck would you say that?"

"Kendall said you were sweeping with Ku-Ku. That's what she calls Numb Nuts, right?"

OMIGOD, OMIGOD, OMIGOD, OMIGOD!

"You know...Gosh, I don't really remember what she calls him."

The line is silent for a God awful uneasy amount of time before he speaks again.

"I think you're lying to me."

I am and I don't want to because I made a vow that I wouldn't, but how do I get out of something that I don't even know quite yet that I'm supposed to get out of? FUCK ME! Oh, geez! I take that back! Please don't let me have been fucked! *Pleeeeeeeeease* Jesus, who I promise I'll start believing in RIGHT NOW! Please, please, please don't let me have been fucked!

"Chrissy, if I fly home right now and ask Kendall if she was with you at the cottage this morning and you were sweeping, what would she say?"

Looking at myself in Kurt's bathroom mirror, wearing nothing but a tank top and underwear, I know I'm fucked...just hopefully not for the second time in twelve hours.

"She'd say...she'd say..."

"Would she say you were at the cottage?"

273

Closing my eyes, I murmur,"No."

So calm it's scaring the crap out of me, he continues, "Would she say you were sweeping with a broom when she handed you the phone?"

My body is now trembling, I'm biting my lower lip, my eyes are closed and my head is shaking "No," but the word won't come out of my mouth.

Calm is now gone when Leo roars, "CHRISSY, WERE YOU IN HIS BED?"

"Leo, please…nothing happened. I came to drop her off and…"

"ANSWER THE FUCKING QUESTION!"

In barely a whisper, I croak, "Yes."

For almost a minute, the line is completely silent and then, now jarringly composed, he says, "I was calling to tell you how sorry I was that I couldn't reach you yesterday and to make sure you got your birthday present, but it looks like you were busy getting another one."

"Leo, It's not like that. Please, I can explain—"

"You don't get to do that anymore, Chrissy. I'm only gonna say this once, so pay real close attention. Do not ever contact me again. Do you understand me?"

"No, Leo! Please! It's not what it seems like! DON'T DO THIS!"

"I'm doing this."

And then the line went dead.

Numb

*W*hat have I done?
Seconds after Leo hung up on me, my eyes drift in the direction of the soft knocking on the bathroom door, but I'm too numb to move.

"Chrissy, come on out."

You.

"Can you hear me in there?"

Bad, bad things happen when there's exposure to you. I knew that. How could I have been so stupid?

"I'm putting your clothes by the door."

I hear Kurt shuffle around and then the bedroom door slams shut.

After getting dressed, I splash cold water on my face, but it does nothing to clear my head or wash away the shame. This can't be happening. I won't accept it. I'm going to walk out of this bathroom and Kurt will tell me I simply fell asleep out of pure exhaustion.

Yes, that's it. I was exhausted.

I open the bathroom door and immediately my eyes focus on an empty bottle of wine on the nightstand.

God dammit, I wasn't exhausted. I was drunk.

Disgusted, I make my way to the kitchen where I find Kurt.

"Where's Kendall?"

"I put a movie on for her in her room so we could talk..." Handing me a cup of coffee, "...Here, I made this for you."

"I don't want any fucking coffee. I wanna know what the hell you did to me."

"Whoa, hold on! I didn't to a damn thing to you!"

275

"Then how do you explain me waking up, *in your bed,* without any clothes on?"

"That was all you, Chrissy."

"What do you mean, '*allllll me?*' I'm engaged to be married, for Christ sakes!"

"Oh, that's right, silly me! I forgot that your moral compass works properly when you're engaged. It's when you're married that it craps out!"

Slamming the coffee cup on the counter, I want to say "How dare you!" Instead, I rest my head in my hands and whisper my pain.

"What have I done?"

"We had a good time for once, that's all."

"And it cost me…my engagement."

"What are you talking about?"

Ignoring him, I talk softly to myself.

"In his mind, just being in your house is justification for ending it with me, and I knew that, so how could I have been so stupid?"

He continues to sip his coffee, stare at me, and listen to my shame.

"Here I am, the failure, the cheater…the bad guy. The big three I *never* wanted to be all over again."

I look up at him, expecting some kind of feedback. Still, he says nothing.

"I thought things were gonna work out for all of us. I mean, despite all of the shit I put us through; I really thought we could have good lives. I thought I was gonna be able to give Kendall everything she deserves, and I thought I could be the partner to Leo he deserves. Even you…I thought you were finally free to find the love you deserve and in one night I fuck it all up for everyone. Well, maybe I didn't fuck it up for you. It's not like anyone got hurt because…" And then I start to cry, "…because we slept together last night."

"He thinks we slept together?"

276

"Duh! Look where I was when he called!"

"And he called off your engagement?"

"Are you listening to a God damn word I'm saying?"

He's just staring at me...Defiant. Saying nothing.

I start pacing the room.

"The pieces of last night fall apart for me right after we looked at that stupid picture. You were telling me how much you fucked up my life and then you...Oh shit, you kissed me! What happened next, Kurt?"

"You pulled away and we drank two more bottles of wine, that's what happened."

"How the hell did I get in your bed, WITHOUT MY PANTS?"

"You were hot and started complaining about me being too cheap to use my air-conditioning, which I am, and then you took them off."

Oh, Jesus.

"That doesn't explain how I got into your bed!"

"You put yourself there."

Son of a bitch.

"But why were you there with me?"

"Sometimes Kendall wakes up with nightmares and it's the place she knows to find me. You were too drunk to hear a freight train hit the house, so I stayed in there just in case she needed me."

"Couldn't you have slept on the floor?"

"Would it have mattered in the end result? You just said yourself he was gonna end it with you just for being in my house..." Then his mood shifts to the irritated. "...Besides, it's my house. You should've slept on the damn floor."

Ignoring his comment, my mind starts racing with ideas. Maybe Kurt can call Leo and tell him nothing happened. Maybe he can tell him I got sick with the stomach flu when I dropped her off and I had to stay! I mean, he can even tell him I shit my pants for all I care! I'll put my humiliation aside if it means I can have Leo back. I might've vowed to never lie to Leo, but Kurt didn't! Maybe this can get fixed!

"I know you, Chrissy, and I know exactly what you're thinking. But stop because I'm not getting involved in this."

"But Kurt! Hear me out...if you tell him nothing happened, then he might forgive me."

Out of nowhere Kurt punches the kitchen cabinet and yells, "WHAT MAKES YOU THINK I WANT HIM TO FORGIVE YOU?"

"Oh my God, what is wrong with you?"

"*What's wrong with me*? Jesus, Chrissy...are you seriously telling me you don't remember anything that happened after that kiss? You don't remember what I told you?"

"I remember we went to the couch...reminisced about old times...I think I got emotional. Oh my God, did we do it on the couch, or in your bed?"

My eyes are zooming around the room, my head is shaking defiantly, my heart rate is sky rocketing. There is no way I would ever do that! I would never betray Leo like that. NEVER!

Literally getting on my hands and knees, I start to beg him, "Please, Kurt, please just tell him nothing happened!"

Pouring himself another cup of coffee, he speaks uncomfortably slow when he says, "Let me get this straight. You want me to call the guy you cheated on me with when I was your husband and tell him you didn't cheat on him with me?"

"Kurt, I'm begging you. If you don't do something you'll ruin my marriage!"

"Oh yeah...WELL YOU RUINED MINE!"

It's silent for several minutes as Kurt tries to calm down and I try to piece together last night. *Am I lonelier than I thought I was?* Is it possible that I slipped and slept with Kurt in a moment of weakness? No! No! No! I would never jeopardize what I have with Leo. Not in a million years.

Out of anger for forgetting that bad, bad things happen when there's exposure to Kurt and that I exposed myself to him, I lash out at him like never before.

"The day I divorced you was the end of the days when you could make me crazy. Never talk to me about anything other than Kendall, ever again. Never talk to me about our past or tell me about your future, but mostly NEVER talk to me about what happened last night."

He says nothing, but I continue, "I will find a way to get Leo to forgive me without your help. Mark my word...I will have everything I ever wanted."

I grab my purse and attempt to walk out of the kitchen, but he grabs my arm to stop me.

"Let's just calm down and talk about this for a minute."

"CALM DOWN? I wish I never went to that graduation party in 1986! If I hadn't, there never would've been a fucking Life List. I could've been anything, had I not met you! Maybe I would've gone to a better college, like the one you talked me out of going to! Or, maybe I never even would've gone to college! Maybe I would've gone to Los Angeles to be an actress, or maybe I would've become a painter or an author! I never would've gotten pregnant and I NEVER would've had an abortion, and I never, never, never would've married you or had to get a divorce! YOU RUINED MY LIFE SO DON'T TELL ME TO CALM DOWN!"

On that note, I yell good-bye to Kendall and walk out of the house. On the short drive back to my cottage I wonder how the hell I'm going to get Leo to forgive me, panicked that it's probably impossible. But there's no way I'm going down without a fight. First thing when I get home, I'll shower and then call him. No, I'll call him first. No, maybe I should send him an email. No, I'll—

"Ho-ly Shit."

Inching into my driveway, I park right next to a brand spanking new silver Porsche Carrera, complete with a big red bow on top, just like you see in those sickening Christmas commercials. With shaky knees, I exit my car and walk over to the card taped to the windshield and open it.

Happy Birthday, Baby. I told you I could make all of your dreams come true. Seventeen days until we're together again. I love you. Leo

Wait, *What?*

August, 2002

" *A* *Porsche?* "
    I lift my heavy head from my desk and nod.
"A brand new one?"
    I exhale loudly, and speak painfully slow, when I answer Slutty Co-worker.
    "So new, I could still smell the bratwurst on the breath of the German who put it together."
    "Ouch. Did you try to call him?"
    "Seven times. He never picked up."
    "Did you leave a message?"
    "Just one. I said I can explain if he'd just call me back."
    The minute after I read the card that was taped to the Porsche, I ran into the cottage, took a quick shower, got back in my car, called Slutty Co-worker and Megan, drove to the yoga studio, and while I waited for them to arrive, I attempted to contact Leo.
    "Of course I can't think of a fucking explanation, so I guess it's a good thing he hasn't called me back yet."
    Staring at my co-workers stunned faces, I plead for some kind of advice.
    "There has to be a way out of this, right? I mean, he'll forgive me when he finds out nothing happened, won't he?"
    "How do you know nothing happened?"
    I snap at Slutty Co-worker, "Because I'd never cheat on Leo!"

281

"I dunno, Hunny. If there's one thing I know for sure, it's that I've never woken up without my pants on and *didn't* have sex."

Megan chimes in with, *"Wait, what?"* And then snaps, "You don't actually think she slept with Kurt, do you?"

Ignoring her, Slutty Co-worker attacks my problem like she's on freakin' Law & Order.

"How does your huha feel? Like…is it sore or anything?"

Megan, who's uncharacteristically unsupportive of my latest Chrissygan, has apparently had enough of my love drama and abruptly leaves my office. I look at Slutty like she's the reason for her departure.

"Okay…one, you've offended the poor girl and two…YOU'VE GOT TO BE KIDDING ME WITH THAT QUESTION!"

"No actually, I'm not! Do a couple of squats right now…you'll know if something was in that thing last night."

"I've been taking yoga classes from you for the last two years! Of course my huha is sore! IT'S ALWAYS SORE!"

"Take a deep breath and think real hard, Hunny. Was there any…you know… gunk in your trunks this morning? You know…something sort of crunchy."

"Are you literally asking me if I woke up with a *crunchy huha*?"

"Well, you're the one who needs to know for sure!"

"No, Psycho! What I need to know is if you think Leo will forgive me!"

"That depends on what you're expecting him to forgive."

Throwing my head in my hands in total disgust, I whimper, "So you think I might've actually slept with Kurt."

"How much did you drink?"

"A lot."

"How long since you've had sex?"

"A long time."

"And what was Kurt telling you before he kissed you?"

"Everything I wanted to hear."

"Where did you wake up this morning?"

"In his bed."

"And what were you wearing?"

"Almost nothing."

"Hate to say it, but it's not looking so good in sex court."

I'm scared that she might be right and getting Leo to forgive me for merely being inside of Kurt's house, let alone the fact that I slept in his bed, is about as likely as my dear old slutty friend abstaining from sex for the rest of her life.

After a long sigh and a discouraging head shake, Slutty Co-worker then walks up behind me and starts to massage my shoulders.

"Hate to say it, Doll, but what you've got here is a full-blown relationship crisis and we all know relationships aren't my expertise. I think there's only one person who can talk you through this mess."

And I think she's right. I leave the studio and head back to my cottage where I find that my dream car has already been taken away. I guess while I was trying to call Leo, he was busy on the phone with the dealership. I rip the notice off of my front door instructing me to call Peninsula Porsche if I have seventy-five thousand dollars to buy it back, drop my purse on the ground and head right to the phone. No need to look up the phone number, it's tattooed on my brain. It rings five times before the familiar voice prompts me to leave a message.

"It's me. Everything has fallen apart again. Leo's back in New York, but unlike before, this time I've done something so unforgivable that I don't think he's ever coming back. I also don't think there's anything you can do to change the situation. I just need some advice and...a friend to talk to."

After hanging up, I walk uneasily toward the dirty clothes I had on this morning. With my eyes closed I reach down and pick-up the underwear. Tensely cracking open one eye, I search for some kind of reassurance that I'm not as horrible of a person as I'm beginning to think I am.

Following (adjective)
fol*low*ing:
Coming after in time or sequence

I don't wanna see, I don't wanna see anything
I don't wanna be, I don't wanna be lost again
("Grace," *Saving Jane*)

Big Gaping Hole

September 11, 2002

Today has been a day of many, many unexpected surprises and it started with my rude awakening from that dream I had with Kelly when I stood up to flag down the waiter at Chili's and my pregnant belly bashed into the table causing our drinks to spill everywhere.

Sure, Kelly's been showing up in my sleep a lot over the last year and she's been making a lot of jokes that a baby was on my horizon. But I have never in my life experienced being that pregnant and it felt so freakishly real. I woke clutching my stomach in panic thinking for sure something was growing in there. What I experienced in my sleep…well, it's just a whole new element of weirdness that I can't make any sense out of.

What bothered me most about the dream is that it painted a painfully realistic picture of what my life would've been like had I never sat down next to Leo at Buckley's that January night in 1998. There's no doubt in my mind that had I never met him, I wouldn't have realized how truly, madly and deeply miserable I was as Mrs. Gibbons. There's no doubt in my mind that I would've ultimately ended up pregnant with Kurt's baby and eating at a Chili's with my best friend as we planned a lame camping trip, while my obliviously adventurous husband was off at some stupid pilot training course in Nevada. *I most likely would've stuck with my life list.*

My day of unexpected surprises continued after the dream, on my drive into the studio. I wasn't prepared to see so many American flag-waving patriots paying tribute to the anniversary of 9/11, and I wasn't prepared for the emotional response it set off inside me. I felt overwhelming sadness for the victims of the tragedy, and for the first time since waking in Kurt's bed, I felt no sadness for myself. How could anyone who's alive and who has the potential to live a good life ever feel sorry for themselves when remembering 9/11? But when the flag-waving patriots became a blurred image in my rearview mirror, the image of waking in Kurt's bed catapulted to the forefront of my mind, causing me to hate those Muslim extremists more than ever. Had 9/11 never happened, Leo never would've left to help Taddeo. He never would've left me…leaving open that small window of opportunity for Kurt to creep back into my life and wreck it.

When I got to the studio, the girls tried their best to make me feel better about my wrecked life. Well, most of them. Something is definitely up with Megan since the fiasco at Kurt's house, and she's been unusually quiet about what may or may not have happened in his bed. But the other two gals…they showered me with support. Barbara, even going so far to say what might've happened that night wasn't entirely my fault. I love her for it, but she knows just as well as I do that my latest Chrissygan was a bombshell that only I'm responsible for. Yep, getting drunk at Kurt's house pretty much ruined my life.

Hitting up the cemetery today might not have been the best idea since it was already such an emotional one with all of the 9/11 business, but freaking Nicole and her crazy doctor schedule gave me no other choice. As usual, I enjoyed my fake conversation with Kelly, but it gave me no insight into the dream I had about being pregnant and no hope that I'd ever get Leo back. What were her exact imaginary words again? Oh yeah, *"Getting him back would probably be just as difficult as getting me back."* Great.

I didn't have the courage to admit my latest Chrissygan to Courtney and Nicole. Until I get some answers, it's best to keep them in the dark...where I still remain myself. I guess the upside about going to the cemetery is that I got to put a beer on Craig's tombstone and see him and Kelly close together. As gross as it sounds, it brought me a little peace.

The unexpected surprises continued at my last stop of the day – Kurt's house. It was the first time I saw him since that wretched night a little over two weeks ago. Oddly enough, despite how weird Megan's been, she offered to pick up Kendall the Sunday after it happened and deliver her back to him on Friday, so I could have a few more days to cool off. But unfortunately Megan had to go to New York for work, and I was forced to face him at the pick up today.

For the life of me, I can't figure out why was he so damn nice to me when I went there. I mean, I basically threatened him with his life when I stormed out of his house that morning. But there he was with his million dollar smile, open...*willing almost*...to talk about what happened. But I have no desire to rehash the bad choices I made that led to the big gaping hole in my heart, and I'm more than happy to leave the question of "Did I sleep with Kurt?" unanswered for the rest of my life. There's no point in knowing, other than to hate myself even more, if the answer is what I fear. So this evening I left Kurt's house in another blaze of anger.

Once back at the cottage, it looked like things had tapered off into the boring and predictable with Kendall's corn dog dinner and bubble bath, but then the most unexpected thing of the day happened when I tucked her into bed.

In the nine months since I've had guardianship of Kendall, I've never heard her refer to her mother as being dead. In fact, unless I bring Kelly up, she hardly ever comes up. So, it really threw me when during our game of eye spy with my little eye, she said, "Cuz I'm spyin' somedin' dat's dead" as she looked at her mother's picture.

Now taking the framed photo off of the nightstand, I sit beside Kendall to have the talk I've been dreading.

"You know who this is, right?"

"Yes."

"Do you wanna talk about your mommy?"

"I don't know her, do I?"

"I guess you really don't, huh?"

Almost shamefully, she shakes her head.

Wrapping my arm around her delicate little shoulders, I ask, "Would you like me to tell you some stories about your mommy?"

"Can't you just...be my mommy?"

I just remembered there was something very important I failed to cover in my sessions with Dr. Vikki. THIS!

Looking over at Kelly's picture, I silently tell her how very sorry I am for what I'm about to say.

"Sweetheart...I...I can be your mommy. If that's what you want."

With a single tear streaming down her cheek, she whispers, "I just wanna be like my fwends."

Knowing it's all Kelly wants for her too, I spring into action.

"Then, you know what, Sweetheart? We can make it happen, right now!"

Reaching across her bed, I grab the magic wand that she was playing with earlier.

"Here! All you have to do is wave that thing, cast a spell, and I'll officially be your mommy. I mean...if that's what you want."

"Looking at Kelly's picture, "But will she be mad at me?"

"No way! Your mommy in the picture was my best friend in the whole wide world and she trusted me to give you all of the love and attention you deserve. That's why you're my...you're my..."

"Ki-Ki, why are you crying?"

"Oh, they're happy tears, Kendall. You see, I've *always* wanted a daughter."

And given the recent course of events in my life, you'll no doubt be the only one I'll ever have.

"Then, it's magical, Ki-Ki!"

"How's that?"

"Because *I've* always wanted a Mommy!"

Wiping the tears off of my face, I jump up on the bed and announce, "Well, what are we waiting for then? Wave that wand and let's make it official!"

Hopping out of her blankets and now standing on the bed right beside me, Kendall starts waving the wand around my head.

"Hocus pocus, swammi Tommy, make Ki-Ki my...MOMMY!"

After she thumps me on the head with the wand, we stare at each other with wide eyes.

"Do you feel any different?"

Her eyes are darting around the room searching for some kind of new feeling.

"Nope. Do you?"

"Nope and you know why?"

"Why?"

Poking her in the tummy, I inform her, "Because I've already been your mommy for a really long time! And now, like all good mommies are supposed to do, it's time for me to tuck you into bed!"

After stuffing her under the covers like a burrito, Kendall excitedly asks, "When do I start calling you Mommy?"

Kissing her forehead, "That's up to you, Sweetheart."

Just as the door to the bedroom is about to close, she blurts out, "Will Weo be my daddy when he comes back or should I wave my wand at Ku-Ku?"

Oh, Christ.

"Well...I...I think we have some time to figure that out."

291

"Can I have two?"

"Lots of kids have two dads. The only rule I have as your...mommy..." Her giggle tells me how much she enjoyed that, "...is when the time comes to pick one...or two, we get to decide together. Sound good?"

"Soopa doopa good!"

"Sweet dreams, Hunny."

"I'm gonna dweam about snipes and my brand new backyard! What are you gonna dweam about?"

Relieved that I already turned out the light so she can't see my sullen face, I speak softly. "Most likely the exact same thing."

"Ki-Ki?"

"Yes, Kendall?"

"How many more days until Weo gets home?"

"Soon, Sweetie...soon."

After closing the door to the bedroom, I stagger to the kitchen sink to splash cold water on my face, hoping it'll magically wash away the mistake I made. A mistake that looks like it's about to prevent Kendall from getting everything she deserves. But minutes later, as I quietly sip my tea, nothing magical happens, there's only bitter acceptance that I royally screwed everything up.

Now, resting my body against the very countertop that Leo placed me on a few years ago, I let out a deep sigh and think about how good it is that Kendall has two million bucks in the bank. She's going to need it to buy herself a nice house with a big backyard, because I sure as hell can't afford to keep the one I bought for her now that I'm...alone.

Done

September, 2002

The yellow ribbons are still tied to the overpasses, but the people from yesterday who stood next to them waving their American flags are all gone. They've returned to their lives...probably nice normal unadulterated ones too.

I did a good job of hiding my latest Chrissygan from Nicole and Courtney at the cemetery yesterday, but it'll only be a matter of time before Kurt tells their husbands what happened. I'll deal with it when the stupid-ass cat gets out of the bag. I have much bigger fish to fry right now. And the conversation I had with Kelly at the cemetery yesterday did little to make me think the fish fry would be easy. Her imaginary voice of reason continues to haunt me... *"Getting him back would probably be just as difficult as getting me back."* Even Kendall's Magic 8 ball gave me a reading of "outlook not good" this morning when I asked it if Leo would ever forgive me.

After I drop Kendall at pre-school, I decide to make a self-deprecating stop at the new house to water the flowers I planted in the front yard just two days before the bottom fell out of my life...for the millionth time. As I'm lost in a daze with the hose, neighbors who I've already become fond of pass by and ask, "When's the big move in day?" I just shrug and murmur unintelligible jibber jabber.

To no avail, I've now left about fifty phone messages for Leo. He's a smart and responsible man, so I know he's fully aware of the financial burdens that are about to hit me with the new mortgage and the extended lease we signed on the cottage. But I'm starting to get nervous that my latest Chrissygan has made him not give a crap. And then I stare down at my ring. I

293

can't bear to take it off, which is ironic seeing as though I barely wore it the first few months I had it. *And why?* Oh, right…because I was trying to protect Numb Nuts from getting hurt. *And what did that get me?* Abso-freaking-NOTHING! *And what did it get me for feeling sorry for him when I found the picture of his college graduation?* It got me drunk! Everything I do and say to protect Kurt's feelings leads to a disaster. It always has and it always will. So why do I do it? Looking down at my watch, I mumble, "Maybe I'll finally figure out the answer to that question in about an hour."

As I'm turning off the hose, I hear my cell phone. Cranking the nozzle faster and then making a run for it, I'm too late. It stops ringing by the time I get to my car. Picking it off of the passenger seat, I scroll through the missed calls and my heart literally stops when I see the number. It's a New York prefix! I hit the send button and hold my breath as the line rings and rings and rings and then…

"Hi, Chrissy."

That's certainly not the voice I wanted to hear.

"Did you call to yell at me? Because if you did, I really don't think I can handle it right now, Taddeo."

"I didn't call to yell at you."

It's a shock and a relief all at the same time. It's shelief.

"Then please tell me he's on his way here to talk to me and you're calling to tell me to pick him up at the airport."

"He's not on his way."

"I swear nothing happened! Please tell me he believes that."

"Chrissy…"

"Damn it, Taddeo! Please tell me what to do!"

"Let him go."

"I can't!"

Obviously uncomfortable, he clears his throat.

"You have to. Look, for some reason you can't let go of your past and it's fucking him up."

"I'm not holding onto anything and—"

294

"Listen…I'm calling to tell you he thinks it's best to cut ties like this. He said you can tell Kendall whatever you want, but he won't be coming back."

"No! She adores him and—"

"That's up to you to deal with. Look, he's done. I'm sorry. As far as the house goes, you can buy him out by covering half of the down payment and assume the loan, or you can…"

Slumping down to the curb, I stop hearing everything Taddeo's saying. I stop seeing my new neighbors. I stop feeling. He's done. It's over. I believe it this time.

"Chrissy! Hello….*Are you there?*"

"I…I think so."

"I know it's a lot to figure out right now. Maybe talk to the real estate agent about your options. Leo's been in touch with her, and she knows what's going on."

Great. My agent knows my fiancé left me. He's done. It's over. I believe it this time.

"Can I talk to him?"

"Not gonna happen."

"If you could just convince him to talk to me…He'll listen to you! I know he will!"

"Chrissy, I tried, and you might not believe me, but I told him to listen to what you had to say. I'm his best friend…I hate seeing him go through this shit. But he doesn't…"

"He doesn't what?"

"He doesn't trust you…for like, the tenth time."

After a long moment of silence, I take a deep breath and ask, "He's done?"

"Yeah."

"It's over?"

"…Yeah."

"I believe it this time."

"Sorry, Chrissy."

"How come you're being so nice to me all of a sudden?"

"I dunno. Guess it's tough to beat someone when they're down. Or, maybe it's all of the 9/11 anniversary stuff. "

"Can't believe it's been a year. How are you holding up?"

I surprise myself by asking the unselfish question…and in the midst of my crisis. Maybe I'm growing up after all.

"It's been tough. Couldn't have done it without Leo. Maybe I feel a little guilty about that. I mean, if he didn't have to come here…"

"You didn't do this, Taddeo. It was all me…" After a long pause, "…Can you tell him something for me?"

"Sure."

"Tell him I know I betrayed his trust and I don't blame him for reacting like this."

"Okay."

"Tell him I know I don't deserve him."

"Okay."

"Taddeo?"

"Yes?"

"Please tell him I'll always love him."

Tough Love

September, 2002

Not a thing has changed since the last time I was here. And since *I'm* here…it seems not even me. The chairs are the same barfy mauve color. The art is the same garage sale looking crap. Even the same old tattered magazines are sitting on the shitty table. The only thing different about the room is that there's no Sad Frumpy Lady. Nope, *Barbara's* at work right now. *Barbara's* a normal functioning human being. *Barbara* isn't a colossal fuck-up that has to return to therapy because *Barbara* doesn't repeat the same mistakes in her life. *Barbara's* made some actual progress that…My internal tirade is abruptly interrupted by the familiar squeak of the door that leads from the offices to the lobby. I lift my head and am at once comforted that perhaps I'm about to make some actual progress too. Peering at me over the rim of her glasses, Dr. Maria exhales, "What did you do now, Chrissy?"

After an embrace that feels more like one shared between a mother and a daughter than a therapist and her patient, we walk silently back to her office. After I settle into my usual spot on the old grey couch, I look up at Dr. Maria and shake my head in total disbelief that I'm here.

"So…did you record my phone message again this time? Will there be another big fake celebration at the end of this process for all of my hard work and dedication to becoming a normal person?"

"I see you haven't lost your wit."

"I think it's the only thing I have left."

"Tell me why you're here, Hunny."

"I need help getting Leo back."

"First, why don't you tell me how you lost him."

One thing's for sure, I've learned not to beat around the bush on this couch anymore because it only takes me five minutes to tell Dr. Maria how I went from almost becoming Leo's wife and all of the fabulous perks associated with it like sex, houses, and fancy cars, to getting drunk at Kurt's house and waking up in his bed the next morning with no pants on.

Slowly removing her glasses, she takes a long sip of tea and then leans back in her chair. Awesome, it looks like she's already got a plan!

"If memory serves me, Leo's a passionate one, yes?"

"Yep."

"He's already forgiven you...*how many times in the past?*"

"At least ten, probably."

"Uh-huh...And he was always honest with you about how he felt about your ex-husband, right?"

"Right."

"Even so, he was...how did you put it, 'digging deep' and working on his jealousies so that he could marry you and be a part of your new life with..." Looking down at her notes, "...Kendall, correct?"

"Correct."

"Kurt has weekend visitation with the child?"

"Yes."

"Did Leo ever give you any indication that it would be okay for the three of you to have sleepovers?"

"No. Of course, not!"

Tossing her pad of paper on the table, she lets it rip.

"Then I don't know what the heck you expect me to do to help you, Chrissy. You screwed up. Now, if you want to talk about your feelings or some sort of depression you're experiencing from the breakup, we can do that. But as far as getting Leo back, you did it on your own before and you're going to have to do it on your own again, because that's not my job."

Who the hell is this woman and what has she done with my Dr. Maria?

"But I thought you could—"

"What, be a bounty hunter?"

"Well no, but I at least thought you might help me figure out why I made the stupid choice to get drunk with Kurt and sleep in his bed. If I'm ever lucky enough to explain what happened to Leo, I'm gonna have to understand it myself first, right?"

"Alrighty, now we're talking therapy. Ready for my assessment?"

"I think so."

"You haven't had any alcohol for nine months, which by the way is very impressive. But I think you forgot about the emotional effects a few drinks—"

"*A few?* I wish."

Ignoring my gross admission, Dr. Maria proceeds.

"We all know emotions will go one of two ways with that much alcohol; you'll either get super happy or super sad. Where did you go?"

"Sad."

"What triggered the sadness?"

"A picture of Kurt's college graduation and what he had to say about it."

"Did he say what you wanted him to say?"

"Yes, finally."

"And how did that make you feel?"

Is it just me or is this woman fast-tracking my therapy?

"Validated, but it was weird because the validation also made me…like I said, sad."

"Why do you think that was the case?"

"I guess I didn't like hearing that after all this time, everything his family failed to do for him that day really did break his heart. I dunno…hearing him say the words kind of broke mine all over again, and it didn't seem fair."

"It didn't seem *fair* that he shared his true feelings with you, it didn't seem *fair* that he was authentic with you?"

"It's way too late for that."

"Who are you to tell him how he should or shouldn't be? Isn't he the one that did that to you for all of those years? Wasn't that the main reason you grew to resent him?

"Excuse me?"

"He can be however he wants to be and as long as you choose to engage with him, you have to accept it. Seems to me we talked about this before."

Omigod, I hate it when she's right. And…she's *always* right.

"Chrissy, you didn't have to stay and chit-chat with him, you didn't have to drink all of that wine, you didn't have to let him expose his feelings to you. Get one thing straight, he didn't do anything to you other than be the thing you always asked him to be. If it makes you crazy, or causes you to make bad choices, then stay away."

"I tried! For like, the last year I've even been walking around mumbling, 'bad, bad things happen when there's exposure to Kurt!' But I always get sucked back in, and I can't figure out why the hell that is!"

"Guilt."

"But Kurt and I have been divorced for almost two years! I'm sick and tired of feeling guilty for making a choice I know was right. When is it gonna go away?"

"You said he broke up with his girlfriend recently?"

"Yes."

"And his best friend died?"

"Yep."

"Maybe you don't think he's moved on to a point where you feel like you can be happy given the pain he's feeling from all of that stuff, *on top* of the pain you caused him before it. I mean, for you to marry the man you essentially left him for…"

"For the millionth time, I didn't leave Kurt for Leo!"

300

"Yeah, but deep down you know he'll never see it any other way and that makes you incapable of making the choice to move on yourself. But remember what I told you a long time ago. Your choices should not be ones that you think will make you hurt less, they have to be the right choices."

"Yeah?"

"Well, as much as marrying Leo and living out your dreams seem like all of the right choices, I think they hurt you because you think they hurt Kurt. That's why I think you always sabotage them."

"I'm still trying to protect him, aren't I?"

"That's what it looks like, my dear."

"When will it end?"

"I also told you this a long time ago…It will end when you put your relationship with Leo first. And Chrissy, I also think you need to quit assuming what Kurt thinks."

Paying no attention to the second half of her response, I stare down at my ring that I still can't bring myself to take off and numbly ask, "What relationship with Leo?"

"That's up to you to figure out." Putting her hand on my knee, "But I'll be here for you if things don't work out the way you want them to."

After giving Dr. Maria a brief update on the only thing I seem to be doing well in my life—Kendall—I stand to hug her and thank her for the tough love. When I reach the door, she asks, "I have to know…off the record. Did you sleep with Kurt?"

"I don't think so."

"You don't *think* so?"

"I was *that* drunk."

"Oh, Lord. Well, what did he have to say about it?"

"Nothing."

"He didn't say one way or the other if it happened?"

Thinking really hard back to my conversation with him the morning after, I come to realize, "No actually. He didn't."

301

"Why do you think that is?"

"Maybe he knows the truth will destroy me."

"Interesting. So, you actually think he's trying to protect you?"

Staring out the window at the sun setting over the beautiful rolling hills of Danville, I whisper, "I'm afraid so."

But what I leave out is just how afraid.

Five Minutes

September, 2002

"So what you're saying is she didn't tell you a damn thing."
"She didn't have to. I already know what I have to do."

Throwing an airline ticket on the table, Slutty Co-worker says, "Me, too."

Numbly staring at her kind gesture, I sigh, "Well, we're obviously on totally different wave lengths because I was talking about sending my engagement ring back."

"No way! You have to see him in person!"

Looking at my bighearted friend like she's out of her ever-lovin' mind, I ask in amazement, "You *actually* want me to go to New York...so he can kick my ass?"

"No. So you can talk to him...work this out."

"I told you what Taddeo said! I can't just show up!"

"*Why not?* Isn't that what you did all of those other times, like at the Lafayette Reservoir, The Red Devil Lounge, The Round-Up, P.J. Clark's?"

"Well, yeah, but—"

"But schmut! Hunny, if there's anything you've taught me, it's to NEVER give up. YOU'RE GOING!"

"But Kendall..."

"Don't give me that as an excuse! It's Friday and Kurt will have her for the next two days. Megan's picking her up from pre-school and she's meeting Kurt at some stupid park. She said they have that Nepal crap to talk about anyway. Not sure what it is with that girl, but she's got a charity bug up her ass that I can't dig out!"

Not taking no for an answer, she rushes me out the door. Within minutes I find myself worriedly driving home to pack, praying Slutty convinced me to do the right thing. Believe me, all I want to do is see him. I feel like if I can just do that I'd be able to convince him of my innocence. *An innocence I have to believe exists.* But Taddeo's words weigh heavy on me and I don't doubt the gravity of them for one second.

"Let him go."

"He doesn't trust you."

"It's over."

And the way he said everything…it's like he felt sorry for me because he knew, this time, it really is over. Once I'm back at my cottage, I walk directly out to the deck and stare at the creek below, continuing to weigh my options, finally accepting the one that hurts the most. I have to set Leo free so he can pursue his own life list. My baggage has and always will be in the way of fulfilling his dreams.

Just like two years ago when I didn't have to tell Kelly if I went to New York to get Leo back, I don't have to tell Slutty Co-worker if I go now. I can go back to doing what I do best…lie. But I wonder….Just like two years ago, how will I ever rid myself of the desire I have for Leo if I don't hear it from him, in person, that he's done with me?

After splashing cold water on my face, I reach over and grab the towel that he left behind after 9/11. All this time, it's functioned as some sort of stupid tribute to his return. I'd look at it every so often and laugh about making him wash it when we finally lived together again or playfully slapping him on the ass with it. But ever since he hung up on me at Kurt's house, it's only functioned as a sad reminder of what I'll never have and I'm sick of looking at it. I yank it off of the towel bar, stomp to the hamper and attempt to throw it in but it gets caught on my ring. As much as I shake it to untangle it, it just keeps dangling.

In a fit of anger, I drop to the edge of the hamper and demand answers.

"KELLY? GRANDPA? CAN SOMEONE PLEASE TELL ME WHAT I'M SUPPOSED TO DO?"

After a few maddening minutes of silence, I tear the towel off of my ring, throw it in the hamper and trudge to the kitchen.

"WHAT NOW?"

Hitting the answering machine so it'll stop blinking at me, I hear the solution I was just praying for.

"Hi Chrissy, it's Dr. Maria. I forgot to remind you of something else I told you last December...Remember to always follow your heart. It'll take you where you need to go."

Without hesitation, I run to the closet and grab my carry-on bag and then to the hamper to retrieve the crunchy old towel and put it back in the bathroom...Hopeful it'll still get the washing I wish for *and* a few ass smacks.

With no time to spare, since I only have until five o'clock Sunday night, I rush to the airport just in time for the red-eye that Slutty Co-worker booked me on. Then, praying the entire flight that this trip turns out differently than my last trip to New York when I hunted down Leo, you know...when he left me hanging on the dark and snowy streets of Manhattan, I land at six in the morning without a plan...just like last time. So far...NOT so good.

With nothing to lose, I hop in a taxi and head to the W hotel where I book a room for one night. I shower, change, and for the first time ever, do very little to impress Leo with my looks. *This trip is all about what's on the inside.* Two hours later, with every ounce of courage I can muster up, I hop back in a taxi and give the driver Leo's address.

Because time is so critical, I don't dilly-dally when I arrive at the apartment like I did nearly two years ago outside of P.J. Clark's. I don't check my ass or my makeup in a window. I

305

don't flip coins, and I don't pace back and forth weighing my options. I exit the cab and promptly push the buzzer to his apartment as casually as if I'm the pizza delivery guy. *This trip is all about time management.* Magically, the front door of the building pops open without any security screening, and I slip inside unnoticed. I enter the elevator and like the addict I am, start to shake when I push the button that I know Leo's finger has pushed a thousand times before. On my way up, my mind gets the best of me and I start to consider the worst. What if, in an attempt to make Leo feel better, Taddeo has some girls over? I mean, thinking back to the Red Devil Lounge…he's been known to do it before. All of a sudden I begin to hit the buttons to make the elevator stop, but it's as if Kelly or my Grandpa are in control because the damn thing ignores me and goes straight to the top. Staring up at the Heavens, I whisper, "You guys better know what the hell you're doing." The elevator opens, and I cautiously peer into the quiet corridor. The door to Leo's apartment is propped open and now I know why I was buzzed in so easily. It looks like whoever's in there really was expecting a delivery.

Listening intently, I quickly surmise that there are no girls inside the apartment, only the sound of a baseball game. I gingerly push the door open a little wider and poke my head inside. He's in there…somewhere. My Leo drug percolates inside of me. I slowly enter the apartment. His trench coat is strewn over the console table, and my hand gently slides across it as my eyes dart around trying to soak up the place that he's called home for all of these months. Turning the corner of the entry way, I poke my head in the direction of the sound and find my love sitting on a leather couch, dully staring at the TV. My God, he's so beautiful. His broad back, his strong shoulders…the little specks of grey that are already peppering his dark black hair. He must've been working tirelessly on T.L. Capital. I'm completely lost in a daze as I study the intensely driven man who was supposed to become my husband…tomorrow. Everything is so calm, and it almost feels like I can fix the damage I've done, until…

"WHAT THE FUCK?"

My heart literally jumps out of my body and I spin around to confront Taddeo's loud and angry voice. I'm completely speechless. I still hadn't figured out what to say. *This trip is all about heart.* My heart that I have to pick up off of the ground.

"Jesus Christ, Woman, what part of let him go didn't you understand?"

Ignoring the big bastard, I turn to face Leo who's now on his feet and glaring at me.

"I had to see you."

From behind me, Taddeo boasts, "I told you he doesn't have anything to say to you!"

Ignoring him, I appeal to Leo, "I have a lot I need to say to you. *Please?*"

"No way, man! Do not let her do this anymore!"

By the look on Leo's face there's no doubt in my mind he's done and even though I have no idea what to say to convince him otherwise, I continue to beg, *"Please…you have to let me explain."*

"Aw, fuck this shit! You'll explain, he'll take you back, and then you'll screw up again. Seriously, dude! Don't fall for this crap!"

Spinning back toward Taddeo, I growl, "I don't get you! You sounded like you actually cared when you called me! Why are you being like this?"

"I told him to be nice."

Finally, his voice. I turn in its direction and plead once again, "Leo, please just let me talk to you."

After a few tortuous seconds, he nods at Taddeo to disappear. The pissed off Italian grudgingly grabs his coat and says he's going to watch the game at the bar down the street. As he storms out, he calls his best friend a stupid ass.

Leo sits back down on the couch, facing away from me.

307

"I'm only giving this relationship five more minutes, so you should probably start talking."

His voice is filled with the same hate he delivered to me on the night of his college graduation. The same hate I'd seen him give to others who had wronged him in the past. Unlike many of those others, I was lucky enough to get a second chance with him, because of dead people or whatever miraculous change of heart he experienced that caused him to take another stab at love with me, but what I'm detecting in him now tells me there will be no more chances.

"I never should've put myself in that situation at Kurt's house, and I'm sorry."

Silence.

"It was my birthday, and he felt bad that I was alone, so he offered me a drink. I accepted too many and it interfered with my judgment."

Silence.

"I dunno…I guess I thought it would be nice for Kendall to see us get along…for her to have some kind of a family night. I know it's stupid and I know it could've waited until you got back, but—"

"Was it nice for Kendall to see you naked in his bed?"

"Leo, I wasn't naked! You have to believe me, nothing happened!"

Hey, if I don't know for sure that anything happened then…NOTHING HAPPENED!

Standing to face me, he says what I already fear to be true.

"He wanted something to happen."

Now I'm silent.

"He wants two things: to get you back and to get back at me, and it looks like he's succeeding."

"No! He doesn't have me back! I'll never talk to him ever again if that's what it'll take for you to forgive me!"

Laughing in my face, he spitefully informs me, "How are you *not* gonna talk to him ever again, Chrissy? You're basically raising a kid together!"

"No! *We're* supposed to raise Kendall together. You and me!"

"GIVE ME A BREAK! IT WOULD'VE BEEN YOU, ME AND HIM AND YOU KNOW IT!" After calming down, he continues, "It's a good thing this happened before I moved back because you know what? I'm not *that* guy, Chrissy. I'm not someone who can share the scene with your ex-husband. Even though I knew it wasn't in me, I tried to dig deep and deal with it because we were already engaged and I *really* like Kendall. But this break up was unavoidable once I moved back to the Bay Area and we both know it."

"That's not true, we—"

"IT IS TRUE! Maybe you didn't have sex with him this time, but you used to and every time I see his face or hear his name I imagine it and it drives me crazy. I can't be with you when he's in the picture and now that you have Kendall he'll *ALWAYS* be in the picture."

"I won't accept this, Leo! There has to be something I can do!"

Confirming that there will be no more chances at love with him; he looks right through me and coldly says, "There's nothing."

He follows my eyes to the clock on the table and recognizes at the same moment as me that I've used up my five minutes.

Refusing to accept everything he's telling me and rejecting the inevitable, I shake my head, and whimper, "I don't think I can do this. I can't walk out of here and never see you again."

"It's why you shouldn't have come."

To the extent that I was praying for it not to be true, *this trip is all about closure.*

Tainted Love

September, 2002

As much as I don't want to admit it to myself, Leo's right. It will always be me, him *and* Kurt raising Kendall, and given the way Leo and I are wired to love, it will never work. If the truly, madly, deeply tables were turned, I'd have to make the same choice as he did and end the relationship.

I shift my gaze from the clock back to Leo and slowly nod my head in defeat. He shakes his in disbelief. Realizing the enormity of a face-to-face good-bye, he suddenly puts his anger aside and speaks to me with his eyes. They're saying, "We could've avoided this pain had you just stayed away." As much as I know his eyes are right and that I should leave, I *cannot* willingly quit my drug.

"Please tell me how I'm supposed to walk away from the only person I've ever been real with?"

Still, he just continues to shake his head.

"How do I flag down a taxi...sleep in a hotel room twenty minutes from you? Leo, please tell me how I'm supposed to get on a plane tomorrow knowing I'll never see you again?"

Demanding I help him right back, he asks me, "How do I tell you to go away when I can barely tell myself to stay away from you?"

All of my past break-ups with Leo were angry and tumultuous. When he told me we were done after my surprise party in 1998, when he told me we were done the night of his college graduation in 1999, when he told me we were done on the snowy streets of Manhattan in 2000, each break-up lacked the love that for the most part we gave so easily to each other and I *think* it was why, each time, I was never able to move on. I felt like I needed to be faithful to the deep loving connection we shared, and I found it incredibly hard to be with another man. I never felt like those thoughts were something anyone could understand, not even Dr. Maria, so I kept them to myself and I struggled with them. I struggled with them when I traveled to Los Angeles and forced myself to kiss the tatted up attorney, Mark Wiseley. I struggled when I, oh Jesus, dry humped the Cal Berkeley quarterback. I fear if I walk out of here right now with all of the angry feelings Leo just expressed, I'll be stuck forever. I'll never be able to move on without him, and I'll always feel the need to be faithful to him. As if he feels the same way, he walks up to me and leans his forehead against mine.

"I wish I could be the kind of guy who could go along with the setup you and he have."

"I know."

"I wish I could put my jealousies aside and share Kendall with him."

"I know."

"I wish I didn't care about you walking out of here, about you alone in your hotel room or flying home tomorrow…I wish so badly it didn't have to be this way…" Pulling back to look at me, "…I have *never* loved anyone as much as I love you…but that love fucks me up, Chrissy, and that's why it has to be this way."

Knowing my relationship with Kurt can't go away because of Kendall, I know my relationship with Leo has officially run out of time. But this break-up is so different than all of our others. Whenever we broke up before, I always had the hope we'd get back together and it was that hope that prevented me from officially turning into a Sad Frumpy Lady. My cracking voice wonders out loud, *"How do I leave here with no hope?"*

"Like I said…how do I tell you how to do something I can't even do myself?"

Doing what I think I need for closure so that I can hopefully get on with my life, I gently cup his face with my hands and kiss him. It's a kiss that starts off modestly and without expectation, but almost as quickly as it starts, it grows into something passionate and familiar. Disappointed in himself, Leo pulls away.

"This isn't a good idea."

The drug, now boiling in my system, compels me to fight for this kind of closure.

I breathlessly beg, "Why? Breaking up the other way never worked for us."

Unmistakably let down in his lack of self-control, Leo tilts his head back and lets out a deep moan. At first he resists kissing me back, but ultimately the deep connection of our tainted love wins over and he picks me up and carries me to his room.

Knowing that words will get us nowhere at this point, we withdraw into our own thoughts and devour each other knowing it will be the last time. Our approaches to what we're doing are completely different. Leo, angry at himself, intermittently shakes his head knowing that making love to me is counter-productive to getting over me. While I, knowing it will be my last time with him, move slowly and methodically. I want…No, I *need* to remember everything.

He removes all of my clothes, gently lays me on the bed, and then takes his self-deprecating time to kiss every inch of my body before he stands in front of me, removes his own clothes and then delicately lies down beside me. Conscious that I'll have to leave his apartment the minute this is over, I nudge him onto his back. I kiss his chest, then his belly, and work my way down to his pelvis where I take him into my mouth. I never thought it possible prior to meeting him, but his adoration of me has always made this a pleasurable act and I'd do it every single night if he asked me to. His pulsations tell me when to back off and not wanting the moment to end, I do.

"Chrissy, what are we doing?"

313

"What we'll never have with anyone else."

"It's making things harder."

Traveling back up to his lips, I beg him to answer the question, "How could it be any harder, Leo?"

Feeling like it's disrespectful to sleep with a woman he's breaking up with, he feels obliged to defend his principles.

"I want you to know, I wouldn't be doing this unless I loved you."

"And I wouldn't let it happen otherwise."

And then, just like he did the very first time we ever made love, he takes my hand and places it on his heart, the beat as steady and hard as it was that night four years ago. And also just like that night, I do absolutely nothing to stop him as he pulls his body on top of mine. And just like the overwhelming feeling I had the first time this ever happened, like a woman is supposed to love a man, I love him. The only thing different about what's happening right now and the night we first made love is that back then he said, "Once this happens, I'm not letting you out of my life." Right now, all I can hear in my head is, "When this is over, you have to be out of my life." But it doesn't matter. Our relationship started with a deep loving connection and I need it to end with one. And when Leo enters my body that's all I can feel. I hold on to him as tightly as possible to hang on to the feeling for as long as possible.

He held me in his arms when the moment was over, and as long as he did I wasn't going anywhere. But when he dozed off, that's when I knew it was now or never. To stay with him until the morning would only result in another sad conversation with the same sad outcome. With Kurt a part of Kendall's life, it will always be constant torment for Leo. *I have to release him from the torment.*

As soon as I hear the soft purr of Leo's sleepy breath, I slip out from under his grasp and stand by the edge of the bed, staring at him until I hear Taddeo enter the apartment, see my

314

shoes in the hallway and say "You've gotta be fucking kidding me," before closing his own bedroom door.

After quietly gathering my clothes and putting them on, I slip my beautiful engagement ring off of my finger and gently set it on his nightstand. Then, I mentally yank the Leo syringe out of my vein that's been stuck there from the moment I met him, walk out of his fancy New York apartment, and away from the man who taught me what real love is supposed to be like...because he asked me to.

Vomit

October, 2002

"You look like shit."

"Screw you! *You* look like shit!"

"No I don't! Look at my rosy cheeks!"

Kelly's right. Ever since last March she's looked amazingly refreshed and it bugs the crap out of me. I should really ask her what spa she's been going to.

Giggling, she asks me, "You wanna know why?"

"Why what?"

"Why you look like shit."

"I already know why! I've been working my butt off opening that new studio in…in… Jesus, my memory is for shit these days! I can't even remember where the damn place is!"

"I know why your memory is bad, too, and boy oh boy is it ever gonna freak you out."

Our food arrives, and the minute it lands in front of me I push it away.

"Not hungry?"

"Not at all. And the smell…it makes me nauseous!"

Kelly flicks a French fry at me and worriedly insists, "Chrissy I think you need to get your head out of your ass and wake up."

"I'm trying!"

Grabbing my wrists, she shakes them and yells, "NO, REALLY WAKE UP! IT'S COMING! IT'S COMING!"

I snap out of my dream just in time to run to the bathroom and throw up.

After wiping up the mess, I check on Kendall to make sure I didn't wake her with the ghastly noise, before heading to the kitchen to make a cup of tea. Steeping my bag, I softly glide my hand across the countertop that Leo placed me on during Holy Fucking Shit night. That night was one of a million exciting firsts I shared with him. My hopes were high so many times during our relationship that we would make it. And so many times I managed to royally screw everything up. I numbly sip my tea. Then, I do what I do every morning…count the days since I last saw the man who was the love of my life.

It's been over a month since I left his New York apartment. Remarkably, I was able to hail a cab without melting down, lay in my hotel bed without wanting to kill myself, and I flew home looking about as normal as anyone else on the plane (which isn't saying much because most New Yorkers look like walking zombies). Because of the little girl in the other room I had no choice but to stay calm and persevere, so that's what I did. Of course, it doesn't mean that every single day since I left him hasn't hurt like a mother fucker.

I think the hardest part about coming home was telling Kendall that Leo and I decided to go our separate ways. After I explained that he wouldn't be moving in with us, she got her snipe-hunting night vision goggles that he sent her a few months back, handed them to me and said, "I guess I don't need these anymore," and then somberly walked back into her room. I definitely won't be winning any 'guardian-of-dead-best-friend's-daughter-mother of the year' awards any time soon.

The second hardest part about coming home has been deciding what to do about the new house in Lafayette. With the

318

money I still have saved from the sale of my Danville house and what I earn at Forever Young, Inc. I can easily buy out Leo's half of the down payment. But it's the monthly overhead of the place that scares me. I'd have to kiss things good-bye like facials, fancy restaurants, and flashy shoes, and I just don't think I'm ready to do that. Even so, Kendall and I are crawling all over each other in the cottage and something needs to be done. I asked the real estate agent if I could have until December to decide what to do, and after running it by Leo, she told me it would be fine. A thought suddenly occurs to me and I slam my tea cup down. *That real estate agent is cute and single!* What if she's flirting with him now that she knows I'm out of the picture? Oh my God, I'll kill her!

Dammit! How come I don't know Leo's voicemail code? No! Calm down, Chrissy! It's for the better. Life will be better for you if you don't know about his love life....something he's bound to have again one day. If you had his code, you'd just go back to being a psycho and dial in ten times a day looking for status updates. It would break you down...it would DESTROY YOU! Yep, Leo's voicemail, while it was a less stimulating drug than the actual physical Leo, it was a drug nonetheless and my life is better without it.

And with thoughts of Leo doing to my real estate agent what he did to me on "Holy Fucking Shit" night, I slam my tea cup down on the counter one more time and run to the bathroom to throw up again.

SAY WHAT?

October, 2002

"**Y**ou look like shit."
       "Wow...First Kelly, now you?"
"Huh?"
"Never mind."
Holding Kendall's hand, I brush past Slutty Co-worker and walk to Megan's little office. It's crammed with boxes.
"*Seriously, Megan?* I mean, you've got to either ship this crap to the Nepanese people or donate it to Goodwill. I can barely find you in here."
"It's *Nepalese*, Chrissy."
"I don't care what the..."
Looking down at Kendall who's looking up at me with wide eyes, expecting a bad word, I rethink my approach.
"I don't care what the *bleep* it is. It's making me crazy!"
"Is that what you came in here to tell me?"
Now trying my best to be sweet, I tell her the real reason I'm here.
"Actually, no...Can you drop Kendall off at school? Pretty please? I feel like..."
Knowing the S word is about to explode from my mouth, Kendall tugs my hand and disapprovingly shakes her head.
"I feel like pooh-pooh."
Looking back down at Kendall, I ask her if that's better.
"Yep!"
"And yep, I can take her to school! Come on Kendall, hop on my back!"
The second they're gone I slide down the wall and hang my head between my legs.

"Been hittin' the bottle again, Hunny?"

I pull my head up and glare at Slutty Co-worker.

"Very funny. Must be the flu or something."

Barbara, who just walked in with a sassy new cut and color, takes one look at me and says, "That's *not* the flu, Sweetie Pie...you're pregnant."

In unison, Slutty and I let out a whopping, "SAY WHAT?"

"Yep, I know that look, and I bet you my next paycheck, there's a baby in that belly!"

Almost not wanting it to be true as much as me, Slutty Co-worker starts rambling off a million questions. I immediately throw my hands in the air to stop the annoyance.

"WHOA, hold on! No one's pregnant! It's just the flu!"

Barbara, who's now laughing, kneels down beside me.

"Is that why you fell asleep at your desk twice last week? Is it why, all of a sudden, you run out of the building when you smell my food heating up in the microwave?"

"Okay, first of all, *helloooooo*, I'm raising a child...I'm tired! And second of all, that Berkeley Indian food cart shit smells like...SHIT! If you haven't noticed, *everyone* runs out of the building!"

The new and improved Barbara stands, waves me off, and walks down the hallway singing, *"Somebody's gonna have a baaaaaby!"*

Slutty Co-worker looks down at my clearly puzzled face.

"You wanna talk this out?"

Scrambling to my feet, I freak, "Let's go find a calendar."

Settling at her desk with our day-timers in front of us, I start shuffling through the pages.

"That day! Look, it's in black and white! I got my last Depo-Provera shot on July nineteenth! See, there's no way I can be pregnant!"

"Hold on there, Fertile Franny. *Are you sure?* Because according to my calendar, you took half of that day off to get the keys to your new house, and before you left to do that you were here the whole time."

"What? Let me see that!"

I nervously grab at her calendar as she moves to look at her computer screen.

"Yep, and see right here? Here's an email I sent to Megan on that day bitching about how much time your house hunting had taken and that I was glad you went to get the keys, and it was finally over."

"Hold up. You guys talk shit about me?"

"All the time…but stay on point, this is serious! Do you think that maybe in the excitement of getting the keys to the house you forgot to go to the doctor?"

Like a shot of lightening…No scratch that. Like baby kicking in the womb, all of a sudden I remember exactly what happened.

"Oh shiiiiiiiiiiit."

"What did you do, Doll?"

"Ohhhhhh, no, no, no, no, no. This is *not* good."

"Oh boy, what's not good?"

"It's coming back to me now."

"Spill it."

"I was *supposed* to get it after I got the keys, but when I called Leo from the new house and he told me the news about postponing his arrival until September, I remember thinking, 'Heck, I guess I don't have to get that shot today,' and I decided to stay at the house and play with Kendall in the backyard."

"And you never rescheduled?"

In total disbelief, I sift through the pages of my calendar and murmur, "How could I have forgotten?"

"Hold on, it *never* crossed your mind that you forgot when you were having sex with Leo last month?"

"No. And I even pulled my calendar out on the flight home to see when my next shot was scheduled."

"When is it?"

Looking down at my calendar, deflated, I tell her, "Tomorrow."

"Guess you can forget about going to that one, huh?"

Nervously staring at my friend, I wonder out loud, "Do you think Barbara's right?"

"Only one way to find out."

Twenty minutes later, after a quick run to the drug store, Slutty Co-worker sneaks a peek at the stick I peed on three minutes ago and vivaciously asks, "Are you ready?"

I never thought, once I became an adult, that being pregnant could be a nightmare. After all, it was engraved on the Life List I made when I was sixteen. Even though that list didn't pan out like I dreamt it would, and I promised myself I was done with lists forever, I couldn't resist and made that new little one right after Leo suggested we get married in Fiji. Everything was falling into place and it seemed safe to start planning my life again. And item number six on my old list, to have children, became item number three on my new list, and I happily dreamt of the day I would become pregnant. However, I happily dreamt about it as a married woman...not as a knocked-up, dumped and dejected single mom who's barely capable of raising the kid her dead friends left her. But all of that stuff is *not* why a positive pregnancy result would be a nightmare. It's what I'm too afraid to admit that makes it one.

Closing my eyes, I whisper, "I'm ready."

"It's negative."

Because the super emotional side of me swears she already felt contractions, I snap open my eyes and look at Slutty Co-worker, shocked and confused.

"Wow. Guess I dodged a huge bullet with that one, didn't I?"

"Why's that? I mean, it's not like I'm into trapping guys by getting knocked up, but you definitely would've gotten Leo back."

"I'm not so sure about that."

"What are you talking about?"

"I didn't tell you this because quite frankly, it scared me a little, but when you were asking me those questions about the night I spent at Kurt's house—"

"Oh God, the underwear...was it crunchy?"

"Would you stop with that!"

In actuality, the peek I had of the underwear the morning I got home from his house revealed no such crunch. Even so, the lack of evidence did nothing to curb my concern over what might've actually happened in his bed.

"What then?"

"Well, you asked me how I knew if nothing happened with Kurt, and I said I knew because I'd never cheat on Leo."

"But?"

"But Kurt never actually denied it."

"Well, this is getting interesting..."

"The thing is I don't remember much of anything from that night. To be honest...I might've slept with him."

"Oh boy."

"The only thing Kurt told me after that night was whatever happened...wasn't his fault. I've been trying to convince myself he was referring to merely waking up in his bed, but whenever I add up the facts...lots of wine...the emotional moment we shared with the graduation picture...the tank top and underwear...all signs point to the obvious. *Don't they?"*

My supportive sidekick knows I'm about to lose it and wraps her arms around me.

"It's been *killing* me that I might've betrayed Leo, but since I knew, or at least I thought I knew, I was protected by the shot, it's been kind of easy to believe what I wanted to believe..."

"...Because there would never be proof to the contrary."

"Exactly."

I turn toward my friend so she can see how disgusted I am.

"Now can you see how being pregnant would've been a total nightmare?"

"Absolutely. You slept with Leo two weeks after that night. You'd have a little baby daddy mystery on your hands, wouldn't you?"

I look into her eyes and insist she tell me the truth.

"Do you think I could've actually slept with Kurt?"

"Not a chance, I know how much you love Leo. But you should probably find out for sure."

"Why?"

Handing me the stick, "Because you're pregnant."

Hush Little Baby

November, 2002

I remember this feeling. It's a larger than life kind of thing. It's a feeling you can only understand if you've been told you're pregnant. In an instant, you're not *just* you, you're two people. Your life is over and just beginning all at the same time. You'll never be ready for it...even when you've been planning for it your entire life. And you certainly can't be ready for it when you don't even know who the father is.

"What did you just say?"

Handing me the stick, Slutty Co-worker giddily says, "See right there? It's blue, and blue means you're pregnant!"

Frantically flipping the box over so I can match the results, it's easy to conclude that, I am, indeed pregnant.

"Why the hell did you tell me it was negative?"

"Just fucking with you. It might be the last time we have fun like this now that you're gonna be all maternal. Pregnant women are so...blah."

"Holy shit, I have a baby...growing inside of me...RIGHT NOW?"

They're the exact words I spoke when I found out I was pregnant at seventeen and even though I'm thirty-three now, they're coming out as frightened and confused as they did back then.

"Yep. And now that we've established that, I guess it'd be a good idea to establish who the father is."

Oh my God! This is a total nightmare! I'm officially a candidate for one of those 'who's my baby daddy' episodes of *The Jerry Springer Show.*

Judging by the look on my face, Slutty feels compelled to make the most horrid of horrid remarks, "That is...if you decide to keep it."

This isn't how it's supposed to be. I'm not supposed to be comparing myself to Jerry Springer trash, and I'm not supposed to be asked if I'm going to keep my baby. I'm a grown-up now! A real live child psychologist even called me one! Someone please tell me, HOW IS THIS MY PATHETIC LIFE...AGAIN?

"Chrissy, you are gonna keep it...*right?*"

Leo doesn't want me anymore. We made our break, and I have no right to ruin his life for the millionth time. I will never tell him about this.

"Hunny, are you in shock?"

And there's no way I'm asking Kurt if this is his. I don't want to know if I slept with him. It would make me sick knowing I did that to Leo. I will never tell him about this.

"You're freaking me out, girl. Can you please tell me what you're thinking?"

But how long can I keep a pregnancy a secret? Leo's no problem because he's on the east coast, but I see Kurt almost every Friday and Sunday when we exchange Kendall. Eventually he'll find out...and if he asks if it's his, then I'll know the ugly truth about what really happened that night.

"You're turning white. Sit tight, I'm gonna get you some water."

How will I tell Kendall? *What will I tell Kendall?* Should we move into the Lafayette house that I can barely afford? I can't bear to sell it though. It's the dream house I was supposed to share with my dream husband as we raised our dream family. I look up toward the sky and internally scream, SOMEONE TELL ME WHAT I'M SUPPOSED TO DO? And then I remember what happened the last time I begged for the answer to that question...Dr. Maria called to tell me to follow my heart, it'll take me where I need to go. Looking at the blue stick I ask myself, *what does your heart want, Chrissy?* Within a nanosecond, my mind answers. *My heart wants a family.* Like a bottle going into a screaming baby's mouth, I'm all of a sudden composed. Kendall, this baby, and I are going to move into that damn dream house, and I'm going to FINALLY do what I should've done starting all the way back at sixteen. I'm going to take it day by day. No lists. No expectations of what the perfect life is supposed to look like.

"Here's your water, Hunny. Now…please tell me what the heck you're gonna do."

I've made a lot of mistakes in my life, but what I did when I was seventeen was, by far, the worst. Sliding my hands down to my belly, drawing strength from my new family member, I answer my old friend.

"Of course, I'm keeping this baby."

"Oh, this is so exciting! When can we start telling people?"

"Never."

The pictures tell the story
I took them off the wall
It's hard enough to get through
I still can feel the fall
Do you even think of me at all?
("Only you," *Matthew Perryman Jones*)

It's Time

November, 2002

It was four years ago that I signed the lease to my cottage. The courage it took for me to put my name on that contract...the courage it took for me to break the news to Kurt that I was leaving him...the courage it took for me to sleep in it alone for the first time, all of it is something I wish I could write a book about. And the first thing I would write is how much harder it was to leave that cottage than I ever thought possible. My little six hundred square foot dwelling has saved my life over and over again. Leaving it, feels like a death.

My landlord, although bummed he wouldn't be getting any more of my money, was accommodating when I had to break the three year lease that Leo and I just signed a few months ago. And knowing I had to break it because we split up and I no longer had a man in my life, he was nice enough to help me pack up the place. Standing in it now, cold and empty just like it was the first time I stepped foot in it, I'm just as alone and scared as I was back then. Before I shut the door for the last time, I take one last tour of my love shack.

First, I scan the vacant bathroom, and my eyes land on the place they had so many times over the last year. The towel I had expected so much out of, is now sitting in the bottom of a box

331

somewhere. When push came to shove, I couldn't bring myself to throw it away. Aside from my Banana Republic ring, it's the only physical reminder I have left of Leo, unless, of course...the human being growing inside of me is his. With that stomach-turning-mystery-of-a-thought, I move on to the bedroom. I stare forever at the outline of where the bed used to be, the bed where I gave everything I had to Leo. The mattress is now in the dump and the frame has been donated. I never want to be reminded of what I'll never experience again. Next, I walk out to the deck and stare blankly at the creek, feeling sad I didn't do it a lot more while I lived here. Finally, I walk to the kitchen, the place where so much happened. I glide my hand across the countertop one last time and touch the wall where Leo placed my hands the night I "bumped" into him at The Round Up. I close my eyes and feel everything all over again. The temptation to change my mind about leaving the cottage hits me hard, and I swiftly move my hands to my stomach to draw the strength I need to move on to the next stage of my life.

My landlord pops his head inside and tells me the U-Haul is ready and he's waiting to follow me to my new house...that I'm now the sole owner of and can barely afford. The real estate agent made the buyout of Leo's share of the home super easy and there wasn't any need to deal directly with him on the transaction. I appreciated her willingness to get the job done as quickly as possible, but I pray it wasn't so she could *do him* as quickly as possible. The thought of Leo even giving her the gift of his voice over the phone sends me into a frenzy, so I have to force any and all thought of him giving more to her out of my mind. Rubbing my stomach, I exhale, "It's not healthy for either of us, is it?"

When I know my landlord is back outside, I take a Swiss army knife out of my pocket and start carving. Before I close the kitchen cabinet, I take a moment to admire my work. Carved deep into the wood are the words, "I loved here." Then I bend down and grab the only box I wouldn't let my landlord help me with, the one containing Kelly's videos. Standing in the entryway, I give my refuge one last glance before saying "thank you" and then I close the door for the last time.

During the ten minute drive to my new house, I mull over my next moves as well as the ones taken over the past few weeks, like my first doctor's appointment. Slutty Co-worker, who so far is the only person who knows about the baby, came along for moral support. Actually, it was more like slapstick support...

"Can you estimate the time of conception?"

Before I have a chance to answer the doctor, my dear old friend chimes in with, "Ain't that the million dollar question?"

"I beg your pardon?"

"Well...she slept with her ex-husband *and* her ex-fiancé within..." looking back at me, "How many weeks between the two, Hunny?"

Mortified, I attempt to clear things up for the doctor.

"I'm not *exactly* sure if I slept with my ex-husband, but if I did, it would've been two weeks before I slept with my...uh, my ex-fiancé, August thirty-first."

Jesus, how is it that a woman who has only slept with two men in her entire life can have so many exes?

Confused, the doctor asks, "You're not *exactly* sure if you had sex with your ex-husband?"

"She was drunk."

I shoot a look at Slutty to stop doing me favors.

"I...um...I had a lot of wine that night, but I want you to know it had been nine months since I had anything to drink. It's not like I'm an alcoholic or anything."

"Yep. Thank God those days are over!"

The doctor peculiarly brushes off Slutty's remark and hits me with the guilt I knew I had coming.

"Being highly intoxicated isn't exactly the most ideal way to bring a child into the world."

Thanks, Fuckhead.

"I'm aware of that, and it scares me. If this baby was conceived drunk..." Seriously! It does NOT get more Jerry Springer than this "...will it be okay?"

"Everything should be fine. I know being a first time parent can be really scary—"

"Oh, she's not a first time parent! She has a daughter!"

I shoot Slutty Co-worker another shut-the-F-up look.

Baffled by the twist and turns of this conversation, my grouchy doctor scratches his head and asks, "You do?"

Oh brother.

"Yeah, I'm the guardian of my dead...best friend's...daughter."

"Where's *that* father?"

Oh sweet Jesus. This is brutal.

"Uh, he's dead too."

I can tell by the look on the doctor dude's face that he's wondering if he should call social services or the police and his judgmental looks are all my big-mouth friend can take. She jumps out of her chair and attacks.

"No! No! No! You don't look at this woman like that!"

I try to interrupt the outburst, but there's no stopping her.

"Sure, she might sound like a fuck-up, *Doctor*, but this is a good woman with a heart as big as her stomach's about to get! Two of her dearest friends are dead, and she's raising their child like she's her own, and she's doing a better job than you or anyone else could do. And yes, she might've slept with two men in two weeks, but she loved both of those guys more than I've ever loved half of one. So just lube up that stick thing, put it inside of her, and tell us everything's okay, because we have a baby to plan for and your asshole looks are holding us up from doing that! Got it?"

And that's how my first doctor's appointment went. Probably not something for the baby books, that's for sure. But I left there that day knowing two things, Slutty Co-worker will do anything to protect me, and I'm due on either June seventh or June twenty-second…depending on who the father is.

Now, just five minutes from my new house, I'm idling at the stop light in front of The Round Up. Carefree girls, who aren't eight to twelve weeks pregnant, wander in and out like remembering to apply their lip gloss is the most pressing thing they have to do. I grab the rear view mirror and stare at my make-up-less mom face. I'd look prettier than this if Leo was with me. We'd be making this drive together, laughing at The Round Up people and excited about meeting the furniture delivery guys at the new house. It would be a day to cross off of our shared life list. But no, we have separate lists now. He's probably hanging out with the types of girls I'm watching go in and out of The Round Up, and you know what? He deserves it. He deserves to be young. He deserves better than my baggage. The light turns green and in the nick of disparaging time, I hit the gas.

Rounding the corner to my new house, I see the delivery guys loading a crib into the garage. Slutty Co-worker bought it for me. It's vintage white wrought iron and it's absolutely stunning. But as beautiful of a gift as it is, it can't go in the house yet…I still have to tell Kendall about the baby. I park on the street and watch from the car as my landlord immediately gets busy unloading what little belongings I have, and a few of my new neighbors start to approach my car with coffee and muffins. Yep, as alone and scared as I was moving into my cottage four years ago, it's nothing compared to what I'm feeling right now. Placing my hand on the box of videos that's buckled into the passenger seat, I whisper, "I think it's time to start watching you."

Interrogation

"What's with the moo-moo?"

It's been months since I've been to the cemetery and months since I've seen Courtney and Nicole. Work, Kendall, the studios, morning sickness...life, have taken over. And in watching Kelly's videos, I know she'd approve of my absence.

I started at the beginning, just like she asked me to do in her letter. The very first night I moved into my new house, after I kissed Kendall goodnight, I made a cup of that damn Nepalese tea, settled into my brand new big bed and put on the first video, titled, *Three years old,* which was Kendall's age when Kelly got sick. I couldn't have done it even two months ago. I still wasn't ready to see her...to hear her. But with each passing pregnant day, I needed Kelly's voice of reason more and more. So, I closed my eyes, blindly aimed the remote at the television, hit play, and there it was.

In classic Kelly style there wasn't any long drawn out dramatic explanation for making the videos, no mention of cancer or death, nor was there any gooshy pronouncement of her love for anyone or anything. Knowing time was of the essence, she got right to the point. She spoke of temper tantrums and healthy snacks and requested that Kendall be read to every single night and taken to the library at least once a week. Eyes still closed, I let out a little, "Uh-oh, better get on that." She encouraged Craig to keep his cool during the times when Kendall would test him and reminded him that she never yelled and hardly used profanity and expected him to follow her model. Knowing I'd dropped the S bomb in front of Kendall at least twenty times, I whispered, "Oh crap." Then, Kelly moved on to the importance of staying ahead of Kendall's needs and that's when my eyes finally opened, literally and figuratively. When she said the words, "Never let Kendall's demands get ahead of what you've planned, even if it means losing sleep and blowing off your friends. Your life and hers will only be as calm as you make it," I froze. It's exactly what I needed to hear, and I paused the video to think long and hard about her message.

For so many months, I've been terrified to watch the videos. I didn't think I had it in me to look at my best friend who knew she was going to die. My best friend, who knew she would not live to see the day her daughter turned four. But I forgot how strong Kelly was, and I underestimated her reasoning. She made these videos in the midst of chaos, knowing her family's life could only be as calm as she designed it to be. And now that I'm in the midst of a little chaos of my own, there is so much I can learn from them. Now that Kendall's turning five next month, and now that I'm going to have my own child, I can't afford to let the videos gather anymore dust. As much as Kendall needs the information on them, I do, too.

Pressing play, the video cut to Kelly reading Kendall's favorite book, *Goodnight Moon.*

"...In a great green room, tucked away in bed, is a little bunny. 'Goodnight room, goodnight moon.' And to all the familiar things in the softly lit room—to the picture of the three little bears sitting in chairs, to the clocks and his socks, to the mittens and the kittens, to everything one by one—he says goodnight."

And then, without shedding a tear, my strong friend said, "Good-night, Sweetheart. I love you, and I'm always with you."

I walked to Kendall's room and repeated the words to her in her sleep, and then headed back to my new bed with plans to fall fast asleep before thoughts of Leo highjacked my mind, but I made the mistake of stopping in the bathroom to pee on the way. In a box, right in front of me as I sat on the toilet, was the towel Leo left behind after 9/11. Feeling overwhelmed and lonely in my new home, I was relieved I hadn't thrown it away and fell asleep that night, and every night since, with it pressed firmly against my heart. The next day, I got a library card, stocked the house with healthy snacks, and Kendall and I started planting a vegetable garden in the backyard. Most importantly, I assembled a swear jar and said good-bye to my two favorite words, *shit* and *fuck*. New baby…new house…new life…new calm.

Now approaching my best friends who are already settled on top of Kelly's grave, I don't feel an ounce of guilt that I haven't been here very much. Kelly would appreciate the calm I've been hard at work creating. She would much rather I live my life than reflect on a life I'll never live, which is usually what happens when I come here. Nevertheless, it's nice to see Courtney and Nicole, and unload a few things that are essential in my quest for calm.

"It's not a moo-moo, Nic. It happens to be Juicy Couture and it's all the rage these days."

"Well, it makes you look pregnant."

"Probably because I am."

Speculating that I might be telling another one of my famous fibs, my doctor friends just stare at me in silence.

"Around twelve weeks, actually."

"Hold on, *you're serious about this?*"

I place Nicole's hand on my small, hard bump and give her an eyebrow raise.

"Holy moley…" Looking at Courtney, "…Either she has some serious gas or the girl's prego."

"Was there a wedding? I mean, I don't remember getting an invitation, do you Nicole?"

"Ahhhhh, *nooooooo*. Jesus, Chrissy! Why didn't you tell us you were pregnant sooner?"

"I didn't know myself until last month."

"It sounds like something that would slip through the cracks with you!"

After my friends pummel me with hugs and kisses, the interrogation begins.

"Are you and Leo gonna wait until after the baby's born to tie the knot?"

"Or, are you gonna be as fashionable as that outfit and be a knocked up bride?"

Opening a bottle of water, I practice what Kelly was preaching in the video and *calmly* tell them, "Leo and I broke up."

Silence again.

"It's okay you guys, I'm gonna be alright."

Not really. But it's not going to do anyone a bit of good if I display my actual state of emotions, which is what I would label as frantically heartbroken. Life is only as calm as I make it, right?

"No you're not."

"Yeah, you can't fool us, Chrissy. You're talking to people who've had to tranquilize you after you chipped your nail polish."

In an attempt to hold back my tears, I close my eyes for a long time before I respond to their spot-on assessment of my emotional state.

"You're right. I'm an absolute mess. But there's nothing I can do about it. It's really, really over this time. His choice. How pathetic would I be if I didn't accept it and begged for him to reconsider?"

What? It's not like the whole world needs to know I was on my hands and knees in New York in September doing that very thing.

"Well…is he gonna be a part of the baby's life?"

Now it's Courtney's turn with, "And what about Kendall? I mean, she *really* liked him."

"Trust me, I hate that another person is gone from her life. But in all honesty, he's been in New York for so long, it didn't seem that tough for her when I broke the news."

"Wait...he's still in New York? Wow, and I thought the visitation you have set up with Kurt was a pain in the ass. Sounds like this will be a nightmare."

Here we go...

"I don't even know if it's his."

The two of them scream, "WHAT?" so loud that the entire funeral service taking place two hundred feet away turns to look at us.

Courtney groans, "You've taken the word Chrissygan to a *whooooooole* new level with this news."

Needing more information, Nicole inquisitively asks, "C'mon...spill it. Who else are you sleeping with?"

"It's not important. Besides, I don't even know for sure if it even happened."

Courtney has no idea what the hell I'm even talking about, but Nicole on the other hand...

"Drunk?"

"Big time."

"Been there. Done that. You think I wanted a kid in my twenties...in the middle of my residency?"

Problem solver Courtney is NOT happy with the direction Nicole's taking the conversation.

"Nic, this is different! You were drunk...with your husband! Chrissy, are you saying you're not gonna tell the father of this baby what's going on?"

"I'm just taking it day by day, Court."

"Okay, ONE this isn't Alcoholics Anonymous, so enough with the sanctimonious holier than thou crap and TWO, that's totally unfair! Leo—or some other random guy— is about to become a father. You can't rip him off like that!"

"I'm not saying that's the plan."

341

Nicole moves closer to me and lovingly says, "What is the plan, Mama?"

"Well, the first step…" looking at Courtney, "…and I'm not trying to rip off Alcoholics Anonymous when I say that…" I wanted to make her crack a smile, but no go, "…is to find out if I even slept with the mystery man."

"Here's an idea, why don't you ask him?"

"I did, Courtney. I think he sort of said no."

"You think?"

And then Nicole is right behind with, *"Sort of?"*

Their logical brains are clearly not built to handle the chaotic intensity in which I *used* to live my life. Watching them self-destruct with all of this is actually the most fun I've had in a long time, and it's a nice vacation from missing Leo.

"I think he was trying to let me off the hook."

"Well, what are you gonna do then…paternity test?"

Clapping her hands, Nicole sings, "That's *soooooo* Hollywood!"

Ignoring her idiocy, I proceed to explain.

"Once he finds out I'm pregnant, he'll come clean because he's a good guy. If he says we had sex, then I'll do a paternity test, but only with him."

"Why not with Leo?"

"Because he asked me to set him free. No, wait…actually he begged me. Telling him I might be having his baby qualifies as the opposite of setting him free, don't you think?"

"Hold on, so if you find out this baby is Leo's…you're *still* not gonna tell him?"

I merely shrug because I just don't know.

Courtney shakes her head and looks away. Nicole though, she knows I need a little love and moves closer.

"When *are* you gonna tell this mystery man that you're pregnant?"

"I'm not."

What I failed to tack onto my response was…You are.

Unraveling

December, 2002

It wasn't my plan to tell Courtney and Nicole I was pregnant. In fact, it was my hope to keep it a secret...forever. Silly I know, but there it is. But I started showing and quickly realized that even the most expensive couture ensembles aren't going to hide the baby I've got growing inside of me. Not long after I shared my secret with my best friends, I shared it with Megan and Barbara, too. Barbara was so excited about the news, she got busy right away crocheting blankets and booties. Megan though...she looked confused. Despite her reaction, I needed a huge favor. I asked if she would continue to deliver Kendall to Kurt every Friday and pick her up every Sunday, so that I could keep my pregnancy a secret for a while longer. Reluctantly, she agreed. I had to run off to a holiday party at Kendall's school, but I made a mental note to talk to Megan later in private about her reaction and apologize for using her as a chauffeur. She's my designer, not my nanny, and I have to get back to treating her accordingly.

On top of the fact that my protruding belly is preventing me from keeping my pregnancy a secret, Kelly's words have been weighing heavily on me and as soon as I started to watch the first video, I decided that my life, Kendall's, and the new baby's will be a lot calmer if I know the truth about who the father is. Some smart person once said, "The truth will set you free," and by unleashing my secret to Courtney and Nicole, and knowing damn well they'd say something to Kurt about it, I hoped to find out if that smart person was full of shit. I guess the bright side is, if Kurt is the father, he'll have both of the kids every weekend and it'll offer me much needed time alone to cry myself senseless.

But it's starting to look like I might not get that alone time *or* answers anytime soon because it's been nearly four weeks since I told my friends about the baby and Kurt *still* hasn't said a peep to me about it. I even asked Megan if he said anything the last time she picked up Kendall, and her answer was a somber, "No." The crazy thing is, I'm not sure if I'm happy about this or not. Let's be real. Leo basically told me to get the hell out of his life. I'm not too excited about bouncing back into it with an entire family. I am completely confused about what to do. That's why Kelly's videos have become my new addiction. They force me to forget about the past and plan for the future. They take my mind off of my problems and force me to find solutions to them. I don't want to rush through them, though. Each one is a gift that I want to make last. I've watched the *Three Years Old* one every night since the first time I popped it in. Tonight, I'm giving myself the Christmas gift of *Four Years Old.*

After Kendall and I put cookies and milk out for Santa, I tuck her in and bring my own cookies and milk into bed and pop in the next video.

Kelly doesn't look that much different than the video she made before it, perhaps she did them just days apart. Glancing at the box containing the other thirteen videos, I cringe at what I'm about to watch unfold. Looking back at the TV, I observe her beautiful shoulder-length auburn hair. I still hate the cut...but the color is to die for. Oh shit...sorry Kel! Bad choice of words! Her weight is still seemingly normal, and her physique is as strong looking as it ever was. Her voice is authoritative, and just like the last time it spoke to me, I take in her every word.

"...I've read that four years old is all about rapid mood changes, explosive and destructive behavior, testing limits, exaggeration, and even fibbing."

Shoving another cookie in my mouth, "Good Lord, I'm like the world's oldest four year old."

"...But do your best to stay calm...be tenderly honest with her about her behavior. Lead by example, and try your best not to react to her outbursts."

The funny thing is Kendall has never been explosive or destructive. Letting out a deep sigh I think, Kelly and Craig sure missed out on a gem.

"... Kids are a lot smarter than we give them credit for, and it'll backfire on you if you hold back the truth from her."

With that reasoning, I turn off the video, roll onto my side, and agree with Kelly. It's time.

The next morning, Kendall woke to a brand new big girl bike from Santa and the news that she's going to get a brand new sibling.

"Really, Ki-Ki?"

As much as she wants to call me Mommy, she's still struggles with it. She writes it on every card and picture she makes, but saying the word is still so awkward for her.

"Really, Hunny! And the baby will be here in June."

"Is dat what Santa brought you?"

Looking under the tree and realizing there's nothing there with my name on it, I nod my head.

"Does it mean you were naughty or nice?"

Ahhhhh, out of the mouths of babes.

"Well, since babies are the most precious gift in the world, I'm pretty sure it means I was nice."

Too nice actually.

"Tell me, how do you feel about being a big sister?"

Thinking long and hard, she makes a pouty face and asks, "Do I have to share my new bike?"

"Probably not for four more years."

"Then I'm SOOPA DOOPA happy! I hope it's a boy!"

"*Really*? I was all about the girl power thing. Why do you want it to be a boy, Kendall?"

"He can pretend he's the daddy."

On that gloomy note, and to thwart anything explosive or destructive from flying out of my four year old mouth, I dully hand Kendall another present to open.

Exposed

December, 2002

"Wow, the garden really looks amazing, Chrissy."
"It's all amazing...the garden, the house, the yoga studios, the pregnancy. I can't believe you're managing all of this stuff by yourself."

Courtney and Nicole left their own families on Christmas day to spend some time with mine, and up until that comment, I was happy for the distraction.

"Yep...all by my lonesome. Thanks for the reminder, Nicole."

The three of us watch Kendall from the kitchen window. She's attempting to ride her new bike in the backyard, and it's just about the cutest thing ever.

"God, she's starting to look more and more like her mother."

Courtney and I nod our heads in agreement, before I say, "And she's got the laid-back temperament of her father. Seriously, the girl is amazing..." Pointing at my stomach, "...I hope to heck that I, and whatever I've got going on in here, don't screw her up."

"Does she know about the baby?"

"Told her this morning."

"*And?*"

"If I told her I was giving birth to Santa Claus himself, she couldn't have been more excited."

Sort of changing the subject, Courtney asks, "Have you heard from Leo?"

"No."

I slam my knife down on an onion so that they think my tears are from its stench as opposed to thoughts of him.

"I told you…he's gone."

"And still no word from the mystery man?"

"Not a damn thing."

"Why can't you just tell us who it is?"

Shaking my head, I tell them, "Later."

"Do you think he knows about the baby yet?"

It's been almost four weeks since I told my friends I was pregnant, so I laugh a little when I say, "I sure thought he would've found out about it by now."

"What does Kurt have to say about all of this?"

Now things are about to get interesting.

"How would Kurt know I was pregnant, Nicole?"

My back-peddling besties are all of a sudden hard at work covering up their big mouths. The same big mouths I was counting on to tell Kurt the news.

"I…I guess I assumed you would've told him by now."

"Yeah, look at you! He must have noticed!"

"I haven't told him, and I also haven't seen him since September, long before I started showing."

My back-up singers let out an impressively harmonized, "*Why?*"

"We had a pretty big blow up back in August, and Megan's been handling the transfer of Kendall for me."

Looking at Courtney, I curiously then ask, "Do *you* think he knows?"

She nudges Nicole who shamefully confesses, "I *kinda* spilled the beans to Kyle about the baby and well…he asked Kurt how he felt about you being pregnant…" She turns to look at Courtney, "…I guess that explains the surprised look on his face, huh?" Then back to me, "…I'm sorry Chrissy. I had no idea he didn't know."

Ignoring her guilt, I go on my own fact finding mission. "When was that?"

"About three weeks ago."

"And what did he say?"

"All he said was, 'I know it was on her list. I hope it makes her happy.'"

"Did he say it in a way that made you think he gave me the baby or was it more like he thinks I'm a big happy family with Leo?"

Once again, I'm surrounded by back-up singers when Nicole and Courtney, scream out, *"KURT'S THE MYSTERY MAN?"*

Christmas day sure isn't turning out to be as ho-ho-ho-hum as I thought it would be, that's for sure.

"Maybe....I still don't know for sure."

"Holy crap, is that why you and Leo broke up?"

"It was more over the fact that since I have Kendall, Kurt will always be a part of my life, and he couldn't dig deep enough to get over it."

Nicole, who's recklessly trying to crack open a bottle of wine to enjoy while she and Courtney process the news, jabs me with, "Well, Jesus, considering you might've slept with Kurt, I guess the guy made the right choice!"

I grab the mutilated bottle from her and jab right back, "You're gonna break that damn thing! Seriously...how do you treat your actual patients?"

After showing Nicole how easy the bottle opening process should be, I pour them each a ginormous glass and get back to my fact-finding mission.

"So, Nic, when Kyle told Kurt the news, did he give off any sign that this could be his?"

"Nope. He just said he hoped you were happy and got back to the football game he was watching with the guys."

"Not true, there's more!" Courtney nudges Nicole again and says, "Tell her."

Nic, who's not happy about being exposed as a blabber mouth, hesitantly confesses, "Okay, I also asked him if he heard the news that you and Leo were officially over."

"*And?*"

"He said he's known about that since sometime in August."

The morning I woke up at his house....What kind of game is Kurt playing?

Courtney, who doesn't think Nicole's handing the meat and potatoes of this conversation as well as she should interjects with, "Chrissy! If Kurt thought for a second that the baby was Leo's, but knew that you guys broke up, don't you think he'd make some kind of a joke about you sharing custody of *another* kid? C'mon, he'd make a crack about you being a mess or something, wouldn't he?"

"Correction, I don't share custody of Kendall with Kurt, he gets visitation."

"Who cares? Don't you see what I'm getting at?"

"Not really."

Actually, I kind of do, but denial is a much more appealing place to be right now.

"Maybe he thinks you and Leo broke up because you got pregnant with his baby, and he's just waiting for *you* to talk to *him* about it."

Then, slapping Nicole on the shoulder, she grumbles, "Wow, anyone else feel like they're on *The Young and The Restless* right now?"

Nicole, in a rare non-sarcastic moment continues with, "Chrissy, I got the feeling he knows exactly what's going on, and he's just waiting for you to deal with the reality of the situation."

Covering my ears, I blurt out, "Don't say it, Nic...I don't wanna hear it."

"Sorry, Sweetie, but it's starting to look like the reality of the situation is that you slept with Kurt and...he could quite possibly be the father of your child."

I shift my focus to my problem-solving friend, hoping for some answers.

"Courtney?"

"It's a possibility that only you can rule out. Just talk to him, okay? He's changed. You might even—"

Knowing exactly where my old friend is going with this conversation I cut her off.

"Hold it right there, Sister. I didn't spend all of those years learning how to let him go to end up with him again."

My friends nod their heads in acceptance of what I just said, but I can still see the hope in their eyes.

Stubborn

January, 2003

"**B**ut is that what *you* believe to be true?"
I haven't been to the cemetery much lately, been too busy with life to hang around dead people. Kids can really fill up a schedule like that. But after the Molotov cocktail of confusion that Courtney and Nicole dropped on me, I had to make the time and get some smart and unbiased advice…from a dead person. Because you know how much that makes sense.

"No. But I believe in leprechauns, so you could say my belief system is a little out of whack."

"Chrissy, c'mon, you have to have some kind of awareness about this. I know you're not *that* stupid."

"Fine. Here's what I believe. I don't care if I had twenty beer bongs shoved down my throat, I would NEVER cheat on Leo. I told you before, he's it for me, and I meant it. And Kurt's NOT the type of guy to take advantage of a girl who's drunk. He's been an emotionally detached son-of-a-bitch more times than I can remember, but when it comes to sex…he's *always* been a gentleman. I can make sense out of that much, Kel. What doesn't make sense to me is why Kurt won't talk to me about this."

"I think the bigger question is why won't *you* talk to *him* about this?"

"I can't."

"Why the heck not?"

"He'll get too much satisfaction out of it."

"Oh, please!"

"I'm serious! Do you realize how close I came to having everything I ever wanted?"

"I do."

"And don't you think he's just a smidge happy that I can't have those things because of my lousy decision to spend the night at his house?"

"I don't..."

HUH?

"...I honestly believe Kurt wants you to be happy."

"You don't think he hates Leo?"

"I absolutely think he hates Leo. Jesus, he cold-cocked him at my husband's funeral. I'd say there's a little bit of anger there. But I also think it's a completely normal reaction to have toward the guy your wife cheated on you with."

"That's kinda harsh."

"Uhhhh, it's kinda true!"

Stupid-ass voice of reason.

"But even though he hates him, he's not the type of guy to do something vindictive, like make you think you slept with him, just to mess up your life. That's not how Kurt's wired..."

Maybe not so stupid-ass after all.

"...It's more like how *you're* wired, but let's stay on point."

Nodding in reluctant agreement, I roll my hand in the air at her to continue.

"There's another thing I honestly believe, Chrissy..."

"What's that?"

"I honestly believe Kurt took your words to heart when you divorced and he completely agrees the two of you aren't right for each other."

"I thought he did, but—"

"Chrissy, did you ever think he might be staying away so that he can finally go after a little bit of happiness himself? I mean, that huge engagement ring of yours sure showed him you had moved on. Maybe the punches he threw at the funeral were all that he needed to leave the past behind. Maybe the drinks he offered you on your birthday were just nice gestures because he saw how lonely you were. Kurt's a lot of things, but he's not desperate and he's not a pig."

"You don't think I slept with him?"

"Nope. Not even if you jumped on him naked. So can you just do yourself *and* your baby a favor and stop being so damn stubborn? Clear this up with Kurt so that everyone can get on with their lives."

The funny thing is, they're the same words Megan said to me when I got back to the office this afternoon. I found her sitting at her desk, buried under mounds of charity clothing with no easy way to escape, so I pounced on her and asked why she's been so weird about the pregnancy.

"I dunno, Chrissy…" Pointing at my stomach, "…There's a baby in there and lives that people are ready to get on with. If you could just ask Kurt the damn question, everyone might be able to finally have some happiness." She pauses before she says, "You might even be able to…"

"I might be able to what?"

"Never mind. I'm staying out of this."

"*Staying out of what*? Megan, why are you being so damn secretive lately?"

"WHY ARE YOU BEING SO DAMN STUBBORN LATELY?"

Expecting me to unleash five months of pregnant hormones on her, Megan winces as she anticipates my reaction. Instead, I apologize.

"You know what? You're right and I'm sorry. I let the mystery of the night at Kurt's house get the best of me…and then Leo broke up with me…and then I found out I was pregnant and…everything has just spiraled out of control. It's like my affair all over again, and I don't know how to put an end to it without someone getting hurt."

"Chrissy, what's the worst that can come out of this if all you did was pass out in Kurt's bed?"

"You mean, what's the worst that can come out of this…if I'm having Leo's baby?"

"Yes."

Slumping down in the chair, I admit the painful truth.

"I'll be forcing him to be a part of my life…a life that I still have to share with Kurt because of Kendall. He begged me to cut him loose of it, Megan, and it's been five months since I gave him what he wanted. *Has he called?* No. *Has he written?* No. He got what he wanted. I have no right to mess things up for him again."

"Would you listen to yourself? He's probably the father of this child! Don't you think he'd want to know that? Geez, Chrissy, *don't you think he deserves to know that?*"

"Megan, it's more complicated than that."

"It sure is. You're more than half way done with a pregnancy you could've been sharing with him the entire time. Chrissy, he's had five months to get on with a life that will never be half as good as it could be if you'd stop being so damn stubborn. Just pick up the phone, ask Kurt the stupid question, and get the answer you need so that we can all get on with our damn lives."

Heart of Hearts

February, 2003

January came and went with not much more to show for it than
Kendall's fifth birthday party to which I purposely didn't
invite the gang or my yoga friends. It was a completely
immature and destructive decision that required trace amounts of
exaggeration and fibbing to pull off, and it came as a result of a
rapid mood change that I'm sure will come back to bite me in
the ass. Yep, it seems like no matter how many times I watch
Kelly's last video, I'll forever be stuck at age four.

Aside from the fact that I was in a room full of dinosaur-
sized blow up slides and jumpy houses that smelled like barf
with people from Kendall's pre-school whom I've never
invested more than five minutes of my time with…the party was
a success. The gang wasn't there to fill my head with beliefs that
Kurt's the father of my child and my yoga team wasn't there to
convince me otherwise.

After the earful Megan gave me at the studio last month, I
thought long and hard about reaching out to Leo. In my heart of
hearts, I just know this is our baby, and I've already lost so much
precious time not sharing the experience with him. I've endured
the morning sickness alone. Other than that first disastrous
doctor's appointment with Slutty Co-worker, I've attended all
others alone. I told Kendall the exciting news alone. The baby's
room sits void of furniture, because I can't bear the thought of
decorating it alone. And because Megan just left with Kendall to
drop her at Kurt's for the weekend, I'm all alone for the next two
days.

Before Megan left with her, she turned to me and asked,
"Did you make the call yet?"

Even though I've thought long and hard about reaching out to Leo, all I could do was shake my head "No." I still can't find the right words to explain myself to her...or him.

Once they were gone, I got busy cleaning up the house. I love my new kid with all of my heart, but I love a clean house, too, and it seems like the only two days I have one is when she's gone. Makes me feel bad for criticizing Nicole and Courtney all of those years for living like pigs once they became mothers. I had no idea how time consuming it was to just keep up with laundry, let alone clean a toilet or empty the dishwasher! Just another takesie-backsie from my pre-mom days. After tripping over one of Kendall's recent birthday presents, I gather up as many of them as I can and resignedly walk to her room to drop them, feeling like it'll be me...doing stuff like this...alone...for the rest of my life. One toy bounces under the bed and I laboriously get on my knees to search for it. When I reach underneath to retrieve it, I grab two.

What's this?

Decorated with glitter and scented marker is a small box with the words, *'For Weo,'* written on top.

Oh, Sweetie...What have you done?

Carefully peeling off the seventy-thousand pieces of tape so as not to expose my invasion of her privacy, I open the box and find the night vision goggles for snipe hunting that Leo had given her a year ago.

I let out a big sigh, and mutter, "I'm so sorry I did this to you, Kendall."

Lifting my heavier-than-it's-ever-been body from the ground, I carry the box to the living room and place it on the coffee table. I put on some mellow music, light a fire, settle into my old wicker couch, and begin to collect my thoughts the only way I know how...with a list. After an hour or so of reflection, I conclude that, just like with my affair, there are only three possible outcomes to this latest nightmare I've created.

1) If I tell Leo I'm pregnant now, he'll wonder why I waited so long and I'll have to tell him the truth that I wasn't sure if it was his...exposing that I might've cheated on him.

2) Leo asked, no wait...he begged me to cut him loose. He wants absolutely nothing to do with Kurt. But with Kendall, comes Kurt. If I'm having his baby, I'll be forcing him to live a life he outright told me he did not want to live.

3) Being adopted and wanting nothing more in the world than his own biological child, Leo will know I contemplated stripping him of that joy and NEVER forgive me.

4) Leo will swoop me up in his arms and tell me he's been in hell every day since I left New York. He won't ask me any questions about the last five months, and he won't care about anything other than the fact that we're together again and we're starting a family. I know...I know... THIS WILL NEVER HAPPEN! That's why I said there are only three possible outcomes to this nightmare.

The thing I feared the most when I was having an affair with Leo was that he would hate me if he found out I was married. Looking down at my newest list...one thing is glaringly obvious and I slump back into the couch. All realistic outcomes to this latest nightmare point to the exact same thing...hate.

"But hold on a minute."

Leo *didn't* hate me after he found out I was married. In fact, he said he was relieved to finally know the truth and had I told him any earlier, he might not have been in love with me enough to handle it. Sitting back up, my mind starts to race. I don't think Leo would've have been able to handle the news of the pregnancy right after the fall out of waking up in Kurt's bed; he was still too angry. But now that he's had time to cool off...maybe...

Then I immediately get deflated when I think back to his college graduation night. What ultimately led to our demise before was that I dragged my feet on the divorce. And I've done just that again with news of this pregnancy. See? Outcome bad. And then I slump back into the couch.

Dammit though. Something's gotta give, because I'm really, really starting to feel the heat from all directions to get to the bottom of this. Everyone wants answers...except, of course, the two guys who might be the father. Maybe the pressure of pleasing everyone around me is stronger than I thought and I'm going back to my old pleasy-pleaserson days. Maybe I'm torn about which crew to make happy and it's clouding my judgment. *What would Dr. Maria say*? Duh, she'd tell me to follow my heart. And you know what? Since I have two of them for the time being....I should really listen.

Twisting my Banana Republic ring, I ask myself, *What do you want Chrissy?*

Blocking out everyone's opinion about what I should do, I pick up another piece of paper and get busy crafting another list...and this one makes me smile.

I let you go
And I watch you leave
And I hold my breath
So you don't hear me scream
("What I didn't say," *Saving Jane*)

Disoriented

February, 2003

"**W**ow, you guys! That was the most fun I've had in a long time!"

My rag tag team just threw me the most awesome baby shower ever. It was just the four of us in the dimly lit meditation room at the studio. No annoying extended family members and no annoying thank you cards to write. No muss, no fuss.

Patting Slutty on the back for a job well done, Barbara, Megan, Slutty, and I are about to enter my favorite restaurant in Lafayette—Postino's—for the yummiest dinner ever when all of a sudden I stop dead in my tracks.

"C'mon, Hunny, it's friggin' cold out here! Get movin!"

But I can't move. I can't talk either. All I can do is stare.

Sitting at a dimly-lit corner table is my Leo, and he's holding hands with a very smart looking, okay…fine, *a very pretty*, brunette. My friend's eyes zoom in the direction of mine and damage control commences.

Megan's hand covers her mouth in horror when she speaks.

"Oh crap! I thought they were staying in San Francisco this weekend. I *never* would've suggested this place if I knew they'd be here."

Disoriented, I continue to stare. Not the case with Slutty.

361

"What the hell, Megan, you knew he'd be in town this weekend?"

"He's here for the whole week, actually. That west coast office finally opened."

"And you know this *how*?"

"My roommate's ex-boyfriend…well, I guess they're more like fuck-buddies now."

"Get to the point, Megan!"

"I'M TRYING! He told her Leo was coming to town and he was… he was…"

"HE WAS WHAT?"

"Bringing his new girlfriend…" Whispering over to me, "…I'm so sorry, Chrissy."

But I can't hear Megan. I can't hear anything but my own thoughts.

Walk over there and show him your stomach. Get him back, Chrissy.

But I can't! I don't know for sure if this baby is his.

Yes, you do! Forget what Courtney and Nicole said, you're carrying Leo's baby and you know it. And if he knew it, too, he'd forget all about Kurt's relationship with Kendall…he wouldn't have to dig deep! The relationship he'd have with his own child would make all of those jealous feelings insignificant. He wasn't capable of seeing things that way when he broke up with you because there was no baby, but all of that has changed now! Forget all of those stupid outcomes you created. Show him your stomach and let him be the judge of his own life. Show him and get him back!

Slutty Co-worker's back to demanding answers from Megan.

"Why would he bring her here? He knows damn well Chrissy lives in this town."

And then I see the answer. Leo's Mom walks out of the coat check room, up to the brunette and introduces herself with a nice big hug.

Oh no... Please, no. Please, please, don't let this be happening. She used to be my biggest cheerleader. *She used to root for me.* Reaching out for the wall in front of me for support, I close my eyes at the agonizing sight. I made myself believe I had lost him. I tried so hard to convince myself he was gone, but when the baby came along, I had hope again. I never talked about it. I barely even admitted it to myself because I knew it was a long shot. But there has always been a pull toward my Leo drug, and I had an unspoken feeling I'd be with him again one day. But watching Leo's mother embrace the woman, who is clearly someone very important to him, I feel him being pulled away along with my courage to approach him. And I'm not the only one who feels it. My baby, who all of a sudden kicks me for the first time, feels it, too.

Shaken by the unfamiliar jolt in my stomach, I hastily clutch it and breathlessly mumble, "Take me home."

In the hustle to get me across the street and into the car, Slutty Co-worker yells expletives to everything standing in our way. Everyone, from the rambunctious kids flowing in and out of The Round Up to the patrons entering the restaurant, can hear her. I take one more glance back at Leo's candle-lit corner table as my friend's usher me to the car, and notice that he can hear her, too. He leans back in his chair to glance out the window to try and connect the sound from his past with a face, and neither Leo's mother or the brunette, notice when he finally makes the connection and whispers, "Oh, my God."

Swiftly and painfully, I turn away from the sight of him.

Now sitting in the passenger seat of the car, door closed, I keep my head pointed toward the ground. I can't stand to see him with her for one more second. Without shifting her gaze from Leo's, Slutty Co-worker asks me, "Are you sure you don't wanna talk to him, Hunny? I mean, maybe he deserves to know what's going on."

"Please...just take me home."

Her eyes still locked on Leo's, she shakes her head in contempt at him for bringing his new girl to my neighborhood and then she gets in the car and drives away.

Great Aunties

February, 2003

O nce we're back at my house, Barbara scurries to the kitchen
to make some tea. Sassy clothes and chic hair aside, she
still hates big commotions and will avoid them at all costs. And
it's not hard to tell by my pacing in the living room that there's
about to be a lot of commotion. Suddenly stopping dead in my
tracks, I ask Megan to tell me everything she knows, and Slutty
Co-worker isn't happy about it one bit.

"Hunny, this can't be good for the baby. C'mon…I'll make
us some food and we'll wait for another kick."

Ignoring her, I glare at Megan and demand, "Tell me. I have
to know."

My over-protective old friend disapprovingly nods her head
at Megan, giving her permission to break my heart.

"He met her in Texas."

"When?"

"I think it was in November."

"Is it serious?"

"Chrissy, don't make me do this."

"Just tell me."

"Aside from bringing her here to meet his mom…they've
flown back and forth between New York and Texas quite a bit."

"Do they work together?"

"I think she has something to do with the new office in
Texas. But Chrissy, if he knew about the baby…"

"Do you know if he's happy?"

"Chrissy, c'mon…how would I know for sure?"

"I know you know, Megan. Just tell me…is he happy?"

Clearly not relishing in my self-affliction, she hangs her head and speaks softly.

"All I know is he's enjoying his success."

He's enjoying his success. He's enjoying his success. It's all I could hear as my friends tucked me in. Then, when they turned out the lights, all I could see was Leo making love to that woman. I could feel his hands on her back and his lips all over her body. I could smell him and I could feel her quiver with every gasp of air she took as he had his way with her. I could see him burying his face in her hair and doing with his body all of the delightful things he used to do to me. I saw his eyes look passionately into hers, and I could feel her knees go weak as his deep voice whispered over and over again, "I'm never letting you go," and then I heard hers say back to him, "I'm never letting you." But mostly, I could hear him ask her about her dreams and how they magically aligned with his. To stop the frenzied visions, I snap the lights back on and reach for the glass of water on my nightstand and that's when I see it, the stupid happy list I made just last night.

> *1)   Pick up Kendall on Sunday night and show Kurt I'm pregnant. Ending all mystery about who the father is...because I know.*
> *2)   Call Leo and tell him the news and that I waited this long because I wasn't sure if he'd be glad.*
> *3)   Let Leo decide what's best for him and stay calm.*
> *4)   Live happily ever after because Leo will decide YOU are what's best for him.*

None of this can happen now because of that woman. He's done. It's over. I believe it this time. I solemnly rip the stupid happy list into a million little pieces, vowing it'll be the last one I ever make. And then, clutching the towel he left behind, I quietly cry myself to sleep as I damn my truly, madly, deeply existence.

I wake in the morning, face swollen from torturing myself last night. I'm instantly hit with the foreign movement in my stomach.

"Morning, little one. Is someone hungry?"

Rounding the corner to my kitchen that I'm still petrified I can't afford, I'm not sure who was more surprised, my yoga friends at the hideous swollen sight of me, or me, to find Larry, Curly and Moe attempting to cook pancakes.

"What are you guys still doing here?"

Slutty Co-worker barrels toward me and boasts, "We have a surprise for you!"

Scared that I'll never feel excitement and happiness ever again, I place my hands over my trembling lips to try and keep my emotions under control. She immediately wraps one arm around me and places the other one on my stomach.

"We're your family, Hunny, and we'll never abandon you, okay?"

Megan then comes up behind me and does the same.

"We're gonna help you through this, Chrissy. You'll never be alone."

Barbara stands in the background with a huge smile on her face and holds up the thirty-third pair of booties she's made.

After pretending to feel better, I chew on a rubber pancake and let them guide me to the surprise. They take me to the room I designated a long time ago as the baby's.

Slutty Co-worker whispers in my ear, "We thought this would help" and then she opens the door.

At the sight, my hands go once again over my trembling lips. My friends stayed up the entire night quietly painting and putting together furniture. They even found a baby store that was open until midnight (who knew those existed?) and after they were sure I was fast asleep, they snuck out to buy every single thing a newborn baby and a stupid ass mom could ever need.

"And if it'll help, Chrissy, I can move in once the baby is born to help out."

"Megan…I'm speechless."

Throwing her hands in the air, Slutty Co-worker, belts out, "Well, me too! That offer makes all of the shit I've done so far seem *totally* insignificant!"

In barely a whisper, because after what I saw last night it's all I seem to have left in me, I say, "But I can't let you do that, Megan. You're a fashion designer, not a nanny."

"I'm a fashion designer…and a friend."

Sitting in the rocking chair, I look all around the room in amazement.

"This is more than I ever could've dreamt of. You guys did good."

Shockingly, Megan then says, "I guess this would be a good time to ask you for a month off then, huh?"

Looking like they know exactly what Megan's about to tell me, Slutty Co-worker and Barbara quietly back out of the room and close the door.

"But don't worry; I'll be back before the baby gets here."

"Where are you going?"

"Nepal. You know…to do my *thang*."

"Oh yeah…the charity thing. Of course…of course…but what about your boyfriend, won't you miss him?"

"My boyfriend?"

It's a weird reaction to a completely innocent question, and it makes me forget for a second that Leo's probably in some expensive hotel room going down on that brown-haired hedge fund bitch.

"Mick…from shipping…at our old company. *Remember?* The guy you told me might be 'the one'?"

Clearly relieved, Megan slides down the bedroom wall and lands on the ground.

"Meggers, are you okay?"

"Guess I'm just tired from being up all night. Anyway, Mick and I broke up like a year ago, Chrissy."

"Oh, geez. How did I not know that?"

"You've been a little busy."

Feeling bad for not being there for her, I apologize and tell her, "You've become like a little sister to me, Megan. I should never be too busy for you. I'm so, so sorry."

"It's not that big of a deal, really."

"This Nepal thing...is it safe? Did Kurt set you up with the right people and all?"

"Totally safe. And well...Kurt's actually going with me."

WHOA...*WHAT*? Sure, the Kurt I've known my whole entire life is like, *seventeen thousand* different non-emotional things, but he'd NEVER leave to go to a third world country without talking to me if he knew he knocked me up. Rubbing my stomach, I say to myself, *See, I knew Leo was your daddy.*

"I agree with everything you're thinking right now."

Surprised that Megan can see right through me, I cock my head up and ask, "What's that?"

"There's no way he'd go if there was a chance it was his."

"I know."

"I've been doing the drop off and pick up of Kendall for what...like four months now?"

"Yeah."

"He hasn't asked about it once."

"I know."

"Does knowing make all of this better or worse?"

"In light of what I saw last night, I don't know anything anymore."

"Should I have told you about her?"

"Now that I think of it...you tried. Last month, in your office when I asked you why you were being so damn secretive lately, you started to tell me I might be able to stop something if I'd just pick up the phone and tell Leo about the baby. But you stopped short of telling me exactly what it was I'd be stopping."

"Chrissy, I think I—"

"No, it's okay Megan. This was bound to happen..." Trying to be strong, "...We broke up five months ago..." Rubbing my belly, "...Life goes on right?"

"About Nepal, I think you should—"

"Right, Nepal...go and have some good ol' fashioned third-world charity fun."

Just then the rest of the crew barrels back into the room to *ohhhhh* and *ahhhhhh* over its beauty.

Welcome To My World

March, 2003

Apparitions of Leo will always linger. I want them to leave me alone, but it's like they're literally growing inside of me, and like the bountiful garden in my backyard, they get more abundant every day. Fortunately, I'm able to get through my days with limited images of Leo and his new girlfriend because they're jam-packed with activities at Kendall's school, doctors' appointments, the yoga studios and Lamaze classes where Slutty Co-worker is animatedly standing in as my lesbian lover. My nights though...they're God awful. In the beginning, I tried to flick on *The Family Feud*, but unlike the distraction he so kindly provided during my divorce days, Richard Dawson did little to stop Leo's new life *and* his new success from flashing through my mind. Most of my nights end with me in some kind of Glenn Close type of scenario where I sit in darkness in my new rocking chair. With each sway, I cruelly envision Leo having his way with that girl. And then I fantasize about her dying a slow and painful death.

It was four weeks ago that I came to my own absolute conclusion that the baby is Leo's. I even let out a little derisive chuckle every now and then that I ever thought it wasn't. Drunk or not, I'd always be true to him. And Kurt...well, he's just not the kind of guy to bang a drunk chick. I let my mind get the best of me ever since I woke up in Kurt's bed and it's managed to ruin the most special experience of my life...and it opened the door for a new one to enter Leo's. Absolute conclusion or not,

I'm not so sure it's fair to break that door down and ruin whatever he's got going on now.

Megan and Kurt left yesterday for mission "whatever," and I'm truly a single mom for the next thirty days. For the first time since our heated conversation in his driveway on September eleventh, Kurt made contact with me last night in the form of an email. It simply said he didn't have a formal will, but in the event that something should happen to him, everything he owns goes to Kendall. I got it last night and two things surprised me: one, he *actually* planned for the future, and two, he didn't mention *anything* about my pregnancy. Shockingly, his lack of interest about the most important thing to EVER happen to me caused me no annoyance. It only further substantiated my absolute conclusion that the baby belongs to Leo.

Plucking some zucchini from my green oasis, I smile and can't wait to show Kendall when she gets home from school. For once, I'll have her all to myself on a weekend and I can hardly wait. She's the most important person in my life now and as sick and twisted as it may seem, I can't imagine her not being my daughter. We have our routines, like cookies and milk after school, tending to the garden well into dusk and casting spells with her magic wand right before bed time. We're also learning how to cook together *and* how to navigate through a library, with her being the more experienced one at both. Sometimes I think Kelly's rolling over in her grave watching it all happen, but I'm quickly comforted knowing all of those experiences are exactly why she left Kendall to me. I think she knew I needed them just as much as her daughter.

I bailed on the cemetery last month because Kendall and I had more important stuff to do, so I didn't get a chance to talk to Nicole and Courtney about all of the conclusions I've come to. But surprisingly their emails further substantiate everything I've been thinking. Both of them admitted Kurt still hasn't brought me up once and they've since recanted their prior assumptions that he's the father. In fact, they think he's even seeing someone new. I know I'll have to talk to Kurt again one day. I mean, something will eventually happen with Kendall, or the gang, that will necessitate a verbal exchange. But until then, I'm kind of enjoying the break.

With every day and every kick in my belly that passes, I become less worried about Leo hating me for keeping the pregnancy from him and why I did, and more concerned about my child having a relationship with his or her father. I've become more truly, madly, deeply about what's growing inside of me than my own love life, and I feel like I'm able to deal with the fallout from the nightmare I've created with grace. And I also feel like even though Leo has a new special experience in his life, I *think* he'd consider mine more special, and he'd want to be a part of it.

Placing the freshly-picked zucchini in the basket that holds the other seventy-five pounds of vegetables I've picked over the last couple of days, I think...there's only one person who can substantiate my assumptions and the time has come to reach out.

Ringing, ringing, ringing and then...

"Hello?"

"It's Chrissy."

Just an exhale.

"How are you, Taddeo?"

"Hangin' in there."

"Don't you wanna know how I'm doing?"

"Things finally got good around here, so no...not really."

"Does that mean Leo still lives with you?"

"Yeah...for now."

Fucker.

"Look, I know about her, so don't think you can hurt me with that, okay?"

Nothing but silence.

"Listen...Remember that night a long time ago when we ran into each other at the Red Devil Lounge?"

"Yeah?"

"And I told you there was more to my life than I had told Leo and I wasn't sure if he could handle the truth..."

"What the fuck is the point of this phone call, Chrissy?"

"There's something going on in my life now that I think he should know about, but I'm not sure if he can handle it."

"Look, I hate to be a dick, but you guys are kinda over, so whatever you've got going on in your life really isn't his problem anymore."

"I'm pregnant."

I could've given birth in the amount of time it took for him to react.

"How pregnant?"

"About six months."

Doing the math in his head, he quickly calculates my visit to New York was exactly that long ago and exhales, "Oh, shit."

"Is that what you think he'll say?"

"Jesus Christ, Chrissy, the guy's finally happy."

"And it's not my intention to change that."

"Then *what* is your intention?"

"I wanna know if you think I should tell him."

"Your timing sucks, you know that? He's moving in with L..."

"DON'T SAY HER NAME! I DON'T WANNA KNOW HER FUCKING NAME!"

"Okay, okay, okay...I'm sorry. Jesus, hormonal much?"

"Hormonal A LOT, Taddeo, so take it easy on me."

Realizing I'm a lot more fragile than I was the last time he saw me, which was pretty freaking fragile, he takes it down a notch.

"Fine. It's just that...dammit, Chrissy, he's getting really serious with this girl and this is gonna...this is gonna..."

"This is gonna what?"

"Ruin everything."

I hang my head in defeat. That's it then. I have the answers I was looking for when I set out to make this phone call. They're not the answers I wanted, but they're answers.

"I guess that's all I needed to know."

"Wait! So you're not gonna tell him about this?"

"And be the one to ruin his life? No thanks. I love him too much to do that."

"But now I know, too! Fuck, I've never kept a secret from him in my whole life!"

"Well I guess now I'm not the only one with more baggage than a 747, am I? Welcome to my world, Taddeo."

And then I hung up.

My next phone call is to the only person in the world who can help me make sense of my decision, and two hours later, I'm on her couch.

Ready?

March, 2003

"Well, well, well…I wasn't expecting this!"
Rubbing her hands on my belly, she continues with, "Do you know what you're having?"

"Nope, let's just say I'm all about the surprises these days."

"Well, you look absolutely beautiful, Hunny."

Faking a smile, I sing, "You know me, Dr. Maria…it's all about what's on the outside."

"Things not so pretty on the inside?"

"Hideous, actually."

After a long pause, she takes off her glasses, points at my stomach, and asks, "You don't know whose that is, do you?"

Letting out an exhausted breath, I tell her, "All signs point to it being Leo's."

"Well, when are you going to start asking the questions that are going to give you the definitive answers you need?"

After plopping into the couch I give her a matter of fact, "I'm not, and I guess that's why I'm here."

"Excuse me?"

"I'm too afraid of the fallout."

"But Chrissy, this isn't about you anymore."

Why is that everyone's favorite thing to say to me?

Throwing my hands in the air, I say in frustration, "Dr. Maria, it's too late."

"Too late for what?"

"Too late for any of this to be good."

"Chrissy, you need answers for this baby. *Don't you see that?"*

"AND DON'T YOU SEE HOW TERRIFYING THIS IS FOR ME?"

I've been brash before with Dr. Maria, sometimes even a little rude. But I've never yelled at her like that and it catches her completely off guard.

"I see your hormones are working a little over time."

After a long while of staring out the window, wondering how I'm going to rebound from having just made yet another ass of myself, Dr. Maria breaks the silence.

"At risk of you biting my head off again, I have to just say...You're smarter than this, Chrissy."

Still staring out the window, I respond in barely a whisper.

"Dr. Maria, if this is Leo's and I go to him now and tell him I kept this from him for six months and why I kept it from him, *can you imagine his reaction?*"

"He'll be pissed, and he has every right to be. But Hunny, if it *is* his, think about the possibilities."

"There are no possibilities. He's with someone new."

"I don't care if he has twelve wives. The man deserves to know!"

Jesus, who's the hormonal one now?

My voice, still barely a whisper, confesses, "Taddeo said it would ruin everything for him."

"Now you're taking advice from a guy who doesn't like you? Again, Hunny, c'mon, you're smarter than this."

"I know I'm a lot smarter than this. But going to him now almost feels like I'm hunting for chaos. I'm so tired of chaos, Dr. Maria."

She can tell I'm lost. Her voice softens.

"I hate to be the bearer of bad news, Chrissy, but right now you're living smack dab in the middle of chaos. I promise you, nothing will be calm in your life until you confirm who the father is."

"In my heart of hearts, I know it's Leo's."

"Then *you* know what my advice is."

Finally becoming part of a back-up singing group myself, Dr. Maria and I simultaneously recite her famous words.

"Follow your heart, it'll take you where you need to go."

As I stand to gather my belongings to leave her office, I turn to confess my real fear.

"Knowing hasn't been my problem for a while now. It was replaced by telling about four weeks ago."

"Just dial his number. When you hear his voice, you'll know what to say."

With not enough time to get anything done at home or at work until I have to pick up Kendall from school, I make a pit stop at the Lafayette reservoir to wait out the clock and beat myself up for what could've been. I park and guardedly walk to the bench where I found Leo sitting...*five years ago*. Just like that day, all I can hear is the crunch of the rocks under my shoes as I approach it. But unlike that day, the bench is empty. There are no strong hands waiting for me, no green eyes to pierce right through me.

Like I used to so often do, I sit and watch the packs of modern day Francescas circle the trail and like I did a few years ago, I eavesdrop on their depressing conversations. They still hate their husbands, they still resent their kids. They still hate the job that they're forced to have to afford their mediocre lifestyle or they hate the fact that they had to give up the job they loved to raise their children. They still look pissed and tired and they still continue to bitch and moan about the great lives they used to have. Even if I wanted to, I wouldn't fit into any of the pathetic packs because I don't even have a husband of my own to bitch and moan about. I guess I'm going to have to start my own pathetic pack. It'll be made up of single moms who never even came close to getting what they wanted in life because they continually sabotaged their happiness. With that thought, my head drops into my hands and I lose it.

After a few minutes, or maybe twenty, of hard core sobbing, I lift my head to find that I'm not alone.

"How long have you been sitting here?"

"Long enough. Did you get it all out?"

"Is Leo waiting for me at home?"

"I don't think so."

"Then I didn't get it all out."

"You're ruining this very special time in your life, you know. A time that you might not ever get to have again."

Suddenly feeling really stupid because of all that she lost and her inability to get it back at this stage of her life, I shake my head in disgust.

"I don't wanna feel this way, Barbara. I thought I had moved mountains in my life so that I wouldn't have to."

"I know you did."

"It took every ounce of courage I had to correct the mistakes of my past to be with Leo."

"I know it did."

"Then why didn't it work out?"

"How do you know it didn't? No one's dead, right?"

Honestly, I do not know how this woman survived the loss of her husband and child. I gently place my hand on her knee to try and draw her strength.

"I'm sorry, Barbara. You must think I'm truly..." Thinking about the new pack I'm going to become the leader of, "...pathetic."

"Not at all. What's going on with you is very sad. But I just don't think it has to be that way..." Pulling my chin up with her index finger so that I'm looking into her eyes, "...Things can still work out the way you want them to."

"I could ruin his life..."

"Or you can make it better than he ever thought possible."

"That's a pretty wide range of possibilities."

"At least both of them will result in some kind of resolution." Pointing at the pack of bitching Francesca's walking by, "At least you won't be stuck in limbo-land like them. Take it from me, limbo-land will suck your life away. Make a choice to do *something* Chrissy, but don't do nothing. No good will come from it."

The difference between doing something and doing nothing is everything. It's what Kelly gave me credit for showing her during my divorce, and it's why she made those videos for Kendall.

"You can't get the past six months back…but you can change for the better what the next six will look like. All you have to do is pick up the phone and call him."

"What about L?"

"L?"

"The girl he's with."

"Ahhhhh. Well, he might choose her, and if he does we'll all be here for you. But Chrissy, he deserves to be the one to make the choice. Take it from someone who didn't have the choice when it came to losing her family…stop this nonsense and give him the option to choose a life that's best for him."

Standing to hug Barbara and thank her for the tough love, I ask her how she knew I was at the reservoir.

"I didn't. I'm in one of the packs of the old ladies. You know, the ones who seem pretty content with life…or they're glad it's almost over. We meet here every other day to make fun of all the young girls who take life way too seriously."

"Girls like me?"

"Pretty much."

Both laughing a little now, she takes my hand and asks, "Are you ready to make the call?"

"Yes."

Answers

March, 2003

"What are we gonna name him?"

"How do you know it's a boy?"

Grabbing her magic wand, Kendall waves it in a circle and then taps my belly.

"Presto! It's a boy!"

"Well I guess that takes care of that! What do you think we should name him?"

"Weo."

Give me a bleeping break. *Seriously?*

"Sweetheart, why do you wanna name the baby Leo?"

"So he'll pway snipes with me."

Silently praying to Jesus, who I wish I started believing in a long time ago so that my prayers weren't in vain, to pull some strings and make it so Kendall can play snipes with the real deal again one day, I kiss her on the forehead and turn out her light.

On the way to make the call I promised Barbara I would make, I enter the baby's room and sit for a long while in the rocking chair to think over everything I need to say to him.

"Am I doing the right thing, Kelly?"

Silence.

"Your dreams were right, by the way. Every single thing you said to me for the last year and a half has been dead on. Oops, sorry…I mean, accurate. Anyway, the pregnancy, the needing to make a choice or one would be made for me…you were right about everything."

Silence.

"What would you do if you were me? Would you tell Leo you were pregnant or would you live with this secret?"

Silence.

"I know, I know…you'd tell him. But you know why it scares me to do that, right?"

Silence.

"A lot of help you are."

Before leaving the room, I open the dresser drawer to admire the baby clothes that the girls bought…Actually, I'm procrastinating. Sifting through the piles, I stumble on a roll of masking tape and a bottle of glue probably left behind when they were decorating the room. Looking up toward the Heavens…*or were they?* I think back to the one and only conversation Kelly and I had on her porch where she lambasted me for always trying to "fix my broken package."

"Kel…are you telling me to stop fixing things or are you telling me to start again?"

Silence.

"C'mon, I need to know! What am I supposed to do?"

Silence.

Just then the phone rings and I quickly wobble to the kitchen to answer it before it wakes Kendall. The whole way mumbling at Kelly.

"Hello?"

"Will you accept a collect call from Kathmandu, Nepal?"

"*Uhhhh, sure.* I can't afford my freaking mortgage payment and I have a baby on the way who I probably can't afford to feed, but…what the hell."

"Excuse me?"

"Never mind…I'll take the call."

"Just a moment while I connect you."

The line is silent for about ten seconds and then all of a sudden it gets incredibly muffled and I hear a faint clatter on the other end of the line.

"*Hello?* Megan? Are you okay?"

"Not…Meg…Kur…I have to…you."

"Kurt? Is that you?"

"Ye...Me."

"I can barely hear you. Is everyone all right?"

"Good...here. Chri...we have...talk...the baby."

For so long I didn't want to know the truth about that fateful night at Kurt's house, fearing it might reveal I betrayed Leo. Then recently, I convinced myself there's no way I ever could have. Like I told my friends, Kurt would never take advantage of me drunk, and like I told Dr. Maria just five hours ago, I know my baby is Leo's. But why is Kurt calling me after not talking to me for months? I look up toward the Heavens and wonder if this is Kelly doing a little gluing and taping on my behalf.

"What about the baby? Kurt! What about the baby?"

"You need...know."

"I need to know what? *Kurt, what are you trying to tell me?*"

"It's...mine. I'm sorry...told...sooner."

And then the line went dead.

I stand there for a moment, in total shock.

"Omigod, he thinks it's his..." And then feeling my breath slip away, "...Oh...my...God. I slept with both of them."

Immediately, everything in my line of vision becomes blurry. I frantically reach down to the receiver to start dialing Slutty's number and that's when a huge fart explodes out of my ass. Trying to support myself on the countertop, I know *exactly* what's about to happen next.

Mommy

March, 2003

I fainted at hearing the news that I was back at square one with my nightmare, not knowing who the hell knocked me up, and came to just as Slutty Co-worker was putting the key I had given her months ago in the door. Apparently, I successfully dialed her cell phone just before hitting the ground. Luckily, she was close by at the studio and drove straight over out of concern for not hearing my voice on the other end of the line. Not needing to be convinced by her, I instantly agreed to a trip to the hospital to get checked out while my Lamaze class lesbian lover/other mother of my illegitimate child spent the night with Kendall who fortunately slept through the whole ordeal.

After an anxiety-ridden five hours of getting poked and prodded and being asked *a thousand times* if I wanted to call my husband, the evening ended with me finally dozing off to the healthy sound of my baby's heartbeat over the monitor.

"I know it's not what you wanted."

"It's just so damn frustrating! We *always* ask for ranch dressing, but they bring us this blue cheese crap every single time!"

Looking around for the waiter, I'm surprised to see that Chili's is completely empty. It's just Kelly and me.

"I'm talking about the baby."

"Oh, Lord…here you go again with that."

"Look down, you big dummy."

It's like all of a sudden I'm magically seven months pregnant.

"Whoa, where'd that come from?"

"That's what everyone wants to know."

"Can *you* tell me?"

"I could, but that would put an end to all of the fun I'm having."

For once I don't deliver the humor back to her. I'm scared.

"Is everything gonna be okay, Kelly?"

"Your baby is fine…beautiful actually. Has the most stunning eyes and brilliant smile I've ever seen."

Cynically speaking, I lower my eyes at my friend and growl, "Thanks for narrowing down where it came from, Kel."

All of a sudden, my voice of reason becomes quietly reflective.

"Speaking of beautiful…I should go now."

"No, please don't. This is the best talk we've had in a long time."

"No, no. She comes first. She needs you."

"Who needs me?"

"Ki-Ki…Wake up Ki-Ki."

Squeezing my hand tightly, her sweet voice then worriedly whispers the words I thought I'd never hear.

"Mommy…Mommy, wake up. Can you hear me?"

I open my eyes to find Kendall and Slutty Co-worker standing by my side. Instinctively, I pull my daughter onto the hospital bed and hug her with all of my might, telling her over and over again how much I love her, that our family is healthy, and I'm sorry if I scared her. Initially, the news that Kurt delivered to me sent me into a shitstorm of panic, but falling asleep to my baby's heartbeat and now feeling Kendall's as I embrace her, I'm experiencing the kind of calm I've been searching so long for. And I'm determined to hang onto it.

After being discharged from the hospital, the three of us return home, where I promptly put a movie on for Kendall, make a fresh pot of tea, and tell Slutty Co-worker *exactly* what Kurt told me.

"Hunny, after what you just told me, I think I'm gonna need something stronger than tea." Then pointing at my gut, "It's anyone's guess what the fuck you've got going on in there!"

"*Shhhhh* with the swearing! Kendall's in the other room!"

When I left the hospital, I promised myself I'd hold it together. I didn't want to do anything else to upset "whatever I've got going on" in my belly, or Kendall. But as I'm pouring my friend a scotch and myself a cup of tea, I can't hold back my tears.

"It's official. I've become the woman I never wanted to be."

Lovingly placing her arms around me, she inquires, "Francesca?"

"Yep."

"But you're not married to Kurt anymore."

"If this is his, it almost makes things worse that I'm not married to him. It won't be like how it is with Kendall. I'll have to share custody of this child. He'll have a say in everything. Worse, I *won't* have a say in everything. This kid will be on a dirt bike by the time it's three years old and there won't be a damn thing I can do about it, because fifty percent of the time I won't even be around."

"And now you know why unhappily married folks stay together...for the damn kids."

"And I knew that. It's why I was so proud of myself to have left the marriage *before* I dragged kids into the picture. For a while it even felt like I could be the poster girl for how to deal with broken dreams and still live a fantastic life. *But now?*"

"Chrissy, you're not a failure."

"Right. I'm so much worse than that."

After slamming her scotch in one gulp, she reaches for the bottle and asks, "So, what's the plan, Doll? What are we gonna do about this?"

"Well, I explained my mortifying situation to the doctor last night, and he recommended a paternity test right after the baby is born."

"Why not now?"

"Kurt's not back yet."

"You can call someone else, you know."

"See how calm I am right now?"

"Yes, and it's kinda freaking me out."

"Well, I'm trying to keep it this way. There's no need to call Leo, ruin what he's got going on, and invite a whole lot of chaos into his life and mine if I don't have to."

"Why do you think Kurt told you this news now?"

"I've been racking my brain over the same question. The only thing I can think is that Megan told him how much I've been agonizing about this and she asked him to put me out of my misery. I'm sure the truth shocked her as much as it shocked me."

"This is just crazy! I don't think anyone saw this coming."

Thinking of Kelly, I whisper as I walk to my bedroom, "Wrong. *Someone* saw it coming."

Far, Far Away

April, 2003

It's been nearly a month since that phone call from Kurt and it has now settled in that I cheated on Leo. I didn't believe it could ever happen. I didn't believe I could be that stupid. Jesus, given what I know now, he's better off without me. Forget a 747, my baggage can't even fit into a freightliner, and there's no room for it in his good life.

It was a blessing that Megan left for Nepal almost immediately after I found out about 'L.' I probably would've tortured her for more information every single day and that wouldn't have been good for anyone...especially me. No matter the outcome of the paternity test, I can never be with Leo knowing what I did to him. Our tainted love is...forever tainted. There's no wondering...no hoping...no scheming or even any yearning for him to return knowing what I did to him. The chapter of my life with Leo in it is closed forever and I'm somehow miserably calm about it. There's something painfully gratifying about getting over an addiction that I've had for so many years. No matter how attractive, chiseled, adoring, good in bed, and successful that addiction was.

I'm still far, far away from knowing some essential truths in my life, but knowing that I can rule out so many what-ifs has been very good for my little misfit family. For the last thirty days...and for that matter, for the rest of my life, my focus is all about them. Welcome home, Francesca.

Kendall is excitedly awaiting the arrival of whom she continues to insist is her new brother. I can't get her to drop the idea of naming the baby Leo, but I still have two months left to crack her. She calls me Mommy one hundred percent of the time now and I hear it about a hundred times a day! I think she's making up for lost time, which is just fine with me. She's grown so much in the last year and a half. Her brown hair is as long as her back and her legs are twice that, and I marvel at the number of strangers who stop to stare at her beauty. She's got the most mild-mannered temperament; I can probably count on one hand how many times she's thrown a temper tantrum in the last year. I don't have enough hands to do the same for myself. She continues to miss her daddy every day, but the tears have since transformed into laughter. Her parents would be so proud of the young lady she's blossoming into, and I continue to try my best not to screw her up. So far, so good. Francesca may have been guilty of a lot of wrongdoings, but not one of them is being a bad mother.

Last weekend, Courtney and Nicole threw me a surprise baby shower at the cemetery and that's when I broke the latest news to them that I did, in fact, sleep with Kurt.

"Ho-ly crap."

"*Holy shit* is more like it!"

"Yep, it's my best Chrissygan to date, don't you guys think?"

I'm trying to make light of the shitshow I've created for myself, but my best friends see right through it.

"You can't possibly be okay with this, can you?"

"Do I have a choice, Nicole?"

"Well, no, but I just thought I'd ask."

Things aren't adding up for Courtney though, and things *ALWAYS* have to add up for her.

"None of this makes sense, though. When Nicole told him you were pregnant, sure, he looked surprised, but after that he didn't say a thing about it."

"Court's right. I mean, the Kurt we all know has been a tad emotionally detached over the years, but about something like this? I don't think so."

"I don't know what you guys want me to say. None of it makes sense to me, either."

Courtney's not ready to drop it.

"And I thought he was seeing someone new."

"Yeah, I don't think he'd do that without..." Nicole then waves her hand in front of my belly, "...cleaning up this mess."

Horrified, I struggle to my feet.

"WHAT THE HELL IS WRONG WITH YOU TWO? Five months ago you were all, 'the reality of the situation is this is Kurt's baby!' Now, you're like, 'there's no way in hell it can be!' Just pick a fucking side and stick with it because I can't take it anymore!"

Reaching her hand out for me to sit back down, Courtney says, "It's not his, Chrissy. There's no way. It just doesn't add up."

With hope I was sure was all but dead, my eyes plead with hers.

"But Courtney...he said it's his. *Why would he say that?*"

"I have no idea."

Nicole is in agreement.

"I don't know, either. But what I do know is, if it's not his, it's Leo's, and that's what you wanted, right?"

"It doesn't matter what I want. Leo's with 'L' now and apparently he's happy and successful and..."

"Who's 'L?'"

"It's the first letter of his stupid new girlfriend's name."

"*Awe,* their names start with the same letter, that's kinda cute."

After Courtney punches Nicole in the arm for kicking me when I'm down, I quietly gather my belongings and set off to leave the cemetery. As I'm walking down the path to my car, my childhood friends stop me with news I was totally not prepared to hear.

"Are you mad at us?"

"I'm mad at the world, Courtney."

"Then I guess there's no better time like the present to drop this on you. Ready, Nic?"

"As ready as I'll ever be. Brace yourself because she's gonna blow."

Wondering how much more I can possibly take, I sigh, "What's going on, guys?"

Courtney's first to blurt out, "I took a job in Zimbabwe. Guss and I leave next month. Your turn, Nicole."

Nicole then fires off, "And I quit my job in the ER. We're moving to Arizona so I can finally go after that teaching thing. It's much cheaper to live there."

I think my water just broke.

"Okay, one...I don't even know where the hell Zimbabwe is! Is it in the South bay, like off of Highway seventeen or something? And what the fuck, Nicole? *Arizona?* Driving to your house was gonna be hard enough with two kids in the car, now you expect me to put them on a plane?"

I know I said I wasn't going to swear out loud anymore, but desperate times call for desperate language.

"Zimbabwe's in Africa, Chrissy. I got a grant to reconstruct a hospital there. I can really make a difference. It's like the biggest thing to ever happen to me."

My problem-solving touchstone is moving to...Africa?

"And our house sold two weeks ago. We leave for Arizona at the end of the month. I finally have a chance to start over."

My sarcasm is going to the desert?

WHERE'S MY GLUE? MY TAPE? PACKAGE IS BREAKING! PACKAGE IS BREAKING!

After pointing at my belly with my mouth gaping wide open for like an entire five minutes, I unleash the cougar that Nicole so sarcastically labeled me almost two years ago.

"AND I'D CALL THIS IS THE BIGGEST THING TO EVER HAPPEN TO ME! I'M THE ONE STARTING OVER! I'M THE ONE WHO NEEDS HELP! ARE YOU TWO SERIOUSLY LEAVING ME...NOW?"

Wrapping her doctor arms around me, Courtney acknowledges what I so badly didn't want to hear.

"Yes, we're leaving you now."

Nicole follows up with a hug herself, and some rare non-sarcasm.

"Chrissy, it's time for us to go after a little bit of what you've got."

Frantically waving my arms in the air to signify that I have absolutely nothing, I ask in complete bewilderment, *"What are you talking about? What the hell have I got?"*

"You got off the hamster wheel a long time ago. All we want is to do the same. You can understand that, right?"

"But you two are the only ones I know who have kids!" Pointing at my stomach, "Who's gonna help me with this if you guys are gone?"

Smiling at me like I might even be dumber than I think I am, Courtney reminds me of something important.

"Chrissy, you haven't called us once since you got Kendall and asked for our advice."

And then Nicole rattles off, "Yeah, and if you had, you just would've done the opposite of whatever we told you to do." Slapping Courtney in the shoulder, "Which probably would've been a good thing, eh?"

Scrambling to say anything to keep the remaining members of the A-BOB's together, I plead, "But you two are my...family."

Now forming a group hug around me, back-up singers are once again in full effect in my presence when they say in unison, "And we always will be."

Courtney whispers in my ear, "Nothing changes between us, other than a few more miles to travel to see each other. Got it, girl?"

Wrong. This changes *everything*.

I crave for you boy…
I'm sure you're on your way
Yes I'm sure you're on the road
("Nowhere Warm," *Kate Havnevik*)

April Showers

April, 2003

My best friends abandoning me would normally be front and center of my focus right now. I'd be dedicating every waking minute of every day trying to convince them not to leave me. I'd literally bust out that tape and super glue them to my side. But no time for arts and crafts at the moment because Megan emailed me last night to notify me she's back from Nepal and to tell me the trip was a huge success. Whatever the hell that means. She also wrote some other jibber-jabber about needing to have lunch with me to talk about the phone call Kurt made from Nepal and feeling bad about something or other. Frankly, once I read the first sentence that she was back, I was too focused on the email I was about to fire off to pay much attention to hers.

Kurt, I know you're home now. I'll be at the Lafayette studio at ten o'clock tomorrow. Please meet me there. You've kept everything a secret long enough and I need you to finally fill in the blanks. Chrissy

Waking in the morning, I take a long hot shower and bravely prepare for my face-to-face with Kurt, if he decides to show up, that is. To calm my nerves, I plan on attending one of Slutty Co-worker's yoga classes before he arrives, so I dress in my comfortable yoga-wear and only apply a small amount of lip gloss. Certainly no need to pile on the make-up. With what I expect Kurt to tell me about our torrid night of drunken sex, I'll just cry it off anyway.

Leaving my bedroom, I tap the box of Kelly's videos and declare, "Today's the day girl…Sorry, no more fun for you."

I arrive to the studio, and it's abnormally quiet. I search for my team and no one's to be found. In fact, there's a sub teaching Slutty's yoga class. Weird, I think I'll skip that. With unexpected time on my hands, I head to my office and fire up my computer to check for a response from Kurt. To my surprise, there is one.

Chrissy, you're right. Too many secrets. Relieved to have it all out in the open now. See you at ten o'clock. Kurt

Glancing at my watch, it's nine o'clock. One more hour until I finally get some answers. I poke my head into the lobby to look for my crew again, hoping for some kind of distraction, but it's empty. I take the opportunity to hit up the mediation room to further prepare myself for whatever comes flying out of Kurt's mouth. Leaving the door open a crack so I can hear when my rag tag team decides to show up for work, I turn on some soft music, light the candles encircling the space and sit criss-cross applesauce (as Kendall calls it) on the floor facing the calming, water fountain-filled atrium. The tranquil sound of the water as it cascades down the rim of the fountain and drops lightly into the small pool surrounding it blocks out the clutter in my head and instantly puts me at ease…for about five minutes.

Almost as soon as my mind is at rest and it feels like I'm gently floating around the room, my eyes snap wide open at what sounds like all hell breaking loose in the lobby. The studio doors burst open, and I hear Slutty Co-worker arguing with a man. I listen a little more, and then swiftly place my hands on my stomach when his voice becomes recognizable.

"*Oh my God.*"

Staying seated, but tilting my head in the direction of the conversation, I listen intently as the two of them argue.

"This was a mistake! She's gonna kill me for doing this!"

"Where is she?"

"You know what, it seemed like a good idea to contact you last night, but now that you're actually standing here, I'm second guessing everything. I shouldn't have emailed you! You shouldn't have flown here!"

"Well I guess you should've thought twice before you wrote me with, 'Chrissy's in trouble, she really needs you.'"

"But I didn't actually think you'd take the first flight out! I thought you'd ease into asking why she needed you with...Oh I dunno, MAYBE A PHONE CALL!"

"Just tell me where she is."

"I can't."

"Why not?"

"Because I didn't tell you what she needed you for. And man-oh-man, is she EVER gonna fire me over this."

"Another thing you should've thought about before you contacted me, but not my problem. Look, I'm only gonna ask one more time before I lose my shit. Where is she?"

"I don't know."

"WHAT DO YOU MEAN 'YOU DON'T KNOW?'"

My slutty old meddling friend apparently took matters into her own hands last night and emailed Leo in what looks like some kind of attempt to give me the fairytale life I've always dreamed of, and which I will undoubtedly kill her for trying to do. Judging by the sound of his voice, she probably knows just as well as I do that he's two seconds away from screaming out my name and alarming over a hundred well-paying patrons, so she resignedly seals her fate in the unemployment line.

"Fine. Stay right here. I'll go find her."

Knights in Shining Armor

April, 2003

Quite frankly I'm torn between the shock of Leo being twenty feet away from my pregnant body, and the audacity of Slutty Co-worker. Forget the unemployment line, that woman will be lucky to make it out of this building alive. I hear her prying little footsteps get closer to the meditation room, and I use up every second until she reaches me to figure out how to deal with the hand she just dealt me. I take notice of the door opening and then closing softly behind, but I don't turn around.

"Hunny?"

Silence.

As sweet as I've ever heard Slutty Co-worker, she chirps, "You look real pretty today."

As mean as she's ever heard me, I sneer, "How would you know? You're staring at my back."

"Well, your back looks real pretty today. Can hardly tell there's an extra twenty-five pounds strapped on to the front of it."

Brushing off her lame attempt to boost my vanity, I unleash.

"Who the hell do you think you are to ask him to come here?"

"Well, technically I—"

Turning to face her, she can now see the look of terror in my eyes.

"You had no right to email him. You had no right to…to make me have to see him again. To have to tell him to his face that this baby could be somebody else's."

"Chrissy, I—"

"Jesus, *don't you get it?* We said our good-bye's and they were good. I had something special to remember him by. *But now?* Now there's just shame, and it's all because of you." Letting out a snide snicker, "Oh, but that's right, you wouldn't get it because you've never been in love. All you have are empty one night stands, and a phone book full of phone numbers of men who could care less about you."

After biting her upper lip to control her own emotions, Slutty speaks slowly and softly when she says, "I'll let you get away with that because I know what I did was wrong and I can see how mad you'd be at me, but Chrissy all I wanted to do was see if his heart was still connected to yours. And look, it is. He flew all the way here to save you."

"Save me from what? *Myself?*"

"No! From making the mistake of throwing good love away."

From outside the mediation room window I can hear a car door slam. I look at the clock and actually start laughing at the insanity of the scenario that's about to unfold.

"Welp, Kurt's here."

"*WHAT?*"

"Yep, while you were busy planning my life for me last night, I was busy setting up a meeting with Kurt…here…at ten o'clock."

Glancing up the clock, Slutty Co-worker starts pacing back and forth muttering, "Fuck, fuck, fuck, fuck, fuck, fuck…." And then she worriedly asks, "What are we gonna do?"

"*We* aren't doing anything. I didn't want any of this! You made the mess. You clean it up."

And then I turn back around and resume my meditation pose, faking calm.

A moment later I hear the door close behind her.

I can't even begin to wrap my head around what's happening out there. *Will there be another fight?* I take a deep breath in and a deep breath out to try and relax. *Who will be the one to tell Leo I'm pregnant?* Deeper breath in. *When he finds out it could be Kurt's, will he bust out in a fit of pathetic laughter at the woman he wasted so many years on?* Deeper breath out. *Will he rush home and into the arms of L, thanking God I'm out of his life?* Now there is no breath to be found. I just sit in breathless silence…waiting to be saved. *By what?* I don't know.

I take notice of the meditation door opening and then closing softly behind.

Wow, that was fast…and quiet.

I don't turn around. I hear the footsteps get closer and my eyes close tighter. I acted cool when I reprimanded Slutty, but I'm a mess, and scared to death about whatever she's about to tell me. But it's not her who speaks.

"She wouldn't tell me where to find you, so I started looking on my own."

Leo.

"I don't know why I'm here really. Things are finally working out for me."

Oh my God, she didn't tell him. He still doesn't know.

"But she said you were in trouble, and it was crazy, I had to get to you."

At once, a million thoughts are shooting through my brain. He still loves me. I love you too, Leo. I love you so much that I couldn't bear to bring this predicament into your life. Maybe, just maybe, there is a way we can make this work.

"I had to get to you even though I met someone new."

With those words, I lower my head in agonizing defeat.

"But all I'm doing is staring at your back, and I feel like a fool for rushing things with her to take my mind off of you. I'm not sure what we have, Chrissy, because it fucks me up. But what I do know is your smile changed my life. And the way you talked to me, I mean *really* talked to me. It always felt like you were the only one who ever really knew me. And I know you

403

feel the same way. I know you feel like we saved each other when we met."

With my eyes still closed as tight as tight can be, he continues...

"Until you, I let no one in. And I've let no one in since..." Letting out a surprised quiet laugh, he mutters, "...To think I realized all of that from just staring at your back."

He takes a few more steps forward, rounding my body, and I hear him catch his breath as he's introduced to my protruding belly. I can sense his mind exploding with the words in the email that Slutty Co-worker sent to him, *Chrissy's in trouble...she needs you.*

With a frog in his throat as big as the child in my stomach, he croaks, "Is that mine?"

My eyes still squeezed shut; I breathe deeply...buying myself meditative time to think of the right answer.

"Please open your eyes, Chrissy...Please talk to me."

Even though my heart rejects the idea that I slept with Kurt, I made a vow to never lie to Leo again, and dammit, that vow meant something to me. I can't break it. I have to tell him the truth. I have to tell him that I don't know if it's his baby.

"Chrissy, please answer me. Is that my baby?"

I slowly open my eyes to look at Leo, hoping to draw strength to tell him the truth. But when our eyes meet, there is no strength to be found. There is only the drug that I unbearably surrendered seven months ago and it rushes in like a tidal wave, causing my baby to do a happy dance inside of my body. Leo's eyes are hopeful and for the first time since I became a mom, I feel like I'm part of a family and the emotion overwhelms me.

Kneeling down beside me, he gently whispers, "Please don't cry."

Likely due to the massive drug overdose coursing through my veins, I no longer care about the end result of the answer I give to Leo, I only care about hanging onto this feeling and keeping him here with me for as long as possible. For more

404

times that I care to count, I've watched things that matter to me fade away. If I have to break a vow to prevent it from happening again, so be it.

He places his hand on my belly and gently asks one more time, "Is this mine?"

Leo and I saved each other before...*maybe it's possible we can we be saved again.* With that hope, I place my hand on top of his, look deep into his hypnotic green eyes, and deplorably confess, "Yes."

As Leo pulls me to my feet to take in my different-than-he's-ever-seen-it body, I see Kurt round the corner to the meditation room and come to an abrupt halt when he looks through the glass door. The seven roses he's carrying drop out of his grip and to the ground as his eyes squarely focus on the man he was not at all prepared to see.

THE LIST TRILOGY

The Life List

The Unexpected List

The Hope List

www.askchrissy.net
@askchrissy
www.facebook.com/chrissyandersonbooks

An excerpt from book THREE of The List Trilogy,

THE HOPE LIST

BY

Chrissy Anderson

CHAPTER ONE

Devoted

September, 2013

"...and it sure seems like this cellular telephone thing is becoming all the rage."

Her skin is as pale as those little white butterflies you see fluttering around in early spring. Her severely cracked lips are a distracting bluish color, and for every five words she speaks she has to take two labored breaths. She's having a hard time swallowing and gets noticeably agitated when she can't remember basic words and facts. Aside from the perfectly positioned bright red scarf wrapped around her bald head, everything I'm looking at and listening to is in painful disarray. My beloved best friend from childhood, Kelly, who died thirteen years ago, is giving this life lesson every ounce of energy she's got, and just like all the other lessons on all the other videos before it—it's absolute torture to watch.

"...But just ask Ki-Ki, even a milkshake in your hand is enough to cause a distraction when you're driving. I swear, that woman never could tolerate a brain freeze...damn near killed us that day. I hate to think of the damage she would've caused if there were actual cell phones in cars when we were younger. Promise me you won't ever talk on one of those things while you're operating a vehicle."

My daughter, Kendall, hasn't called me Ki-Ki for nearly ten years, and her hand instantly goes to my knee at the mention of

411

the term of endearment she used to sing at the top of her lungs every single time she saw me when she was a small child. As always, the memory of the silly name makes her smile. Then, as always, the memory is immediately hijacked by the bitter reality of why she stopped using it. Her face morphs from a sweet smile into something resembling a tightly scrunched-up troll doll, and I see her mind teeter between wishing everything happened differently and being happy that everything turned out exactly like it did. It's a guilt-ridden battle I don't wish on anyone. Can you imagine the mental struggle of being sad your parents are dead, but at the same time, happy your life turned out exactly as it has? I can't. With that thought I squeeze her hand to let her know I sympathize with her battle.

"I'm not gonna lie to you, your Ki-Ki, Auntie Nicky, Auntie Courty and I used to break a lot of rules when we first got our drivers licenses. We even stole beer from our parents, parked at the top of Mission Peak, drank it all, and then drove back home like we were invincible. But we weren't...we were just dumb and incredibly lucky we didn't kill ourselves."

I purposely avoid eye contact with Kendall to dodge the shame of one of my many poor adolescent choices. Even so, I can see the critical look on her mature-beyond-its-years face out of the corner of my eye. I wanted to be the first one to tell her about all of my near-misses with cops that took place back in the day, but it looks like Kelly beat me to the punch on this one. Glancing over at the box containing only a few remaining videos, and listening to the strain in her voice, it's highly unlikely my beloved old friend will get around to too many more of my mess-ups.

"Don't think for one second you'll get lucky like my friends and I did with the whole drinking and driving thing, Kendall. In fact, there was a boy in our high school who died from doing it.

It literally destroyed his family and they were never the same. Obviously, when that happened, my friends and I stopped playing with fire. But what if one of us had been him instead? I beg you to respect yourself and your life enough to take the privilege of..." She stops for a long while to catch her wheezing breath, before continuing. "*...to take the privilege of driving a car seriously.*"

Kendall and I let out a simultaneous sigh, silently acknowledging the morbid correlation between what Kelly just said and the fatal drinking-related car accident that *literally* changed *our* lives forever. At the time Kelly made this video, she had absolutely no idea the very heartbreaking scenario she just spoke of would take her husband's life, too.

"Now, let's talk for a minute about curfews..."

Kendall hastily reaches across the bed, grabs the remote, and presses pause. Then, in her usual grown-up and concerned nature, she lays in on me.

"Mom, *really?* Auntie *Courty*...Auntie *Nicky?*"

Actually, it is a little silly considering...

Now pointing at the television screen, she interrupts my thought and continues, "*And, would you look at her?* This is getting beyond brutal, don't you think?"

The thing is, I completely agree with her. It's been brutal for four years now, ever since we watched the video titled *Twelve Years Old,* when Kelly damn near threw up in the middle of talking about super absorbent tampons. However, I don't think it was the chemo making her sick. The woman never could discuss feminine hygiene without gagging a little.

"I know, Sweetheart. It's just that...I made a promise."

"Mom, *puleez.* I might only be fifteen-and-a-half, but I'm smart enough to know you've broken a few promises in your day."

A few? Ha! She doesn't even know the half of it.

Pointing back up at the television screen, she protests, "I appreciate that she made these for me, I really, really do. But you and Daddy have already talked to me about this stuff, and well…"

"Yes?"

Lowering her head, she whispers, "It's kinda hard to say."

Lifting her chin up so our eyes meet, I gently press, "It's okay to tell me what you're thinking, Kendall. Besides, we're probably thinking the same thing."

After a long pause she lets it all out.

"It's just that…It's like we're a perfectly normal family for three hundred and sixty-*four* days a year and then one day a year, on this stupid video day, I get reminded we're not. I know she was your best friend, and I know you made a promise to show me every last one of these things, but can't we just stop at this one? I mean, geez, I don't even want a car, I want a horse. Something, you know about and she doesn't…because *you're* my mom."

Kendall's right. For three hundred and sixty-*four* days a year we have swim meets, equestrian show-jumping competitions, theatre productions, dentist appointments, flu shots, backyard barbecues, wardrobe malfunctions, temper tantrums, and end of the school year pool parties. We wake on Christmas morning in our matching footy pajamas (*including* my mortified husband), we hunt for Easter eggs, bake cookies, participate in school talent shows, have slumber parties, and meticulously tend to our much-loved vegetable garden. For all but *one* day of the year, it's normal family operating procedure, and I adore every single second of every single one of those days. But then comes this day—video day.

Video day is on auto-reminder in my Outlook calendar. On this same day every year I'm prompted to pull the archaic VCR out from under my bed and plug it in. Then I glumly saunter over to my closet, uncover a large box of dust-covered videos,

414

and summon Kendall to come into my room so we can watch the latest installment in private. I tried to leave the ritual up to whenever the mood felt right, but that only resulted in a lot of procrastination (and a lot of potential promise breaking). So one day, many years ago, a day was picked at random by playing pin the tail on the calendar with Kendall, and this was the day selected as the one day every year we'd watch the recorded life lessons her mother made for her before she died of pancreatic cancer in 2001. It was a task originally appointed to Kelly's husband, Craig, but unbelievably he died too. So that left me, Kendall's legal guardian, as the one showing her the sixteen videos—one made for every year of her life beginning at three years old and ending at eighteen. But they're becoming incredibly difficult to watch and quite frankly I'm not so sure it's fair to ask that Kendall does…regardless of the promise I made.

Yes, Kendall and I were thinking the *exact* same thing. We both want to be a perfectly normal family for three hundred and sixty-*five* days a year and not get reminded on this one day that we're different. In fact, aside from a few individuals who know otherwise, you'd *never* know her father and I weren't her biological parents, and you'd never *ever* know she wasn't the full-blooded big sister to the ice-cream-stained-smiley-face who just barged into my bedroom.

Acknowledgements

Because I'm extremely committed to my tagline, "the difference between doing something and doing nothing is everything," I feel it's necessary to acknowledge those who have offered me love, genuine encouragement, and selfless guidance while writing *The List Trilogy*.

First and foremost, I want to recognize my husband. The irreplaceable love I have for him is the inspiration behind every word I write. From the moment I met him, I felt compelled to write about our love story. And once I started, I became obsessed with sharing it. I appreciate his understanding when it comes to my commitment to helping others find true love and I pray to God I have honored him in the process of doing that, for his love and respect means everything to me. My daughter, who was four at the time I began writing *Part I of The List Trilogy*, is nine now. My baby has demonstrated a level of patience with my "hobby" that blows my mind and warms my heart. *The List Trilogy* is for her to read with an open mind and a willingness to learn…when she's an adult, of course!

There were many times over the last five years when I almost chickened out of publishing my work. If it wasn't for my best friend, Eva, who took my panicked phone calls, stressed out texts, and rambling (almost psychotic) emails about how stupid I think I am, and turned them into rejuvenating and motivating therapy sessions, *The List Trilogy* would never exist. Thank you, my dear old friend, for all of your recommendations and for protecting me *once again* from making a total ass of myself. You are the definition of what a true girlfriend is and no matter how many miles separate us, we will always be close.

I have to bow down to my dear friend and publicist, Vikki Espinosa. Without this woman, I'd think Facebook was make-up and Twitter was a venereal disease. Okay, maybe I wasn't *that* socially-challenged, but I needed help, and she gave it to me…big time. To this day Vikki continues to inundate me with marvelous marketing ideas to take my trilogy to the next level. I love you for being you, Vikki, and I'm so incredibly grateful I met you eight years ago.

I have to acknowledge Peter Baxter for the charitable work he's done on my website, waskchrissy.net. Like me, Peter is one of those freaky left-brain/right-brain people. He's an accomplished author of several works of non-fiction about smart stuff like Africa *and* he's a web developer. Who even thought a species like that existed? Our style of writing could NOT be more different, yet he's offered me subtly valuable advice that's no doubt taken my work to a more polished level.

And speaking of polished level…I'd be a total literary laughing stock if it weren't for Amy Metz of A Blue Million Books and professional wordsmith and editor, Margie Aston. Both of these incredibly selfless women picked-up first editions of *The Life List* at random, read it, and loved it. But they could've loved it even more if I knew how the hell to use an ellipsis or how to spell "fuck's sake," so each of them contacted me to offer their professional and much needed support. Words can't express how indebted I am to these two women for their brains, generosity and overall conviction that I had a really great story that could become phenomenal if I knew how to punctuate…and spell, for fuck's sake! (They'd be so proud.)

Lastly, I have to thank all of the mini-Chrissys and forsaken-Francescas out there. While "Leo" was my inspiration for my convoluted and chaotic love story, you were the ultimate courage to tell it. I don't want anyone to ever feel as lonely, scared, or confused as I felt during those years of my life. No matter if you're at the beginning of an arduous relationship, or deep into one that you wish you left a long time ago, I hope I've made you feel sane and supported. I want you to know you have a friend. Maybe my story will be *your* difference between doing something and doing nothing. And if it isn't, well no one knows why better than me.

Oh wait…there is one more very important thing. If you've read this far, please tell me why. Reviews are the breath of life for authors and every single one left on Amazon will increase the visibility of my work. Without your review *The List Trilogy* will most definitely get lost in a book abyss. I'm begging you to not let that happen. Please click to Amazon right now…two minutes of your time is all it will take to make a staggering difference.

xoxo,
Chrissy Anderson

Made in the USA
Lexington, KY
17 October 2016